## SHIVERS OF SWEET PLEASURE

Gavin pushed up out of his chair. "I apologize for my questions. I only asked of your past in curiosity. I really don't care what you did or where you came from."

Ellen took a step back. "I've had a lovely evening, but I really must go. Richard will—"

He came around the table so quickly that she didn't have time to retreat. Before she could think, he had her hand. He took her in his arms.

His nearness was making her head reel. She wanted to pull away. She knew she should. But there was something about the way he looked at her with his green eyes . . . something about the way his arms felt around her.

Gavin's lips touched hers and her eyes drifted shut, intoxicated by the heady nearness of him. She felt her hands lift and then fall as they settled naturally on his shoulders. His kiss was brief, no more than a brush of his lips against hers, but he left her breathless.

"Come home with me," he whispered, caressing her cheek with his fingertips. "Let me make love to you, my elusive Ellen."

# COLLEEN FAULKNER

# Sweet Deception

**ZEBRA BOOKS**
**KENSINGTON PUBLISHING CORP.**

ZEBRA BOOKS

are published by

Kensington Publishing Corp.
475 Park Avenue South
New York, NY 10016

First printing: October, 1992

Printed in the United States of America

# Prologue

*Essex, England, 1654*

Thomasina adjusted the black Puritan cap on the back of her head as she slipped into her father's library. "You called for me, sir?"

Her father, the Viscount Greenborough, stood facing the bookshelves, flipping through a dusty volume, his back to her. His thin shoulders were hunched beneath a black coat, and even from behind she could see his frail hand tremble as he turned an onionskin page.

The room was dim, lit only by the yellow light of a few stinking tallow candles. All was silent save for the eerie scratching of a limb on the windowpane, left bare by an unlatched shutter.

Thomasina clasped her hands. "Sir?"

The viscount returned the leather-bound book to its proper place and turned to face his only living heir. He looked at her, yet took care not to make eye contact. "I'll not mince words, daughter. I've grave word from London."

She lifted her chin, her dark eyes settling upon her father's beaten frame. "You've lost your lands," she

5

whispered, shocked but by no means surprised.

Greenborough tugged at his goatee. "I have."

"But what of Lord Waxton's promise?" Thomasina asked.

The Earl of Waxton, a prominent man at Parliament, had befriended her father more than a year ago, promising to aid him. Though he made Thomasina's skin crawl, he had become a frequent visitor at Havering House. Her father had insisted the earl's intentions were naught but good.

"You said he swore you would be safe if you left the church and vowed your allegiance to Cromwell." She could feel her heart wrenching beneath her breast. All she could think of was her dead mother and the pain her father had caused by closing the chapel here at Havering House and sending away the household priest. Unable to practice her religion any longer, Lady Greenborough had withered and died in six months time. "You abandoned your faith to save these lands!"

"I did not abandon my faith, daughter. I but made a prudent political decision, so it will do you well to hold your tongue against such words!"

Thomasina set her jaw in bitter anger. Though barely thirteen, she was not such an innocent that she didn't know what it meant to lose one's lands to Cromwell. Since the beheading of Charles I, she had seen it happen to neighbors and friends, to those not willing to sign allegiance to the Protector. Those who were lucky traveled from one relation to the next seeking food and refuge; those who were not so lucky had been beheaded. Her voice was barely a whisper when she spoke again. "He swore he would protect the family seat. Lord Waxton—"

Greenborough gave a quick wave of his hand, not allowing her to finish. "Silence, woman! Lord

Waxton has saved my head. He could do nothing more!"

"But, Father," she balled her hands in anguish, "for how many hundred years has this land belonged to our family? How can you give it up so easily? Surely there are means to—"

"Silence, I said!" His face had turned scarlet. He lifted a long, bony finger and held it beneath her nose. "It would be best if you learned to hold your tongue. To be a scold is unbecoming in a bride."

Thomasina felt the blood drain from her face. When she managed to speak, her own voice sounded strange in her ears. "A bride, you say? But you promised my mother that you would not sell me to save yourself."

She touched the lace of his sleeve, searching his haggard face for a glimpse of the man he had been before the wars. "You promised, sir . . ."

"Deathbed pledges made in haste are soon regretted." He pulled back his hand, made uncomfortable by her touch. "I did what I had to for your own good. This is the only way I could protect you." Then he added, as if in consolation, "You're nearly of marrying age. This agreement should be of no jolt to you."

She lowered her gaze to the grey slate floor, numb with shock. "I take it that he who has been granted your lands has also been granted my maidenhead?"

"Crude words for a young woman, but aye."

Thomasina's hand went to the crucifix she still wore pinned inside her bodice. She had never had much use for her mother's religion, but the tiny gold cross was all she had left of her. "May I ask who this gentleman is, or is his identity to be a surprise as well?" Of course, she knew the answer before her father spoke. She had seen this coming a year ago.

7

Only her father had been too blind to not know what would become of them both.

"The Earl of Waxton."

Thomasina bunched her skirts in her hands to retreat. "I won't marry him!" she shouted, her dark eyes narrowing in determination. "I'll take the veil before I marry that olden dupe!"

Her father's laughter echoed in the high-ceilinged room. "You cannot take the veil, daughter. Your mother's beloved Catholic Church has been dissolved."

Her father's heartless laughter echoed in Thomasina's ears, and her vision clouded as she fought back her tears of injury and anger. She looked up into the dome ceiling painted in Italian fresco. The faded winged cherubs and horned beasts seemed to be laughing, too, laughing at her as they whirled overhead. Suddenly, this place that had been her haven would be her prison. Her father, the man who had been her defender, was now her whoremonger. "I . . . I won't do it, sir. I vow, I won't." She lifted her stiff skirting and whirled around. "I'll run away," she cried over her shoulder as she marched for the doorway, her head down. "God a'mercy! I'd take my own life before I'd marry an abhorrent caitiff such as Waxton."

"An abhorrent caitiff, the lady says?"

In her haste, Thomasina had not heard Waxton's approach. She stopped so near to him that the hem of her drab olive petticoat brushed the toes of his polished shoes.

"Step aside, sir," she muttered between clenched teeth. She did not lift her head to look at him.

When she tried to push past him, he caught a handful of her thick, shining hair and jerked so hard that her head nearly snapped from her shoulders.

Thomasina looked up, her lower lip trembling with a mixture of fear, pain, and utter condemnation. The earl was a tall, painfully thin man some forty years her elder, with a hooked beak nose and black rodent's eyes. He wore a great powdered wig and the rich melancholy suit of a man of Cromwell's government. In his hand he carried a silver-tipped walking cane.

Waxton stared at her and for a moment he made no effort to conceal the lewdness of his thoughts. His sinister gaze flicked to her father's nervous one. "Is there adversity here, Greenborough?"

"Adversity? No, most certainly not, my lord." Her father's voice was strained. It was apparent he was frightened of Lord Waxton and his power. "It's naught but an attack of the vapors, isn't it, daughter?"

When Thomasina hesitated, Waxton, still holding her by a handful of her hair, tapped his cane on the cold slate floor. "Come, maid. This union is one of prudence. We'll not be wed immediately . . . not at least until your woman's flow has come. You'll learn to accept me in time."

Oblivious to the pain that brought tears to her eyes or the embarrassment of his words, she lifted her dark lashes until her gaze locked with Waxton's. "No, sir," she murmured, the venom plain in her voice, "I should think I will, instead, come to despise you even more than I do at this moment."

# Chapter One

*Havering House, Essex, England*
*January 1662*

Thomasina halted on a stone step and pressed her back to the wall to steady herself, knowing that if she stumbled she would fall to her death in the blackness below. With no railing on the winding tower staircase, the damp, sweating wall was her only safeguard.

Her hand fell to her breast and she felt the rapid beat of her heart. The only sounds she could detect were those of her own breathing and the squeak of a few mice that scurried along the crumbling steps. The passageway was dark and dank, and even through the thickness of her ermine-lined cloak she could feel the biting cold of the January wind.

There had been few times in the last eight years that she had ventured up these precarious steps into the tower, a full four stories above the ground. It was here that Waxton's laboratory was located, a room he said women had no need to set foot in.

But the hour was right. Thomasina knew it was time to make her move, to strike a bargain with the

Earl of Waxton. For eight years she had endured the farce of marriage between them. For eight years she had remained imprisoned here in Havering House, given no opportunity to leave the boundaries of the land. She was not permitted to seek out female companions in neighboring homes, nor to visit sick villagers, nor to even shop for her own goods.

Since her marriage and the suicide of her father that had quickly followed, Thomasina has been kept under lock and key to prevent her from cuckolding her husband. She was nearly imprisoned in her own apartments in the third wing of Havering House, only to be paraded before her husband's cronies as the virgin bride. For eight years she had endured Waxton's cruel verbal and physical assaults, the foul touch of his hands as he struggled to take what he could not, and the loneliness that had become the most difficult to bear.

All these long years Thomasina had sought an opportunity to escape the marriage. Just when she had nearly given up hope of ever being free, her prayers were answered. The solution had come in the simple form of a letter she discovered pigeonholed in a secret drawer of her husband's bedchamber writing desk. The letter contained a brief message and a list of twelve names of noblemen engaged in the business of attempting to overthrow the newly crowned King of England. The punishment for treason to the Crown, imagined or real, was the immediate beheading of the accused.

Like most of the Roundheads of Cromwell's brief era, Lord Waxton had turned the tables at Havering House and welcomed his new monarch with open arms, just as Charles, upon restoration of the crown to the Stuarts, had welcomed his stray sheep back into the fold. Waxton, along with many other members of the Protector's government, had declared his loyalty to King Charles and vowed to defend his crown forever more. For in the two years of semi-anarchy following the death of Cromwell, most Roundheads had joined their onetime enemy Royalists in yearning for the return of the monarch.

But Thomasina now knew the earl had lied when he had gone to Whitehall Palace to make his oath. The hidden slip of parchment was her proof, and that proof was what would finally free her from Waxton's iron grip.

Thomasina, having caught her breath and gained her courage, lifted her heavy velvet skirts and walked to the crude planked door of her husband's laboratory. A candle burned in a sconce on the wall, illuminating the entryway. She rapped on the door with her fist.

Just as she pulled her hand back inside her cloak, the massive door swung open. To her surprise, it was not her husband who answered her knock but the Duke of Hunt.

Thomasina swallowed hard against her fear, taking an involuntary step backward. She had not known Hunt was here at Havering House, for had she been aware of his presence she'd have remained safely in her apartments until his departure.

"I vow," Hunt murmured, raking his eyes over her, "a good even to you. I had hoped I might have the pleasure of your company before the night was over, but your husband thought you to have retired for the night."

She looked up at his stark white face and white hair. If there was one man she feared more than her husband, it was this albino, the Duke of Hunt. A friend of her husband's, the duke had made it obvious to her that it was only a matter of time before he

13

himself took the maidenhead Waxton was obviously unable to claim.

For six months he had been stalking her, patiently biding his time until he stole what Waxton seemed to treasure most. The man was frightening enough just to look at, with his ivory skin and inhuman pink eyes, but Hunt himself was more terrifying. He was in a powerful position at Whitehall, a friend to the king and a man known to always get exactly what he set out for, destroying anyone in his path.

"Lady Waxton?" Her husband appeared in the doorway, obviously annoyed. "What is it that is so compelling that you must disturb me in my laboratory? You should have sent Warren if you had need of me."

"I . . . I'm sorry, sir." She turned to go. "I . . . I'll speak with you on the matter later."

"Nonsense." Hunt lifted to his shoulder the albino ferret he often carried in a pocket. "Come in, my dear lady. I was just bound for my apartments. I'm weary from my travel from London. The road was muddy. Quite rough, my trip."

Thomasina lowered her gaze, feeling caught in the spider's web. This was not a good time to confront her husband, not with Hunt here. His name had been at the head of the list.

"A good night to you, then," Waxton offered his houseguest. "I'll have Warren make arrangements for hunting come morning."

Hunt gave a nod to his host and passed Thomasina in the doorway, letting his hand, invisible to Waxton, brush against the curve of her breasts above her busk. Thomasina sucked in her breath as he went by, suddenly all the more determined to escape the wretchedly hopeless life she saw stretching out before her.

14

The duke's footsteps echoed hollowly on the stone steps as he made his descent. Waxton walked back inside his laboratory, signaling Thomasina to follow. He closed the door behind her.

The laboratory was an ill sulfur-smelling room, with tables piled high with various object of scientific interest. There were several human bones with tags hanging from them, jars of pickled remains, several wire cages of mice and bats, and bottle after bottle of medicinal concoctions such as cow dung mixed in vinegar, no doubt purchased in the hopes of curing the earl's impotency.

Waxton walked around behind a scarred wooden table and began to sprinkle a green powder onto a scale. "Yes, what is it, madame? You can see I'm engaged." He brought a lit candle closer and leaned over the table in concentration.

Thomasina breathed deeply as she drew her ermine cloak around her trembling shoulders. She was cold, cold right through to her very bones. *Now or never*, an inner voice warned. *Say it whilst you still have the courage!* She glanced up at her surroundings, stalling for time.

The laboratory, a circular room, was flocked with glass windows and heavy crimson drapes falling from the ceiling. Candles sat on several window ledges, turning the glass into eerie mirrors that reflected distorted images of her and Waxton. Outside she could hear the howl of the wind and the pounding of rain on the dimpled glass. The smell of the damp sweating stone walls mingled with the odors of the laboratory, making Thomasina's stomach lurch. She turned away from the tagged human skull that rested on a pedestal.

"I . . . I've come to ask for an annulment, my lord." Thomasina heard the remarkable words

15

escape from her lips clear and steady. For a long moment there was silence, save for the tick of a table pendulum. She began to wonder if the earl had heard her at all.

Finally, his voice shattered the shocking silence. "You have come to ask for a *what*?" Still, he did not look up, nor did he cease measuring the powder. But his voice was like liquid steel.

She swallowed the lump in her throat and spoke louder than before. "I said I've come to ask for an annulment. I wish to leave Havering House. The lands and my dowry are yours to keep." She knew she would have to sacrifice any financial security her father had left her, but at this point all she was concerned with was escaping Waxton with her life and her sanity.

He threw back his head in laughter, his bass voice taking on a sinister tone as it echoed off the bare stone walls. *"You"*—he was so amused that he could barely speak—"have come to ask *me* for an annulment?"

"It is obvious, sir, that we do not care for each other." She forced herself to look up at him. "It is also obvious, sir, that there will be no children of this union."

He slammed down the measuring spoon, his eyes boring down on her as he leaned across the table. "And what makes you think I would free you now, my little virgin strumpet? Now, after all of these years? You are mine to do with as I please, though I do not see that I have treated you ill. You wear the finest clothes, you drink the richest wine, you eat the most splendid food."

Her gaze locked triumphantly with his. "I have information . . . information I fear you would not wish made public."

His rodent eyes widened, his full attention sud-

16

denly tapped by her words. "Information? I don't know what you talk of." He started around the table. "Speak up, you worthless chit. What idle threat is this?"

She watched him come toward her as a predator stalks his prey. "'Tis not idle, I assure you, sir."

He stopped a few feet from her and reached up to smooth his grey mustache, watching her face as he tried to discern the truth of her words. "Come, come, what is it, then?" he asked, a hint of amusement in his voice again. "What possible information could you have that would be of significance to me?"

"Quite significant, I'd wager, for it could mean your head in the Tower." Since the return of Charles Stuart to the throne, punishment for treason, even suspected, was dealt with swiftly and with a heavy hand. Charles II had no intention of allowing any situation to get out of hand. His father had lost his head in his own courtyard, a fate Charles II was determined to avoid. Already more than one nobleman had been beheaded in the Tower of London for less than what Waxton's letter suggested.

Her husband crossed his arms over his chest. He was dressed superbly as always, in a burgundy velvet suit with a broad linen collar. No doubt it was Thomasina's money that had purchased the clothing, for though he had come to Havering House with a title and a small home on The Strand in London, he had little more. His family had lost everything in the wars.

"Pray tell me, then, what this vital information is, and we will see what it is worth to me."

Filled with a new sense of confidence, Thomasina stepped away from him and went around the table toward the windows. She kept one eye on him as she walked. "I have a letter, sir."

"'Sdeath, woman! Speak sense. A letter? What is a letter to me?"

"A letter with a list of names . . ." She glanced up to see Waxton turn notably pale.

"Names?"

"Twelve, to be exact. A list of names and a brief description of a purpose to the assembly."

He swore a foul French oath beneath his breath. "You cannot be serious? You mean to blackmail me? You are even more a lackwit that I thought, wife."

"I want a horse and an escort to London. A few pounds to see to my lodging—"

He gave a little laugh. "An innocent such as yourself in London? You'd not last a week in that decadent fetid city. Londontown devours pretty, naughty little girls like you, my child."

"—and an annulment. I don't care what reason you give. Say I'm barren if you like." She folded her hands. "As long as you leave me be, your secret will be revealed to no one."

Waxton took a sudden step around the long wooden table toward her, lifting his upper lip in a sneer. "You're serious, aren't you, you little bitch?"

She took a step back, her voice haughty. She had him now. There was truth in the letter and he was afraid of her. He would have to comply with her wishes. "Entirely, my lord."

He held out a wrinkled palm. "Give me the letter and I will forget this conversation took place."

"I can't do that."

"Where is it?" he shouted, shaking his fist. "Tell me where it is or you will severely regret your actions." His fist came down hard on the wooden table, knocking an empty glass beaker to the stone floor.

The sound of the shattering glass was frightening

18

in the tension of the room. "I . . . I will not give it to you," Thomasina whispered. "You will let me go tonight or the information will be in the king's hand by the dawn's light."

"Who else knows of this? Who is in conspiracy with you?" In rage, Waxton balled his fists at his sides. He was a man to whom control meant everything, and he did not like it when he lost control. "Tell me who!"

Of course, Thomasina had taken no one into her confidence. It was a bluff of sorts. She really didn't know how she could transfer the information to the king. Of course, she had realized she wouldn't have to. She had known that Waxton would have to meet her demands, aware she knew what she did. "It matters not who is with me. All that matters is that you free me from this abortion of a marriage and that I keep your secret safe."

Waxton's eyes narrowed. "The groom. What is his name? Lester." He snapped his fingers. "I knew that you must be lying with him!"

"Not Lester."

"Cook's son, then?" He looked up at her. "I suppose that my rein was not tight enough, for you still somehow managed to spread yourself for another man despite my efforts."

"I have given myself to no one. I'm still as virginal as the day you took me as your bride on my fourteenth birthday," she said, enjoying just a little the power of being able to remind him of his failure to perform as a man. "For all you know, my accomplice could be female."

"That 'twould not be unheard of," he accused.

She frowned, her voice taking on a gentler tone. "Come, Waldron." Thomasina had used her husband's first name but two or three times in eight

19

years. "Let me go. I won't tell anyone what the letter said. I swear, I won't. I couldn't give a hang for your politics or anyone else's. I just want to be free of you."

Waxton hung his head, shaking it wearily as he made a clicking sound between his teeth. "Oh, my silly girl, my silly little girl." He looked up at her. "You truly thought this would work? You truly thought that I would ever let you go?"

"You must. If you want to save yourself and the others, you have no choice."

He began to come slowly toward her, still shaking his head. Thomasina took a step back.

"You don't have an accomplice, do you, my darling child?"

She took another step back. "I do."

"You don't. I know you too well. You're too concerned for others' welfare to endanger anyone, no matter how insignificant a creature that person might be. Yes, you have the letter," he agreed, still moving closer, "but you thought I would just let you go. Oh, silly little Thomasina. I can't let you go. I can't even let you live knowing what you know."

She half smiled in disbelief. "You wouldn't murder me, not your own wife."

"The pity of the matter is that no one will even know you're dead. No one will care."

Thomasina's mouth dropped open in the sudden realization that she had made a terrible error in judgment. She had never thought her husband a murderer, but she had been wrong. She could see it in the glimmer of his dark eyes. He meant to kill her . . .

Just as Waxton dove forward, Thomasina let out a bloodcurdling scream and dodged around a small table under one of the windows.

"Go ahead and scream," Waxton taunted, coming toward her. "No one will hear you up here. And even if they did, they would not come. My servants are loyal only to me. I have made certain of that."

She lifted a glass beaker and threw it at him. He raised his hands to protect his face and the glass shattered against his hollow chest.

He cursed her, brushing away the broken glass from his clothes. She lifted another container, this one tin, and threw it. He yelped as it glanced off his head.

"Let me go!" Thomasina screamed, tears running down her cheeks as she reached for another projectile. "You had no right to keep me locked up here all these years!"

"I had every right as your husband," he bellowed.

She watched him pick up a knife from the table behind him, and Thomasina shook her head in terror. "Let me go, Waldron. Just let me go and I'll never tell a soul."

"Tell me where the letter is!"

She threw another glass beaker, but this time he ducked and it missed him entirely, hitting the drapes behind him before it crashed to the floor.

"I won't tell you!" she screamed, her entire body shaking. "Go ahead and kill me, but you'll never find the letter! You'll never know when the king's men will come to take you to the Tower, will you? You'll never know!"

In a rage of fury, Waxton lunged forward, the knife in his hand. Thomasina screamed and fell back against the musty drapes as the tip of the knife nicked her left breast. She shoved the little table at him, catching him across the groin. Waxton doubled over and groaned in pain. Seizing his moment of incapacity, she ran along the rough-carved wall. If she could just reach the doorway!

"Come back here, you malapert slut!" Waxton

shouted. "I will have that letter or your death will not be without pain!"

Thomasina's heavy skirts and tight busk made it nearly impossible to run, but she forced herself forward. No matter how terrible her life had been these last eight years, she still wanted desperately to live. Just another few feet and she would reach the door!

But suddenly she felt his grip on her arm. She screamed again and again as he sank his long fingernails into her flesh and whirled her around. He slammed her against the stone wall so hard that the impact jarred her teeth. As she clutched at the drapes, trying to keep her footing, a candle in the windowsill tipped, igniting the velvet. Flames shot up the wall as Thomasina twisted, trying to escape her madman husband.

"Where is it? Where is it?" he cried as he grasped the bodice of her gown and ripped it, letting her breasts fall bare from the torn velvet. He tried to bring the knife up beneath her chin, but she raised her knee sharply against his elbow and the weapon went clattering to the floor.

"Fire!" she screamed. "Fire!" If his servants would pay no heed to her screams for help, perhaps their fear of fire would bring them.

"You're going to die! You're going to die and no one will miss you a wit, you little sneaking jade!" Waxton wrapped his bony fingers around Thomasina's neck and pressed her back against the window, oblivious to the flames around them.

She felt his fingers tighten around her windpipe as she clawed at his hands. *Not this way. I won't die this way.* Despite Waxton's age, she was still no match for his strength. Already she was growing lightheaded, though she could still feel the pressure of his hands and the heat of the fire on her face.

Thomasina knew it would only take a few seconds without air before she would lose consciousness. And then he would win. She would be dead and no one would be any wiser. What Waxton said was true. No one would care, for there wasn't a soul on earth who gave a hang about her. But she deserved better. She deserved happiness, even love, and she wasn't going to let Waxton's twisted wickedness rob her of that right.

Somewhere deep within herself Thomasina found a surge of strength. Though her hands had already gone limp, her sight blurry, somewhere she found the power to twist around. She kicked hard with her left leg, catching Waxton in the shin, and then shoved him as he lost his balance.

Thomasina heard the glass window shatter before she saw it, and then it took a moment for her to realize what was happening as the bitter winter wind came whistling through the room. Time suddenly seemed to slow, so that every action was exaggerated, every sound intensified.

By the orange light of the blazing drapes, she saw an instant of stark terror on Waxton's face as he continued to fall backward. He flailed his arms and grabbed for her, catching Thomasina's sleeve. She looked down in mute horror as she felt herself begin to pitch forward into the darkness. But the sleeve cuff tore from her gown . . .

Waxton uttered a terrifying scream as lost the final resistance and went tumbling through the window toward the ground, four stories below.

Suddenly, Thomasina was alone in the blazing laboratory. Rain pelted her face, the wind tearing at her hair as she stood immobilized by fear and shock.

But her inner self, the survivalist in her, called out

23

to her. *Run! Run! Run far from here and never look back!*

Suppressing the urge to peer out the window at Waxton's broken body below, Thomasina lifted her skirts and ran for the door.

"Fire! Fire! Above in the tower," a servant screamed from somewhere in the house.

Thomasina sailed down the steps, passing two men with buckets of water. They called to her but she kept running.

She raced through the maze of hallways and down two back staircases, knowing it would be only moments before someone discovered the dead master. Thomasina could hear the shouts of servants and the clatter of feet on the stone floors as she darted through the long kitchen toward a back door.

Outside she ran across the compound, oblivious to the driving rain and harsh wind. She ducked inside the stables. One of the grooms lay asleep on a pile of straw. She touched him with the toe of her slipper. "Saddle me a horse—astride," she ordered, panting.

The groom sat up, blinking away his sleep. "My lady?"

"I said, saddle me a horse!"

He looked up at her exposed breasts, and she quickly lifted the torn material to make herself more decent. There was blood streaked on her hands, from whence it had come she didn't know. "Now, I say!"

He shook his head. "My . . . my Lord Waxton won't a . . . allow me to saddle up for you without his permission."

Spotting a pitchfork leaning against the wall, she grabbed it and thrust it at the boy. "I said, saddle up one of the mares, or I'll run you through with this, I swear by the heavens, I will."

The round-eyed groom darted into the nearest stall.

Spotting a woolen cloak and an old hat with a drooping feather, Thomasina snatched them up. She pulled her hair up on her head and pulled the hat over it, then threw the cloak over her shoulders and tied it around her neck.

When the boy led a saddled mare out of the stall a moment later, she made him give her a lift up. He opened the doors and she sank her heels into the horse's flanks and sailed out of the barn, the woolen cloak flapping behind her.

Thomasina reined around Havering House, intending to take the main road toward London. Flames shot from the windows of the tower, the room fully engulfed, filling the sky with orange light and shooting sparks. As she circled the house, she spotted the lantern light below the tower. They had found Waxton. She pulled hard on the horse's reins and the beast slid to a stop in a slick of mud. Thomasina debated which way to go, fearing someone would see her. But, then, what did it matter now? Waxton was dead, and a houseful of servants had seen her flee the tower. Murderess! She had killed her husband, and the punishment for her crime would be to hang from her neck until dead. The fact that her husband had tried to kill her was inconsequential.

Thomasina lifted the reins and urged her mount forward. This path was the quickest way to the road. If she had any hope of escaping, it had to be this way.

As she raced past the tower where men and women gathered, she caught a glimpse of Hunt by the yellow light of the lanterns. He held Waxton by the shoulders, and for a moment she thought for certain that she saw her husband's lips move.

"Stop her!" Hunt suddenly shouted above the cry

of the wind as he pointed an accusing finger. "Stop the murderess!"

Thomasina lowered her head and urged her mount faster. There was no turning back now. She sped down the long lane and onto the road that led to London.

Not a mile down the road, she heard the pounding of hoofbeats behind. She didn't know how he had gotten a mount so swiftly, but she knew it was Hunt. And as surely as she knew her own sire, she knew in her heart of hearts that Waxton had lived long enough to tell Hunt of the incriminating letter.

Thomasina tried to get the mare to run faster, but she was a delicate mount, no match for the war-horse Hunt rode. Thomasina didn't know how long she could ride at this jarring pace or how long the mare would hold up. Mud splashed up from the rutted roadway, onto her skirts and even into her face. Again and again the horse slipped, nearly going down in the mud and pouring rain. But she gave no thought to her discomfort as she tried to concentrate on the road ahead. Surely the good Lord would not let her die this way, here on a lonely road by the hands of the devil incarnate?

Hunt was gaining on her. He was no more than a quarter of a mile behind her now. She could hear his horse's hoofbeats; she could feel his pink eyes boring into her. But there was nowhere to go, no pathway to turn off onto, no woods for cover. She could do nothing but ride and pray for God's mercy.

Suddenly, Thomasina made out two flickers of lamplight. A coach! A coach ahead! She began to scream and wave one hand, while struggling to keep her seat on the slippery saddle. The weight of her sodden wet skirts was pulling her down and throwing her off balance. "Help," she cried. "Help me!"

Baron Richard Chambray sat on the leather bench seat of his coach with his long legs stretched out, his arms folded over his chest, his eyes closed. The rain beat down on roof and the wind blew so hard that the vehicle swayed precariously. Richard thought of the poor coachmen out in the downpour and wondered if he should not have stopped at that roadway inn nearly two miles back. But he wanted to get back to London, by morning if possible.

He had been to visit his widow mother in Essex, a duty that always left him fatigued. But since he had returned from the Turkish wars to find his father dead and his mother alone in the country, he had made it a ritual to visit the ailing woman once a month. Richard dug beneath his brocaded coat and pulled out a flask. He took a sip of the fiery liquor, as much to chase away the memories as to quench the chill of the frigid night.

Five years ago he had left England a young man, anxious to see the world. After a year in France he had joined several mercenary friends on a lark. They had wound up captured prisoners, and Richard had lost his manhood to a Saracen's blade. He was a eunuch. The word still echoed in his head as his mother had sobbed it. But the bitter resentment had passed, the psychological pain long gone and nearly healed along with the scars. He had his life here in England now, and a good life it was. With the title of baron left by his father and a reasonable sum of money, he spent his days gambling, supping with friends, and enjoying the freedoms of life he had nearly lost in that hellhole cell in the sand.

27

Richard took another sip of the brandy and corked the flask, returning it to his coat. As he laid back against the leather backrest, he thought he heard a faint voice. The wind, he surmised . . .

But then he heard it again. Stronger, more clearly. Someone crying for help!

Richard parted the back leather curtain of the carriage and peered out the window. Through the darkness and downpour he saw the outline of a horse, its rider flailing his arms.

Richard considered not stopping. These days the roads were amuck with highway robbers known to pass themselves off as travelers in distress, only to rob a man and leave him to die on the roadway. But there was a tone to the voice that made Richard think differently.

He rapped his fist on the ceiling of the coach. "Paul! Stop!" he ordered.

Throwing his cloak over his shoulders, Richard stepped out into the mud the moment the coach ceased to roll. He shaded his eyes from the rain and squinted. Yes, yes, definitely a rider.

"Help! Help me!" the strangled voice still called. Richard could hear another rider a quarter of a mile behind, most obviously in pursuit.

Richard ran across the rutted roadway to where the horseman had pulled up his mount. By the time he reached the rider, he had flung himself down.

"Holy, hell," Richard murmured, spotting the tangled skirts. The rider was a woman—most definitely a woman from the flash of her bare breasts beneath her cloak as she dismounted.

"You have to help me," she begged, running toward the coach.

"What is it?" Richard demanded, turning to follow her. "Who chases you?"

She flung open the family-crested door of his coach and somehow managed, even under the burden of her cumbersome woman's skirts, to get inside on her own.

Richard stuck his head inside the coach. A corner of her petticoat had caught in the hinge of the door, but before he could release it, she snatched the material, tearing it away. "Madame? I say, who pursues you?"

"Thieves," she shouted, gasping for her breath. "Thieves."

Richard stared out into the darkness. Peculiar, he thought, for a single thief to be chasing a woman on horseback in the dark of a rainy night.

He watched her pull back the curtain in the rear of the coach and stare. Richard could see that the rider had reined in some one hundred feet from the coach.

"Your horse?" Richard asked the mysterious woman. "Shall I have the coachmen tie her to the rear?"

"Leave her. Please—" she turned back in the seat to face him, her hands clasped as if in prayer, "please tell your driver to drive on. I beg of you."

The baron hesitated for only a moment, the rain running down his angular handsome-featured face, and then he called to Paul. Richard stepped back into the coach, pulling the door closed from the inside, and the vehicle rolled forward, leaving the "thief" behind.

For a long moment Richard regarded the young woman by the light of the single candle that burned in a sconce on the coach wall. Shaking from head to toe, she had pulled off the battered hat she wore and now pushed back long locks of wet, matted hair. She was a tall woman with ivory skin and dark eyes. Richard recognized that look in a person's eyes. He'd seen it too many times in the wars. This woman had just escaped death . . . and barely, he was certain of it.

She was a tearing beauty, whoever she was, and of nobility. But what touched Richard's heart the most was the courage he recognized in her frightened face. He knew that he could never have this woman in the way he wanted her at this moment, but a strange sense of protectiveness came over him. If he could never make love to her, at least he could protect her, and God willing, he would.

"Don't be afraid," he murmured, offering her his drier cloak so that she could cover the torn bodice of her gown. "I know the man who followed you was no thief. Now tell me the truth of your circumstances, and I'll see what I can do for you."

She lifted her lashes, and for the first time he saw a tear trickle down her pale cheek. "How . . . how do I know I can trust you?"

He considered her words for a moment before he spoke. "Have you anyone else you can trust?" he asked gently, guessing the answer.

She shook her head.

Richard slid across the coach into the seat beside her and took her trembling hand. His blue-eyed gaze met hers. "Then you've no real choice, have you, madame?"

# Chapter Two

*London, 1664*

Gavin Waxton, the Earl of Waxton, leaned back on the coach seat and nodded absently in response to a comment made by one of his companions. Having arrived in London only two days ago, Gavin would have preferred to remain in his rented rooms at Covent Garden and tend to some business. But he had run into an old friend, James Knowles, in the Royal Exchange, who had insisted Gavin accompany him and his companions to the Royal Theater tonight. James had promised it would be a night to remember.

James's coach, with its family-crested doors, swayed down Drury Lane, its progress hampered by the vendors, apprentices, beggars, hackney coaches, and hired chairs that thronged the street. The afternoon din was so loud, between the vendors calling out their wares and the roll of coach, cart, and hackney wheels, that a man could barely hear himself speak, let alone hear what anyone else had to say. The fetid stench of the summer air pouring through the tiny coach windows was enough to make even someone of strong constitution retch.

As Gavin glanced out the open window, he couldn't help but be astonished by the change in London in the last three years. He had left the summer of 1661, immediately after King Charles had awarded him a land grant in the American Colonies as payment for his family's loyalties and funds during the war years. London, then, had been on the verge of violent change, with the passing of an age of Puritanism, but Gavin had never anticipated that it would be so swift and mighty.

Restoration London was vibrant with the putrid smell of the open sewers, the site of crowded streets, and the taste of smoke in the air. In three years time it had become a bawdy city in sight and sound, alive with activity both honest and dishonest day and night.

To Gavin, it seemed as if every man, woman, and child on the street, in an ale house, or in a shop was frantically involved in some task or another. There seemed to be no difference between a countess hurrying through the exchange or a pickpocket slitting strings of gold buttons from gentlemen's coats; each was inexhaustible in his or her quest. All of England was prospering, yet Gavin saw little happiness in the faces of royalty and beggars alike.

Two days in London, and already Gavin missed the fresh, clean air of the American Colonies, the vastness that was so silent and enveloping. Here he felt anxious, fearful he would be swept up in the same tide as every other Londoner. Here he felt smothered by the masses, but there on the Chesapeake Bay of the Maryland Colony, he had come to experience the true meaning of freedom.

Gavin had intended to remain in the Maryland Colony and send a representative to the king to request another land grant, but it was the letter sent by his brother Waldron's solicitor that had brought him back across the sea.

The letter, misrouted for nearly two years, bore the disturbing news that Waldron, Gavin's elder brother, the Earl of Waxton, had been brutally murdered by his young wife, and Gavin was now heir to his brother's title and lands, as well as small fortune. But it was neither the title, nor the lands, nor even the needed money that brought Gavin back across the ocean. It was the need to see justice done.

The murderess had not been arrested. In fact, Gavin had been informed yesterday that she had escaped the very night she had killed her husband in cold blood, and now she walked free while Waldron was buried beneath the earth. Gavin was determined to find the sister-in-law he had never met and to see her hanged for her gruesome deed.

James Knowles repeated his question to Gavin, who glanced up. "Sorry, James, what was it you said?"

James reached across the coach and shook his friend's arm good-naturedly. Both men were fashionably dressed in fitted velvet suits, with scrolls of gold braid at the neckline and cuffs and low-crowned cavalier hats with plumes. Gavin had chosen a more traditional forest-green, but James wore a vibrant red, reminding Gavin somewhat of a barnyard cock.

"I said," James repeated, "London has changed since last you were here."

Gavin looked out the window of the swaying coach again. "That it has. I don't remember it being so dirty. There are so many people—more pickpockets, I'll vow, than honest men."

"They say they've come from the villages to share in the good fortune Stuart has brought—to some, of

33

course, more than others." He flashed his other two companions an all-knowing look. They were all aware of Gavin's financial success after he had received a letter of marque two years ago allowing him to seize foreign vessels in the name of the king, for which he was well paid. He crossed his legs. "True, the crime has increased, but that's just part of the city's allure. And I can vouch to you there have been some prudent changes. Wait until you see what walks across our stages these days."

Gavin lifted an eyebrow, trying to appear interested, wishing he had remained in his apartment. He had several documents belonging to his brother that he was hoping would lead him to the dear widow. "And what might that be?"

"Women."

Gavin gave a lazy smile. "Women, you say?"

One of the others, a man in a lavender suit, slapped his knee with his purple-plumed hat. "They sing, dance, strut across the stage half naked, and entertain at private parties for a fee." He nodded to James. "Our good friend here has made just such an arrangement. After the performance, a Madame Lucy Maynor will be accompanying us to The Strumpet and Bull tavern."

Gavin returned his gaze to the window as the coach pulled up to the playhouse, where a yellow flag flew declaring a play would be performed that day. "The woman of my dreams," he murmured with good-natured sarcasm.

The men burst into rowdy laughter as the coachman threw open the door and the gentlemen stepped out into the dirty street.

Inside the Royal playhouse, one of the only two licensed playhouses in the city, James led them to a box above center stage. The play, a performance of

34

one of Shakespeare's comedies, had not yet begun, but the playhouse was alive with an electrifying energy that could be found nowhere else. It was here that the royalty came to see and be seen; the play was almost an afterthought.

The curtained stage was apron-shaped and directly in front of it was the pit, where a hundred or so young men sat on benches calling to each other and climbing over the seats. Young girls selling oranges and sweetmeats called out their wares from the pit and shouted at the harlots who had accompanied the men in the pit. Directly above the pit but near the stage was a center balcony divided into boxes meant for the king and his guests. Another balcony above the royal boxes was filled with ladies—faces painted, necklines heavy with jewels—and their gentlemen. Gavin guessed that there were more women attending the afternoon play with their lovers and men with their whores than husbands with their wives. It seemed that Londoners had so long lived under the iron rule of the Puritan Cromwell, where playhouses, face paint, and bright clothing were prohibited, that they were going to make up for those lost sixteen years. Faithful marriage had apparently gone as far out of fashion as farthingales.

Gavin took his seat between James and the companion in lavender in the front row of one of the upper boxes. He listened to their conversation but made no attempt to participate. Finally, the minstrels began to play and the curtain lifted. The audience grew quieter but by no means hushed.

The comedy began and Gavin tried to become involved in the story, but it wasn't until a woman walked out on the stage that his attention was suddenly drawn. Gavin leaned forward in his seat, looking down at the redhead who had materialized in a group of several other actresses.

Her part was a minor one, but the moment she stepped foot on the gas-lamp-lit stage, the audience was captured. The younger men in the pit began to holler and clap, stomping their feet until the lines of one of the actors could barely be heard.

The actress wore her brilliant red hair long and wavy down her back and over her shoulders, to frame her heart-shaped face. Beneath her costume was evidence of a perfectly shaped female form, all curves and soft spots with long, lithe legs. But it was her eyes and the tilt of her smile that caught Gavin's attention. The actress's dark brown eyes gave off a sparkle of life that showed a woman who was content, even happy, something he did not see often here in London or abroad.

Gavin sank his elbow into James's side. "Who is she?"

"Who?"

Gavin indicated with his chin. "You know damned well who I mean, Knowles. The redhead."

James chuckled, leaning forward in his seat to admire her with him. "A beauty, isn't she?"

The redhead spoke and Gavin paused, holding up a finger for James to be silent. The actress's voice was low in pitch, almost gravelly, but utterly feminine and extremely provocative. The redhead's lines ended and another spoke.

Gavin watched her as she made her exit. "Is she for hire like the others?"

"Ellen Scarlet?" James gave a little laugh and reached inside his coat for his snuffbox. "I fear not."

"I should like to sup with her."

"As would every other man in this box . . . in this theater, for that matter. Choose another and I'll see what I can do, Gavin."

36

"Ellen Scarlet . . ." Gavin said aloud, enjoying the taste of her name on his tongue. Never in his life had he been so thoroughly captivated by a woman. Though never an abstainer from womanly wiles, Gavin had never before sought out a woman; they always seemed to find him. In his lifetime, he hadn't met a woman he'd consider getting to know better outside his bedchamber. There'd just never been the interest. But seeing Ellen Scarlet, for just those few moments, convinced Gavin she would be a woman worth becoming acquainted with.

He turned back toward James. "And what makes her so unobtainable?"

"She's Lord Chambray's mistress."

"I imagine she wouldn't be the first kept woman to see another man."

"The circumstances are different here, friend. Richard Chambray, Baron of Chambray, is not a man to cross. He is a nephew or something to the Lord Chancellor. They say he's very protective of his woman. Not six months ago there was a duel at Ridgely field. He killed the offender with a blade through his heart."

"She must be a very special woman."

"You're not listening to me," James insisted. "You've been away from England a long time. Things have changed. I'm telling you, you don't want to get involved with Madame Scarlet."

Gavin leaned back in his seat, forgetting about the play. "What does she think of her keeper's protectiveness?"

"They say she's in love with him. She socializes very little with the other actors and actresses and seems completely content to spend her time away from the theater in the arms of her lover." James turned back toward the stage and touched Gavin's sleeve. "Now, there's Lucy . . . A tearing beauty, isn't she? She's the one I was telling you about. The one that will be accompanying us."

Gavin glanced down toward the stage at the blonde who was singing as she danced around a circle of swains. She was beautiful, but nothing compared to Ellen Scarlet.

Gavin said no more about the redhead, but when the play was over and James led him backstage to the tiring-rooms, where they were to meet with Lucy, Gavin hung back from the others.

"This way," James called through the crowd of actors and actresses and equal number of admirers. He waved his scented handkerchief as they became separated by a swarm of students.

"I'll meet you at the coach," Gavin answered.

"I'll not be your second at a duel," James warned.

Gavin only laughed and waved. He certainly had no intention of dueling over the redhead. He only wanted to speak with her. What harm could there be in that?

Ellen Scarlet stepped behind a curtain in the far corner of the woman's tiring room and sat down at a mirror to wipe the stage makeup from her face. She couldn't resist a smile as she caught the reflection of the redheaded woman that looked back at her.

She brushed back a lock of the hair that had once been chestnut-brown. It was all Richard's doing. Dear Richard. It was he who had come up with this brilliant way to protect her from arrest for the murder of her husband.

Even after they had bleached her hair until it had become this shade of red, even after she had changed her name and Richard had sworn to protect her,

38

Ellen had still not felt safe. She was plagued by nightmares of her husband returning from the dead, of the Duke of Hunt finding her. But when Richard had suggested she audition to be one of His Majesty's actresses, Ellen had seen light at the end of a dark tunnel. As a sworn servant of the Crown, no actor or actress could be arrested for a crime with a signed warrant from the king himself. Locked into her new identity with her new appearance and the safety of her appointment, she could live again.

Countess Thomasina Waxton was gone forever. She saw herself as Ellen now. She felt like Ellen. Her past was nothing but a nightmare now, which dissolved with the coming of dawn. She had her job at the theater that she loved, and she had Richard whom she loved just as fiercely.

When Richard had first told her of his terrible injury, she had been shocked, then saddened by the thought that he would never be able to marry. Not her, not anyone. But she soon discovered that Richard was not a man to be pitied. He was too full of life. He had too good a heart. He wanted no pity. He was content with the life he had been given and encouraged Ellen to be content in her own lot of life.

And suddenly Ellen had so much with which to be content! For the first time in her adult life, she had someone to love and be loved by. This love was such a glorious gift that the fact that their relationship would never be the same as between other men and women mattered little to her.

Ellen heard her name and looked back up into the mirror. The curtain behind her had parted and in the reflection she saw a man. He was as handsome as Richard, but in a different way. His rich brown hair was cut to just below his shoulders, his cheek-bones high, his nose angular. He had the most startling green eyes.

"Madame Scarlet?"

For a moment Ellen didn't answer. Although the women's tiring room was always filled to capacity with admirers after a performance, few people bothered with her. Word had gotten around that she was Richard's and that she was not interested in admirers. That combined with the fact that Richard often stood guard, waiting for her after every performance, kept most men away.

When Ellen said nothing, Gavin went on. She was even more beautiful up close. "My name is Gavin Merrick."

"And what can I do for you, sir?" She couldn't resist a hint of a smile.

Men sometimes still frightened her, but somehow she felt immediately at ease with this strikingly handsome gentleman. Unlike most of the fashionable peacocks these days, he wore a sober suit, but expensive nonetheless and well fitting. He was tall, though not quite as tall as Richard. But where Richard was slenderly built, this man was all muscle and bulk. His shoulders were broad and his legs muscular beneath his silk stockings.

He smiled a lazy smile and looked away, then back at her again. "I'm not sure. I . . ." His green-eyed gaze met hers.

She went back to brushing her hair. Something about him made her stomach flutter in an unfamiliar way. "Yes?"

"I was wondering, would you sup with me tonight?"

Ellen lowered her gaze, immediately wary of the stranger. Richard had warned her she must be very careful with strangers. If she were to keep her identity a secret, she could not allow anyone to become too familiar with her. She could not afford to make friends.

"I'm afraid that would be impossible, sir."

Gavin watched her pull the brush through her waves of magical red hair. "You're married?"

She reached for the hat she had worn into the theater today, wondering where on earth Richard was. He was usually here to pick her up by now. "Kept, and I must say, my keeper is quite a jealous man."

It was part of the ruse Richard had conceived. She would pretend to be Richard's mistress and therefore off-limits to other men. This way she could live with him in his apartment and enjoy the safety it afforded. Once upon a time Ellen would have been horrified to have thought that anyone might think her a harlot, but it was a way to stay safe. And safety was all that mattered these days.

"Excuse me." She rose. She was a tall woman, but not as tall as Gavin. "My lord is most likely waiting for me outside."

He stepped back to let her pass, handing her the fan she had left on her dressing table. Their fingertips touched, and she felt the warmth of his hand as well as his smile. "May I escort you?"

She quickly moved past him. "I can assure you that won't be necessary." She started through the noisy crowded tiring room, but he followed.

"I mean you no harm," he told her, taking only one long stride to catch up with her. "I want only to talk."

Ellen laughed, throwing her light cloak over her shoulders. Though it was quite warm outside, the overgarment was needed to protect her gown from the filth of the streets. "You want only to talk? I find that's quite untrue when it comes to the male of

41

the species, sir.''

"Bring your Richard with you, if you like.'' He didn't know what was making him so generous, except for the fact that he was suddenly desperate to talk with this mysterious woman. "He can protect you. I've just come back from the American Colonies. I've brought with me some fascinating artifacts.''

She stopped in the doorway of the hall that led to the rear of the theater. Men had asked her to supper before, but she'd never been tempted. She wondered what it was about this man that drew her. "I'm sorry. I thank you for your kindness, but I have to go.'' Ellen lifted her skirts and hurried down the long hallway, leaving him behind.

She had almost reached the rear door when he called to her. She thought it best not to respond, but she turned anyway. He was leaning against the plaster wall in an easy stance, his arms crossed over broad chest.

When she met his gaze, he spoke, his voice casual but sincere. "I'm not an easy man to pawn off. Not easy to forget.''

She smiled again, in spite of herself. "No, I don't suppose you are.''

"I think it only fair that I warn you: I'm going to make you fall madly in love with me.''

Ellen laughed, knowing she blushed. "That's ridiculous. I don't know you and don't care to. I told you, I'm quite taken.''

"As am I. By you.''

The smile slipped from her face, and for a moment she just stood looking at the handsome suitor. Then, suddenly a little frightened, she turned and ran out of the theater and into the evening air.

Luckily, Richard's coach was just pulling up when she walked out. She was relieved to see him inside when the coachman offered her his hand and helped her up the step. She slid into the seat beside Richard and kissed him on the cheek. "I missed you today."

He grinned. "Did you, now?" He took her gloved hand and raised it to his lips. "And I you." The coach lurched forward and they rolled away from the theater. "Now tell me all about your day."

Ellen glanced outside the window as they passed the backstage door. Standing there watching the coach part was the mysterious Gavin Merrick. She looked back at Richard. "Nothing of interest. My part's changed for tomorrow. A better one." She pulled on her gloves and leaned back against the leather seat. She didn't know why she hadn't mentioned the stranger, Gavin, to Richard. She told herself it was because she didn't want to concern him. Gavin was harmless. But deep in her heart she feared there was more to the matter than she cared to think.

# Chapter Three

Deep in thought, Gavin ran a finger through the thick dust that had collected on the mahogany mantel. The moldy crimson draperies had been thrown open to let in the sunlight, but the library still seemed dark and ominous with its shelves of musty books and the strange fresco paintings that decorated the domed ceiling of the room.

Gavin had come to Havering House to see what he could discover about his sister-in-law. Finding the stately stone and brick home to be in ill shape, he had fired the inebriated caretaker and immediately engaged several servants from the village to see to the estate's upkeep. Gavin intended to sell the house as soon as he was free to do so. In the meantime, he would not have such a beautiful work of architecture crumbling at its foundation because of neglect.

"I'll expect the place to be kept tidy," he said to the widow with the hardy face standing next to him. He had found Mrs. Spate down in the village and had hired her to see to the upkeep of Havering House until it was sold. "You'll be held responsible, but the others are to do your bidding. Hire and fire as you see fit, and I'll see that payment is made."

"Aye, sir."

Gavin lifted a silver candlestick from the mantel. The candle had melted into a puddle and hardened on the carved piece. "There's been no looting?" he asked curiously. The house had been standing empty, save for the caretaker, for over a year.

Mrs. Spate dropped her hands to her plump waistline. "Most people's too fearful to come up to Haverin' House, even for silver."

"Fearful? Of what, pray tell?"

"Of the ghosts, my lord."

He smiled in amusement. "Ghosts?"

"Yes, my lord." She twisted her bare foot on the dusty slate floor. "Them in the village says Haverin' House is haunted."

"By my dead brother's spirit, no doubt?"

"Some in the village says that late at night you can see flickerin' lights in the tower where Lord Waxton's laboratory was before the fire. That pollute Joey was the third caretaker the gentleman from London hired. None a' the others would stay more than a night."

"Afraid of the mysterious lights?"

She chewed on her lower lip pensively, as if deciding whether or not to say more. "No sir, on account of they say there's a ghost woman that runs screaming through the hallways."

"The man I just sent off said nothing of screeching savages."

She shrugged. "They say there's some with the sight, some without. Mayhap his head was just too clogged with ale to see more than the pimpled nose on the end of his face."

Gavin set down the dusty candlestick and glanced at the widow. "You said you would be willing to stay here in the house and sleep in the servant's quarters.

Aren't you afraid, Mrs. Spate?"

"I got four boys and no husband to feed 'im since he drowned last summer past. I'll not let a ghost or two get in the way of me feedin' my boys." She crossed her arms over her lumpy bosom. "I fear nothin' but the wrath of the Lord. He'll protect me from goblins same as he protects me from a win'er storm."

"Wise woman." Gavin nodded. "It sounds as if you're precisely the person I'm looking for. I've no more time for specters than you do, Mrs. Spate. Now go speak with the others in the kitchen, assign them their duties, and come back to me with any questions you might have."

"Yes, sir." She bobbed a curtsy.

"I'm going to look around just a little longer and then I'll be on my way. I'll let you know before I go."

Mrs. Spate took her leave of the room and Gavin began to explore the large house. Before he had left London, he'd done a little research. He found that Havering House had been awarded to his brother Waldron by Cromwell in the fifties. Before that transfer of title, the lands had been in the Greenborough family for almost three hundred years. Apparently the young woman, Thomasina Waxton, had more or less come with the property. Shortly after Waldron had married the mistress of Havering House, her father, the Viscount Greenborough, committed suicide while hunting stag.

Gavin wandered from room to room, running his hands along the dusty furniture tops and staring at the walls lined with portraits. The main reason he'd come was to see a portrait of his brother's wife; he wanted to become familiar with what she looked like. He knew there had to be one here; it was tradition to have a wedding portrait painted. But so far he hadn't found any picture that could possibly be the Lady Thomasina Waxton. Those that hung on the walls covered in cobwebs were old ones. Everywhere Gavin looked he saw white-haired men in stiff collars and black suits. The few women whose portraits hung in the hallways or going up the front staircase were dressed in fashions from long ago.

Gavin went to the second floor and then the third. Most of the rooms had obviously been unoccupied for much longer than the two and a half years since his brother's death. But in a wing there on the third floor, Gavin discovered the apartments his brother and his wife must have occupied.

The first bedchamber he stepped into had to have belonged to the Lady Waxton. It was a room paneled in oak, and above the fireplace it was carved in scrolls and flowers. The heavy drapes seen in the rest of the house had been replaced with lighter curtains in a pale green, which allowed the sunlight to pour through the glass panes. More of the same filmy material hung from the bed, and every chair and stool was also covered in the same pale green.

The room was neat though dusty. A basket of needlework rested near a chair in front of the fireplace, as if just left there by an owner who had meant to come back. Inside the heavy oak chest of drawers were a few gowns, slightly out of style and in somber colors, but made of obviously expensive material by an excellent dressmaker.

Gavin stood back and stared for a moment, his gaze flickering from one piece of furniture to the next. The room gave little clues as to the personality of the woman who had slept here. She was neat. She was not terribly vain, for the only mirror he saw was a small oval one in a gilt Italian frame that hung near the doorway to the hall. No books lay open anywhere, despite the extensive library downstairs, so she was not a reader. Her lady's writing desk was neatly closed.

Gavin walked through a doorway on the side wall and stepped into a small rectangular parlor. There was a table with a lamp resting on it against the wall between two windows . . . for gaming perhaps. Two upholstered chairs were arranged near a small fireplace, with a round oak table between them. Several books were stacked neatly on the table, scientific volumes and one small leather-bound book of Shakespeare's sonnets. Gavin ran his finger along the spine of the book. *So the lady does read.*

He walked through another door and into the connecting bedchamber. Heavy velvet drapes covered the windows, nearly blocking any sunlight. But even in the semidarkness, Gavin could see that this room was filled with masculine subtleties. There was the dark mahogany paneling, furniture in a heavy florid style, and piles of books everywhere. There were several articles of clothing flung here and there and a man's silk dressing gown left out on the bed.

"So this is where you slept," Gavin murmured thoughtfully. "Not with your young wife, brother?"

Slowly, he turned from where he stood in the center of the room. Then he saw it, the portrait he'd been looking for! There, hanging over the paneled fireplace, was a painting of a young woman.

Gavin ran for the windows and yanked open the drapes, one after the next, allowing the full strength of the afternoon sun to pour in. When he turned to face the portrait again, he was immediately disappointed.

The portrait was indeed of a young woman approximately the same age as Thomasina was said to be. The subject had been painted in full length but, oddly enough, with her face turned away so that Gavin could see nothing but a sweep of dark, shining hair.

Gavin crossed his arms over his broad chest in utter fascination. The woman was wearing a dark green velvet gown, with a small tiara of emeralds in the hair she wore down her back in the fashion of a virgin bride. Gavin could see nothing of the young woman but the curve of her face, yet there was something about the portrait that he couldn't tear his gaze from it.

"Thomasina, is that you?" he asked. "Why do you look away? Are you scarred by the pox? Are you harelipped?" Then a strange thought came to him. *Or did your husband not wish to share your beauty with anyone, not even with the artist?*

Gavin stared at the painting for another minute, then, on impulse, grabbed a stool and dragged it over the hardwood floor toward the fireplace. He stood on the stool, grasped the portrait of the young woman, and pulled it down. It was heavy and cumbersome, but he managed. And when he had it down on the floor, leaning against the bedpost, he touched the outline of the woman's cheek.

For the first time in hours, Gavin thought of Ellen Scarlet. The actress had said she would not see him, but there had been something about the way she had said it that made him think she could be persuaded. He smiled to himself. She had only to be persuaded in the right manner.

Suddenly anxious to return to London, Gavin lifted the portrait of Thomasina Waxton and took it out of his brother's bedchamber and down the hall. He would have one of the servants load it into the coach for him and then he'd be on his way. With Mrs. Spate in control of Havering House, he could return to his business in the City.

*      *      *

Ellen rolled her head on her pillow, moaning as she sank deeper and deeper into fitful sleep. Her mind was filled with the terror of black swirling clouds and thundering hoofbeats as the man of her nightmares bore down on her.

"No," she murmured, clutching at the bedsheets that were damp with perspiration. "No, please!"

But it was always the same.

She was running through the hallways of Havering House. But the hallways seemed to lead to nowhere. She could smell the stench of the fire in the laboratory and feel its heat on her face. She could hear Waldon's screams echoing off the stone walls. She ran faster but made no progress. There seemed to be no escape.

Hoofbeats clattered on flagstone. Ellen knew the albino was behind her, though she didn't dare look back. With every turn in the corridor he was gaining on her, growing closer and closer on that great white steed of his.

Suddenly, a hand reached from behind and grasped her by the shoulder. As he forced her to face him, Ellen opened her mouth and screamed in fright . . .

"Ellen! Ellen!"

She thrashed about, struggling to escape but knowing it would be impossible . . . knowing what would happen . . . what always happened . . .

"Ellen, wake up, love. It's a dream. It's only a dream."

"Richard?" Her eyes flew open. She saw Richard, stark naked, leaning over her. Richard?"

"Yes, yes, it's Richard."

She could feel her entire body trembling with fear.

51

"Another nightmare?" she asked. She never remembered them when she woke.

"But you're all right now, aren't you, sweetheart?" He sat down on the corner of her bed, where a candle on the nighttable illuminated his handsome face. "I'm here and you're safe." He took a glass of water from the table and pushed it into her hands. "Now drink this."

She sat up in obedience and drank the water laced with wine. "I can't believe this is still happening. It's been more than two years."

He ran his fingers through her long red hair, pushing thick locks over her shoulder, soothing her as a father would soothe a young child after a nightmare. "It'll take time, I told you that."

She looked up over the rim of the glass. "I feel foolish waking you like this. It's the second time this week."

He leaned foward and kissed her forehead. "Don't." He grinned mischievously. "I like getting the chance to come racing into your room minus my drawers."

She laughed with him. The first time she had seen Richard's mutilated genitals, she'd been shocked, then ashamed of her reaction. But nowadays they were like an old married couple past their years of sexual pleasure. Their relationship was platonic, but it was comfortable.

In the last year, Richard had taught her how to be comfortable with the person she was. Not just with the nudity that Waldron had somehow convinced her was something evil and to be hidden, but more importantly it was herself that she had come to accept, to even like. Richard's gentle tutoring had taught her confidence; he had taught her happiness. Somehow he had washed away the unfounded shame she had felt all these years, replacing it with confidence.

She patted the spot beside her in the bed. "Lie down with me. I don't want to be alone."

"Ellen—"

She took his hand, looking up at him. "Please, Richard. I just want to feel your arms around me. I just want to feel safe."

Reluctantly, he climbed over her and beneath the covers. He lay back on a pillow and allowed her to rest her head on his shoulder. "Better?" he whispered.

She smiled in the darkness. "Better."

Richard kissed her temple and then closed his eyes. "Then go to sleep. I have to be up early in the morning. I've business at Whitehall."

Ellen sighed and snuggled against him. As she rested her head on his shoulder and listened to the steady rise and fall of his breath as he drifted off to sleep, her mind wandered.

Against her will she thought of Gavin Merrick, the man she had met at the theater. For two weeks now he had been sending her gifts. Some were expensive, others without value yet touchingly precious nonetheless. One day it was a bowl of oranges or a single wildflower picked from the outskirts of the city, the next a pair of emerald earrings. In the past she had always returned the gifts from admirers out of respect for Richard, but for some reason she'd kept those from Gavin. The earrings, necklace, and Chinese vase were hidden in a chest at the foot of her bed. She'd shared the exotic fruits and sweets with the other actors and actresses at the theater.

She didn't know why she kept the gifts. All she knew was that there was something about Gavin Merrick that excited her . . . that made her stomach flutter each time she thought of him. Richard made her feel secure, but this giddy feeling associated with Gavin was different. He made her feel deliciously unsteady.

With each gift, Gavin sent a note. It always read the same: "Sup with me just once," it always said. And it was always signed simply "G."

*What would be the harm?* Ellen thought, rolling over so that her back was pressed to Richard's bare chest. *It would hurt Richard. I can't hurt Richard,* her mind echoed.

*But he wants me to be happy.*

Ellen smoothed her pillow and laid her head down again. It still felt like betrayal. Why else would she not have told Richard about Gavin? Because nothing was going to come of it. Because there was no need, she told herself. It was too soon to really go out in the world. Too soon to think of faraway thoughts like a husband and children. Hunt was still out there. She still had to be careful. Time, Richard said. It was all going to take time.

She sighed and closed her eyes, determined to push away all thoughts of Gavin Merrick. The fright of her nightmare had passed and she was suddenly tired. *The next time he sends a gift, I won't accept it,* she decided, nestling deeper into the soft bedding. *I'll send it back and that will be the end of him.*


"Good afternoon, madame!" *Squawk!* What a beauty you are. Tearing fine! Tearing fine!" *Squawk!*

The crowd of actors and actresses that had gathered around Ellen's dressing table laughed and clapped their hands, all talking at once.

"Where did it come from, Ellen?"

"Is it African?"

"Who taught it to talk?"

54

Lucy, one of the women Ellen often switched roles with, ran her fingernail across the gilded wires of the parrot's cage. "They say Lady Dumois has a parrot that talks, but only in French. She can't teach it to speak a word of English. Imagine that! What an uncivilized bird!"

The parrot flapped its blue and green wings and leaped to a swing that hung from the center of the cage. "My name is Sir Gavin." *Squawk!* "Come sup with me. Tearing fine beauty. Tearing fine!" *Squawk!*

Lucy glanced at Ellen. "So where did he come from, this Sir Gavin the parrot?"

Ellen stared at the beautiful bird. It was large, with blue and green feathers tipped in gold. It had a long, shiny yellow beak and beady black eyes speckled with gold highlights. The bird had been delivered by a young boy and had come with no note, but Ellen had known immediately who had sent it.

"Well, who sent it to you?" Lucy arched her painted black eyebrows. "That exquisite Richard of yours?"

The parrot swung on his perch, lifting one clawed foot and then the other. *Squawk!* "Tearing fine beauty, tearing fine! Come sup with me." *Squawk!* "Sir Gavin! Sir Gavin!"

"A friend." Ellen lifted the purple velvet cage cover and dropped it over the gilded cage with a smile. "A friend sent him."

With the bird silenced, the group of actresses and actors dispersed, all busy talking about other parrots they'd seen. Ellen waited until they were gone, then pulled her curtain around her dressing table and sat down to remove her stage makeup. Just as she was completing her task, she heard a masculine voice from the other side of the curtain.

"Knock, knock."

Ellen knew who it was. She made no response. Of course, she had to return the parrot. He was too expensive a gift. Too precious. But he was so beautiful!

"Anyone in there but a parrot?"

Ellen laughed and drew back the curtain to let Gavin in. "He's beautiful. But you shouldn't have sent him."

"I thought you might find him intriguing. He can imitate anything you say with a little practice."

Gavin's smile was infectious. "Wherever did you find him?"

"A friend who's just come into port from the islands had him in his ship's cabin, but his wife wouldn't let the bird in the house. He's an orphan." Gavin gave a wave of his hand. "The bird, I mean, not my friend."

Ellen ran her hand over the velvet cage cover. "Let me pay you for him, at least."

Gavin nodded. "All right."

Ellen looked up. The quarters were so close behind the curtain that she could have reached up and touched Gavin if she'd wanted to. She rose up out of her chair so that she could look at him eye to eye. "Name your price. I don't carry coin with me, but I can give you a note for my goldsmith."

Gavin caught a lock of her bright red hair and twisted it around his finger, mesmerized by the color and the way the light played off it. "My price is higher, Ellen. The bird for one supper."

She pulled back. "I told you I can't possibly."

"Just one." His gaze met hers as he slowly released the red curl. "And then I swear I'll never come back unless invited."

"You wouldn't just rather have the money? I'd

pay you well for him."

He took her hand and turned up her palm, pressing a kiss to its middle. "One supper," he murmured, "and I'll be gone from your life."

A quiver of cold heat ran up her arm. She shouldn't. She knew she shouldn't. But his hand felt so warm in hers. His lips had made her shiver. "Not tonight." Tonight she was meeting Richard and some of his friends at the Partridge and Plume for supper and cards. "Tomorrow night."

"I take it you don't want me to come for you?"

"I'm free to come and go as I please, but I'll not hurt my Richard's feelings."

*My Richard's feelings* . . . An odd sense of jealousy came over Gavin. "I'll be discreet, madame."

Ellen reached for her cloak and the bird cage. If she didn't hurry, Richard would come looking for her. "I have to go. I'll rent a hackney. Just tell me where to meet you."

"At the Six Pence. Do you know it?"

"The new tavern on King Street?"

He smiled as she passed him. "Exactly. Seven?"

"Eight."

Gavin lifted his plumed cranberry hat, lowering it onto his head as he swept into a bow. "Your servant, madame. I'll see you tomorrow night."

She waggled a finger. "But just this once, and then you must swear you'll let me be." Her gaze caught his. "I've no place in my life for you, Gavin Merrick."

He laid his hand over his heart, his voice laced with amusement. "I swear it."

Ellen turned away before he saw her smile and she hurried down the hall, swinging her bird cage.

# Chapter Four

Gavin leaned back in a comfortable chair, one booted foot propped up on a stool as he sipped his glass of burgundy. In ten minutes time he would leave for the Six Pence and his assignation with the beautiful actress Ellen Scarlet.

Across the room, leaned up against the wall, was the portrait Gavin had brought from Havering House last week. He studied it thoughtfully.

His search for the woman who had murdered his brother was not going as well as he had hoped it would. The Lady Waxton had no friends, no living relatives. So where had she fled? Who harbored her? There was no place for a woman of her station to go in the late of night in the middle of a thunderstorm. There was no place for her to hide. Yet that night she had vanished without a trace. It was almost as if she had never existed.

Yet Gavin knew she had. The haunting portrait was proof.

In anger, he set down his glass with a clatter. It was because of her that his brother, his dear half brother who had been so kind to him as a child, rested in a grave in the churchyard near Havering House. It was because of her that Gavin had been forced to leave Maryland, to cross the ocean he had sworn to never cross again.

Gavin stared at the woman who had turned her face away when the artist had painted her. "Where are you?" he inquired softly. "Where have you gone without money, without friends? Without a person left in the world who knew you?"

No. That wasn't quite true. There had been the servants. But Gavin had been unable to locate even one of them. They, too, had fled or been dismissed by someone within a day or two of Waldron's death.

The only lead that remained was something his brother's gossiping goldsmith had said. Despite his sister-in-law's cloistered life, there was supposedly one man who had known her, a Duke of Hunt who had been out of the country for some time now but was soon to return. The Duke of Hunt had been a friend to Gavin's brother and apparently had known Thomasina. There was even rumor that Hunt had been there at Havering House the night Waldron was murdered. But details were sketchy. Because Gavin had been unable to find a single servant in the village who had actually worked at Havering House, it was only through a cousin of one of the housemaids that he had learned what little he had about the night his brother was murdered.

Perhaps this Duke of Hunt would be the stroke of luck Gavin needed. Gavin had visited Hunt's home, and according to his housekeeper, he was expected back from France any day now. When he arrived, Gavin would call on him. Perhaps this Hunt could shed some light on what had happened that night at Havering House. Perhaps he would have some idea as to where the Lady Waxton had fled.

Of course, there was always the possibility that she

was dead. Dead or had left the country. Gavin knew that.

He looked back at the portrait that leaned against the wall. "But you're not dead, are you?" His voice reverberated off the dark wood-paneled walls. "You're not dead and you haven't run far, have you? You're right here in the City. I can feel you out there, trying to lose yourself in the masses. But you won't get away, my lady." He slid forward in his chair, staring intently at the portrait. "I'll find you, wherever you are, and I will see that you pay for my brother's life with your own."

"Seven o'clock on a warm summer's night and all is we—ell," the watch down below called as he walked down the street.

Gavin rose from his seat and reached for his coat. His coach waited down below on the street for him. It was time he went on to the Six Pence. He wanted to arrive there early to be certain everything was prepared to his liking. He wanted nothing to go wrong tonight. This Ellen Scarlet had caught his eye, and if he tossed his dice wisely, he'd have her between his sheets by midnight.

The fact that Ellen was obviously cheating on her keeper didn't concern him. She was a woman who walked the boards. She was an actress who traded her body for a place to live and food on her table. No more could be expected of such a person and he didn't hold it against her. What did he care, anyway? He wanted no long-term relationship. Once he received his land and found his brother's killer—and he would find her—then he would be on his way back to the American Colonies, never to return to mother England again.

Gavin took one last look at the mysterious portrait of Lady Waxton, then grabbed his green worsted coat

61

from the back of a chair and stepped out of his apartment, closing the door softly behind him.

King Street, where the Six Pence was located, was a muddy fashionable street that ran through the Whitehall palace grounds. Along its east side were a great many large residences, while on the west were several taverns patronized by the wealthy and poor alike. By the time Ellen's hired hackney pulled up beneath the weather-beaten sign bearing six shiny pence, she was so nervous that she felt lightheaded.

After Richard had left the apartment, she had dressed carefully. She wore a sage-green smock with full sleeves and abundant skirting, laced all in ribbon. Her short, tight busk made her waist small and her breasts stand high and firm. With green silk stockings, lacy garters, and flat black slippers, she knew she was dressed in the height of fashion. But as she had curled her hair and dusted her face with rice powder, she had wondered if Gavin would care what she wore.

She thought not. Though Gavin Merrick dressed well in coats cut of the finest cloth, he wore them without the air of most of the court fops. While it had become all the mode for a gentleman of Charles's court to take more care with his wardrobe than a lady did with hers, Gavin had somehow escaped that eccentricity. No, this was a man who judged another by the person he or she was, not by the weight of a purse or the popularity of a dressmaker.

By the time Ellen stepped out of the coach and paid the driver, Gavin was coming out the door of the tavern to greet her. He took her hand, kissing it roguishly, and then led her inside the Six Pence.

Several heads turned as Ellen passed the tables of

men in the common public room. Someone gave a low whistle, but the threatening glance Gavin threw in the direction of the offender was enough to make him turn his attention to the bottle of sack in his hand. Ellen kept her eyes fixed ahead and prayed none of Richard's friends were supping here tonight. She cursed herself for not having thought to wear a mask and vizard.

"I'm so glad you didn't change your mind," Gavin whispered in her ear as he directed her to the steps in the rear of the common room. "I feared you wouldn't come."

"I'm a woman of my word." She was relieved to reach the second floor, where private rooms were rented to the nobility.

Gavin took her light cloak from her shoulders and dropped it onto a peg beside the door.

The proprietor of the Six Pence hovered behind Gavin. "Your meal will be sent directly." He clasped his chubby hands, craning his neck to get a glimpse of Ellen, who had walked to the window to look down on the street. "Is there else I can do for you, my lord? Perhaps a ballad or two while you dine? I can send one of the minstrels up."

Gavin held open the door, inviting the tavern-keeper to take his leave. "Thank you. If we've need of else, I'll ring you."

Gavin closed the door behind the nosey proprietor, then he turned to study Ellen for a moment.

She returned his gaze, though a little hesitantly. This tenacious attraction she felt for this man who was a complete stranger was overwhelming. At this point when her new life was still in its infancy, Ellen knew she could not afford to reach out beyond the bounds Richard had so lovingly constructed for her. It just wasn't safe, not yet. Nonetheless, she found

63

herself staring back at Gavin with the eyes of a woman who wanted to touch and be touched.

Gavin had taken off his coat, so he stood in a pair of trim fawn-colored breeches and soft linen shirt with a lace cravat. The shirt was well fitted to accentuate the width of his broad chest and shoulders. His breeches clung to the hard, long muscles of his thighs, leading to an apex that left no doubt this was a male of the species. Gavin's stockings were silk, but rather than shoes he wore polished black boots that came nearly to his knees. A fashion from the colonies, no doubt.

He wore a thin mustache that hung above a smug grin, emphasizing the unsparing good looks of his rugged suntanned face. His dark, silky hair fell straight to brush his shoulders as he turned his head to catch the last rays of the afternoon sunlight.

Ellen felt her cheeks grow warm with her own intimate scrutiny, and she looked away from the dark-eyed gaze that followed her movement. "You say you've just come back from the Americas. I've heard others speak of the colonies but never met anyone who's actually been there." She ran a finger along the windowsill, watching a cart full of drunken students roll down the street.

"I've land there." She heard a chair scrape against the wood floor as he sat down. "I'm a planter in a colony called Maryland."

She turned back to see that he had seated himself at the long, narrow table that dominated the small room. He was making himself busy removing the linen napkins that covered their supper.

"Is it the desolate place they say, with naked savages and wild beasts?"

"A few naked savages and wild beasts, yes." He was obviously amused. "But desolate? Definitely not. It's

64

the most beautiful place I've ever seen, and I've been to many a land in my travels." He pointed to the chair that was across the table from him. "Sit before the food grows cold, and I'll tell you about Maryland whilst we eat."

Ellen sat down to the sumptuous meal of steaming leek soup, duck stuffed with oysters, crusty bread and cheese, and peas swimming in a cream sauce. Gavin talked and she listened, fascinated by his tales of the forest wilderness across the ocean called Maryland.

As the evening progressed and Ellen shared a bottle of white Rhenish with him, she became more talkative. She asked questions about his plantation, about the people who lived in the colonies, why they went, and the reasons they stayed.

Ellen was amazed that she felt so comfortable alone in a tavern room with a man she didn't know. But he made her laugh. He made her think. He had a good sense of humor, not only about the world but about himself, too.

A serving girl came into the room to clean away the remnants of dinner, bringing a bowl of nuts to crack and a plate of dried fruits for dessert. When the two had had their fill, Gavin produced a deck of cards and they proceeded to play a game of slur and knap.

Ellen loved to play cards. Though both her father and husband had rarely permitted gambling in their homes, with Richard's tutoring, Ellen had become quite proficient at various card games.

Another hour passed as she and Gavin took turns winning, talking and laughing as if they'd known each other a lifetime. It was not until Gavin began to question Ellen about herself that she grew uncomfortable.

She focused her attention on her hand of cards, laughing uneasily. "There's nothing to tell of

65

myself. Honestly."

Gavin planted his elbow on the scarred table and leaned in toward her. "Nonsense. You've not been an actress your entire life. When I left in '61, there were no women yet on the stage of the Royal Theater. Tell me where you're from. Tell me how it is you find yourself gracing the stage."

"You mean, what brought me to such a low station."

"No. I don't. I only—"

She laid down her cards and stood abruptly. "It's late. I must go."

"It's still early." He pushed up out of his chair. "I apologize for my questions. I only asked of your past in curiosity. I really don't care what you did or where you came from."

She took a step back. "I've had a lovely evening, but I really must go. Richard will—"

He came around the table so quickly that Ellen didn't have time to retreat. Before she could think, he had her hand. He took her in his arms.

The smell of him so close, mixed with the strong wine she had drunk, was making her head reel. She wanted to pull away. She knew she should. But there was something about the way he looked at her with his green eyes . . . something about the way his arms felt around her.

Gavin's lips touched hers and her eyes drifted shut, intoxicated by the heady nearness of him. She felt her hands lift and then fall as they settled naturally on his shoulders. His kiss was brief, no more than a brush of his lips against hers, but he left her breathless.

"Come home with me," he whispered, caressing her cheek with his fingertips. "Let me make love to you, my elusive Ellen."

For a moment she did not react. *Make love.* She

66

knew what he meant, though what Waldron had tried to do to her so many times could not possibly have had anything to do with love. But that was what Richard called the sexual act between a man and a woman. That was what he said he could never do. He could never make love to her.

Ellen's eyes flew open. "Mary, come up! Let go of me!" She was suddenly indignant. Gavin thought her a whore! Of course. So did everyone else. Common actress and whore. It was all part of the role she portrayed; it was what protected her. It was what she and Richard wanted people to think. But for some reason, it hurt to think that Gavin believed she sold her body.

"I have to go. I'll be late." She pushed his arms down so that he was no longer touching her.

"I'll pay you if that's what you want. Handsomely."

She whirled around and hurried for the door, fighting tears of anger and heartfelt injury. She had never before cared about others thinking her a whore. Suddenly, though, she had come to the realization of what it really meant. There was a price for everything, wasn't there? And this was the price she paid for her freedom.

Gavin watched her for a moment, his arms crossed over his chest. "I've offended you. I'm sorry. It's just that—"

"Just that I'm an actress. I'm another man's mistress. I must be a whore." She tried to snatch her cloak off the peg on the wall, but the material caught and refused to come free. She gave it another tug.

"I . . . I know you're kept," Gavin said, coming to her, obviously puzzled. "You said that much yourself. I just assumed that you were for hire for a price.

Most kept women are." He didn't say it in an accusatory way, but rather stated a fact they both knew to be true. He reached above her head and freed her cloak.

Ellen turned around, almost bumping into him. "Well, you assumed incorrectly. Now if I may beg your leave, sir . . ."

"Whoa, whoa there." He caught her by the shoulders and peered into her face. Her cheeks were flushed, her mouth drawn taut in anger. "I apologize for my error."

"Yes, Richard is my protector, but it's not what you think. I'm not his trollop!"

Ellen didn't know what had made her say it. She knew she was never to even hint to anyone that Richard was anything but a man who kept a mistress, or that she was anything but a refined whore.

Gavin gripped her shoulders, refusing to set her free. "Life's like that, isn't it? It's never what it appears to be."

She looked down at the sanded floorboards, embarrassed by her behavior. She liked this man. She liked him a lot. And she was scared. "I really do have to go," Ellen said softly. She looked up to meet his gaze. "But I enjoyed myself, and I thank you for the evening and for your kindness."

He returned her smile. "Can I see you again?"

"Again?"

"No questions. No indecent propositions unless they come from you. You name the time and the place."

She searched his handsome face for understanding. "Why? I belong to another man. That cannot change."

"I don't know why." He caught a lock of hair that rested on her shoulder and fingered it lightly.

68

"There's something about you that draws me. I can't sleep for thought of you. I can't attend to my business for wondering what you're doing, what you're thinking . . . who the man is that holds you in his arms at night."

"Isn't this the sort of thing men say to women when they want to seduce them?"

"Some men, I'm sure. But me? No. I'll not say I don't want to lie with you, Ellen, because I do. God knows, any man would want to." His gaze met hers in an act of sincerity. "But I'd be happy if you'd be my companion on occasion . . . at least for now."

Ellen knew she had to say no. She had no business becoming involved with a man. And she couldn't hurt Richard. He loved her so. Besides, what did she know of Gavin Merrick except that he had sailed the world and owned a tobacco plantation in the Maryland Colony? To see him again just wouldn't make any sense.

But Gavin had said he wouldn't be in London long. He had mentioned that he was looking for someone and that he was waiting on a land grant from the king. But then he would be returning to the colonies. He'd never be coming back. What harm could there be in taking supper with him a few more times?

"Richard cannot know."

Gavin lifted a palm solemnly. "Discretion is one of my finer points."

"And you can't keep coming to the theater. One of Richard's friends will see us."

"Send me a message when you can make it. I'm staying at the Tres Fleurs in Covent Garden."

She dropped her cloak over her arm. "Gavin," she said gently, "I really must go."

Reluctantly, he stepped back. "When will I see you again?"

She shook her head. "I don't know."

"A day from now? A month?"

"Somewhere between the two, I should think."

He opened the door for her. "I'll get you a hackney."

"I'll have the innkeeper get me one." She hung in the doorway, not really wanting to say goodbye. "I really did have a good evening."

"Only because you won more hands at cards."

She laughed. "Good night, Gavin." She knew he wanted to kiss her again, at least as badly as she wanted to be kissed. She turned away and hurried down the hall before one of them lost their willpower.

Gavin stood in the doorway of the private room long after Ellen's footsteps had died away. Another man's woman? This wasn't like him. He had no desire to cuckold anyone. But after one evening with Ellen, he just couldn't turn away. She was delightful. She was intelligent and intuitive, with a sharp, subtle sense of humor. She was unlike any woman he had ever met.

So what if she was this Richard Chambray's mistress? Gavin fought a pang of jealousy. He had never taken a woman into keeping, so it was better if she stayed with her man, anyway. He merely wanted to borrow her, just for a few precious hours.

Gavin stepped back into the private room and tipped his glass, finishing the last of the white Rhenish. He reached for his coat and shrugged it on. He would go downstairs and pay the innkeeper, then he thought he might ride past the Duke of Hunt's home and stop in, just to see if he'd yet returned.

# Chapter Five

Gavin leaped into the coach, a fistful of wild-flowers in one hand and two bottles of ale in the other. Ellen smiled as he comically offered her first the dusty green bottles, as if in error, and then the bouquet.

The coachman closed the door behind his master and the vehicle rolled westward down Piccadilly Street. Gavin had picked Ellen up at the theater after rehearsal and he was taking her on an outing, though where she didn't know. It was a surprise, he promised her, like a young boy not yet willing to pass out yuletide gifts. After several stops at the market and at a cookshop, they were finally on their way.

Nearly a month had passed since Ellen had met Gavin that night in the Six Pence, and since that time they had enjoyed each other's company as often as could be managed without Richard suspecting something was amiss. Sometimes Gavin took her to some public event like a bearbaiting or a puppet show, or to watch the changing of the guard at the palace. Once they'd even gone to see the king and Buckingham playing croquet in Spring Garden.

At first she had thought it too risky to go out in

public. But Gavin had convinced her that dressed in a vizard and a mask, she could walk at his side without fear of being recognized by one of Richard's friends.

Though it was exciting to be out in public and see the sights she had missed the first twenty-odd years of her life, Ellen's favorite times were those spent alone with Gavin. Usually she just met him at a tavern, but twice she had been bold enough to have him to the apartments she and Richard shared. Alone, without the distractions of crowd or entertainment, the two could while away the hours talking. Ellen hoped today would be one of those private times.

The longer she knew Gavin, the more she liked him. In fact, Ellen liked him so much that she feared she was falling in love with him. He was quite unlike Richard, and her feelings for the two men were decidedly different. Against her will, she found herself constantly comparing them.

While Richard tended to be thoughtful and pondering, Gavin could talk for hours on any subject. He had a sense of humor that kept her laughing, but he could become serious in a moment's time. Richard was a content man who was happy to simply be alive, whereas Gavin was a passionate man, unwilling to accept the merely acceptable in any situation. He expected the best from himself and the same for those around him. While Richard was gentle in word and deed, Gavin could be caustic at times, but he always truly believed in what he spoke of.

Gavin had kept his promise not to inquire of Ellen's past, but the longer she knew him, the more fearful she became that she might inadvertently reveal some tidbit of information that would make him begin to probe again.

To play it safe and hopefully stifle his curiosity,

Ellen had provided him with some information about her life before she came to London. She tried not to alter her true past any more than necessary, while completely leaving out the Earl of Waxton and the years she had spent as his wife. Ellen told Gavin about her father and the lonely but content years she had spent growing up. She talked of her father's political errors and the eventual loss of his lands and his subsequent suicide. She explained that she had lived with a maiden aunt until the woman died and it was then, penniless and desperate, she explained, that she had come to London and became an actress.

"So where are you taking me?" Ellen asked, eyeing a large hamper on the floor beneath the seat, which he had picked up at the cookshop. "And what's in there?"

"I told you, it's a secret."

She glanced out the window. "Out of the City? Are you kidnapping me, sir?"

Tossing his coat onto the seat beside him, Gavin stretched out his long legs and folded his arms over his chest. "I have to admit the thought has crossed my mind. I care more about this business of sharing you than I thought I would. I've never been a man to sneak about the shadows."

She looked away. "I thought you understood. I can't hurt Richard. He's done too much for me." She had pretty much left the story of how she and Richard had gotten together the way it was. Of course, she had left out the fact that Richard was a eunuch, so he and Ellen were not truly mistress and keeper in the way that everyone assumed.

Gavin nodded, not wanting to quarrel unnecessarily. His time with Ellen had become too precious. Besides, in a way, he found her loyalty to Richard

73

Chambray very admirable. Just the same, he felt his jealousy growing thicker beneath his skin with each passing day. He wanted to possess Ellen, and not just her body but her heart, the way that Richard possessed her.

Gavin glanced up at Ellen after a few minutes of silence, which found them both staring out the window at the countryside as they left the City. Rolling green hills stretched out on both sides of the roadway, their symmetry broken up only by the dot of cottages on the horizon. "I received word that my land grant may well be approved shortly."

She smiled, thankful he had changed the subject. "That's wonderful!" But then her smile fell, her disappointment obvious in the tone of her voice. "But that means you'll be leaving soon."

He shook his head. "I think, perhaps, I'll wait until spring. I'm not too anxious to make a winter Atlantic crossing, and besides, I've still business here in London. I've not been terribly successful in my search."

After a moment she asked softly, "Why won't you tell me who it is you look for? Who is she? A lover who jaded you? A wife who's run off with your fortune?"

He chuckled. "I told you, my family lost their wealth in the wars. And as for this person I seek, who she is isn't important."

Gavin had decided that he would not reveal to any more people than necessary who it was he sought, for fear the Lady Waxton would catch wind of it and flee. Besides, he was not completely comfortable with this terrible urge for revenge that burned in him. He had no desire to reveal such a dark side of himself to a woman who brought bright shining light into his life. He feared she just wouldn't understand. "Who

74

she is or what she's done matters not. But I can assure you, I have no feeling for her but hatred.''

"So what will you do with her once you find her?"

"Just see a wrong righted."

Ellen nodded. Despite her curiosity about this woman, she knew that Gavin honored her right to her own privacy and so she must honor his.

For the next hour the coach rumbled along the rutted road, and Ellen and Gavin talked. They discussed the present politics between France and England, and the king's sister who was married to Philippe, Duc d'Orleans, King Louis's brother. Gavin seemed surprised that Ellen knew so much about a subject supposedly of interest only to men, but then he was reminded that there was much about her that surprised him.

In some ways, Ellen seemed so naive, so sheltered from the world, yet at other times her understanding of mankind was as clear as the waters of the Jamaican Islands. Unlike most women he had encountered, she was hungry for knowledge. Every subject seemed to interest her, from astronomy to anatomy. She wanted to know the whys and wherefores of everything, and she was a superior student. Her memory amazed Gavin, for once she had heard, seen, or read something, she never forgot it. He assumed this ability came from her training on the stage. After all, as often as the play was changed at the theater and her part changed, she had to have a good memory to know all her lines.

The coach finally came to a halt, and when Gavin helped Ellen down, she have a sigh of delight, spinning on her toes. They had stopped at the foothills of a small town along the Thames. Here the open field of grass that ran along the river's edge was a brilliant green, speckled with the yellow flowers of late summer. There was not a soul to be seen save for a young girl far in the distance, tending to her family's small flock of sheep.

Gavin flipped the coachman a coin, and the servant started off toward the little town and the nearest tavern, no doubt. Then Gavin and Ellen were alone. He spread out a blanket down near the water and began to unpack the hamper. It was apparently filled to the brim with various delicacies.

"A picnic!" Ellen dropped down on the blanket beside him in delight. "I've never been on picnic, but I've read about them!"

"Never been on a picnic!" Gavin set out a loaf of fresh bread and two wheels of cheese. "What a crime against nature to have reached your tender age and never been on a picnic."

She picked at a bit of crust on the bread. "I told you my father was stern and never one for frivolity."

Gavin lifted an eyebrow. "Picnicking, a frivolity. Certainly not. I'd, in fact, consider it a necessity of life. One of those experiences that makes a man," his green eyes twinkled, ". . . or a woman whole."

All too quickly the afternoon in the warm sun passed, and soon it was time to make the trek back into London.

"We could stay the night in a tavern and return in the morning," Gavin suggested as Ellen put the remnants of the picnic into the straw hamper.

"You know I can't do that, Gavin. Richard will be home this evening and I have to be there."

Gavin knelt on the blanket in front of her. "I don't know that I can stand this much longer, you being in his arms when I want you in mine." He lifted his finger. "I've kept my word, Ellen. I've not laid a hand upon you, but my constitution is wearing thin."

She kept her eyes averted. "Just companions, you

76

said . . . I agreed to meet you only to talk, only to share your company."

He pressed his hands to his muscular thighs and leaned toward her, forcing her to meet his gaze. "It's not enough." Slowly, he reached out to caress her cheek with the tip of his finger. "And I think you feel the same. You're just not willing to admit it."

She tried to tear away from his gaze but he caught her chin with his hand. "Tell me you don't feel the same, Ellen, and I'll not pursue this. Just tell me the truth, love."

Tears filled her eyes. She couldn't lie, not to Gavin. Not about this. Too much of her life was a lie. "Yes," she whispered, almost fearful of her own voice. "I want you." She couldn't tell him how hard this was for her, how she had never wanted a man in this sense. He thought her wanton. He thought her experienced. She had to play the part. "I want you, Gavin Merrick, but I belong to another man."

"Leave Richard and come live with me. Tell me what he pays you. What he provides. I'll match it. I'll better him. Just tell me what you want, Ellen."

She caressed his hand that still held her chin. "It's not that simple."

"Make it that simple."

She shook her head. "There are things you don't understand. Things you don't know . . . that you can't know."

Gavin groaned. "Ah, Christ's bones, Ellen." Without thinking, he pulled her across the blanket and into his arms.

As his mouth crushed down on hers, she could do nothing but hold tightly to his shoulders. She was powerless against his strength. She couldn't protest. She didn't want to.

His mouth was wet and hard against hers. But the

77

hurtful pressure of his impatience set aflame sensations deep in the pit of her stomach. She had been kissed, but never like this.

As his tongue touched hers, her breath quickened. A part of her wanted to pull away, but the rest of her wanted to stay here in Gavin's arms beneath the setting sun forever. When his hand came up beneath her busk to caress the swell of one of her breasts, she moaned softly. She could feel her nipples harden beneath the layers of clothing; she could feel her body arch against his, wanting more despite all reason.

When Gavin broke their kiss, her eyelids fluttered open. They were so close that she could feel his warm breath on her numb lips. "Tell me now that you don't want me," he whispered.

She exhaled with a shuddering breath and sat up, untangling her arms from his. "We have to go, Gavin, else it will be my head."

He opened his mouth to speak, then thought better of it. He rose and offered her his hand to help her to her feet. "All right, sweet," he murmured. "I'll take you home." He picked up the picnic hamper and draped his arm casually over her shoulder. She rested her cheek on his arm, savoring the feel of his hard muscles beneath his linen shirt and the scent of his masculinity.

The coachman appeared over the crest of the hill, and in a few minutes time their things were packed and Ellen and Gavin were headed back toward London.

Gavin took the seat beside Ellen and she rested against him, made drowsy by the warm afternoon, the abundant food and drink, and the burden of her feelings. Comforted by the strength of his arm wrapped around her shoulders, she drifted off to sleep.

Ellen awoke with a start sometime later. The coach was rocking violently to and fro as it pulled to an abrupt halt. Gavin leaped up and snatched a pistol out from under the seat cushion. He tucked it into the waistband at the back of his breeches, beneath his coat. Its twin he held drawn in his hand.

Outside, Ellen could hear the coachman shouting in terror. "Don't kill me! God a' mercy, don't kill me!"

"What is it?" Ellen tried to rub the confusion of sleep from her eyes.

"Highwaymen, I think." Gavin's fingers tightened around the carved mahogany wood of his pistol. "No matter what, you stay inside. Do you understand me?"

She nodded, frightened but not wanting to be a coward. "I've little cash; Richard says it's not safe to carry much." She fingered the small velvet bag she wore around her waist. "But you can give them what I have."

Gavin shook his head. "Just stay inside. We keep handing over our possessions to these thieving bastards and there'll be no end to it!"

Gavin's hand touched the knob of the coach door, but before he could push it open, it was yanked from his hand. He leaped out into the darkness, and Ellen heard a gunshot and saw a streak of light. A second and then a third shot followed.

Ellen pressed her balled fist to her mouth in terrified indecision. She could feel her legs trembling beneath her petticoats. All she could think of was that dark night Hunt had chased her down. Was it Hunt? Was that who had stopped the carriage? Had he come for her after all this time?

But then she thought of Gavin. He'd been so good to her these last weeks. He'd taught her so much about the world . . . perhaps even about love. Suddenly, she realized that her fear that he was hurt or dead was stronger than her fear of Hunt or whoever stood aside. With a scream of anger, Ellen jumped out the carriage door and onto the soft dirt of the highway.

"Well look, pray tell, what we got here, Jeremy!"

In the semidarkness of twilight, Ellen could see two men standing a few feet from the carriage, one aiming his unfired pistol at her. Gavin lay there unconscious, his discharged weapon clutched in his hand. The coachman was to her left, down on his knees, begging for mercy.

"Looks like we got us a gen'leman an' his whore out on assignation, Billy." The man snickered. "What we gonna do with 'em? Strip 'em naked an' tie 'em to a tree like last pair, Billy Bulbo?"

The blond with stringy hair chuckled. "You just cover me whilst I tie up the coachman and get the horses. Them bays'll pull a might price at the fair come Saturday." He slipped his unloaded pistol into his breeches and started for the horses.

Ellen's eyes narrowed with fury as she took in the sight of the two men. These were no handsome, gallant highwaymen the girls at the theater talked of. These were common street thieves that smelled of a pigsty. "What have you done to him?" She fell to her knees, running her hands over Gavin's still body. She could see no blood save for a streak at his temple. He was still breathing. Ellen looked up, her hand finding the hard metal of the pistol tucked into the waistband of his breeches. "Well, what do you want?"

The one called Jeremy took a step closer. He was wearing a gentleman's suit, but it was ill-fitted. Ill-gotten, gains no doubt. "Well, let's see." He crossed his arms over his chest. "We could start with them there fancified earbobs, couldn't we? Then we'll move on to the likes of you, missy."

Ellen touched her emerald earrings possessively, worried more about them than her virtue at the moment. The earrings had been a gift from Gavin. When he sailed to America, she would have nothing left of him but his baubles. "I think not."

Jeremy broke into a grin, tipping his cavalier's hat brim with the barrel of his pistol. "Ye hand 'em over, little lady, else I'll take 'em."

Ellen eyed Billy, who was busy unharnessing the horses from the coach. Her gaze strayed back to Jeremy. As she spoke, she brushed her fingers down Gavin's back and slipped her hand under his coat, hoping the movement was lost in the material of her abundant petticoats. "They were a gift. You'll not have them. Take the horses and I'll let you go."

"You hear that, Billy Bulbo? The *laidy* says she'll let us go." Jeremy slapped his thigh. "Ain't that the funniest thing you 'eard all day, Billy?"

"Get the jewels and tie 'er up, Jeremy. We ain't got time to dawdle. Someone else'll be comin' along."

Jeremy took a step closer to Ellen.

Ellen's fingertips touched the hard, smooth wood of Gavin's pistol handle and tightened around it. "I warn you. Not a step closer." Her gaze was locked on the outlaw's face, but her mind was on the pistol.

"Ye warn me, do ye?" Jeremy laughed again in his high-pitched nasal voice. "Hear that, Billy Bulbo? She's a-warnin' me!" He took another step closer. "And what you gonna do, little lady, if'n I do come closer?"

With one smooth movement, she slipped the pistol out of Gavin's breeches and raised it level with Jeremy's stomach.

81

"Sweet Jesus!" Jeremy took a step back.

"You don't go now and I'll blow a hole through your middle, that's what I'll do." She steadied her trembling hands.

"Hellfire!" Billy called, coming around leading the horses. "I thought you were holdin' 'er up, not the other way 'round, Jeremy!"

Jeremy shook his head. "She . . . she got a pistol, Billy Bulbo. What do I do now?"

The outlaw exhaled loudly. "For the cryin' tears of Mary, you take it from her, you dull-witted jacka-nape! You take it before her finger slips on the trigger and she blows your balls off!"

Ellen rose up off her knees, both hands gripping the pistol. "You take another step, Jeremy, and I most certainly will remove your most intimate parts." She was surprised by the strength she heard in her own voice.

Jeremy gulped. "Hear that, Billy?"

Billy glanced over his shoulder at Ellen. "She's only got one shot, Jeremy. Most likely she'll miss 'em. Now take the blessed pistol, get the earrings off her if you want, and let's get the hell out of here." He cuffed the side of Jeremy's head for good measure.

"Ouch!" Jeremy massaged his temple.

"You've got the horses. Don't be greedy," Ellen warned. "It's true I've only got one shot, one of you will most certainly be dead, if not instantly, then of a rotting belly within a fortnight. I understand it's a painful way to die, a gunshot through the entrails. The worms and maggots set in before you're dead, you know."

Jeremy swallowed hard and took another step back. By the light of the carriage lamps, Ellen could see he was making a cautious retreat.

Then she heard Billy Bulbo swear and make a

sudden move toward her. She jumped but not fast enough, and he hit her with his fist as he threw his body against hers. Without thinking, Ellen raised the gun and pulled the trigger, hitting Billy point-blank. His body jolted and fell backward under the impact of the musket ball and heavily loaded charge. The recoil of Gavin's pistol nearly knocked her over.

Through the smoke she saw Jeremy drop his pistol and take off into the darkness, crossing himself as he ran.

"Jeremy! Jeremy!" Billy called from the ground. "God's bowels, wait for me!"

Billy started to crawl away, dragging one leg behind him. In the confusion, she had fired low and struck him in the thigh instead of the stomach. Billy was now headed straight for the pistol his partner had dropped in his escape.

Ellen tossed away Gavin's discharged pistol and ran the few steps to reach Jeremy's weapon in the grass. Billy lifted his head to stare up at Ellen. "Don't kill me," he grunted. "Don't kill me, miss."

Ellen looked up to where Jeremy had come to a halt behind a knotted oak tree a hundred feet from the road. "Let 'im go. We didn't really mean no 'arm. I swear we didn't!"

Ellen thought she should probably wait for a constable, but how long would that be? All she wanted now was to be rid of the highwaymen and to see to Gavin's injury. She thought for a moment and then motioned with the pistol. "Jeremy, get back here and see to your friend. He's bleeding all over the grass. He'll need the attention of a surgeon, I fear."

Though Ellen didn't have a good view of the thief, she could hear the trembling in his voice. "You . . . you ain't gonna shoot my nuts?"

83

"I'll step back. You come and get him, and then you take yourself from this road. I'd suggest you find yourself another occupation." She paused. "One a little less hazardous to your manhood, perhaps." When Jeremy didn't come from behind the tree immediately, she brandished the pistol again. "Come, come, my patience wears thin."

Finally, Jeremy came creeping from the shadows of the tree, his hands cupped between his legs. Ellen stepped back beside the carriage but held the pistol aimed in Jeremy's direction. After a few cautious steps, the man came running, his wig askew. He grabbed his moaning partner by the ankles and started pulling him through the grass. Ellen watched him until he disappeared from view, then she knelt to see to Gavin.

She stroked his forehead. Already a purpling bruise was beginning to spread across his temple. "Gavin . . . Gavin?" She brushed her fingertips across his high cheekbone. "Wake up."

Gavin groaned.

"M . . . ma'am, could you see to untying me?"

Ellen looked up to see the coachman crawling toward her, his feet and hands bound. She had forgotten him entirely. She quickly unbound his ropes and returned to Gavin's side. "Get me some water or something," she ordered the coachman. "Then see to the horses before they wander away."

He brought her back a bottle of water and then went to do her bidding. Ellen dampened the corner of one of her petticoats, and as she bathed Gavin's blood-encrusted forehead, he began to move.

"Ellen?"

"I'm here." She bit down on her lower lip. "Are you all right?"

"What the hell happened?" He touched his

forehead with his hand as he slowly sat up. "Ouch, damn."

"You were hit in the head."

Slowly, he opened his eyes. "The highwaymen?"

She nodded. By the dim light of the coach lamps, she could see that the color was beginning to return to his face. "So much for my defending milady. Did they take off with everything we had, including the horses?"

She shook her head. "The horses got loose, but the coachman's seeing to them now." She peered into his face, wanting to be certain he really was all right.

"What did they take, then? Just money and jewels?"

She couldn't suppress a smile. "Nothing."

He looked up at her, squinting, as if focusing would hurt his head. "Nothing?"

"In fact, I think we gained an extra pistol."

Taking a moment to get his bearings, Gavin stood with a little help from her. "What are you talking about? Highwaymen who leave items rather than taking them?"

"Ah, you should have seen the lady, sir. Proud of her, you would have been," the coachman offered, approaching with both horses. "Sent them packing, she did. One with a hole clear through his leg."

Gavin looked up at her. "You chased off the thieves? With what?"

"Your pistol. The one you stuck in your breeches."

He broke into a grin. "I'll be damned straight to hell." He reached out to her, his face suddenly a mask of concern. "You're hurt. They hurt you?"

She tried to brush away his hand. "It's nothing, really." But she couldn't push him away. Instead, he took her in his arms to get a better look.

"You're bleeding."

She touched the place beside her eye that now stung. Her fingertips came away stained red. "I'm all right, really I am. We have to go, Gavin, else we won't get back in time."

"I can't believe this happened. I feel like a fool. I got knocked out."

"You were shot. You could have been killed."

"It was a graze!"

She brushed her fingers over his lips. "I'm just glad you're all right," she whispered, feeling a lump well up in her throat. Now that the incident had passed, she was frightened again. Frightened for her own safety and for Gavin's as well.

On impulse, Ellen pressed her lips to his. At first it was only a kiss of thankfulness, but at the feel of his lips touching hers, the kiss blossomed. Suddenly, there was something desperate about the need she felt for him, about the sorrow of knowing he would soon be gone.

"Come home with me tonight," Gavin whispered against her lips. He kissed the tip of her nose, her cheeks, the lobe of her ear.

She shook her head. "No, I can't. Please." She pulled away and lifted her skirts to step into the coach on her own. "The horses are harnessed, Gavin. We have to go."

The ride to London was quiet as Ellen and Gavin sat side by side, his arm draped over hers. They said little because there seemed little to say. Once they finally rode into London, Ellen tried to convince Gavin to let her off down the street from the apartments she shared with Richard, but he refused.

"You said yourself you don't expect him for another hour," Gavin said, taking her by the arm to help her down from the coach. "Look, you said yourself there aren't any lights burning in the window."

"I know, but . . ." She stumbled as her feet touched the dirty street.

Swearing softly beneath his breath, Gavin swept her into his arms and carried her in the front door. "Which way?"

She pointed up the steps to the second floor and to the right, too drained to struggle. "Just inside the door, and then you must go."

"I'll go. I'll go. I just want to see you inside safely."

At the top of the steps, Gavin lowered her to her feet and took the key from her hand. He unlocked the door and pushed it in.

"Ellen? Ellen, is that you?"

Ellen looked up at Gavin in shock. "R . . . Richard?"

Richard came out of the darkness, his face etched with concern. "Ellen, I . . . What the hell! Who are you?"

A heartbeat passed as a tense moment of silence stretched between the three of them there on the landing. Then Gavin stepped forward and swept off his hat. "Gavin Merrick, your servant, sir . . ."

# Chapter Six

Richard glanced at Ellen, at Gavin, and then back at Ellen again. "Christ's bones, what happened to you? Who is this man? Has he injured you?" He touched the swelling beneath her eye where the highwayman had struck her. "You're bleeding."

She pushed his hand away gently. "I'm all right. Gavin is a friend. He just brought me home."

Richard looked so dubious that for a moment Ellen could only stare at him, mute. So many thoughts were running through her mind. Should she lie about what happened tonight? Should she say she had been attacked here in the the City and that Gavin, a stranger, had rescued her? Or should she tell him the truth? Should she tell Richard, who had done so much for her, that she had been seeing Gavin behind his back? Could she tell Richard that she was afraid she was falling in love with this man?

Ellen pushed past Richard. "I can explain everything. But please, let's take the conversation from the hallway, else everyone in the queen's drawing room will be repeating our words by midday tomorrow."

Richard followed her into the apartment, leaving Gavin to trail behind. "What happened, Ellen? Are you certain you're not injured? You look as if you've been through Hades' gates."

She swept a hand over her torn, dirty smock. "It looks worse than it is."

He touched the sore spot beneath her eye again.

"Really, Richard, it's naught."

Gavin hung in the doorway, his feathered hat still in his hand, watching the transaction between Richard and Ellen. "I'll go," he said stiffly.

Ellen shot him a thankful look. "I think that's best."

Richard glanced at Gavin, as if suddenly remembering his manners. "I take it you saved my Ellen from some sort of danger . . ." He searched Gavin's face for some clue as to the relationship between him and Ellen. "Let me express my gratitude."

Gavin looked to Ellen. "More the other way around, I think." There was a hint of a smile on his rugged face.

Richard frowned. "I don't understand. How did you come upon her?" He turned back toward Ellen. "Where were you that you could have encountered such danger? You know I prefer you not to go out after dark without me. I thought you were here safe at home." He rubbed her hand in his. "I was sick with worry when I found you gone."

Ellen looked from the man she loved to the man she was falling in love with. She knew she couldn't have both. In fact, she couldn't truly have either. At this point, all she wanted was to keep from hurting them.

She lowered Richard's hand and walked to Gavin. "Go home and have a surgeon attend to the gunshot, else it will turn on you." She laid her hand on his shoulder, hoping the gesture wouldn't seem too intimate to Richard but wanted Gavin to understand

90

how she felt at this moment. "I'll explain to Richard what happened. Good night."

Gavin glanced up at the tall, slender dark-haired man. "You certain you'll be all right?" he asked Ellen, his voice tight.

She could tell by the tone of his voice that he meant, *Would Richard harm her?* He was obviously resentful of him. He was jealous that it was Richard she would spend the night with and not him.

"I'll be fine," she whispered insistently. "Richard would never strike me. Now go."

With a last challenging glance at his opponent, Gavin nodded his head in a modified bow and slipped out the door. Ellen closed it behind him and leaned back, focusing on the bleached floorboards.

"Where have you been, Ellen? I was afraid something had happened to you. I was afraid Hunt—"

"The coach was held up. Gavin was grazed by a musket shot, but no one was seriously hurt." She walked to the cold fireplace and sat down heavily in a cushioned chair. She rubbed her temples with her thumb and forefinger. "Have we some claret? My head is pounding."

Richard came to her and went down on one knee. He took her hand and turned it in his. "Ellen, look at me."

She lifted her dark lashes to meet his gaze. *Heavens, but he's a handsome man*, she thought idly. *Why could he not be the one that makes me tremble as Gavin does? It would be so much easier. So much more fair to all of us.*

"You've been with him. Tell me the truth, because I'll find out, anyway. You've made a cuckold out of me, haven't you?"

With an incredulous laugh, she threw aside his

91

hand and leaped up. "Made a cuckold of you! How in God's name could I make a cuckold out of you when you haven't the ability to even take my virginity?"

The moment she said the words Ellen was sorry, so deathly sorry. Richard looked as if she had slapped him in the face.

A heavy moment of silence hung between them.

"Oh, Richard!" She ran to him. "I'm sorry, I'm so sorry. I didn't mean to say that. It's just that I—" She wrapped her arms around his shoulders and rested her head on his broad chest. "I didn't tell you about Gavin because I didn't want to hurt you. I didn't tell you because nothing has come of it."

"You've been seeing him for a long time, haven't you?" He held his body stiffly, not returning her embrace but not withdrawing.

"No, no, Richard." She touched his clean-shaven face with her palm. "I haven't. It's only been a few weeks. We're just friends. He's not laid a finger on me. I vow it!"

"And you expect me to believe that?" His blue eyes narrowed. "A woman of your beauty. A man with that swagger. You think me a fool that I didn't see the way he looked at you?"

"Richard—"

"If he's not found his way beneath your petticoats, I should think it would not be for want of trying!"

Ellen's lip trembled and she lowered her gaze. She could feel a lump rising in her throat. Her eyes stung as she fought back tears. She had thought her tears were spent when she'd rid herself of that abhorrent husband of hers and the albino, Hunt.

Ellen swallowed hard. "Please try to understand, Richard. Gavin came to the theater. He was nice to me. We had supper a few times, that's all."

"The parrot. He gave him to you . . . Sir Gavin. It's no wonder you're so fond of the cursed thing."

"He's leaving for the American colonies soon. Nothing can come of it."

"It's not safe, Ellen." He rested a hand on her hip, searching her eyes for understanding. "You know nothing of him. What is he, some lord's son?"

"He owns ships. He has land in the American Colonies."

"What if Hunt sent him to spy on you? Or kidnap you?"

She backed away, throwing up her arms, her anger rising again. "We've not seen Hunt. I've changed my name, my hair color. He'll never find me. You said so yourself."

Richard shook his head, going to the fireplace, where he leaned against the mantel. "It's too soon. You know nothing of this Merrick. It's just not safe to make acquaintances of strangers."

Ellen looked him square in the eye. "Why have you suddenly become so possessive of me? You always said I would be free to go when the time came."

Richard looked away. Ellen thought she detected a tear in the corner of his eye. "Is that what you want? To be free to marry him?"

She laughed without humor. "No. No, that's not it at all. Gavin's made no such proposition. Besides, I told you I would never marry again."

"So what is the point of your words?"

"My point is that I like him. He makes me laugh. What harm could there be in that?"

Richard lifted a decanter from the mantel and poured two generous portions. "I've not kept you from making friends. I've never forbade you to go anywhere or to see anyone. Anything I said or did was only for your protection."

93

She rose and took her glass from his hand, letting her fingertips brush his. "I know. I know that, Richard. You've been so good to me, and for that I will always be grateful. For that you will always hold a very special place in my heart. But you're being too protective." She took a long sip of the heady wine. "It's I who killed my husband, not you. And ultimately, I must take responsibility for that."

He swirled the claret in his own glass, watching the tiny whirlpool it made. "What? You're going to turn yourself in? Confess your crime?"

"No. I'm not."

He thought for a moment before he spoke again. Ellen could tell by the light of the many candles in the room that he was wrestling with his own emotions. "If you want to move out of here, I'll put you up in your own apartment."

She smiled tenderly. "I don't want to move. I don't want to leave you, Richard."

"A man who is not a man," he said thoughtfully. "I can't say that I'd blame you." He forced himself to look at her lovely face. "You told him about me, I suppose? About my inadequacy as a man?"

"No!" She stared at him as if he were a madman. "No, of course not. I would never tell anyone. You know that."

"Yet he knew you lived with me . . . "

"I told him there were special circumstances." She drank the last of her claret and rose to set the empty glass on the carved mahogany mantel. "I told him I loved you, Richard, and that I wouldn't hurt you."

"So Gavin Merrick is a man content to take another man's woman, if only on loan?"

"It wasn't like that. I told him I wouldn't bed him. That he could take my friendship or take his attentions elsewhere."

"And he still wants to see you? Then it is serious."

She shook her head, arguing as much with herself as with Richard. "No. No, it isn't. It's just been two friends enjoying a meal together. We just talk."

Richard reached out and caught a lock of her red hair. "I knew you wouldn't be mine forever. I knew it, Ellen, but I didn't expect to lose you so soon. I didn't—"

"I won't see him anymore if you wish."

"That would be wise." He let go of her lock of hair and watched it swing to her breast. "But only because I think it would be dangerous. If you wish for the company of a man, choose one of our friends. Someone I know you'll be safe with."

She stared at the flickering flame of a candle on the mantel. "I never wanted to see anyone before I met Gavin. I haven't wanted to be with anyone but you." She glanced up. "But you're right about Gavin. I truly don't know much about him." She folded her hands in resignation. "I'll send him a message not to call on me again."

"Do what *you* think is right, Ellen, not what I think is right."

She rubbed her shoulder. Her entire body was sore, from the struggle with Billy Bulbo the highwayman, no doubt. "I think I'll bathe and go to bed. Could you call Rose?"

"It's her evening off, remember? She went to see her sister who's just lain-in." Richard turned Ellen around and began to work on the long row of buttons on her gown. "I'll help you out of your clothes and have bath water brought up."

She leaned against him for a moment, thankful for his touch. "I didn't mean to hurt you, Richard," she said softly. "I didn't mean for any of this to happen."

He kissed the back of her head. "I know you didn't.

95

Now let's get you into bed. We'll forget Gavin Merrick and this silly quarrel."

She squeezed her eyes shut. *I only hope that I can forget him*, she thought wishfully. *I only hope that I can . . .*

Gavin studied the artwork that lined the seemingly endless stucco wall of the narrow gallery running along the length of the gardens below. The Earl of Hunt had a keen eye for art, though his taste was not to Gavin's liking. Hunt had paintings from the brush and palette of the finest Italian, Flemish, and English artists in the world. But he tended to choose those canvases that were dark and foreboding, pictures that left Gavin with an ill taste in his mouth. There were also several pieces of sculpture on pedestals throughout the gallery—an armless Greek statue, an ebony bust from the Far East, even several ancient works of pottery—but they, too, all seemed to hold some tragic secret.

"Viscount Merrick?" a timid voice questioned from the doorway.

"Yes?" Gavin turned. He provided one of his father's lesser titles, when necessary, to give his family name some credence without having to use the title he had inherited upon his brother's death.

"The Duke of Hunt," the duke's secretary announced.

For a moment Gavin was shocked into silence as the duke made an entrance into the room. He had not been warned that Hunt was an albino. Gavin had seen a dead one once on a Dutch ship, but still he was unprepared. The Duke of Hunt had a startling shock of white hair, translucent skin, and inhuman pink eyes.

96

"Quite all right, Merrick," Hunt said, sweeping into the room. "Most have the same reaction when first they see me."

"My apologies, sir." Gavin swept off his feathered hat and bowed deeply. "I'm pleased that you were able to see me on such short notice."

"Yes, well, I've just had the house opened upon my returning from France, so it's as mad as bedlam. You understand?"

Gavin noticed that not only was Hunt dressed in clothing worthy of the king but also that both his hands were laden with jeweled rings. He was obviously a man of great station at court. "I won't take but a moment of your time."

Hunt tucked his hands behind his back and strode down the gallery, studying the artwork that hung on the wall. "What do you think?" He stopped before a stark swirling nude portrait of a deformed woman who had three breasts. "I brought the piece back with me from France just this week. Buckingham will be green when he sees it."

Gavin nodded, coming to stand beside the duke. "Quite interesting, Your Grace." He wasn't certain what else he could say. *Sick* was the word that came to mind, but he held his tongue.

Hunt nodded. "I saw the piece in an Italian's villa and I had to have it." He looked hard at Gavin with his rodent pink eyes. "Do you know what price a woman with three breasts brings?"

"No, no, I can't say that I do."

The duke smiled an odd smile. "More than perhaps you've seen in a lifetime."

Gavin glanced at the portrait for a moment, then back at Hunt. He made him uneasy, but this was his only lead. If he were to find any information on the Lady Waxton, it would be here. "I came to ask about

97

my brother, Waldron."

"Your brother?" Hunt turned inquisitively.

"Yes, the Earl of Waxton. I understand you were friends."

Hunt scrutinized Gavin. "You're not Viscount Merrick, then?"

"'Twas one of my father's lesser titles. I've just returned from the American Colonies, news of my brother's death was delayed in coming. Upon my arrival, I decided not to accept my brother's title quite yet."

His attention immediately captured, the duke smiled as if the two shared some sinister secret. "You seek the courtesan?"

"I seek my brother's wife."

"Well, well." Hunt made a clicking sound between his teeth. "How very provocative. And might I ask why you seek her? You have your brother's title and wealth. The trollop is nowhere to be found. What makes you pursue this avenue?"

"It is my understanding that my brother was murdered in cold blood. If this is indeed a fact—and the facts are sketchy—I will see justice done. I will see the woman hang for her crime."

Hunt crossed his arms over his chest thoughtfully. He was tall, though not quite as tall as Gavin, and well built for a man in his mid-fifties. "The fact is true enough that she killed him. But so is the fact that she has not been seen since that night."

"I understand that you were there that night, Your Grace. Is that true?"

"Did you know her?" Hunt glanced at the three-breasted portrait. "Thomasina?"

"I did not, which is why I have come to you. I understand you did know her."

Hunt walked across the narrow gallery to the

windows and stared down at the lush gardens below. "Know her I did, too well, I'm ashamed to say."

Gavin stood still, watching Hunt's freakish reflection in the wavy glass of the windows. "Sir?"

"Though your brother and I were friends, I fear that I committed a severe indiscretion with his wife, for which I am greatly sorry."

"You slept with my brother's wife?"

"Many times. She was a temptress and I a weak man, unable to resist her charm or abilities."

"You think this is why they fought that night in the laboratory? I'm told there were obvious signs of struggle."

"Quite possibly. I was not the only man who cuckolded your brother. But he never held it against any of us. He knew of Thomasina's wiles. He knew her to be a pathological liar, always weaving extraordinary tales. But Waldron himself was once bewitched by her . . . before he grew to learn of her true treacherous nature. It was the reason he married her in the first place."

Gavin took in this new information, carefully sorting it in his mind. "Have you any idea where I might find her?"

Hunt laughed, tracing a pattern in the glass with his finger. "If I did, I can assure you I would have had her taken into custody immediately."

"Have you no clue?"

He shook his head slowly, as if considering his response. "None." He turned to face Gavin. "But I've been gone a long time. I left, in fact, shortly after your brother's death. But"—he held up a finger—"I would be most interested in speaking with her before you turn her over, should you find her."

"Do you know of any friends or relations she might have here in London?"

"You think she's in London, Merrick—I shall call you Merrick to aid you in your cover."

Gavin nodded. "'Twould be appreciated, sir. And yes . . . yes, I believe she is here. I have no proof, of course, but where would you try to hide if you had committed such a heinous crime? What better place to lose one's self than London Town?"

"You are clever, Merrick." Hunt nodded his approval. "Much like your brother, I should say."

"Waldron was a good man. He didn't deserve to die thusly."

"Indeed he did not."

Gavin toyed with the feather of his wool hat. "Should I have any questions concerning my brother or Lady Waxton, could I call on you again, Duke?"

"You're more than welcome. In fact, I should like you to keep me *abreast*"—he chuckled at his own boyish pun—"of any information you might discover"

"That I will." Gavin paused. "Well," he bowed, "I'll not keep you any longer, sir."

Hunt gave a curt nod. "Come again when I've unpacked the remainder of my art treasures. I'm certain you'll find them most intriguing. Your brother and I always shared a love of finer things. He'd have been quite green with jealousy over my latest acquisition."

Gavin's forehead creased. Surely they weren't talking about the same man. His elder brother had been a man of outstanding propriety. Such crude, twisted excuses for art would never have interested him. "Waldron?"

The duke nodded, a smile crossing his pale face. "Shocked, are you, young man?" He seemed immensely pleased.

Gavin lifted his gaze to meet the duke's. He didn't

smile. "Not shocked, just surprised." He paused for a moment's time. "Well, I thank you, sir. Good day." He replaced his hat and started out the room, but when he reached the doorway, he turned to address the duke one last time. "Sir?"

Hunt had returned to the portrait of the deformed woman. He looked up. "Merrick?"

"Would you recognize her?"

"Thomasina?"

"Yes. I can find no portrait but one from my brother's chambers and it doesn't reveal her face. Besides, it occurred to me that she may have changed her looks, gained weight, suffered the pox . . . who knows."

Hunt broke into an eerie grin, and when he spoke, his voice was thick with an odd sense of finality. "I would recognize Thomasina anywhere."

Gavin paused for a moment, looking directly into the duke's face. *What was it about this man that made him so uncomfortable?* Gavin couldn't quite place his finger on it; he wasn't a man easily unsettled, but Hunt repelled him. Hunt sent up flags of caution in every recess of Gavin's mind.

"Good day to you." Gavin touched his cavalier's hat and walked out of the gallery.

"Good day, indeed," Hunt whispered, turning his attention back to the three-breasted woman. He ran a finger along the gilded frame thoughtfully as he listened to the sound of his secretary, Robards, letting Merrick out the front door . . .

*So, your brother has returned to seek vengeance, has he, Waldron? I didn't even know you had a brother. How very interesting. The important question of course being, Does he know of the letter the bitch stole? A pity you didn't live a moment or two longer so that you could have given me the entire*

101

*story, Waldron.*

*But tell me, was your little brother's name on the letter? You never told me who our conspirators were, Waldron, only that they lay in and out of the country. Is that the true reason why the boy travels under an assumed name and seeks your wife with such determination? Is it more than honor he must defend, but his own life as well? Does he fear his neck will stretch in the tower beside mine if Thomasina shows the letter to anyone?*

Hunt moved on to the next painting, one of a man and woman obviously copulating, though beneath a veil of linen sheets. The woman's hands were tied above her head, her face grimaced in pain or ecstasy, Hunt had not decided which. He folded his hands over his chest, studying the Oriental painting.

*You are out there, aren't you, Thomasina, my little harlot? Your brother-in-law believes it, too.* He smiled, pleased with the turn of events.

The Duke of Hunt had left the country immediately upon the death of the Earl of Waxton, leaving spies behind to listen for word of whether or not Thomasina reached anyone with her condemning information. Only after more than two years of silence from the jade had he thought it safe to return to London.

Of course, he knew he had to find little Thomasina the virgin. Hunt felt his palms go warm and damp, and he grew hard beneath his breeches at the thought of her. He had to have the condemning letter, and then, of course, she could not live with the knowledge of having seen the letter. But there was no sense wasting a life without a taste of it first. Hunt smiled as flashes of sexual fantasies passed before his eyes. Yes, he would enjoy her, and then he would kill her. Of course, this would have to be carefully orchestrated. King Charles or his cronies could not get wind of it. Hunt had worked too hard to reach his position at Court.

How convenient of Waxton's little brother to appear on the scene. Now *he* could bring the little bitch to Hunt.

# Chapter Seven

A knock sounded at the door. Ellen glanced up from the script of *Cleopatra* she was reviewing for next week's new performance. The Royal Theater changed its production so often that she found that once she had a play memorized, she had only to look over the lines of the particular character she would play for the coming performances. Next week she would play Cleopatra, a part she'd played so often that she had only to refresh her memory.

"You want me to get it?" Richard was playing a game of solitary cards at a small gaming table across the room. It was late afternoon, a comfortable time when Richard and Ellen simply enjoyed each other's company.

The knock came again, more insistent this time.

She glanced at the door. "Please. It's probably just a messenger from the theater. I told John to let me know if the rehearsal schedule changed."

Richard laid aside the deck of cards and strode to the paneled door.

"For Mistress Scarlet," a young man's voice stated.

Ellen looked up to see a boy in dirty breeches trying to hand Richard a basket of out-of-season fruits.

Richard looked over his shoulder as if to ask if he should turn the child away. Ellen got up and came to the door to push a farthing into the boy's hand. There was no need to ask who had sent the gift; she knew.

"I thought you told him not to send anything else," Richard said stiffly.

Ellen took the basket from the boy, who bobbed his head and ran down the steps. "I did." She closed the door with her bare foot.

Richard eyed the note nestled among the exotic fruits. "So, does your mouth say no whilst your eyes say yes?"

She watched him return to his card game. She hated this friction between them, but there seemed to be no easy way to soothe. Even if she never saw Gavin Merrick again, Richard would know Ellen had cared deeply for him. He would know.

"I haven't seen him since the night he brought me home, Richard, you know that."

"I know what you tell me."

Ellen frowned but made no comment as she extracted the note from beneath an orange and unfolded it. *Just one last time,* the floral script of Gavin's handwriting read. *Come.* She refolded the note carefully.

"I tell you the truth and you know it, Richard Chambray. You cursed well know it!" She set down the basket but held onto the note.

*It's only fair that I say goodbye,* she thought. *I owe him that courtesy.* She tried to push from her mind the thought that she needed to see him one last time. She needed to make him understand that there was danger in their meeting, without revealing the nature of the danger.

She'd just go to his door. She wouldn't go in. She

106

wouldn't give him a chance to wile her with his charm. She'd just say goodbye and thank him for what he had done for her.

Of course, she could never tell him how much his friendship had meant to her. How he had healed her wounds, much in the same way Richard had. Gavin had made her aware of her own sexuality and convinced her that all such emotions were not sordid or wrongful. He had brought her one step closer to recovering from her husband's abuse. He had convinced her that perhaps someday she could love a man and be loved.

Ellen looked up. "I think I should tell him myself, Richard."

He looked up from the card game he was pretending to once again be occupied with. "I'll not argue with you, because I know it's senseless. At least let me go with you."

She went to him and rested her hand on his shoulder. Her dear Richard, her dear, gallant, loving Richard. "I need no protection from Gavin. The coachman will be enough. I'll even take along Rose if it will make you feel better."

Richard started to speak but, seeing the look in her eyes, remained silent. "You have to do it alone," he said finally.

She smiled bittersweetly. "I have to do it alone, Richard, because I could have loved him."

Richard looked away, trying to control the emotions he struggled with. "Are you certain you don't?"


Ellen hesitated at the door of Gavin's upstairs apartments at the Tres Fleurs, on a fashionable street in Covent Garden. She had left her maid in the coach below, ordering the coachman to wait. She'd only be a moment, she'd said.

But standing here at Gavin's door, she was having a difficult time even bringing herself to lift the doorknocker and allow it to fall. She fiddled with her mother's crucifix worn around her neck. Ellen wasn't certain what she should say. Should she be abrupt and unemotional, simply saying she didn't want to see nor hear from him again? Or should she tell him how much he meant to her and how it hurt to break off their relationship? Should she speak of love, something she knew so little about? Somehow that didn't seem appropriate in this age, when there was no love between the ladies and gentlemen who came to the theater. Love was out of fashion for certain folks in Stuart's court.

But didn't that make the seed of her emotions all the more precious? Wasn't Gavin the kind of man who would think so?

Ellen sighed. There was no need to get into this with him. Gavin had made no proclamations of love. She was under no obligation to say anything other than to please not try to contact her again.

Ellen rapped on the door before she lost her nerve. For a moment she heard nothing, then a door from within opened. She heard hearty male voices, then light footsteps.

A blackamoor boy of ten or twelve, wearing colored robes and a turban, answered the door. He spoke perfect English, but with a liquid smooth accent. "Yes, mistress, might I tell the master who calls?"

She twisted a piece of ribbon at the point of her bodice. Gavin had visitors. He hadn't expected her to come immediately. "Tell . . . tell your master it's Ellen."

"Won't you come in?" The boy swung the door open a little farther.

She stepped out of view of the men gathered around a table. "No. I'll wait here. Tell him I'll only take a moment of his time."

Reluctantly, the blackamoor closed the door, leaving Ellen alone on the stair landing. Not a minute passed before it opened again and Gavin's tall frame filled the doorway.

"Ellen." He was surprised but obviously glad to see her. He was dressed casually in heather-blue breeches and a light linen shirt cut in the colonial style. His hair was braided in the back the way she had seen in paintings of savages, but it was dashingly attractive on him.

Their gazes met and he reached for her hand. "Come in. I didn't expect to see you. I have guests . . . friends from America. I want you to meet them."

She pulled her hand away, fearful his touch would weaken her resolve. "No." She looked down. "I'll not come in."

"Of course. You don't want to be seen. You don't want Chambray to know you've come. I'll send them away." He turned to call to his servant, but Ellen stopped him.

"Please, Gavin. It's not Richard; he knows I'm here." She twisted her hands. "I can't stay, and I don't want you to make what I have to say any more difficult than it must be."

He studied her face for a moment and then stepped into the hall, closing the door and blocking out the sounds of his friends' laughter. The smile was gone from his face. "Richard's turned you out? Don't be upset, love. I'll take you in. I said so before. Why, you could well come here. The apartment is large and

109

I'm hardly ever—"

*He's going to make this difficult, isn't he?* "Please listen to me, Gavin. Richard didn't turn me out."

"But he's forbade you to see me, else he will, so you've come to tell me there'll be no more suppers, no more picnics."

"No, no." She shook her head, looking away. "I can't see you any more, but it's not Richard's decision." She forced herself to look up at him. "It's mine and mine alone."

It was Gavin's turn to look away.

She watched him for a moment, and when he didn't respond, she touched his sleeve, barely a brush of her fingertips against the soft linen. "You don't understand . . ."

"By the king's cod, Ellen! No, I don't understand. What kind of man is this Chambray that he would give his woman permission, whore or nay, to see another man? What the hell has he got on you that you must make this choice?"

She held her temper. "I told you when first we met there were things you mustn't know."

"Things Chambray is aware of and holds over you, no doubt?" he snapped.

"No. No, that's not it at all. Richard is trying to protect me."

"Protect you? From me!" Gavin's baritone voice echoed in the plastered hallway. Somewhere below a door opened and then closed.

"No."

"Then from whom? What?" He wrapped his arm around her waist, holding her tightly so that she couldn't back away. "Tell me your dark secret and I'll protect you, Ellen." When she said nothing, he went on faster than before. "I told you, I don't know who you are or what you've done! I know you could never have done anything so terrible that the wrong

110

cannot be righted."

Her lower lip trembled. "You truly care for me, don't you?" Her voice was barely a whisper.

He brought his face so close that she could see the speckles of amber in his dark eyes. "I do, more than I want to admit even to myself. You've gotten under my skin, Ellen. I'm enamored, entranced. I can't give you up . . . not yet, Ellen. Not this way."

"It's dangerous."

He brought his lips to hers. "Tell me what Chambray knows that I don't. It's the only way I can aid you."

She shook her head with the slightest motion, intoxicated by the warmth of his lips. "I can't."

He kissed her again, the pressure of his mouth more forceful this time. She couldn't resist her own response and she wondered, as she leaned into him, wrapping her arms around his broad shoulders, if he could taste her desperation.

She wanted Gavin. Ellen could deny the fact no longer. No matter how much she loved Richard, she wanted this man. But the physical want that ached inside her didn't alter the fact that what Richard had said was true. She knew nothing of Gavin Merrick. There was no way she could be certain that any involvement with him might not lead to a confrontation with Hunt or one of his men. It was true Hunt was said to be in France, but as Richard reminded her, how long would he stay away from home?

Gavin ran his finger through the curls at Ellen's temples. His mouth touched hers again and again, sending her mind swirling and her thoughts askew.

She felt the rough plaster wall against her back. Somehow Gavin had turned her around and now pressed her against the wall, his mouth on hers, his tongue delving deep. She could feel his hand on her breasts, squeezing gently, sending shivers of sweet pleasure through her limbs as she tightened their embrace.

"Gavin . . ." She whispered his name, her fingers finding his crown of dark hair as he kissed a trail of lingering heat down her neck and across the bare flesh that rested above the line of her deeply cut bodice. When he slid the neckline of silk taffeta down off her shoulder to reveal yet more of her breasts, she caught his shoulders.

"Gavin . . ." She was breathless, wanting more yet fearful that if she didn't stop him now, she'd lose her virginity here in this dark hallway. At some point Gavin had thrust his knee between her legs and she had shamelessly tightened her thighs around it, savoring the throbbing heat of the steady pressure against her woman's mound.

"Gavin, please, not here."

"Tell me you'll not leave me. I'll be here but a few months longer and then I sail, Ellen." He brought his lips to hers again, his voice as raspy with passion as her own. "Tell me we still have this time together, Chambray and secrets be damned!"

She closed her eyes, flattening her palms against the wall. "Yes." She lifted her chin to receive yet another brush of his lips against hers.

"Yes?"

"Yes, but I must be careful." Her dark lashes fluttered as she opened her eyes and studied his. *It could mean my life, Gavin.*"

He rested his cheek in the hollow between her shoulder and neck. Carefully, he lifted the neckline of her gown and replaced it as best he could. "I didn't mean to fondle you in the stairwell," he apologized. He smoothed the taffeta, unable to resist touch-

112

ing her soft skin with his fingertips. "I'm sorry. I didn't intend for it to happen like this. I thought myself a scant more romantic, or at least more sophisticated."

She laughed, taking his cheeks in her damp palms. "No apologies. Suddenly I crave your touch. I'm a wanton woman, it seems."

"No." He kissed her gently. "Not you. Not my sweet Ellen."

She cut her eyes away from him. "Your *sweet* Ellen who walks the boards of the king's stage and lives with a man not her husband?"

He touched her breast lightly. "The heart tells the end truth in all matters, don't you know that?"

"I know not much of the heart. I've little experience with that. But what I do know is that I have to go. If Richard's coachman comes up the steps to see us groping in the hallway, he may try to defend me." She laughed, her voice still husky, as she untangled herself from Gavin's arms.

"Come again—tomorrow night. There'll be no fumbling in the hallway, I can assure you."

She shook her head, taking a step back as she attempted to make herself a little more presentable. Her gown was twisted and wrinkled, her hair in slight disarray. "I can't come tomorrow night. Not here. An inn, perhaps."

"If you're afraid to be alone with me, I swear I'd not force you to do anything against your will. I'm not a man who finds pleasure in rape."

She smoothed her cheeks, knowing they were flushed. Even standing here at arm's length from Gavin, she could feel a magnetism that was difficult to resist. She wanted to feel his arms around her, she wanted to taste his lips. She wanted to know what it was to lie with a man, but Ellen knew that making

113

love with Gavin would only bring heartache, if not tomorrow, then the next day.

"It's not you I worry about, it's myself." She watched his face for evidence of understanding. "I'm not free to give myself—to you or to anyone, Gavin. I have no right to lead you into thinking otherwise."

He grinned roguishly. "Your virtue should be safe enough at the Six Pence tomorrow evening after your performance."

Ellen hung on the polished stair rail, feeling younger than she had in years. "The Six Pence, then."

"And what of Chambray? Is he to be out of London?"

Her gaze fell to her kid slippers that peeked from beneath her petticoat. "I told you, Richard knows I came. I'll tell him where I'm going tomorrow night."

"I'd rather not have to duel for you, Ellen. Too many good men have died over insults, feigned or otherwise." He brushed back a lock of his own dark hair that had come loose from his savage's braid. "But if it comes to that, I'll meet him at Goodman's fields."

"Richard would not challenge you to a duel. He's not that kind of man."

Gavin's eyes narrowed speculatively. "Just what kind of man is Chambray, then? He has me more than perplexed."

"I have to go, really." She turned away and started down the steps, but he caught her hand.

"A farewell kiss?"

She pulled back before his lips touched hers and broke away, tossing her head of red hair saucily. "Mary, come up! I should think I've had enough

114

kissing for one evening, don't you?" But when she reached the bottom step, she turned back to him and blew a kiss in his direction. He was still leaning over the rail watching her as she slipped out the door and into her coach.


"You've *what?*"

"Richard, please don't be angry with me." Ellen sat at her dressing table in an azure silk robe with matching silk mules hanging on her bare feet. She was expected at the theater in less than an hour's time.

"Don't be angry with you!" He snatched the hairbrush from her hand and slammed it down on the table. "I thought you had gone last night to say goodbye. I thought we had agreed that we didn't know enough of this Merrick for you to become involved with him."

Stubbornly, she retrieved the silver-handled brush and yanked it through her hair. "It's too late. I'm already involved."

"You mean you already laid with him?"

She looked up at Richard's reflection in the mirror. *"I mean I wanted to."*

He swore softly in French. "This couldn't be at a worse time, Ellen."

"What do you mean?"

"I mean, Hunt has returned from France."

Ellen's fingers gripped the handle of the brush tightly, her hand frozen in the air. "When?"

"A week or more ago. I'm not certain."

"Why didn't you tell me?" She tried to control the hysteria that rose in a great lump in her throat. "When did you find out?"

He perched himself on the end of her bed. "I didn't

tell you because I only found out myself last night."

The shock passing, she set down the brush carefully and rose to dress. In action she remained calm, but her voice was shaky when she spoke again. "You saw him?"

"No, but I heard Lord Edmond speak of the albino who returned to court this week. Who else could it be, Ellen?"

She sat down on the edge of the bed beside Richard to roll on her sage-green stockings. Only moments before she had been lighthearted, excited by the thought of meeting with Gavin if only for a quiet supper. Now suddenly her world, the world she and Richard had so carefully constructed to protect her, was crashing in again.

"What are the chances he'll ever see me except perhaps from the royal box? With the red hair, the costume, and my country accent gone, he'll never recognize me. He'll never look for the Countess Waxton in a common actress."

"Probably not. And even if he does, I would guess that he is clever enough to know that as long as you hold the letter with his name upon it, you control him and his actions, not the other way around. Surely he knows that if he were to have you arrested for Waxton's death, not only would the authorities have you, but the letter as well." He frowned. "But then comes the next complication."

Her stockings on, she rose to continue dressing. "I'm afraid even to ask, but what complication is that?"

"I heard last night by the way of the same Lord Edmond that there's a mysterious man about town claiming to be the brother to the late Earl of Waxton. Edmond says he's in search of the woman who killed his brother."

Ellen slipped off her dressing gown and reached for the new smock the maid had left out for her on the bed. "But Waldron's only brother is dead. He died at sea years ago."

"So the man isn't Waxton's brother. There are certainly enough fortune hunters these days traveling under false pretenses. And the assets are still sitting there, waiting for you or someone to claim them. Just the same, the man could be dangerous."

She took her time before speaking, knowing what was coming. "So what is it you suggest I do, Richard?"

"We'll close up the apartment and go to my family home in Essex." He took the smock from her and dropped it over her head. "I'm certain Mother will welcome the company."

"I'll not flee, not ever again," Ellen murmured through the folds of material. The moment her head came through, she turned around to face Richard. "I'll not do it," she resounded firmly.

"You're being absurd. Just a few weeks. A month or two until we see what Hunt's intent is, and this man gives up and seeks easier money."

She turned for him to lace her up. "No. I ran once out of terror, but I'm no longer a frightened child. I won't run again. Besides, I can't leave the theater. Even if Hunt were to try and have me arrested, he couldn't do it without causing a great deal of trouble. Only the king himself can have one of his own servants arrested."

"It's Merrick, isn't it?"

She broke away and went to the chest to find her slippers. "You're wrong. And you're jealous."

"I am jealous. Jealous that Merrick could have what I can never have. Jealous that I've done so much for you and you've fallen for him so easily."

117

Locating the shoes, she slipped her feet into them. "Whatever I may feel for Gavin has nothing to do with you, Richard." She looked up at him. "I love you and I will always love you."

"But you love him as well."

"Perhaps." She looked away, lost in her own thoughts for a moment, then back at him. "I don't know. I only know that what I feel for Gavin is different. More physical . . . unsteady."

Richard turned away. "You love the bastard, all right."

She stared at his stiff back for a long moment and then went to him, brushing her hand across his shoulder blades. "But I told you. Gavin won't be here long. He won't be a part of my life long. Just the same, my life is here in London now. It's the theater. It's our friends. It's the freedom to come and go, to speak my thoughts without fear of punishment, something I was never able to do in either my father's home or my husband's." She took his hand and rested her head on his shoulder. "Richard, I can't go back to being the woman I was. I just can't."

"Don't you see, I'm not asking you to." He faced her, resting his hands on her shoulders. "All I'm asking is that we take some precautions. That we avoid the possible trouble before it smacks us in the face."

"I understand what you're saying, but I'm not going to Essex. I'm not going anywhere except to the theater." She looked up at the German clock on the mantel. "I'm going to be late as it is."

"Please at least think about it?"

She smiled and lifted up on her toes to kiss him on the cheek. "I'll think about it, I'm sure. But I won't change my mind. Now, are you going to drop me off at the theater or must I call a hackney myself?" She went to her dressing table to check her face. She'd put on her stage makeup when she reached the theater.

"I'll take you." Richard crossed his arms over his chest. "So when can I expect you tonight? Late?"

She picked up her cloak from the bed, sailing by him and out the bedchamber. "Early. I promise."

# Chapter Eight

As Ellen stepped out of Richard's coach, she saw Gavin standing under the weathered tavern sign of the Six Pence. He waved casually.

She waved back.

Richard rose to help her out, but she declined his aid with a shake of her head. "I'll see you this evening, Richard," she said firmly.

"If you think I'll embarrass you or make a fool of myself, you're wrong. I only want to warn the man that it would be in his best interest to take care with you."

She patted Richard on the knee. "He wouldn't harm a red hair on my head, nor would he let anyone else."

"Does that include highwaymen?"

She rolled her eyes heavenward. "Anyone can be held up, and there was no harm done." She brushed her painted lips against his cheek. "Now, have a good evening with your friends, don't lose too many pounds, and I'll see you at home later."

Richard scowled but kept his seat, allowing a footman to help her out of the enclosed coach. Once out on the street, she stuck her head back inside.

"Don't worry. I vow I'll be fine." Then, before he could answer, she turned away and walked toward Gavin.

He took her hand and kissed it. "Now, we can dine here, or if you like, we could go to a friend's house. I was invited for an informal supper but wasn't sure whether or not to accept." He gave her a sly grin. "Of course, we could skip the meal and go back to my apartments; I've a very inviting bedchamber I'm most anxious to show you."

She sank her elbow into his side, knowing that though he obviously desired her and indeed wanted her in his bed, he was just teasing. "No lewd comments or I'll go home, I vow I will."

He opened his arms, appearing the innocent. "Can you blame a man for trying? Admit it, you'd be disappointed if I didn't."

Ellen couldn't resist a smile as she took in Gavin's easy grin, his comfortable stance. She would guess he had taken less time to dress this evening than any other gentleman walking down the crowded street, yet he stood out among them. He was dressed in a fawn-colored coat and breeches, with a feathered cavalier hat. He wore no periwig, but instead had pulled his dark hair back in a savage's braid again. Ellen decided she liked the radical hairstyle; it said something about the man who wore it.

She took his hand, paying no mind to the steady flow of foot and vehicle traffic around them. "Let's go to the supper."

"You don't mind being seen in public with me? I don't know who will be there."

She shrugged. "Richard knows I've gone out for the evening with you. In fact, he brought me himself." *As for anyone else seeing me*, she thought, *I'll cross that path when I come to it.*

122

"That was him, peering from the coach like a jealous nursemaid, I take it?"

"Please, let's not talk about Richard tonight." She smiled up at him as he led her toward a hackney that had stopped to pick them up. "Tell me instead about who this is that's invited you to sup. How is it you have so many friends here in London when you've been gone so long?"

"Germaine's grandfather was a friend of my father's. Germaine and I knew each other as boys." Reaching the hired open coach, he helped her up and gave the ragged coachman directions. They turned in the middle of the street and headed toward The Strand.

"Your father, really?" Ellen found herself suddenly curious about Gavin's family. He had said almost nothing about them, and what he did say was rather vague . . . as vague as what she had had to say about her family. "Where was it you grew up? Here in London?"

Gavin, who had been gazing intently at Ellen's sparkling dark eyes, looked away. He had been feeling guilty these last few days, not having told Ellen the truth about why he had returned to London. What harm could there be in telling her the tragedy of Waldron's death? She could, perhaps, even offer some insight into the mind of a woman who would have committed such a horrendous crime.

But the instinct of the man who had once wintered with Indians told him to keep silent. On his last visit to see Hunt, the duke had indicated that perhaps he knew more of the night's events than he had originally led Gavin to believe. If Gavin were to gain the confidence of a man of such importance as Hunt, it would be better to lay low just a little longer. He knew that Ellen would not purposefully give away

123

any information he provided, but he thought it best not to take any chances.

Ellen's brow crinkled. "Gavin?"

He blinked. "I'm sorry. I was lost for a moment in memories, silly boyish memories," he lied. He gave her his full attention once again. "Actually, I grew up in no particular place. My father was a traveler. He had estates in several counties, liked to winter in the city, and made trips abroad frequently. I was dragged around like a piece of extra baggage."

"But the estates are gone?"

He nodded. "Gone in the wars, the same sad tale as half of the court's. The only thing I have left is an old country estate that I'm in the process of selling."

"But couldn't the king return some of those lands?"

"I'm not interested at this point. They were sold off a long time ago. Were they returned, innocent parties would suffer. After all these years, my land grant in the Colonies is far more important to me."

She nodded. "And your mother? What of her?"

"She died when I was very young. My father remarried once, but the girl died in childbirth a year after they were married. After that he gave up with women." At least that much was true.

Ellen fingered Gavin's coat sleeve thoughtfully. From the tone of his voice, she got the impression that Gavin was not being completely honest with her. But who was she to question another's honesty? Perhaps there had been some dishonor in the family name in the past, some dishonor Gavin preferred to leave buried with his parents.

Still, she couldn't resist just one more prying question. "Had you any brothers or sisters . . . that lived, I mean?"

He made a face. "What is all this with questions

124

tonight? The Spanish Inquisition? Or have you become a spy for Buckingham? I understand half of London is under his hire."

She laughed with him. What did it matter who Gavin's family had been, anyway? Richard was paranoid to be so concerned about who Gavin was. "I'm sorry. I didn't mean to meddle." She looked up, studying his heavenly green eyes. "I only want to know more about you. Is that so wrong?"

He took her hand, cradling it warmly in his own. "Wrong? No, I suppose not. But rather boring, for certain." He glanced out at the darkening street. "Look, we're here."

The hackney pulled into a drive and to a halt in front of a home with Tudor origins and recent updated refurbishing. Every window in the formidable house was glowing with candlelight, and the sound of music wafted through the air. Several coaches were pulling up the circular lane, with ladies and gentlemen in handsome outfits disembarking.

Gavin paid the driver and lifted Ellen down. "We'll stay as long as you like. Just let me know when you've had enough indecent propositions from these fops."

"Only if you let me know when you've had enough batting of eyelashes, tapping of fans, and indecent suggestions from the ladies."

The two laughed at their joke, amused that they both saw the social life of London in the same humorous light.

Gavin linked Ellen's arm through his. "Shall we go?"

Suddenly self-conscious, she wished she had called Madame Dubois to come and do her hair in a more elegant coiffure. Tonight Ellen had worn it in a simple style, pulled off her crown to fall in waves of curls down her back, much in the same manner she had worn it as Thomasina in a time that seemed a thousand years in the past. "Are you certain your friend won't mind my coming?"

He brushed his lips against hers. "You look so lovely, you're bound to be the gossip of the evening." He tightened his hold on her arm and started up the lamp-lit walkway toward the front door and winding stone stairs. "As for Germaine, he'd be glad to see me if I had a harem in tow."

A servant in emerald-green livery escorted them in the door and announced their arrival. "Lord Merrick and Madame Ellen Scarlet."

As they came down the marble steps into a grand ballroom, Ellen stared at him, taken off guard. "Lord? You didn't tell me you were titled."

He shrugged. "In America titles mean little. I suppose I've gotten out of the habit of using it. Viscount means little to an Indian trader or a field of tobacco."

Ellen started to say something else but was interrupted by a blond-wigged gentleman, dressed in scarlet with a great deal of gold trimming. He hurried across the marble floor, his high-heeled red shoes tapping loudly. "Gavin! Ods fish! I didn't expect you to actually come, else I'd never have invited you, you filthy colonial savage!" He took his hand warmly, then hugged him.

Just as he withdrew, he pretended to see Ellen for the first time. "And this must be the Madame Scarlet, who's captured our hearts from our theater boxes and simply refuses to let them loose." He took her hand and kissed it, making a great event to the gesture. "Tell me, dear, how is it you dare be seen with this Saracen? His fashion taste is simply archaic!"

Gavin clapped Germaine on the shoulder none too

126

gently. "Enough of the dramatics, Germaine. Go see to your other guests and let mine alone."

Nonplussed, Germaine patted his periwig, making puffs of white powder billow in the air. "*Mon Dieu!* I must see to my Lady Richardson, the old bawd. But swear to me, Gavin, love, that you won't carry Madame Scarlet off before I get a chance to dance with her."

"I'll let you know before we go."

"There's some of that fabulous new French champagne to try, heaving tables of tidbits, and gaming in the far gallery." He lifted his painted eyebrows. "Of course, there's entertainment for gentlemen upstairs, but I don't suppose you'd have any interest in partaking of that, Gavin, with such a luscious female companion of your own. Oh, well! Enjoy!" Germaine swaggered away, waving a handkerchief to a guest just being announced.

Ellen was uncertain what to say as she watched Germaine depart. He certainly didn't seem the type of friend she thought Gavin would have.

As if reading her thoughts, Gavin leaned over to speak in her ear. "Ignore the antics and the face powder; he's a damned fine man. I swear, though, he belongs on the stage as well as anyone."

Ellen turned to gaze at the round ballroom they stood in. "From the looks of this, I'd not think he'd be seeking employment."

Twenty or thirty crystal chandeliers hung from the painted ceiling, casting thousands of diamonds of lights over the one hundred or so guests. The house swarmed with earls and dukes and countesses and duchesses, all dressed in silk and weighted down with glittering jewels. Green liveried servants numbering almost as many as the guests made haste seeing to their needs, serving delicacies for the palate

127

and drinks for the spirit.

Gavin swept up two glasses of champagne, and side by side he and Ellen moved from anteroom to anteroom, chatting to those one or the other knew. Ellen could feel all eyes following her, admiring her, and it made her tingle inside. Women flirted outrageously with Gavin from behind fans, but his attention was always wholly on Ellen.

They danced dance after dance until Ellen was breathless. "No more, no more," she protested as a piece ended and couples scattered. She fluttered her fan. "My busk is too tight. I'm going to faint if I turn once more."

Gavin laughed, his voice rich with the closeness of her and the indulgence of fine wines. "Let's step outside onto the balcony, then, and take a breath."

He ushered her out of the ballroom to a balcony that overlooked darkened gardens. Here beneath a canopy of stars, he eased her against the railing and brought his lips to hers. "I've waited all night for that kiss," he whispered.

There were several other couples enjoying the fresh night air and relative privacy, but in the cloak of darkness no identities were obvious. Ellen felt alone with Gavin even if she truly wasn't.

She touched his lower lip. "You taste like champagne." Her voice was husky. She'd had too much to drink, too many dances; she was flushed and intoxicated as much from the evening as from the libations.

"Come home with me, Ellen," he whispered in her ear. He held her tightly around the waist, his cheek nestled on her bare shoulder.

"I can't."

"Come home and let me make love to you." He caressed her bare arm in a slow sweep of his palm.

128

"Let me touch you the way I've dreamed of touching you."

Ellen lowered her gaze. "Something to drink." She looked up with a little laugh. "But no wine. Could you get me something to drink?"

His eyes narrowed suspiciously. "Are sending me off so that you can make your escape?"

"I'll wait right here, I swear it." She lowered her arms from his shoulders. "Just one drink and then we'll go."

He touched her chin, forcing her to look him in the eye. "To my place?"

"Home. I have to go home, Gavin. I promised Richard."

He started to say something, then checked himself. With another quick brush of his lips against hers, he went off in search of something to drink, leaving her in the darkness.

Ellen turned and leaned over the rail to stare down at the lush gardens below. A lighted fountain sprayed a mist in the air, creating a veil of magic over the greenery below. The cool breeze off the Thames blew the wisps of hair off Ellen's face, cooling her.

Just as she was about to turn back, she heard footsteps as a couple walked onto the balcony, then a voice that sent a chill of terror down her spine. For a moment she stood frozen, praying beyond reason that she had imagined it but knowing she had not.

Then she heard it again. Laughter this time in the midst of a conversation with a young woman.

Directly behind Ellen stood the Duke of Hunt.

She didn't know what to do. She had known that someday she would see him again. He was too important a man in London to simply disappear. She knew he would probably not recognize her with her dyed hair and painted face, the innocence of her past gone forever. But still deep inside, Ellen was afraid that if she turned, if Hunt saw her, he would point an accusing finger and she would be carried off to Newgate, only to hang for her crime of murder.

Ellen gripped the iron balcony rail, listening as Hunt and the woman moved to the right. After taking several deep breaths, Ellen forced herself to turn her head and look. She had to be certain it was Hunt. She had to see him with her own eyes.

Even by the dim light of the moon and the candlelight from within the ballroom, she could see the deathly white of his skin and hair. Even hidden in the darkness she imagined she could feel his pink rodent eyes boring down on her.

She turned back. Of course he hadn't seen her. He was lost in conversation with the young woman in the false curls. All Ellen had to do was walk away. Hunt would never know she had been there. He would never suspect how closely he had come to her this night.

But even after Ellen commanded her legs to move, her muscles made no response. Her heart was pounding so loudly beneath her breast that she feared she would give herself away. She was breathing so heavily that it was difficult to inhale in the confines of her tightly laced gown. *Just a few steps*, she told herself. *Four, maybe five, and you can make your escape.*

Completely poised in appearance, she uncurled her fingers from the iron rail and walked the few steps into the safety of the bright room. But even out of sight of Hunt, she didn't feel safe. She felt trapped . . . by the gay music, by the laughter, by the closeness of the strangers.

Ellen hurried through the ballroom, the ladies and gentlemen nothing but a blur. Someone caught her sleeve but she tore away. She lifted her petticoats and made a dash for the door. Like a wild animal pursued by its most dangerous predator, the only escape seemed to be flight.

Ellen bumped the elbow of a servant carrying a tray of empty wine glasses, but even the sound of the shattering glass on the Genoese marble didn't slow her. She ran up the steps two at a time, through the small receiving room and out the front doors that had been left open to receive latecomers.

"Madame, might I help you?" One of the liveried servants appeared at Ellen's side, his face etched with concern.

Ellen could do nothing but shake her head mutely. All of this time, all this distance, all the careful planning, and still Hunt had found her.

Suddenly, Ellen felt even more desperate than she had that rainy night she had fled Havering House. The night Waldron fell to his death, Ellen had had nothing to live for but life itself. But now . . . now she had Richard, she had the stage . . . she had Gavin.

Ellen ran blindly down the curving steps, down the drive, and out onto The Strand, not hearing the sound of Gavin's voice as he called to her from the top step of Germaine's home.

"Ellen! Ellen!" Gavin turned to the servant, shoving the two glasses into the young man's hands. "What happened?"

"I don't know, my lord. She just came running out like the banshees of hell was upon 'er!. I tried to—"

Gavin raced down the steps. "Ellen! Ellen, wait!" The dark street was no place for an unescorted woman. There were thieves, kidnappers, and murderers on every corner in the City these days, all looking to take advantage of the wealthy.

By the time Gavin reached the end of the drive, Ellen had turned off the street down a narrow alley. "Ellen! Ellen, wait!" He traced her steps, gaining on her.

Just a few feet before he reached the alley entrance Gavin heard Ellen scream. He whipped around the corner to see two sailors grasp her by the arms and push her roughly against the dilapidated wooden fence that blocked the alley.

Gavin's first thought was to draw one of the pistols he wore at his waist, but fearful he might accidentally hit Ellen, he knew he would be better served to meet them flesh against flesh. Giving a blood curdling cry he had learned from his Shawnee companion in the Colonies, Gavin threw himself into the attackers.

"Gavin!" Ellen screamed as she attempted to twist free. "Help me!"

Gavin grasped one sailor by his tarred pigtail, jerking back his head so hard that the bones in his neck cracked.

The sailor gave a wail as he was forced to release Ellen. "Bloody cur!" he cursed, swinging a powerful fist.

Gavin returned the man's attack twofold, catching him first in the stomach with a punch, then square in the jaw.

"Gavin!" Ellen cried.

Gavin turned to catch a glance, out of the corner of his eye, of Ellen twisting free of the sailor's grip. But her attacker caught the tail of one of her petticoats and tripped her.

Gavin ducked as his opponent swung a hard right and turned to reach for Ellen, but the sailor swung again and knocked him off balance, sending him tumbling. As Gavin scrambled to his feet, he saw Ellen pick up a splintered board from the ground and slam her attacker in the face. Blood spewed from the sailor's nose as he fell backward under the impact.

Suddenly, Gavin's opponent stood in front of him in a low crouch, a curved-blade knife in his filthy hand. "You want to play, Mister Fancy Coat, Abner can play." He grinned to bare a set of wooden teeth.

Ellen backed away from the three men, not wanting to get in Gavin's way. The man she had hit with the board still lay on the ground, semiconscious.

"Behind me, Ellen," Gavin murmured with a wave, all the while keeping his eyes on the sailor with the knife. "Get behind me and get out of the alley."

Shaking with fear, Ellen sidestepped the sailor on the ground and walked behind Gavin. She held her hand to her mouth to keep from crying out as she slowly backed out of the moonlit alley.

"Come on," Gavin urged with a beckoning gesture. "I've not got all evening.

Ellen watched as he crouched and began to circle the sailor with the knife, becoming the predator rather than the prey.

The tarred pigtailed sailor lunged for Gavin, who stepped easily out of harm's way. With a flick of his wrist he brought his fist down on the sailor's forearm, and from just a few steps away, Ellen heard the bone crack. The sailor grunted and doubled over in pain.

Gavin took advantage of the moment and, with a second swift motion, captured the weapon. Grasping the panting sailor by his ragged collar, he brought the knife up beneath his neck.

"You broke me bloody arm!"

"Better than a slit throat, I should think." Gavin touched the tip of the blade to the sailor's flesh, drawing a drop of blood for effect. "Now, my suggestion would be for you to take your friend and be gone

133

from here, else I'll string up the both of you by your heels and slit you from end to end."

The sailor shook with fear. "We . . . we didn't mean the lady no 'arm, honest we didn't!"

"Just going to escort her home, no doubt . . ." Gavin shook him until his wooden teeth rattled. "Eh?" He paused. "Now, I'm going to count to ten, and if you and your friend are not long gone from here . . ."

"We're going, as God is my witness!"

Gavin loosened his grip and the sailor dropped to his knees. He grabbed his partner by the armpits and hauled him to his feet. "If you don't move, you're on yer own, Sandy," he warned as he began to back out of the alley.

Ellen stepped out of the men's way and watched them pass. Gavin followed behind them to be certain they followed his instructions. It wasn't until they disappeared from the alley that Gavin turned to Ellen.

"Are you all right?"

He opened his arms to her, but Ellen couldn't move. She shook so hard from fear and shock that she was suddenly helpless.

Gavin swore as he tucked the curved knife into the back of his breeches and came to her, enfolding her in his arms. "Why the hell did you run off like that, sweetheart? You could have been killed!"

Ellen buried her face in his shoulder. The two sailors meant nothing. It was Hunt. It was Hunt she saw when she closed her eyes. A sob escaped her throat.

"Ellen?" He grasped her shoulders and pushed her back enough that he could look at her. She was deathly pale but seemed unharmed. But it was her eyes that concerned him. She looked as if she'd seen

Satan himself.

Realizing he'd do better to get her off the street than to try and get any answers now, he pulled her against him and led her out of the alley. They walked up the street the short distance to Germaine's house and up the walk.

The moment they approached the house, Ellen began to shake. "I . . . I don't want to go back in there. I—" her mind reeled, "I don't want anyone to see me like this."

"We'll just step inside. I want Germaine to send around one of his coaches."

She shook her head. "I . . . I'll wait here. I'll be well enough."

He studied her ashen face for a moment. "You won't run again?"

She shook her head again. "I won't."

After a moment's hesitation, he nodded. "I'll be right back. You stand here. No one will see you in the dark."

She looked after him as he strode away. "Hurry, Gavin."

He glanced over his shoulder. "I will."

Rather than tracking down Germaine, Gavin went to one of the servants on the steps. "Have one of your lord's coaches sent around immediately."

The tall, lanky young man shifted weight from one foot to the other. "My lord?"

"You heard me. I said have one of the Lord Lawrence's coaches brought around this instant."

"I . . . I don't know that I can do that, my lord, not without word from Lord Lawrence."

Gavin grabbed the boy by the gold braid of his green livery suit. "Either you send for a coach this instant, or it will be your head, man!"

"Yes, yes, my lord. Right away, my lord."

Gavin released him. "I'll wait at the end of the drive. "You may tell your master Lord Merrick borrowed his coach and it will be returned shortly."

"Yes, sir," the servant called over his shoulder as he ran for the rear of the house to have the coach called for.

Gavin walked back to where he had left Ellen and stood holding her in silence as they waited. Not five minutes passed before a coach with the coat of arms of Germaine's family pulled up.

A footman opened the door and Gavin helped Ellen inside. He gave the man hushed directions to his apartment in Covent Garden and stepped in beside Ellen. The moment the coach rolled forward, he pulled her to his side, wrapping his arm tightly around her, and pressed a kiss to her damp temple. She smelled of wildflowers, clean hair . . . and fear. By the light of the candle that flickered in the sconce on the coach wall, he studied her face.

"They didn't hurt you, did they?"

"No." She kept her gaze lowered, afraid to look him in the eye. "Wh . . . where are we going?"

"Home."

"Home to Richard?" she asked hopefully.

"No, my home." He smoothed a thick lock of her fiery red hair that had come undone from its pearl comb. "I'm going to take you home with me and then you're going to tell me what the hell happened back at Germaine's. Something or someone made you run, and I want to know what or who it was." He squeezed her cold, lifeless hand. "It's time we buried some of these secrets, Ellen."

# Chapter Nine

Ellen allowed Gavin to escort her upstairs to his apartments. She knew she shouldn't be alone with him like this, not when she was suddenly so vulnerable. But it was that very vulnerability that made her want to be with him so desperately.

A light, steady rain had begun to fall as they had left Germaine's, and now the September air had grown cool. Gavin ordered his blackamoor servant to light a fire in the main room and then dismissed the boy to the servants' quarters on the third floor, saying he'd not have need of him again this night.

Gavin then unrolled a Turkish carpet in front of the blazing fire and brought pillows from his bedchamber. All the while Ellen sat stiffly in a chair, watching the flickering flames. He sat across from her in a velvet cushioned chair and removed his shoes, then knelt in front of her on the hardwood floor and reached for her trim ankles beneath her petticoats. He slipped off her slippers and rubbed the soles of each foot.

Then he rose, took two glasses and a bottle of claret from a sideboard, and set them on the Turkish carpet. When he came back to Ellen, he took her hands and beckoned her.

"Come sit with me," he whispered, his voice as smooth as the champagne they had sipped from the same glasses hours earlier.

"Gavin, I shouldn't be here," she said, speaking her first words in an hour.

"Do you want to be here?" They stood facing each other, their fingers entwined, their lives entangled.

"Yes."

"Then stay with me." His lips sought hers and she lifted her chin to receive his kiss. She felt cold, so cold inside. Only Gavin could make her warm again. Only he could take away the paralyzing fear she felt from the tips of her toes to the dyed red hair on her head.

When their lips parted, she looked up into his green eyes that studied her so intently. She smiled. "I'll stay."

He led her to the elaborately designed Turkish carpet and knelt, patting the floor, indicating for her to sit beside him. "And now will you tell me what it is that scared you?"

When she made no reply, he reached for the glasses and poured a drink for each of them. "It has something to do with your secrets, doesn't it?"

She accepted the glass he offered and sipped deeply, thankful for the warmth of the liquor. "It does."

"Will you tell me?"

Ellen gazed back into the flames of the fire. She was calmer now. Her hands no longer shook. Her mind was clearer. As the fear was subsiding, it was being replaced by anger . . . bitter anger that the Duke of Hunt could appear in her life again and threaten all that she had.

She took another sip of the smooth claret. "I can't

tell you, Gavin." She laid her hand on his thigh and swept it in a caress, enjoying the feel of his muscular strength beneath the tight breeches. "I can't tell you, not ever." She lifted her lashes to meet his gaze. "So I'll ask that you not press the issue."

He took her hand and lifted it to his warm lips. "I don't understand."

"I don't expect you to." She paused. "But can you accept it? Can you take me as I am with Richard, with my secrets, neither of which I can give up?"

"You ask me to share you with another man? Even a scoundrel like myself would find that difficult."

"Just the same, I won't leave him, not even for you."

He draped his arm over her shoulder, pulling her close. "But how can I not accept your terms when I've made it clear to you that I'll be gone in the spring . . . that I can make no promises to you, no sort of promises that most women seek."

She touched his lips with her fingertips. "I want no promises. My life is here in London with Richard, yours is with your tobacco and wild Indians." She leaned into him, daring a kiss. "What I want now is to love and be loved, if only for a short time."

Ellen knew that with her words she was giving away the one thing she had to give to a man . . . only once. But it didn't matter. It didn't matter that Gavin would be gone soon, even if soon were tomorrow. What mattered was this moment and the feelings she had for Gavin, be they reciprocated or not. What mattered was that if she made love with this man, it would be something her dead husband and Hunt could never take from her. If Hunt had her arrested and hung tomorrow, she would have had Gavin and would take that in her heart to her grave.

Gavin brushed Ellen's hair back and deepened the

kiss she had initiated. His mouth pressed insistently against hers, as his hand caressed her cheek. Slowly, he lowered her onto her back, stretching out beside her, his mouth still crushing against hers.

His tongue delved deep, but rather than being frightened by his pressing ardor, Ellen was excited by it. Before this, the only thing she had known of the physical coupling of a man and woman was the harsh groping, pinching, and cursing of an impotent, bitter man. But this . . . this was wondrous, this touching, this tasting, this mingling of masculine and feminine scents.

"Ellen, Ellen," Gavin moaned, completely overcome by her sudden abandon. "I've wanted you since that first time I saw you on the stage, and now that I have you, I'm at a loss." He laughed as he leaned to kiss her love-bruised lips. "Look at my hand, it's shaking." He lifted a hand.

She laughed with him, threading her fingers through his as she looked up into his heavenly green eyes, now clouded with growing passion. "It is not. Now touch me, Gavin." Her eyelids drifted shut as she lowered his hand to her bosom, remembering what it had felt like there before. "Touch me. Chase away the demons I can never share with you."

Gavin cupped his hand beneath her breasts, and even through the thickness of her clothing, she could feel her nipples bud in response. His mouth touched hers again, then lower, covering the exposed flesh above her neckline with smoldering kisses.

When Gavin went to push away the shoulder of her gown, she sat up. "Unlace me," she whispered, a bare smile on her lips. "It's grown warm in here."

As he kissed that soft spot between her shoulder and neck, Gavin's nimble fingers found the laces of her gown and quickly loosened them. Then Ellen lay down again and with his help removed her gown, her busk, and even her petticoats, until she lay before him wearing nothing but a sheer linen shift.

"Now you," she urged, running a hand over his shoulder. "Unseemly or not, I want to see what it is I touch."

His eyes locked with hers as he pulled his linen shirt over his head and tossed it into the pile of discarded petticoats. But when he went to stretch beside her again, she shook her head. "The breeches, too." She lifted her lashes to stare at him boldly. "I want to see *all* of you."

Gavin couldn't resist a smile as he reached behind him to slip the laces that held up his breeches. Then he rose and peeled them off to stand before her nude.

By the glimmering light of fire, she watched him, unashamed by her curiosity. Gavin was more muscular than Richard, the only other naked man she had seen in her life. Gavin's shoulders were broad and tanned from months at sea, his chest well-shaped in muscular planes and sprinkled with dark curling hair. His stomach was flat and hard, a dark line of hair leading to his most intimate parts.

Ellen felt her cheeks color as she stared at his hardened shaft, but she couldn't look away. He was beautiful, this man of hers, beautiful as only a virile man could be.

Made suddenly self-conscious by Ellen's attention, he knelt beside her, running a hand up her leg, over her belly, and across her breasts. "You're so beautiful," he told her.

She lifted her arms and he came to her, resting his body against hers so she could curl against him, hard muscles meeting soft, feminine curves. They kissed a kiss of lovers, gentle and probing at first, but building with intensity.

141

As their mouths met again and again, Ellen stroked his body with her fingertips, exploring, fascinated by his hard male body and the scent of him.

Her mind was awash with sensation, a heat rising from the pit of her stomach and radiating into a pulsating yearning that mystified her.

Gavin's hands brushed over her damp flesh until she lost all sense of time and surroundings. The light of the fire and the feel of the wool carpet faded into the recesses of her mind as the sensations of Gavin's mouth and hands intensified.

The first time he lowered his mouth to touch her nipple with the tip of his tongue, she cried out in surprise, lifting up. But as he bent closer, taking her nipple in his mouth to tease it to a stiff peak, she relaxed, sighing smiling in full enjoyment of the gifts of the flesh.

"I didn't know it would be like this," she whispered in his ear, kissing the soft hair at the nape of his neck. "Had I known, I'd not have put you off so long."

Gavin kissed her forehead in response. Then he caught the hem of her linen shift and slowly lifted it up, taking his sweet time as if unwrapping a lover's gift on Christmas Eve. Finally, he pulled it over her head and tossed it aside.

Ellen had been fearful this inevitable joining between her and Gavin would bring bad memories . . the fear, the frustration, the bitter anger of the years spent with Waldron. But as Gavin raised up and lowered himself over her and pressed her into the carpet, there were no ill feelings, only feelings of joy and delicious, pulsating anticipation.

As Gavin brushed his fingertips over her glowing flesh, she felt his hardened shaft against her.

Instinctively, she parted her thighs, wanting him, needing him to fill some void that cried out to be satiated.

Guiding with his hand, Gavin began to slowly slip into her. When he met with slight resistance, his heavy-lidded eyes widened with surprise. Ellen moved against him, gasped, then breathed deeper as the resistance was torn. Gavin opened his mouth to speak. *A virgin. How could she possibly be a virgin, a rare creature indeed in Stuart's London*, but as she began to move rhythmically against him, all thought of logic escaped him.

Ellen was rising and falling beneath him, moaning, her nails digging into his shoulders. He covered her face with hot, damp kisses, forgetting all else for the moment but her sweet, tantalizing movements and the feel of her body melding with his.

"Gavin," she whispered, struggling, reaching for what she didn't know. Her body was aflame with a heat so intense that it took complete and utter control of her. All that mattered was the rhythm Gavin set with his hips and the fulfillment she sought.

Suddenly, Ellen felt a wave of intense, shattering pleasure sweep her up and carry her. The rapture was there for the briefest moment in time and then it began to subside, but for that moment it had been more powerful than she could have ever imagined.

Vaguely, she became aware that Gavin was still moving within her, his movements becoming faster with each stroke. He drove home only once more and then groaned, every muscle in his body tensing. Then he relaxed over her, burying his face in her hair, his body still.

As shivers of ecstasy slowly faded, Ellen once more became aware of the world around her. Her mind gradually filled with a hurricane of thoughts. She

143

once again saw the blaze of the fire and smelled the pleasant, pungent scent of charred wood.

Content to lie like this forever, with their bodies still joined, she ran her fingers through Gavin's dark hair, thinking how perfect life could be if it were always as simple as it was at this moment, one man and one woman entwined in love.

When Gavin could find his voice, he slid off her and onto his side, pulling her against him to cradle her in his arms. "Ellen, you were virgin." He spoke gently but with obvious concern.

She smiled at her secret. "Yes."

"How . . . how can that be possible?"

She traced the line of his chin playfully. "How? All women are born virgins, *Lord* Merrick. It is men that alter that!"

He lifted up on his elbow to look at her, his green eyes stern. "That's not what I mean and you damned well know it. What of Richard?"

"What of him? I told you our relationship was difficult to explain, even harder to understand."

"I would say so, considering the fact that he keeps you as his paramour but has obviously not fulfilled his keeper's rights!" He paused, waited, then went on. "I suppose you don't intend to offer any explanation."

She rested her head on his arm, smiling up at him. "I don't."

Gavin shook his head as leaned to kiss her mouth. "You should have told me you were a virgin, Ellen. I wouldn't have—"

"You wouldn't have what?" She slanted her eyes with amusement. "So perhaps you are a nobleman, but a *man* nonetheless. You'd have been a fool not to accept what I so boldly offered."

"I wasn't going to say I wouldn't have made love to

144

you, because that would be a lie." He cupped her breast with his hand, his thumb brushing the bud of her nipple. "But I'd have at least tried to control myself. I was a little rough there at the last minute."

She closed her eyes, enjoying the feel of his rough hand on her breast. "It was wonderful, Gavin. Far more than I expected."

He shook his head, unable to resist her smile. "You forever intrigue me, my mysterious Ellen. Just when I think I have you figured out . . ." His voice trailed off into silence.

For a long time they lay on the Turkish carpet before the fireplace, watching the flickering flames and enjoying the heat of the fire and of their spent passion. After a while Ellen became drowsy. She wasn't aware that Gavin had gotten up, but soon she was snuggled down in soft quilting, encircled in his arms.

Sometime in the middle of the night Gavin awoke her, his hands sending delicious rivulets of pleasure through her body. They made love and then again slept. It was not until the sun was well up that Ellen woke to find Gavin seated in a chair on the far side of the room, watching her.

She stretched lazily like a cat, unable to resist a smile. He was so blessedly handsome! "What are you looking at?" she asked, covering her bare breasts with the coverlet as she sat up.

"You."

She ran a hand through her tangled hair. "Why?"

His gaze bore into her. "Because you're so lovely. Because you intrigue me. Because I wonder how my life was ever whole without you."

"Ods fish, Gavin, I don't want to hear such silliness. I told you, I expect nothing, and certainly not silly declarations." She opened the coverlet to

145

bare her nude body. "Now hush and come to me."

He picked up a silk dressing gown with dragons embroidered across it. "'Tis tempting, love, but I think it would be best if I take you home. Richard will be concerned."

She rose up on her knees to accept the robe. "Richard . . ." She covered her mouth with her palm. "I almost forgot about Richard. God's teeth, he must be frantic." She looked up. "I told him I would be home by midnight."

Gavin gathered her clothing and carried it through the double doors, through an antechamber, and into his bedchamber, with Ellen following. "I've no maid to help you dress, but I think I can do a fair job."

She sat down on the tester bed and reached out to stroke the hardened muscle of his bare buttock. "I would imagine you've had a great deal of experience."

"Jealous?" he teased, leaning to kiss her mouth.

She shook her head. "I've been too fortunate of late to waste time with jealousies." She reached for her stockings and rolled one on. "I'm a woman who lives for the day."

Gavin went to a chest of drawers and removed a freshly pressed shirt, pair of breeches, and stockings. "Sounds reckless."

"Perhaps for some, but for me, after the things I've experienced, it just makes sense."

Gavin thought to ask just what those experiences were, for the longer he knew Ellen, the more convinced he was that in her brief twenty-odd years, she had indeed witnessed great tragedy. But he held his tongue, not wanting to pressure her. For today he would have to be content with what she offered.

"Dress and I'll escort you home."

She gave a chuckle as she rose to tie her garters.

"You'd best just send me in a hackney. Richard may well run you through with his grandfather's sword should you appear at his door this morning."

"I'll see you home, Ellen."

She shrugged. "Suit yourself, but I don't want you coming up. I want to face Richard alone."

Gavin slipped his colonial linen shirt over his head. "This makes me feel the rogue." He looked up. "But I don't know why I care. I have to admit I've been in this position before—another man's intended, even wife." *But you didn't love those women,* an inner voice echoed in his head. *You never loved before.*

Ellen dropped her shift over her head and came to Gavin. She rested her hands on his broad shoulders and looked into his heavenly green eyes. "So accept this as different and be content." She kissed him. "Now let's hurry. I want to get home."


"I suppose there's no need for me to ask where on God's bloody earth you've been." Richard stood in front of the door, well dressed with his hair neat but with the bloodshot eyes of a man who had sat vigil all night with a bottle of brandy.

Ellen closed the door behind her. "I should have sent you a message, Richard. I'm so sorry."

He stared at her for a long moment, then turned and walked into the parlor, where a table had been set up for the morning meal. There were two place settings. The aroma of hot chocolate rose from a small carafe . . . Ellen's favorite morning drink.

He's been waiting for me, Ellen thought as she slipped into her chair. He's been waiting all night, fearful for me but knowing he can't interfere.

Ellen dropped her napkin into her lap and reached

for the fresh baked rolls Richard must have had sent from the bakeshop early that morning. "I didn't intend to stay out all night, Richard. I didn't intend to hurt you like this."

He took a roll and smeared it with rich, fresh butter. "It's not as if I didn't know this would happen eventually, if not with Merrick, then with another." He took a bite of the bread and chewed slowly. "But somehow I had it in my head that I would have you a little longer."

She reached across the table and took his hand. His was a strong, comforting hand. "You still have me."

"You're in love with him," he accused softly.

"I love you both."

"You can't love two men, Ellen."

She smiled bittersweetly, refusing to allow him to take his hand from hers. "But I do. I may have made love with Gavin last night, but I came home to you. Can't that be all right just for now, Richard?"

He covered her hand with his so that he clasped it. "I would hate to be in your position right now, sweet."

"Oh, it's not so bad, two men who care for me after a lifetime of uncaring." She withdrew her hand and poured hot chocolate from the carafe for them both. "Perhaps it's selfish, but I can't give you up, Richard. Gavin will only be here through the winter and then he sails for his America. *He won't ever come back.*"

"You could go with him." Richard made the suggestion out of a sense of obligation.

"No." She sipped her hot chocolate. "I don't want to go to the Colonies. I want to stay in London. Besides, Gavin doesn't care for me in that way, not like you do. I'm a dalliance, nothing more. He said so."

"And do you mind?"

"If things were different, I would. But do I? No. No matter how I like to pretend there was never any husband or Duke of Hunt, I cannot change what happened. I cannot change my past or reveal my secrets. I told you, I'll never marry again. I couldn't live like that, I just couldn't. I could never live the lies." She lowered her head. "I was reminded of that last night."

"Last night?" He frowned. "What happened last night?"

She took her time in answering, but when she did, her voice still quivered. "I saw him."

"Hunt?"

She nodded as if confessing. "At a supper on The Strand. A friend of Gavin's was hosting a party." She smiled. "It was wonderful." Then the smile disappeared. "Until I saw him."

"Did he see you?"

"No. It was dark. Gavin had gone for a drink." She sighed. "I lost control for a few minutes. I was scared, Richard. I ran. I ran out of the house and down the street." She purposely left out the part about the ruffian sailors who had accosted her. "Gavin found me and took me home."

"He took advantage of your vulnerability!"

She laughed, picking up a pear and slicing it onto her plate with a paring knife. "I took advantage of the excuse I could use to do what I had wanted to do for a very long time."

Richard rose, scraping his chair on the wood floor. "Well, that does it. We have to go, Ellen. We'll go to my estates, where you'll be safe."

"I'm not going, Richard. I already told you that."

"But he could have seen you!"

"And if he had, he might not have recognized me. And even if he had recognized me, what would he

149

do? Murder me there on the balcony in front of a hundred guests?" She bit into a slice of pear on the end of the knife. "I think not. I have the list of names, and as long as I have them, he can't hurt me."

"You're being a reckless fool. Your lust for Merrick is clouding your reason!"

"I'm being perfectly reasonable. Now sit down and eat." She pointed to his chair with her knife. "I told you, Richard, when Hunt finally returned to London I wasn't going to flee. And I've not changed my mind."

"So what are you going to do?" He leaned into the back of the chair.

"Do? I'm going to drink my chocolate and then I'm going to dress to go to the theater."

"Very amusing. I mean about Hunt, and you damned well know it!"

She shrugged, her heart too light with the memory of Gavin's lovemaking to allow herself to fall into a pit of fear and worry. "I suppose I'm going to cross that duke when I come to him!"

Ellen was still laughing at her own joke when she heard Richard slam his bedchamber door behind him.

# Chapter Ten

Ellen stepped out of Richard's crested coach and squinted in the sunlight as she searched for Gavin's ship. The *Maid Marion* was being completely overhauled this winter, Gavin had explained to Ellen, so that the ship would ready to set sail in the spring.

The wharfs were teeming with men, all hurrying to complete some task or another. There were pigtailed sailors moving barrels and crates of merchandise, while tradesmen hammered on the decks and young boys scraped barnacle-encrusted hulls. There was such a din from the construction and the confusion of the busy day that Ellen could barely hear the footman, Adam, beside her when he spoke.

"I can ask which one she is," Adam repeated.

"No. I see her," Ellen answered loudly. "He said her name would be painted across the bow."

Sure enough, several slips down was a great two-masted sailing ship, with the name *Maid Marion* painted across her bow in gold lettering. Mounted on the bowsprit was the beautiful life-size carving of a woman-mermaid with russet hair. Men crawled

151

across the deck of the ship like ants on an anthill, while others hung high on the masts as they made repairs.

Ellen lifted her skirts and hurried toward the gangplank, ignoring the whistles of several men and the call of a one-legged beggar. "You wait for me here, Adam," she ordered as she started up the wobbly bridge that allowed men to board the docked ship.

"M . . . Master Richard, he . . . he said to stick right with ye, ma'am. Said the wharfs was a dangerous place for a woman."

Somewhere a sailor blew on a boatswain's pipe, announcing Ellen's arrival.

"Just the same," Ellen called to Adam from the gangplank, "you stay put. I see Lord Merrick now."

Gavin came to her immediately, taking her arm and leading her down below to his cabin. "I didn't mean for you to come aboard. The wharfs are no place for a woman."

She wrinkled her nose and passed him, stepping into his captain's cabin. "That's what Richard said." She pushed back the hood of her ermine-trimmed cloak. "I just came to see you before I was off to the theater."

He leaned to kiss her and Ellen smiled. Despite the chill in the late September air, Gavin had stripped down to a working man's breeches and shirt without a cravat. He wore a three-cornered hat carelessly over his dark hair, which was pulled back in a queue. He smelled faintly of wood chips, tobacco, and hard work, but it was not an unpleasant smell.

Stepping back from him, she glanced at the tiny cabin he called home for the long trip across the Atlantic. "So this is where the captain sleeps?" she questioned, taking in the narrow bunk built into the

152

wall and the chart table that hung down on hinges.

"Actually, I no longer captain my own ships. I hire someone. I had this cabin built to match the one on the other side, in case passengers were ever aboard."

Spotting a hideous black and white wooden mask hanging on the wall beside the single porthole, Ellen studied it with curiosity. "Is it from the Africas?"

He lifted down the mask and placed it in her hand. It was carved intricately in a scowl with holes cut for the eyes, nose, and mouth. "No, it's from the American Colonies. There are Indians far to the north of my plantation. They're called Iroquois. A friend captured it on a raid and brought it back to me. It's worn for ceremonies and sometimes to scare the enemy in an attack."

Ellen ran her fingers along the smooth carved wood in fascination. "You know many of them—the savages, I mean?"

He went to his chart table and began to shuffle through several stacks of papers. "A few. I once spent a winter among the Shawnee. There's a village not far from the western boundaries of my land. The friend I spoke of comes from that village. He often stays in my home when the mood suits him."

"But he's not one of the savages that wears these masks?" She handed it back to him.

"No." He chuckled. "Azoma is Shawnee."

"Azoma." She liked the sound of his name on her tongue. "Does it mean something?"

"Eagle water." He set the mask on his chart table and plucked at a lock of her freshly washed hair. "Now if you've no more questions, I've work to be done and you need to get to the theater."

He laid her hand on his chest, not caring that his shirt was damp with perspiration. "I'd rather stay here

153

with you. I could be your cabin boy." She grinned mischievously.

"I would imagine you would be content to stay in this eight by eight cabin for about twenty minutes before you went mad."

She lifted up on her toes to kiss him. "Not if I was with you."

Their lips met and then he laid his hands on her shoulders, pushing her back. "You continue with that, and I'll be compelled to rip off your clothes, sweet, and take you here on this filthy floor."

Ellen sighed. "Promises, promises," she mimicked as she lifted the hood of her cloak to cover most of her rich red hair. She really did have to get on to the theater.

He caught her hand and led her out of the cabin. "I can promise you, you'd want no part of me until I had a bath, Ellen."

She stopped at the ladder that led up to the deck and turned to face him. "Tonight?"

"Would you like me to come to your apartment?"

She shook her head. "I wouldn't feel right. Not at Richard's."

"Then mine. I'll send a coach for you at the theater after your performance." He brushed the ermine trim of her hood. "Chambray won't expect you home?"

She kissed him again, this time her lips lingering over his as she thought of the evening of lovemaking to come. "I told him I wouldn't be home until after the play tomorrow night."

He shook his head. "I just don't like this, Ellen. I'm a selfish man; I want you to myself." He took her soft hand and rubbed it with his own one that was callused from the ship's work. "Move in with me."

"I told you I don't want to. What we have is enough."

"When I think of living without you, of sailing in the spring without you at my side, I begin to wonder, Ellen"—he glanced up at her, his eyes intense— "could we—"

She pressed her finger to his lips, silencing him. "Remember, your place is in the Colonies and mine is here. Don't talk to me of permanence, Gavin. *It just can't be.*"

Gavin heard the sincerity in her voice and saw a look of determination in her eyes. He wondered what ailed him to be thinking of such things. Of course, he couldn't take her to America. Ellen was an actress, for heaven's sake! Besides, her life was here with her theater, gay parties . . . and her Richard, be he whatever he was to her. And Gavin certainly needed no wife. Look where a wife had gotten Waldron—six feet under.

Gavin brushed Ellen's cheek with the back of his hand. "Go on with you now, wench, and let me get back to work. I have an appointment in Whitehall later in the day."

"Is it about your land grant?"

"I hope so. I'd like to have the deed secured so I can start buying seed and supplies. I figure I can fill one ship with my own needs, and two more with things my friends have sent me to purchase and with merchandise I intend to sell in the Colonies."

Ellen stepped up the first rung of the ladder and turned back to face him. "You're very wealthy, aren't you, Gavin?"

He grabbed the rail. "Sailing in the king's name was profitable, the tobacco trade perhaps even more so."

She smiled. "A self-made man. I like that. Too many men in London live on what belonged to ancestors two hundred years back."

"It's the English class system, Ellen. It's the way it's worked for a thousand years."

"But that's not the way it is in the Americas, is it?"

"No. It's not." He swatted her buttocks through the mountain of skirting and petticoats. "Now get topside and stop blocking traffic!"

Up above, on the deck of the *Maid Marion*, Gavin escorted her down the gangplank, where the footman waited to take her back to the coach. He kissed her one last time and sent her on her way, saying he would see her that evening.

Gavin had been back on board ship no more than five minutes when the boatswain's pipe announced the boarding of another visitor. He handed his hammer to a workman on the bridge, then walked down to the gangplank on the stern, to find the Duke of Hunt. As always, he was dressed impeccably, today in a fashionable French-tailored suit of maroon and navy, with a sword on his hip.

"To what do I owe this pleasure, sir?" Gavin had not seen Hunt in nearly a month. He removed his hat out of respect for the man's title and bowed slightly.

The albino tucked his hands behind his back and walked along the ship's rail. "I came to see what progress you've made in locating your brother's murderess. I've not heard from you."

Gavin dropped his hat back onto his head, slightly irritated by the man's tone of voice. "That's because I've found out almost nothing. I'm beginning to wonder if perhaps she died of the pox or married some Frenchman and escaped to Paris. It would have been the wisest thing to do for a woman in her position."

Hunt walked from well out of earshot of the worker on the deck, leaning over the rail to peer down at the filthy water in the harbor. He watched

156

with great interest as a rat floated by on the lid of a crate. "I've champion news for you, then." He paused, enjoying the suspense he created. "I believe Lady Waxton has been seen."

Gavin's attention was immediately riveted. "Here, in London? By whom? I thought you said no one knew her!"

Hunt watched the rat leap off its vessel and onto a line running down the hull of a ship in the next slip over. "There's been no confirmation, so I hesitate to speak just yet." He turned to face Gavin. "I only wanted you to know that your time and money spent may well not have been futile."

"Can you tell me at least where she was seen? Where should I be looking for her? A whorehouse on Threadneedle or a bakeshop in Cheapside?"

"She was at a supper at the Barkely House on The Strand not two weeks ago."

Gavin leaned on the rail in thought. "The Barkely House? That of Germaine Barkely?"

"His father's, I do believe."

Gavin glanced into the harbor, amazed that he could have been so close to his brother's murderess and not known it. "I was there that night."

"Were you? I was, as well, for a brief time."

*"You saw her then?"*

"I told you, there's no certainty as of yet. It was dark. She looked much different."

"So I should begin looking in the homes of my friends?" He swore softly.

"For now I would advise you to simply take caution. When she is found, she must be dealt with carefully. There is a delicate matter I have to resolve. I should like to have a chance to speak with her before you turn her over to the authorities."

"What sort of matter are you talking about?"

157

The Duke of Hunt began to walk back toward the gangplank. "It's naught to concern yourself with."

"So what do you suggest I do now?" Gavin asked, knowing the duke must have a suggestion.

"I think you should commit more time and pounds to your investigation. I could recommend some very discreet spies. I would put my own to it, but considering my circumstances, it would be unseemly." He glanced at Gavin, who stood tall and masculine in the bright sunlight, and felt a pang of jealousy for the dashing good looks he had never had. "I would also recommend that you come to a supper in my home two weeks hence."

"I thank you for the invitation."

"It will be on the twelfth. I'll send an invitation to you, but I wanted to invite you myself." He stopped at the gangplank. "I understand you've no wife. Have you a suitable woman to bring? No whores, of course. The king has promised to attend. It will be my first social event since my return from France."

Gavin dropped his hands to his hips. "I can think of a woman quite suitable."

"The actress?"

Gavin's brow creased. "How did you know?"

"I told you, I know some excellents spies for hire. I'd put them up against Buckingham's any dark night."

"Yes, she is an actress at His Majesty's theater, but I can promise you, she's cut of a different silk than most there."

"I've heard from others that she's a striking beauty. I've not seen her, only because I do not frequent theaters. I've much better ways to spend my time than watching strumpets walk across the stage babbling Shakespeare gibberish."

"Well, sir, I thank you for the invitation, and I'll

surely be there. In the meantime, I would ask that you let me know if you hear else of Lady Waxton. I'm anxious to put my brother's death behind me.''

"No doubt you are,'' Hunt said, going down the gangplank. ''Good day.''

Hunt stepped down onto the dock and headed for his coach. He didn't know where Thomasina was, but he would find her. He would find her and have Merrick bring her to him. Of course, once Hunt had possession of the letter, he would be free to dispose of her as he saw fit. If there was any backlash—which he seriously doubted there would be—there would always be the dashing naive fool Merrick to blame.

"So what do you think?'' Ellen spun on her toes in the center of the bedchamber as Richard looked on. ''Is it appropriate to meet the king in?''

Richard smoothed his mustache, not allowing the smile that tugged at his lips. Appropriate? She was damned well stunningly beautiful. Not only would she catch the king's eye in such a costume, but it might well warrant words with Castlemaime, the king's jealous mistress.

Ellen wore an emerald-green taffeta gown embellished with scrolls of gold. There were green stockings and shoes to match, and a black velvet cloak and mask. At her throat she wore the emeralds that belonged to Richard's father's estate. Emerald earbobs hung from her lobes and her hair was piled high in a *tour*.

Ellen's smile turned downward in a frown. ''You don't like it.'' She brushed her gloved hands over her scanty neckline. ''Too much skin? I look like the stage whore, don't I?''

The look on Ellen's face, the tone of her voice,

made Richard's resolve crumble. He came to her and very gently, so as not to wrinkle her gown, kissed her on the lips. "You're as lovely tonight as I think I've ever seen you. I hate to admit it, Ellen, love, but that Merrick has brought a glow to your face I could never give you."

She smoothed his cheek. "I don't want you to be unhappy, Richard."

He sighed, walking away to lift his brandy glass from the carved mantel. "It's not a matter of being happy or unhappy, Ellen. That's what I continually try to make you understand. It's your safety that concerns me, not my own jealousies."

She turned to a Venetian mirror framed with gold cupids and smoothed the rice powder on her cheeks. Richard went on. "It's just that this is madness, your going to Hunt's home. He's going to see you."

"And then what?" she challenged defiantly as she spun around. "What's he going to do to me? Drag me out of the house in front of the king?" She lifted a gloved finger. "You forget, I have the letter. I know he knows I have it. I'm certain that's what Waldron told him of before he died. Why else would he have come after me like that?"

"You speak as if this is some game. This is your life you talk of!"

"Exactly, and that's why I intend to never again let any man control my life, not even you, Richard."

He swirled the brandy in his glass. "Tell me where the letter is. Perhaps—"

"You know I can't do that! We agreed, Richard. If you know where the letter is or who else is mentioned in it, you, too, will be endangered."

He brought the glass down hard on a carved oak side table. "I just feel so damned inadequate!" He looked up at her. "I feel as if I should be doing

160

something to protect, and yet you will let me do nothing!"

There was a rap at the door.

Ellen glanced away, then back at Richard. "That will be Gavin. I have to go."

He let out an exasperated sigh. "Will you come home tonight?"

"I will." She went to him and lifted up on her toes to kiss him. "I swear it."

The knock came again and Ellen hurried to the door. Gavin stood in the hallway dressed in evening finery. He bowed cordially to Richard, who nodded.

Before either man could speak, Ellen grabbed Gavin's arm and pulled him out the door. "I'll see you tonight, Richard. Good night!"

Richard stood in brooding silence, watching the door swing behind them.

Ellen laughed gaily at the snide remark made by a gentleman standing in the group. She sipped her champagne and smiled up at Gavin. What an enchanting evening this had been. Hunt's home was even more beautiful than Germaine's and the guest list far longer. Gavin had explained to her that anyone at court who was anyone had been invited tonight.

Ellen had kissed the hand of the queen and the king, so enthralled that she had barely been able to speak. Gavin had teased her later, suggesting that it was Charles's good looks that had left her mute, but she had sworn Gavin was more to her liking. Ellen had even met Lady Castelmaime, the king's current mistress. The woman was indeed as beautiful up close as she appeared in the royal box at the theater, and Ellen had learned firsthand that her

161

tongue was truly as vicious as she had been led to believe. But not even Castlemaime's rude reference to Ellen being an actress could dampen her spirits. The night was too magical.

Gavin had danced with her dance after dance, surrendering to other partners only under duress. They had dined in the popular buffet fashion, seated on little chairs in the gallery that ran along the lighted gardens. Gavin and Ellen had then walked up and down the gallery, studying the unusual, sometimes shockingly hideous artwork Hunt was so proud of.

Much to her surprise, she and Gavin had not yet been introduced to the host, who had been attending to his more important guests all evening. After several glasses of French champagne and an evening on Gavin's arm, Ellen felt she could face anything, though. In fact, she almost wondered if she should seek out the Duke of Hunt and face the fear of the last years.

It was well past midnight when Gavin suggested that he and Ellen call for their coach to take them home. Tired but giddy with happiness, she agreed, wishing she could just go home with Gavin but knowing she had promised Richard she would return tonight. She and Gavin were making their way through the crowd, saying their goodbyes, when a familiar voice spoke up from behind them.

"Good evening. I hope you've enjoyed yourselves. My apologies for having not sought you out earlier, but the duties of host without hostess can be taxing."

Gavin turned to face the Duke of Hunt, with Ellen on his arm. He bowed formally. Ellen curtsied, her heart tripping as she avoided eye contact with the albino. No matter how well she had prepared herself for this moment, now that it was here, she was afraid.

162

"We've enjoyed ourselves immensely, Your Grace." Gavin indicated Ellen with his chin. "This is Madame Ellen Scarlet. Ellen, the Duke of Hunt."

Ellen forced a smile as she looked up to defiantly meet Hunt's rodent eyes. She didn't want to give Gavin any suspicions that she and the duke had been acquainted before. "Your servant, sir."

He smiled ever so slightly. "Gad, Lord Waxton, and where did you find such a paragon of beauty? Since Lady Marmont went into the country with the pox, I vow we haven't seen a single decent face at court."

A numbness washed over Ellen as her mind ground its gears in utter confusion. The voices of Gavin and Hunt faded into the background of her mind until they were nothing but a buzz. *Lord Waxton? Had Hunt called Gavin Lord Waxton? Was this some sick joke of the duke's?*

But she knew it was not as she looked up at Gavin who had gone on chatting with the duke. Ellen suddenly felt so cold that she thought she must now know what death felt like.

*Intuitively, Ellen knew that Gavin Merrick was Morley Waxton, her late husband's dead brother . . .*

# Chapter Eleven

"Ellen, are you all right?"

She looked up in stunned confusion to see both the wicked Hunt and her darling Gavin staring at her, their faces, in her perception, twisted oddly.

"I said, are you well?" Gavin repeated, grasping her arm.

Ellen realized she must have swayed. She suddenly felt smothered . . . trapped. She couldn't take a deep breath. She was surrounded by enemies but unable to flee. Her thoughts tumbled as she struggled to remain in control of her words and actions. How in the Holy Mother's name could Gavin be the brother to such a monster as Waldron had been?

Worse, did Gavin know who she was? Were he and Hunt together in this game of cat and mouse?

"Ellen?"

"It's . . . it's overly warm in here." She pulled from Gavin's grasp and fluttered her painted fan, stalling for the time she needed to compose herself. "I'm just a little faint." She breathed deeply, wishing her damnable stays weren't so tight.

"Let me call for a servant. You can lie down, madame." Hunt reached to touch her elbow, but she shrank back.

"No." She swallowed against the repulsion she felt at the thought of Hunt's touch. She remembered the disgusting, perverted things he had once whispered he was going to do to her when he finally took her maidenhead. "No, that won't be necessary." She forced herself to look at Gavin . . . her Gavin, who had so obviously played her false . . . her Gavin, who may have well betrayed her tonight. "Please, just take me home."

"Are you quite certain, madame?" Hunt went on in his host's voice.

She stared at him for a moment, memories flipping through her mind in rapid succession. Somehow in the time that had passed, she had allowed herself to forget what a loathsome man her husband had been. But seeing Hunt standing here, the memories were once again all too real. And the worst of it was that no matter how abominable a man the Earl of Waxton had been, Ellen knew Hunt was worse.

With abrupt determination, she turned and walked away from Hunt's smirk, which lurked just below the surface of his feigned concern.

Gavin watched her go, then turned back to the duke, puzzled by Ellen's impertinent retreat. "Excuse us, Your Grace, will you?" He bowed, hoping Hunt was not insulted, but concerned about Ellen. Something was obviously very wrong.

Hunt made a grand sweep of his arm, the gold garnitures at his elbows fluttering. "By all means, see to the lady."

Gavin turned away to hurry after Ellen.

"Oh, and Merrick . . ."

Gavin turned back. "Yes?"

"Contact me soon." He smiled as he tucked his hands behind him. "I may well have some information on the woman you seek."

"Thank you. I'll do that, Your Grace." Nodding farewell, he followed Ellen, who had nearly reached the door. A servant was bringing her her cloak and mask when Gavin reached her.

"Are you certain you're all right, sweetheart? You're ashen." He reached to stroke her cheek but she lifted her mask, interrupting his movement.

Ellen was far enough away from Hunt now that she could think more clearly. Gavin didn't know who she was, she was certain of that; she could see it in his eyes. A woman couldn't sleep with a man and not know something of his character. But he had still lied to her. He had not told her his true name, why, she could only guess. Was *she*, in actuality, the woman he spoke vaguely of seeking months back? The thought seemed so preposterous that it might well be true.

Without speaking, Ellen strode out the door, her head held high to combat her rush of emotion. He had lied to her, and as silly as it seemed in the scheme of things, she was deeply hurt that he had done so.

"Ellen, what is it?"

Their coach pulled up and a footman helped her climb in. The moment Gavin pulled the flimsy leather door closed behind him, she spoke. Her days of hiding and holding her tongue were over. She would speak and be heard.

"You lied to me, you rotting knave!"

He went to sit beside her but thought better of it, sliding into the seat across from her instead. "What by the king's cod are you talking about? I lied to you about what?"

"Who you were!" she spat. "First I find out you're an earl. Then I find Gavin isn't really even your name!"

"That . . ." He looked away.

"Yes, that!" She struck her knee with her fan, snapping it in half. Her anger felt good. Anger made her strong. It was fear that made her weak. She threw the fan to the floor. "Why did you do it, Gavin—or whatever the blast your name is?"

He crossed his legs at the ankles, taking his time in answering. When he spoke his voice was hushed, his words carefully chosen. "My name is Gavin. Morley Gavin Waxton, the Viscount Merrick. If your father had named you Morley, you'd have well gone by another name."

"And what of the Earl of Waxton?" She couldn't control the bitter sound in her voice. If it had been a thousand years, it would still have been too soon to hear that surname.

He purposefully directed his gaze toward her, holding her in the spell of his green eyes. "I've only recently inherited the title. I've been using my father's lesser title for reasons I'd prefer not to have to go into. But by any name, Ellen, I'm still the same man who walked into that house tonight. I am still the man you've spent so many days and not enough nights with."

A sob rose in her throat and her eyes clouded with tears. She looked away. Was life always like this? Did God aways give, only to snatch away? She thought of Gavin's words. There was honest, bitter truth in what he said. In a way, he was still the same man she had loved these past few months, whether she had professed that love or not. And truthfully, at this moment, her love for him was unchanged. The fact that he was Waldron's brother and that she had murdered Waldron was also unchanged. The only difference between now and a few hours ago was that now she and Gavin must part. She took a deep, shuddering sigh, fighting tears.

"I just want to go home, Gavin." Her voice trembled. "Please, just take me home."

Gavin wanted to say something, but he could think of nothing to say. He wanted her to understand why he had kept his identity from her. He wanted to tell her about Waldron and about the woman who had killed his brother. But he couldn't, not yet. He told himself it was reasonable not to share the information in order to protect his quest, but he knew he still protected himself. As long as he didn't tell all there was to tell of himself, he could still hold himself apart emotionally from Ellen. He could keep from admitting that the thought of sailing to the Colonies without her seemed more impossible with each passing day. He wouldn't have to tell her he loved her.

Gavin rode the remainder of the distance to Richard Chambray's apartment in silence. When they reached the address, Ellen leaped from the coach before he had a chance to speak. Stepping out into the darkness, he watched her run up the front steps. He wondered if he should just go home and wait until tomorrow to speak with her. Perhaps he should just let her go to her precious Richard and let him soothe her anger.

But the jealousy Gavin felt in his chest wouldn't allow him to let her go like this. If he continually allowed Chambray to step in with Ellen when matters became complicated, he would always lose out to her keeper in the end. If Gavin wanted to win her love from this man, who kept her as mistress but did not use her as such, then he had to follow Ellen.

Taking the steps two at a time, Gavin caught up with her.

"Go home," she murmured, throwing open the

door. "Go home and let me be, Gavin."

"Ellen, you can't run from me. Let me talk to you. Let me explain." He caught the door before she could slam it in his face, walking into the apartment behind her.

She strode through the room that was lit only by a few sputtering candles, tossing her cloak and mask on a chair as she sailed by.

"Ellen!" Gavin shouted in anger.

Richard appeared in the doorway that Ellen had disappeared through. He was barefooted, wearing a long silk dressing gown. His hair, cropped short for periwigs, was tousled from sleep. "What in holy hell is going on here?" he demanded.

Gavin yanked his hat off his head and tossed it carelessly onto the same chair Ellen had dropped her cloak on. "This is private, Chambray. Stand aside."

Richard blocked the doorway, and though he was not as brawny a man as Gavin, he was still an imposing figure in the semidarkness. "What's happened? What have you done to her, Merrick?"

"I said step aside. What passes between Ellen and me is not of your concern!"

"It damned well is! Now I suggest you take your leave, sir, before I lose my temper and escort you myself!"

Gavin shook his head. "I can't leave her like this!" His voice suddenly softened. "I have to explain to her . . . I have to make her understand that no matter what the secrets are between us, I can't live without her."

Richard stared directly into Gavin's eyes, as if weighing the truth of his words. Then suddenly he sighed, relaxing his stance. "Would you care for a brandy?"

Gavin looked over Richard's shoulder, down the

dark hallway. "I honestly need to speak with her. I've hurt her, Chambray. God knows I didn't mean to, but I have."

"Haven't we both?" Richard walked past Gavin and to the table near the fireplace, to pour them both a drink. He indicated a chair with a nod of his head. "Let her be a few moments. She's always more sensible after some time alone."

Gavin glanced down the hall again, but suddenly curious about Chambray's puzzling behavior, he came back toward the center of the room. He didn't know what he wanted to say to this man, but he felt there was something that needed to be said.

Gavin took the brandy Chambray offered him, but not the chair. "I don't understand the relationship between the two of you," he said flatly.

Richard walked to the fireplace and leaned against it. "What explanation has Ellen given you?"

"She says she loves you." Gavin felt a physical pang of jealousy as he watched Chambray smile faintly. "She says she won't leave you . . . not for me, not for anyone."

"She thinks she owes me something," Richard offered, swirling his brandy to watch it whirlpool in the stemmed glass.

"I think not." Gavin paused. "I think she honestly loves you."

"But she loves you, too. And you can give her what I can never give her."

Gavin frowned, puzzled. "And what is that?"

Richard looked up over the rim of his glass as he took a long sip. "Marriage . . . children . . . a future."

"She was a virgin." Gavin had never had such an intimate conversation with another man, and yet for some reason he felt no discomfort. This was Ellen they spoke of, his mysterious Ellen, and this man

171

Chambray seemed to be the only person who could unlock Gavin's understanding of her.

"She was indeed."

"It doesn't make any sense, Chambray. She says you are her keeper. Those at the theater say you are her lover, but that's obviously false. Just who are you? Her brother?"

"No." Richard caught the tie of his silk dressing gown. "I wish that I were, because it would make loving her easier. No. This is why I have never made love to her. This is why I can never possess her as you can . . ."

Gavin knew his jaw must have dropped when Chambray tugged on the tie of his gown, letting it fall open to expose himself. "Christ," was all he could manage as he stared at the man's grotesque disfigurement.

Richard let the gown fall open for only a moment, then covered himself. "I found Ellen at a time in her life when she needed someone desperately. I fell in love with her." He retied the silk gown. "Who wouldn't? And our love, perhaps, could have developed into what I fear yours has. But for obvious reasons," he splayed his hands, "that was impossible."

Gavin grimaced. "I'm sorry." What else could he say? What comfort could he offer this man who had bared his soul . . . who had admitted to another what Gavin could never have admitted? "I'm sorry," he repeated.

"Not half as sorry as me, my friend." Richard went to pour himself another brandy. "So though I love Ellen and she me, it's a different love. It couldn't help but be. Ellen is just having a difficult time dealing with that fact."

Gavin was still at a loss for words. He felt as if he

wanted to reach out and touch this man, to comfort him in some way, an odd feeling indeed. Instead, he spoke with all the compassion he felt in his heart. "I take it this is not a recent wound." Having been in battle, Gavin recognized the mark of a Turkish blade.

"No. Ellen knew when she came here to live with me."

"Then why set yourselves up as mistress and keeper?"

"To protect her." It was now Richard who chose his words carefully. "She came at a time in her life when she needed protection as well as guidance."

"But you're not going to tell me who you were protecting her from?"

Richard smiled. "You know I cannot."

Gavin set down his glass on a small table near a chair. "All this time you've been playing mistress and keeper to the world, and no one has set your plan astray."

Richard glared morosely. "No one until you."

"I would never purposefully endanger her, I want you to know that, Chambray."

"I think I do." Richard paused for a moment, deep in thought. "You know I realized I would lose her one day. I knew she wouldn't be mine forever, but it's too soon." He sipped his brandy. "I suppose it would always be too soon."

"She refuses to move into my apartments. And I have to admit that I'm jealous of you, Chambray. Even now that I know you don't lie with her, I'm still jealous. I want to possess her heart the way you possess it."

"Have you told her so?" Richard watched him by the candlelight.

Gavin began to pace the length of the room, his heeled shoes tapping on the hardwood floor, his

173

shadow shortening and then growing longer, only to grow short again as he passed a candle sconce on the wall. "No, I admit I haven't."

"Why not?"

"Christ's bones," Gavin glanced up. "You sound like her nursemaid."

"I've played that role among many. Now tell me, Gavin Merrick, why have you not proclaimed your love for the woman who tugs at your heartstrings?"

"A million reasons. None good when each stands alone, but together . . ." His voice trailed off into silence.

Richard waited.

"She's made it clear she wants nothing permanent." Gavin felt oddly defensive. "I'm going back to Maryland with the first spring winds. She says she'll not leave the stage or you." He shrugged his broad shoulders. "It seemed less complicated to keep words of love to myself."

"And has it made it so?"

"Less complicated?" Gavin ran a finger along a carved floral Venetian mirror frame, avoiding eye contact with himself. "In some ways, yes. Others . . . no." He glanced up at Richard through the reflection in the mirror. "Do you know Ellen is the first woman I've laid with more than once that has not spoken of love?"

Richard sat in his favorite chair and crossed his legs. "You're much alike, the two of you. Both making yourselves unhappy, I would guess."

"So you know her so well, what am I supposed to do?"

"Why should I tell you? I would lose a part of my very being if I lost Ellen. Besides, it's not safe for her . . . being with you, knowing you."

"It's not that I want to take her from you, but only

174

that I must have her, Chambray."

"Offer to marry her, then. Take her to your precious Colonies and love her the rest of her days."

Gavin gave a little laugh. "Marry her?"

"If you love her. If you cannot live without her as you proclaim, marriage seems the only solution. I know it's what I would have done the first night I met her were it not for my circumstance."

Gavin turned away from the mirror to study the man he had once thought his enemy but whom he now admired immensely. "You would give her up—for me?"

"For her sake, not yours, and not happily. But I want what's best for Ellen, even if it means you."

Gavin leaned over the back of the chair that sat opposite from Richard. "She'd never agree. It's not what she wants."

"Ellen is not certain what she wants, except happiness, which she blessed well deserves."

Gavin watched him rise and head for the darkened hallway.

"If you'll excuse me," Richard said from the shadows, "I'll be back in a moment."

Gavin barely had time to contemplate all that had passed between him and Chambray, when the tall, dark-haired man appeared again, this time fully dressed and carrying his cloak. "Where are you going?"

"Out." He lifted his aristocratic chin in the direction of the hallway. "Ellen is in her bedchamber. I'll be back in the morning."

Gavin followed him to the door. There was nothing the two men could say that had not been said, but as Richard passed through the outside doorway, Gavin, on impulse, reached out to lay his hand on the other man's shoulder. Richard stopped

175

but didn't turn. A silence of understanding passed between the two men. Then Richard disappeared into the dark stairwell.

Ellen heard her bedchamber door creak open, but she didn't lift her eyelids. Rose had helped her to undress and now Ellen lay in her shift on top of the coverlet. She could hear her own steady breathing and her parrot scratching the paper in his cage. "He's gone, isn't he?" she asked, knowing she had heard the outside door close, knowing Richard had sent him away, knowing Gavin was gone forever.

"He's gone."

Ellen's eyes flashed open. This wasn't Richard, it was Gavin! She didn't want Gavin . . . but oh, she did. She needed him. Brother to Waldron be damned, she needed to feel his arms around her one last time.

Gavin stood hesitantly in the doorway. He had loosened his lace cravat and his well-groomed hair was now slightly disheveled. The shadows of the room cast an eerie light across his rugged features, etched with concern. He was as handsome standing there in the semidarkness as she had ever seen him.

"Where's Richard gone?" Ellen asked, barely trusting herself to speak.

"I don't know. Out, he said. He'll be back in the morning."

Richard had left them alone, here in his own apartment? Richard, who completely disapproved of the relationship? It didn't make sense. "I heard your voices," she said softly. "What did he say?"

"It doesn't matter right now."

"He told you about . . . about his injury, didn't he?" She squeezed her eyes tighter. "He told you about us."

"It doesn't matter. None of it matters, Ellen."

She laid her palm on her forehead. She felt clammy

176

and flushed at the same time. "What do you want?"

He came to the bed and sat down, shifting her weight on the bed so that she naturally was turned toward him. He leaned over her until their lips nearly touched, until she could smell the brandy on his breath and hear the rise and fall of his breathing.

Ellen felt forced to open her eyes and stare up at him. His green eyes were the color of the ocean in the wake of a storm, dark and smoldering. "Tell me what you want."

"I want to tell you I love you, Ellen."

# Chapter Twelve

Ellen blinked. "What did you say?"

His lips brushed hers in a kiss so faint it was like the tender, fleeting brush of a moth's wings. "I said I love you, Ellen. Secrets be damned, yours or mine, I love you."

She shook her head. "Don't say it," she whispered. "It won't work; this can never work. It'll only make it hurt more when we part."

"Then we won't part. We'll find a way. We'll make it work!"

He was so intense in his conviction that Ellen couldn't resist a smile. "It's impossible, I tell you. If you only knew what I'd done—who I was—you'd hate me, Gavin."

"I've done things in the past to be ashamed of as well. So I don't care about your past." He took her hand in his and kissed one knuckle at a time. "You are who you are today . . . now."

She pulled her hand away. "You're not listening to me. You're not being sensible."

"Tell me you don't love me, Ellen." He grasped her shoulders. "Tell me that you don't love me and I'll go."

Caught in the countenance of his sea-green eyes, she sighed. "It's not that."

"Say it."

"All right! All right!" She sat up, leaning against the headboard so that they were eye level. "I love you. I love you, Gavin Merrick, Morley Waxton. I love you whoever in God's Holy name you are!" There. She'd said it. She'd finally said it after all these months. She'd finally admitted it, not just to Gavin, but to herself.

For a long moment neither moved. They only stared at each other, lost in the moment. Ellen could hear her heart pounding beneath her thin shift. She could feel her pulse quicken as he reached out to her. When their lips met, it was no gentle virgin's kiss; it was a kiss of fire and fury. It was a kiss of pent-up emotions finally freed.

Gavin's mouth pressed so hard against hers that it hurt, but she didn't care. The pain was real; it was evidence of their passion. Her hands found his thick hair and she plucked at the ribbon that held it back. As his tongue delved deep in her mouth, she threaded her fingers through his dark hair, fanning it out over his shoulder. Frenzied by his kiss, she ran her hands over the familiar planes of his muscled back, excited by the sheer power of his physical strength.

When their lips parted, Gavin kissed a path to the bodice of her shift. Through the sheer linen he found her nipple, and she rose up with a moan of pleasure as his wet mouth closed over it. Shudders of sweet, torturous pleasure swept her breasts, flowing outward until her entire body tingled with excitement.

"Gavin, Gavin," she whispered huskily in his ear. "Say it. Say it again." Ellen knew that after tonight she could never see Gavin again. It was too dangerous, surely for her, perhaps even for him if he didn't know what part Hunt played in this deadly game. But if tonight were the last night she would ever spend in his arms, then it would have to be a night in which the memories could last a lifetime. "Tell me you love me," she urged.

"I love you, I love you, I love you, sweet, mysterious woman of my dreams." He buried his face in the swell of her breasts. Then with a sweep of his hand, he caught the gathered neckline of her bodice and yanked it.

Ellen only laughed at the sound of the tearing linen, aroused by the knowledge that he wanted her as badly as she wanted him. As he caught one nipple between his teeth and tugged gently, she pushed away the shredded shift. Now only his breeches and shirt were the barrier between flesh and flesh.

"Wait," she whispered. "Take off your clothes." She ran her hand over his shoulders, pressing her breasts against his chest. "Take it all off so I can see you. So I can touch you." She lifted her smoldering gaze to meet his. "So I can taste you."

Gavin turned on the bed and hurriedly removed his shoes and silk stockings, throwing them on the floor. Then he rose to turn and face her as his hands found the buttons of his tight breeches.

He watched Ellen draw her knees up against her chest to sit and watch him, her hair flowing down over her shoulders to conceal most of her lithe body in an erotic curtain of fiery red.

A smile crept across her face and she felt her cheeks grow warm as she watched him watch her as he peeled away the breeches and tossed them aside. The last thing he removed was his shirt, and when he lifted it over his head, she sighed in awe. What a beautiful creation a man's body was, all sleek and hard in comparison to her own soft curves.

She put out her arms to him and he came to her. They stretched out side by side on the soft bed, she on her back, he on his side. With a tantalizing slowness he began a dance of love, caressing every inch of her pale flesh with his fingertips, adding a kiss here and there. Each time she tried to sit up or reach for him, he lowered her arms. "Let me do this," he whispered. "For you. For me."

When he lowered his mouth to the soft triangle of curls at the apex of her thighs, she moaned, sucking in her breath. The air in the chilly bedchamber had grown warm and musky-smelling with the heat of their lovemaking.

Ellen's fingers grew tangled in his hair as she twisted beneath the ecstasy of his touch. Again and again he brought her to the crest of fulfillment, only to let her slide down again.

Finally, when she could take his exquisite torture no longer, she sat up, pushing him aside so that she could climb on top of him and sit astride his hips.

"Where are we going?" he teased, his voice throaty with desire. "I wasn't finished."

She leaned over to nip his lower lip with her teeth. "Hush," she ordered. "You would drive me mad if I let you."

His only reply was a husky laugh, as he let his eyelids close when she caught his hard nipple between her lips and suckled it as he had suckled hers.

Ellen was still in awe of the pleasure the two had found in each other. What was amazing was that it seemed it was not just a surface physical delight but one that went far deeper, one she carried in her heart in a glow for days after they made love.

*Is this what is is to love and be loved?* she wondered as she kissed her way down his flat belly. *Is this what*

182

*Richard spoke of when he spoke of a love so many seek yet so few ever find?*

Driven breathless by Ellen's attentions, Gavin grasped her forearms and tugged. "Now," he whispered urgently. "Now, sweet Ellen."

She started to roll off him so that she might lie flat on the bed, but he caught her hand. "No, stay where you are, just slide forward."

A shy smile crept across her lips as she realized what he meant. A little afraid but wickedly curious, she followed his husky whispers, slipping over his tumescent shaft.

She cried out in delighted surprise at the new sensation, and after only a moment or two of adjustment she began to move, enjoying the thought of being in control of their lovemaking.

Gavin tucked his hands behind his head and stared up at her with heavy-lidded, smoldering desire. Their gazes locked as she moved up and down, forward and back, exploring her own realms of pleasure while taking delight in his.

Again and again, Ellen ceased her movement when she heard Gavin's breathing change in near fulfillment. Again and again, she brought him to the edge of ultimate pleasure, only to let the moment slip away, just as he had done to her so many times.

With a growl of frustration, Gavin finally caught her buttocks with his hands and began to guide her in her rhythm. Growing lost in her own pleasure, she gave up her control, letting him lead them to a sudden conscious-shattering moment of climax. She reached the summit of her pleasure and collapsed over him in breathless wonder, burying her face in his damp, pungent hair, for the moment utterly content.

For a long time Ellen lay on top of him, still

feeling the heat of him inside her, bathing in the pleasure of his hand that stroked her hair.

"I love you, Ellen," he murmured sleepily.

"I love you," she whispered.

Then reluctantly she slid off him. She blew out the single bedside candle and snuggled in his arms, peacefully drifting off to sleep.

When Ellen woke in the morning, Gavin was already up and dressing. He smiled from where he sat rolling up his stockings in a ray of sunshine on the far side of the room. "Good morning."

She stretched with feline grace. "Good morning. Off so soon?"

"I've an appointment at Whitehall. I need to go home and bathe and change."

She lay back on a pillow, pulling up the corner of the coverlet to partially conceal her nakedness. "But I thought we might have a little more time." She kept her voice light and teasing, but suddenly her heart was heavy. Gavin had made her so happy these last months, how could she say goodbye? But he was Waldron's brother, and he would hate her if he ever knew the truth. No, it was better to part now and save herself the agony of Gavin despising her one day.

Gavin rose, tying his stock. "I really do have to go. Besides," he winked, "I think you've well worn me out."

Their laughter joined, echoing in the bedchamber.

As Gavin finished dressing, he went to the bird cage that hung near the window and pulled off the cover. He stuck his finger through the wires and into the cage. "When will I see you again, Ellen?"

The parrot plucked his head from beneath his wing. "See you again, see you again . . ." *Squawk!*

"When will I see you again?"

Ellen gripped the coverlet until her knuckles went white. She just couldn't bring herself to tell Gavin "never." Not when he was so happy this morning. Not when she could still taste his lips on hers. "I don't know," she lied. "I'll send you a message." She forced a smile.

Gavin snatched his finger out of the cage just in time to prevent being pecked by the parrot. "All right, then." He came to her and leaned down, giving her a husbandly kiss. "But soon. We have plans to make. Things to discuss."

She reached up to brush his stubbled chin with her fingertips as he pulled away. "Goodbye, Gavin."

He walked to the doorway, then turned back to her as if deep in thought. "Ellen . . ."

"Yes?"

"Tell Richard thank you for me, will you?"

She smiled. *Another time, another place, and this could have worked,* she mused bittersweetly. *We really could have been happy together.* "I will."

It wasn't until she heard the front door close that the first tears trickled down her cheeks.


"You think he's who?" Richard stood frozen in the doorway, a silver coffeepot in his hand.

Ellen swept back the hair from her shoulders, pulling her knees up to her chest to curl up in the chair. She had lain in her bed for more than an hour, listening to the silence of the room, wishing she could change the past but unable to bring herself to regret her husband's death. If losing Gavin was the price she had to pay for her freedom, then pay she would. Whatever had made her think there would be no price for her escape—and a dear one at that?

Ellen pushed her china cup toward him. "I think . . . no, I know he's Waldron's brother."

Richard swore foully in French. "What do you mean the brother to Waxton? You never told me Waxton had a brother!"

She shrugged. "Yes I did. He was supposedly lost at sea. It's been years, Richard. I've forgotten the details."

Richard came to the table where Ellen sat toying with a sugar spoon. He poured them both a cup of thick, steaming brew, then took the chair across from her. "Why didn't you tell me this last night? Why didn't you tell me that was why you were so distraught? Here I thought the clod had insulted you or something else petty!" Richard rested his forehead on the heel of his hand. "Why in the bloody hell didn't you tell me before I told him to marry you?"

Despite the graveness of the situation, Ellen couldn't resist a smile. "You told him to marry me?" Her gentle laughter filled the small antechamber. "Whatever would have possessed you to say such a thing?"

He took a sip of the coffee and swore again as it burned the roof of his mouth. "Because I thought you loved him. Damn you, jade, for laughing! I thought he loved you."

Still smiling, Ellen reached across the table to cover his big hand with her smaller one. "I'm not laughing at you but at myself, at the silly irony of it all." She stroked the back of his hand. "But never at you, Richard." She paused. "I do love him. I think perhaps he even loves me. That was a gallant thing to do, suggesting such a thing."

Richard looked up. "But you can never see him again now that you know who he is."

"I can never see him again," she echoed as she

withdrew her hand and reached for her coffee, not wanting the tears to start anew. "I know that. I knew it last night."

"That's why you were so upset."

"No." Her voice grew stronger. "I was upset. . . . I was *angry* because he lied to me. He lied about who he was!"

"The question is, why did he lie, Ellen?"

"I don't know. I'm afraid. . . . I'm afraid he's looking for me, Richard, and he just doesn't know it."

"Looking for you?" He reached for a slice of bread and the plate of anchovies. "You're not making any sense."

She sighed heavily. "When I first met Gavin he mentioned a woman he was looking for, but he didn't want to speak of the matter and it seemed unimportant."

"It seemed unimportant!"

She pushed away from the table angrily. "Don't look at me like that! Who would have thought in a city so large I'd have met the one man who could be my downfall!"

"It seems that in one night you've managed to meet both men who could see you hanged."

She paced the floor in her bare feet, her dressing gown swishing behind her. "Hunt."

"Yes, Hunt." Richard turned in his chair, wood scraping wood. "And what makes you think they're not in this together? What makes you think your lover didn't know who you were from the start?"

She walked to a window and brushed aside the heavy draperies so that she could watch the activity in the street below. Vendors were beginning to fill the streets now, peddling their fresh meats and cool milk. A young towheaded boy pulled a dogcart filled with kindling, a puppy following closely at his heels. "I just know he didn't. He doesn't know who I am. Not yet, at least."

"But Hunt did?"

"Oh, yes." She turned away from the window, letting the draperies fall into place. "He knew. I could see it in his eyes. I could hear it in his voice." She thought for a moment. "But he's not going to turn me in, Richard."

"And why not?"

"Because he wants the letter."

"If he has you arrested and thrown into Newgate, you'll be of no harm to him. They'll stretch your neck for the murder of your husband and you'll tell no tales."

"Too risky. What if I were to give the letter to someone? No, he wants the letter in his own hand. As long as I have it, I'll be safe enough."

Despite the early hour, Richard poured himself a drink. "So what if Merrick . . . Waxton . . . I don't know what the hell to call him now . . ."

"You could call him Gavin."

"All right . . . Gavin," he conceded angrily. "So what if Gavin and Hunt are working together to corner you?"

"Hunt wouldn't confide in anyone. I would wager not one of the men on the list knows who else is on the list."

"And you're positive Gavin's name does not appear in any form?"

"I read the list, remember? I'm certain Gavin's not on it."

"So why did Hunt make such an issue of letting you know who Gavin really was?"

"I think he saw an opportunity and he took it. I think he was just trying to frighten me." She ran a hand through her hair. "And I have to admit, he did a fine job of it."

Richard walked to the cold fireplace and leaned on the mantel. "Well, at least we finally agree that you can't see Gavin anymore. We pack up and go to the estate in Essex. You'll be safe enough there."

"I'll not see Gavin anymore." She looked up at Richard defiantly. "But I'll not leave London."

"But it would be suicide to stay now, knowing both men seek you! You'll hang for your cocky games, Ellen, as sure as I stand here!"

She made a fist. "As long as I have the letter, I'm safe from Hunt. He can frighten me, he can intimidate me, but he can't have me arrested."

"And Waxton?"

"It's nearly Christmas. In two or three months time he'll sail for his beloved Colonies. He has his inheritance now. Why would he pursue finding the woman . . . me?" She took a deep breath. "Besides, I'm still protected by the king as long as I remain on stage. Gavin wouldn't have the time nor the power to pursue getting a writ from the king to have me arrested."

"This is insanity!"

"Richard, it's my life! I told you, I'll not run. Not ever again! If I have to live in constant fear as I did when I lived in Waxton's house, then I'd rather be dead."

Richard wiped his mouth with the back of his hand. "I feel like you're killing yourself one day at a time, and I can do nothing but stand and watch you."

She walked to him. "Do you want me to go?"

"Go?"

"I'll pack and find my own apartment near the theater."

"So this is what it comes to?"

It was hard for Ellen to look up at him, to see the fear and pain in his handsome face. It was even harder to know she was causing the pain and fear when he loved her so much. "Richard, without you I'd never have survived. You helped me to become whole again, but now it's time to stand back. I'm strong enough to make my own decisions and I want to do so."

"You want to leave me. . . ."

She looped her arm through his and rested her cheek on his shoulder, ignoring the fact that he remained stiff and unyielding. "I don't want to leave you, so don't make me. Let me be responsible for my own choices." She reached up to touch his chin, forcing him to look her straight in the eye. "You know, if they came and took me away today, I'd have no regrets. I'd hang not being sorry for all I could have done, but being happy I had done what I had. Isn't that the point of life? Isn't that what you have done?"

"Christ's bones, Ellen." Richard wrapped her in his arms. "It's only a matter of time until this shatters in our faces, don't you know that?"

She rested her head on his chest, comforted by his touch but feeling guilty for wanting Gavin. "Mayhap, but mayhap not."

He stroked her hair. "You told Gavin you'd see him no longer?"

She shook her head. "I couldn't do it. Not here. Not after I'd lain in his arms."

"But you will tell him." Richard gripped her shoulders, pushing her away from his body. "Swear to me, Ellen."

"I'll tell him." She laid her cheek against Richard's chest again, clinging to him. "I'll tell him."

# Chapter Thirteen

Gavin brushed back a wisp of dark hair that had escaped his queue and tapped the marred wooden table with his knuckles, signaling the serving girl. He was in some drinking house down near the wharfs, though where he wasn't certain.

The Sea Serpent, a dilapidated wooden structure on some fetid alley, catered to sailors and other waterfront ruffians. The food was putrid, the ale stale, and the whores old and snaggletoothed. Gavin had only come at the urging of an old friend, Julius, the man who would captain his ship on the return voyage to the Colonies in the spring.

When the serving wench, who was seeing to another customer, didn't respond to Gavin, he pounded his fist on the table so hard that it rocked, knocking over Julius's bottle and spilling the remainder of its contents.

Cocking her head sideways, the dark-haired girl flipped him an obscene gesture. "I'm comin', my lord, but you'll have to wait yer turn same as the rest of these salts!"

Gavin scowled.

"Easy. Easy there, old boy," Julius soothed,

mopping up the spilt ale with his sleeve. "There's plenty to go 'round. Just give the poxbox a chance."

Gavin looked up across the table through the haze of his alcohol-clouded mind. Julius Reason was not ten years older than Gavin, but he looked to be a man of at least sixty. His hair had gone grey, his skin dark and leathery from the years in the sun. His hands were wrinkled, his clothing worse, but he was a man Gavin knew he could trust. He was a friend worth having.

"Why'd you bring me, Julius? A man could die of thirst here, if he don't die of food poisoning first."

"You seem to have had no problem taking your fill, friend," Julius responded good-naturedly. "You're soused."

Gavin lifted his empty sack bottle to his lips to catch the last drop. "If I am, it's not drunk enough."

Julius chuckled as he leaned across the table to shake a knurled finger. "Admit it. You love her, else why would you have yourself turned inside out like this?"

Gavin tossed the empty bottle over his head. He waited for the satisfying crash of broken glass before he responded. Several other breaking bottles echoed in the dark, smoky alehouse. "So what if I love her?" He hiccuped. "I told you. She won't see me, Jules. She sends back my gifts. I sent her an emerald—I swear to Christ, it was the size of a goose egg—and she had the messenger return it!"

"You tried to talk to her?"

"She must nearly break a leg running off the stage at the end of the play and she goes home in her costume. That jackanapes Chambray guards her like a hawk in their apartment. I can't get near her. I can't get the chance to try to make her understand why I lied about who I was. And the one time that I did get to speak with her, she just kept saying she was sorry." He looked up. "I can't eat. I can't sleep. I can't concentrate on my work. What the hell am I going to do?"

"Find a whore?" Julius suggested with a grin.

"Tried that." Gavin slapped the table with his palm. "First time since I was fourteen I couldn't get my pecker up!" He sighed dismally. "I'm telling you, she's ruined me, Jules. I've got saltpeter on the brain. I don't want anyone else but Ellen. Don't know that I ever will again." He wiped his mouth with the back of his hand. "I've got to have her."

At about that time, the serving girl came sashaying by. "What you need, gen'lemen?"

She stopped directly behind Julius, who rocked back in his chair to nestle his balding head between her sagging breasts. "A little tit, mayhap?"

She took a quick step back and he lost his balance, nearly falling to the floor. She chuckled good-naturedly. "'Sides that, boyos?"

"Sack." Gavin demanded, hitting the table with his fist for emphasis. "Two bottles each. You're so damnable slow, we'll drink 'em waiting for you to find us again."

The girl smirked and walked away. "Be right back."

Gavin watched in slight awe when she took a sudden running step and kicked a rat with the toe of her worn slipper. The animal squealed as it skittered across the floor and disappeared under another table. The tar-tailed sailors sitting there let out a few hoots and a round of applause.

Gavin felt his stomach toss as he looked back at Julius. He knew he shouldn't be here. He wasn't a drinking man anymore. Now he was hallucinating.

193

"That blessed rat was as big as a dog!"

Julius smirked. "What do you think that meat was you had for sup?" He smacked his lips, rubbing his washboard stomach. "Damned tasty, I vow!"

Gavin's sea-green eyes narrowed doubtfully as he stared across the table at his friend. The worst thing was that the man was probably right. They probably had eaten rat meat! "You're a sick man, Julius. I don't know why I'd let you take my ship out of the harbor, much less to Maryland."

Julius opened his arms in a grandioso gesture. "Because I'm wise . . . wiser than you!"

"Oh, you are, are you?" Gavin leaned on the table and propped his cheek on the heel of his hand. "So tell me, wise man of the sea, what would you do with Ellen Scarlet if you were me?"

"I told you. Get a whore. An expensive one . . . one of them acrobats from the Orient."

"*After* the whore, Jules. I mean, if the whore didn't work. If you still weren't over the jade."

The older man broke into a grin. "I guess I'd kidnap her."

"Kidnap her?"

Julius drew his chair closer. "Look, you say the problem is you can't get to her to talk to her. You say if you could just explain, you know she'd see to your way of thinking and the hull would be patched, right?"

"If she's reasonable, yes."

Julius shrugged. "So there you go. Tie 'er to your main m'st and she have no choice but to listen to you."

The serving girl came back with four dusty green bottles of sack. Gavin snatched them from her hand before she had a chance to set them on the table. "That's insane!"

194

"Look, I told you the whore was your best wager." Julius took the other sack bottles from the girl and dropped a couple of farthings down her bodice. "The kidnapping is only my second idea. After that"—he wiped the neck of a bottle with his sleeve, then took a long pull—"I'm fresh out of ideas."

"Kidnap her." Gavin took another sip of the sack but it tasted sour in his mouth. He set down the bottle. "She'd hate me."

"Sounds like she hates you now."

"Chambray'd lose his mind if she disappeared," Gavin mused aloud. "I'd have to leave him a note to let him know she was all right and that I'd bring her back safely."

"I don't know why you're so light-footed about stealing another man's female. This certainly wouldn't be the first time you've done it. What about that little mademoiselle in Paris back in '57? You remember the little thing with the dark eyes and the mountainous—"

"Chambray's a good man, Julius. Ellen doesn't want him hurt."

"You sail off to the savages for a few years and suddenly you get a conscience, friend." He took another drink. "I'm bloody disappointed."

Gavin leaned forward to keep the conversation private, though who would be listening, he didn't know. He and Julius were by far the most sober men in the tavern, and probably the only two that had any wit to begin with. "You think it could work? You see, I thought what I could do is take her somewhere . . . somewhere out of the city where we could relax and talk. If we just had some time together alone, I'm certain I could convince her that my intentions were never to be deceitful."

Julius twisted the point of his short-cropped grey

grizzled beard. "You'd need a partner. You can't pull off something like this alone—not a gentleman like you. It's not in your blood. No, you need someone who's got the gall to go in and get her out of the theater or her apartment whether she's willing or nay."

"You?"

"I once kidnapped a princess in the Caribbean Islands. Worth her weight in gold to her father, she was, literally." He winked. "Made me a rich man . . . at least for the year or two it took me to piss it away."

"I don't want Ellen hurt in a struggle. You hurt her and I'll kill you, I swear by the virgin I will, Jules."

"No, no, no. You just leave this to me, old boy. A man like me gets ahold of her and she'll be as timid as a mouse."

Gavin lifted an eyebrow. His mind was still a little cloudy from the sack, but he was thinking more clearly. Yes, he'd take Ellen into the country, where they could be alone to enjoy each other's company. There he could make her understand why he'd lied. He could make her understand that he truly did love her. "Ellen's not the timid mouse sort, I'm afraid. She's a redhead with a temper to match."

"Not with me, old boy. I guarantee I'll bring her to you packaged like a docile little lamb." He took a knife from his belt. "Now, you say she lives on the second story." He drew a sputtering oil lamp closer and scratched a square in the table. "Tell me what street she's on and what surrounds the building . . ."


Ellen watched through the window as Richard jumped into the hackney beside two friends and the

196

vehicle rolled away into the darkness of the London night. Morosely, she let the drapery fall from her fingertips.

Richard had wanted her to come tonight to sup and play cards with friends, but she just wasn't up to it. It seemed that in the last two weeks she wasn't up to anything. She had to drag herself out of bed in the morning to make it to rehearsal on time, and once at the theater, she felt a keen lack of interest in the performance. She found herself argumentative with Richard and so restless that she was beginning to think she had been too hasty in making her decision concerning Gavin.

Ellen wandered over to the table where she and Richard had left chess pieces set on a board. They had ended the game only halfway through because she'd been unable to concentrate long enough to make her moves. She lifted a rook and rolled it in her fingertips.

She missed Gavin so much. She kept going over and over in her head that last night when they'd made love. She recalled every caress, every kiss, every word of passion exchanged. It all seemed like a dream now, even Gavin's words of love, but just the same, she kept conjuring them up again and again.

Now that time had passed and Hunt had not showed up at her door, she began to think that perhaps she really was safe. Perhaps he'd realized that the wisest way to protect himself and the men on the list was to simply leave her alone.

Ellen dropped the chess piece back on the board and wandered back toward her bedchamber, toying with the tie of her Chinese silk dressing robe. The maid had filled her bath half an hour ago. If she didn't get into the tub soon, the water would be too cool. Perhaps a bath and a little reading, Ellen

197

thought as she went down the dark hallway, clopping in her silk mules.

She was just unwrapping a bar of French soap when she heard a noise in the front antechamber. Thinking for certain Richard had dismissed the maid before he left, she called out.

"Rose? Richard? Is someone there?"

"Rose!" *Squawk!* "Richard!" Sir Gavin chanted from his bird cage.

"Oh, shut up, or I'm going to send you to the cook house to be made into stew!" Ellen threw a towel at the bird cage, and the parrot screeched and leaped, fluttering its wings.

"Oh, shut up! Made into stew. Shut up!" *Squawk!*

Ellen shook her head. Now she knew why Gavin had given her the blasted bird. It was to drive her insane after he was gone.

Standing at her doorway, she listened for another moment, but when she heard no other noise, she went back to her dressing table to find her brush and comb. Richard was making her as jumpy as he was, with all of his watching for hackneys following them and fearing there were eavesdroppers in every tavern.

Ellen had tossed the bar of soap into the copper bathtub and had begun to remove her robe, when she heard another noise, this time the distinct squeak of the kitchen door.

She tightened the tie of her robe and peeked around the corner into the hallway. In the semidarkness she saw nothing but the familiar shadows of doorways and furniture.

When she heard the floorboard near the kitchen door groan, she was certain there was an intruder in the apartment. Without thinking, without taking time to be frightened, she went to her dressing table and pulled a loaded pistol from a hatbox. It had seemed rather silly at the time when Richard had hidden it there, but now she was thankful.

If it was thieves in the house, they could have what they wanted, but if it was Hunt or if it was someone sent by him to harm her, she'd blow their head off. She'd decided that two weeks ago when she'd seen Hunt. She'd decided she wouldn't be afraid to walk on the street or stay home alone. She wouldn't live with that kind of paralyzing fear of a man, not ever again.

With her fingers tight around the handle of the pistol and shaking only slightly, Ellen crept down the dark hallway. She knew she had the advantage over the intruder, as she knew her way around the apartment in the dark while he—she heard a thud as he struck a piece of furniture—must feel his way through the rooms.

At the end of the hallway Ellen stood stock-still, staring at the shadows of the hulking furniture and fireplace, looking for something that appeared to be out of place.

She saw nothing.

But she could feel someone's presence. She could smell the salt tang that clung to his clothing. She could almost hear his breathing as he watched her from somewhere in the room.

Ellen pulled back the hammer of the pistol, the sound loud in her ears, and took a step into the front room. Still she saw nothing. She took another step, her bare foot making a slight slap on the hardwood floor. It was not until she took the third step that she realized the intruder was behind her, and then she only felt him rather than heard him.

Ellen reeled around, swinging the pistol. She immediately caught sight of a figure in a wool cap with a sack thrown over his back. *Thieves.* "I'll give you to the count of three before I shoot," she warned in a voice that sounded strangely sincere in her own ears. "There'll be no thieving here this night."

There was a chuckle in the darkness. "Christ's bones," he said in a raspy voice, "You do have a spine, wench. Wasn't kidding, was he? Now put down the weapon afore you shoot yourself in the foot!"

Ellen's eyes narrowed as she tried to make out the figure. "*He?* Who's *he?* If it's Hunt who sent you, tell him he'd best come for me himself."

The intruder made a cautious step forward. "He only wishes to speak with ye. Now lay aside the pistol like I said!"

She straightened her elbows. "I'll shoot you. It's no jest."

He swore. "I'll give you but one more chance, wench, and then—"

"Then what?" Ellen was surprised by her own boldness. Here was one of Hunt's men come to kidnap her and she was standing her ground with little fear, with even a measure of aggression. What a long way she'd come since that night at Havering House.

"I'll—"

Ellen saw his intention to move and squeezed her eyes shut as she pulled the trigger. There was a blast of sound and a streak of white light. Ellen felt herself being struck in the middle and hurled backward as the acrid smell of gunpowder curled in her nostrils.

She went tumbling to the floor, with the man gripping her waist. The pistol flew from her hands as the back of her head struck the ground.

The intruder groaned as he wrestled her backward. "You could have killed me, you little bedlamite!"

"Let go of me! Let go of me!" Ellen screamed. Her

200

hands found his face and she sank a finger into his eye socket.

"Son of a poxed whore! Ouch!" In the struggle that ensued, the man somehow managed to catch both of her arms at the wrists and pin them to the floor with his hands.

"Get off me!" Get off!" Ellen screamed, bucking beneath him, trying to get a leg up to kick him.

"If you don't shut your mouth, madame, I'll be forced to knock you in the teeth! Now calm yourself!"

She struggled, though the weight and size of him was obviously too much for her to fight against. "Who are you? What do you want? Tell the filthy pink-eyed bastard to come himself if he wants me!"

"Saint Satan! You've got a mouth!" He let go of one of her hands just long enough to pull a handkerchief from his coat. "The name's Julius. I know no pink-eyed bastard. A friend sent me and he'll be sore displeased if you get hurt, so cease your struggling, wench!"

"I'll not go! I'll not go anywhere with you! Now let me go, else I'll—" Ellen was cut off by the handkerchief he stuffed into her mouth. When she tried to scream again, no sound came out and she almost gagged on the silk.

He let go of her hands and sat back a little, the pressure of his body still holding her down on the floor. "Now will ye be more reasonable?"

She balled her hand and struck him with her fist so hard that he swayed.

Julius swore again as he yanked another piece of cloth from his coat. "As I was saying," he went on as he caught her hands and rolled her over to tie them behind her back. "You could walk out of here sensibly, or I could carry you."

Ellen could only grumble through the gag.

"Well enough! Suit yourself." Julius stood and lifted her up.

The minute Ellen was on her feet, she kicked him as hard as she could in the groin.

Julius doubled over with a growl and came up swearing as he whipped out another length of cloth. "Docile as a lamb, I say. Quiet as a cathedral mouse. As sweet as a dairymaid on May Day," he went on, muttering to himself as he caught her ankles in an iron grip and tied them together.

He straightened up to see Ellen glaring fiercely at him through the darkness.

Julius flashed her a grin. "Can you stay put long enough for me to fetch ye a bit of clothing?" He winked. "Not that you're not rather fetching as you are."

Unable to make a sound or move, for fear of toppling herself over, Ellen could only glower at him as he turned and went down the hallway.

She figured she was in no immediate danger. It was obvious this wharf rat had been sent to bring her to Hunt and that his instructions had been not to harm her. But what would happen when he turned her over to Hunt? She squeezed her eyes against the tears that threatened to spill forth. She'd get out of this. She didn't know how, but she'd not be bested this easily.

Julius returned from the bedchamber a minute later with his sack filled and thrown over his back, nursing his finger. "Damned bird bit me!" he complained, sucking the offended finger. He looked at Ellen. "Dangerous, that parrot is. Were he mine, I'd bake 'im in a eel pie." He stopped in front of her. "Ready, sweet?"

She muttered at him through the silk cloth. He

202

laughed as he lifted her and flung her over his shoulder.

With her hair brushing the floor, he carried Ellen out of the apartment, through the back entrance, and into the black starless night.

She shivered with cold in her thin dressing gown, which blew in the wind. She was dizzy from being held upside down but was determined to keep her thoughts clear. If she was going to escape, she had to know where he was taking her.

Julius walked half a block down the street and stopped at the wheels of a covered coach. She heard the door swing open. Then her kidnapper lifted her gingerly off his shoulder and through the door of the coach.

"By the king's cod, what have you done to her?" a familiar voice said. "You swore you wouldn't hurt her."

"She put up a hell of a struggle, friend," Julius declared as he took a running step and leaped on to the sideboard as the coach rolled off. "I'm lucky I came away without having my private parts blown off!"

As Ellen hit the seat, she lifted her chin to meet Gavin's gaze. Unable to speak, she could only stare at him in fury.

He reached across the narrow space and pulled the handkerchief from her mouth. "Ellen, I apologize—"

"Black-hearted whoreson!" she spat as she raised her feet, still tied at the ankles, and struck Gavin hard in the shins.

Julius's laughter echoed in the deserted street as he swung through the door, closing it behind him, and the coach careened around the corner in its getaway.

# Chapter Fourteen

"Ouch! Hell and fury, Ellen!" Gavin massaged his wounded shin.

"Son of a poxed whore! What are you doing sending someone to kidnap me? You scared the life out of me! I thought it was H—" She turned her head, ashamed of the tears that burned beneath her eyelids.

Gavin slid across the coach to sit beside her. He reached out to stroke her cheek, but she jerked back. He sighed. "I don't know who it is you're avoiding other than me, but if he's had half the trouble catching up with you as I have, I imagine you're blessedly safe."

Julius rapped his knuckles on the ceiling. "I'd love to stay and see how this all turns out, but this is where I take my leave, friend." He swept his knit sailor's cap off his head and half stood, stooping beneath the low ceiling. The sway of the coach made him clutch for something solid. "Your servant, madame."

Ellen glared at him, her green eyes snapping in fury.

Julius gave a laugh and, with a shrug of his shoulders, opened the coach door. Without a moment's hesitation or thought about the fact that the coach was still moving, he leapt out into the darkness.

Ellen heard Gavin's hunchbacked coachman give a fierce, muffled curse.

"A good night to you, Gavin," Julius called as the coach rolled away. "And a good luck to you! You're going to need it."

Gavin pulled the door closed and the vehicle picked up its speed again. For a few moments Ellen and Gavin sat in silence, regarding each other until finally she spoke.

"Well, are you going to untie me, or am I to remain bound like the Yuletide pig?"

"That depends on whether you're going to injure me or not again." There was amusement in his voice, but a hint of aggravation as well.

"Then mayhap you'd best leave me tied." Her gaze met his in defiance. *What right did he have to be out of sorts? She was the one who'd been kidnapped in her nightdress!*

Gavin studied her face for a moment, then made a motion indicating she should turn around. His hands found the ties that bound her wrists behind her back and he loosened them. "You gave me no choice, Ellen. I tried every reasonable way I knew how to talk to you. This was the only way I could think to get you alone."

"So now *I* have no choice."

"You didn't even say goodbye." He threw the cloths on the floorboards and leaned over to free her ankles. "No explanation, nothing. Just no, I won't see you anymore." He lifted his head to look at her. "After that last night in your bedchamber, it wasn't right. You owe me more than that."

She rubbed her chafed wrists, trying to hold on to the anger she felt so quickly subsiding. *He loved*

206

*her so much that he'd kidnapped her! Well, perhaps not love, but at least want. He had wanted her.* "I didn't want a fight. That last night, it was—"

"It was magic . . . sorcery." He took her hands in his and rubbed her wrists with slow deliberateness. "I'm sorry that I lied to you about who I was. I told you that. I thought you accepted my apologies."

She shook her head, wanting to pull away but wanting at the same time to feel his touch. She'd been so lonely these last two weeks without him. Not only had she ached for the stroke of his callused hands, but also for his voice, his laughter. "It's not just the lies, Gavin, mine or yours." She struggled to find the right words, to convince not just Gavin, but herself that this union could never be.

He brought his lips to the pulse point of her wrist. "What then?"

She exhaled, letting her eyes drift shut. "It's everything, Gavin. It's Richard, it's your lies, my deceptions, my past, perhaps yours." She opened her eyes to meet his gaze. "You forget who I am. Barely more than a common street whore. An actress, a woman who works for her keep. You're an earl. You have a position to uphold. Can't you see the impossibility of it all?"

"Nothing is impossible. I don't care if you're an actress or whore to an army of men. Now I want you to tell me who you're afraid of. Who did you think had come to take you tonight?"

"It doesn't matter."

"Have you a husband?"

She shook her head.

"Because if you do, I'll take you, anyway. I'll kill him if you prefer."

She traced the line of his chin, taking notice that he hadn't shaved today. She liked the rough feel of his

207

beard beneath her fingertips. "I almost think you're serious when you say that."

"I am, entirely."

Ellen leaned back in the leather seat, suddenly feeling the chill of the night air through her thin gown. Seeing her action, Gavin immediately shrugged off his burgundy coat and wrapped it around her shoulders.

"Where are we going? I have to let Richard know I'm all right."

"I had Jules leave him a note saying you would return three days hence."

"The theater. John will be furious when I don't show up for rehearsal tomorrow at noon."

"Taken care of. You were feeling poorly so you sent word this evening that you would be traveling to the Springs in Marchion and will return three days hence, rested and ready to continue."

She gave him a dry smile. "It seems you've taken care of everything."

The flicker of yellow lamplight shone across his handsome face. "Does that mean you'll come with me?"

"Have I a choice?"

"No."

She leaned back against the seat, drawing her legs up beneath her. She could feel his fingertips brushing the nape of her neck. "Are you going to tie me up again?"

He leaned to nip at her earlobe with his warm lips. "Only if you want me to, sweet."

She punched him in the shoulder, and their laughter mingled as she snuggled against him and let her eyes close. She knew this didn't make any sense. She knew she was taking chances with her own life to be with Gavin, to even consider seeing him again.

She knew that she would be hurting Richard again, salting the wound she had already created. But somehow all of that didn't matter. Gavin loved her. He loved her! Even if their time together would be brief and riddled with uncertainty, how could she give that up?

The truth of the matter was that she couldn't.

That night Ellen and Gavin stayed at an inn on the outskirts of the east side of the City. Though the establishment was small, the food and drink the host and hostess served was tasty, the room neat and clean. That night Ellen and Gavin did not make love, but instead lay in each other's arms, both strangely pensive but nonetheless content.

In the morning, they broke their fast with fresh pullet eggs baked in cream, fried fish, and bread with sweet butter, all washed down with cups of warm milk. After thanking the host and hostess and paying them handsomely, Ellen and Gavin returned to the coach.

"Where are we going?" Ellen asked, her eyes bright with the thought of the excursion. Wherever Gavin took her, it was always an adventure. He knew so much about the world and she so little that each moment with him seemed magical.

"It's a surprise," he answered, his breath clouding in the sharp morning air. It was almost Christmastide and the weather had turned cool, a refreshing relief from the stagnant heat of the unusual fall.

"A surprise?" She couldn't resist a smile. Gavin looked so young and dashing this morning in a pair of tight black breeches, a simple white shirt, and a black cloak with a matching hat. He still wore the silly colonial boots and his hair pulled back and braided like a savage's, but she had grown used to it. In fact, she actually liked the idea that the man she loved would always stand out in a crowd, whether it be on some foreign wharf or in Queen Catherine's drawing room.

A short time later the coach halted near the winding Thames, and Gavin and Ellen got out. Carrying a carpetbag with a change of clothing for himself and the few things Julius had stolen from her bedchamber, they approached a small dock, where a private bargelike sailboat was tied up.

"This is the surprise?" Ellen's brow creased. "A barge with sails?"

"But a very special barge." He kissed her cheek. "One created for your pleasure."

After giving the coachman directions to return to London, Gavin caught Ellen's arm and led her down the rickety dock. To her surprise, Julius appeared from below. "A good morning to you!" he called cheerfully as he picked up a piece of line and began to coil it.

Ellen stopped. "Don't tell me he's going?"

"Someone's got to steer the boat." He winked as he leaned down to untie a line from a bulkhead. "And I have other intentions."

She frowned. "The man kidnapped me!"

"*I* had you kidnapped and you slept with *me* last night."

She pushed back the hood of her cloak and dropped her hands to her hips. "It's not the same thing!"

"Come now! Jules is a good man. He's my friend, and the best thing is that he'll leave us to our privacy."

Ellen hesitated. It was the principle of the thing! This scruffy man had tied her up and snatched her from her apartment in her nightclothes, for sweet Mary's sake!

Gavin brushed her back with his hand. "It'll be fun, sweet, I promise you."

She eyed the boat, not fully trusting its seaworthiness. "Where are we going? You said I'd be back in London in three days."

"Just down the river."

"I thought floating down the Thames was just for the summer."

He linked his arm through hers and led her down the dock. "I suppose you thought picnics were just for summer, too, but just wait. These will be three of the finest days of your life, I'll promise you."

By the time the sun had peaked in the blue sky, Ellen was convinced Gavin would stand up to his promise. Once boarding, they had set out down the river into the countryside, with Julius sailing the vessel and remaining inconspicuous.

Gavin and Ellen rested on the bow, where there were comfortable padded lounging chairs and canvas walls, which not only served as windbreaks but for privacy as well. Despite the fact that it was early December, Ellen was pleased to discover how warm it was on the bow of the boat lying out in the sunshine, safe from the north wind.

Sitting side by side in the chairs, Gavin and Ellen talked about nonsensical things, simply enjoying each other's company.

As Gavin told a tale of an adventure with the Indians in Maryland, Ellen let her mind wander.

*I should end this deceit and tell Gavin who I am. I should tell him what his brother did to me. Surely Gavin will believe me when I say Waldron's death was accidental, or at the very least self-defense. Surely he will believe me once he realizes what a monster his brother was!*

But a paralyzing inner fear kept her from speaking up. What if he didn't believe her? At least with the lies, she could have him today, tomorrow, maybe a few more months until he set sail. But what if he didn't believe her? What if he didn't understand? What if he hated her?

Gavin finished his tale and was silent. Before Ellen could work up the courage to attempt any conversation about the truth of her identity, he spoke again.

"Ellen, I want to tell you why I wasn't entirely truthful about who I am."

She pushed her cloak she had been using for a blanket onto the deck and stretched like a cat in the warm sunshine. "I've no intentions of sharing secrets, if that's what you seek."

He crossed his arms over his chest. He had shed his linen shirt and lay taking in the sun's rays, his broad pectorals already beginning to brown. "I'm not seeking anything. I just want you to know."

She sighed. "Don't you see, I don't want to know, Gavin. I don't care."

"If you didn't care, you'd not have tried to end our relationship so abruptly. I lied about my name and my identity, or at least deceived you, and you deserve an explanation."

Ellen reached between the chairs to take his hand. "I'd rather make love."

He kissed the back of her hand. "Later. I'm confessing now."

She glanced away, watching the countryside as it passed. The boat moved so slowly, so gently through the water, that it seemed as if the hills and small villages were moving instead. She smiled at the sight of a fisherman on the bank, his young son beside him, imitating his every move.

She glanced back at Gavin, admitting to herself that she was curious as to what his explanation would be. Would he lie? Or would he tell her the truth? Would he admit he was Waldron's brother? Would he say he sought his murdering sister-in-law with the help of the Duke of Hunt? Or would he tell half-truths? She didn't know which was worse.

She lifted her dark lashes. "I'm listening. Confess if you must, but don't feel compelled. I can love you whoever you are, at least for today."

He shook his head. "Such a fatalistic attitude for one so young."

She looked away to avoid eye contact, as images of her father, her husband, and the Duke of Hunt flashed through her mind. "If you'd lived the life I did, you'd be fatalistic, too."

"Tell me," he entreated softly, half rising out of his chair. "Trust me when I say I won't care. Trust me when I say I can help you."

"Remember, this is your confession, not mine."

Realizing he was pressing her too hard, he lay back in the chair and began his tale. "I am Viscount Gavin Merrick, in that that's one of my father's lesser titles."

"But you have another title?"

"I'm also the Earl of Waxton. The title was inherited through my brother, who died while I was in the Colonies."

*So he is to tell the truth,* Ellen thought. *Or at least part of it.* "So why hide your inheritance, title or otherwise, if the inheritance was legal?"

There was a long pause, as he seemed to debate whether to tell the truth or how much to tell. Ellen waited, feeling frightened yet having to know the truth.

"Because my brother was murdered."

She forced herself to meet his gaze, hoping he

213

wouldn't see the flicker of fear in her eyes. "And?"

"And I seek the woman who murdered him. His wife." He exhaled as if a great weight had been lifted from his shoulders.

There had been obvious pain in his voice as he spoke, and that pain disturbed Ellen. He had cared for his brother! This wasn't just justice being sought. It was vengeance!

"You knew her?" Ellen's voice was barely audible above the swish of the water as the boat glided up the Thames in the direction of Essex and Havering House.

"I did not." He ran a hand through his hair that now fell loose on his shoulders. "You see, my brother Waldron was almost twenty-five years my elder. I was gone when he met and married his wife. He spoke of her several times in letters, but then we lost contact with each other. I was a man for the Stuarts, he for Cromwell." He looked at her. "But to Waldron that made no difference. We were still brothers. He encouraged me to follow my heart, as our father would have encouraged me." He looked away, as if lost in the past. "Apparently, sometime in '57 Waldron received word of my death. A ship I was supposed to be aboard was sunk by the Spaniards, but actually I was in Paris laid up with a musket ball in my thigh. I sent word I was safe, but he never received it."

Ellen vaguely remembered her husband's mention of his little brother's demise, but the memory was dim. Waldron had seemed unaffected at the time. In fact, she did remember him making some comment about his brother Morley getting what he deserved like the other sinners. "You never saw each other again?" Ellen prodded carefully.

"We did, in London in '60, just after the king

214

returned, but the visit was brief. I don't know if you were here in London that May, but the city was mad. I was busy getting my land grant. Waldron had business in Europe. I never even got a chance to go to his home and meet his wife."

As Ellen flipped back through the pages of time in her mind, she remembered Waldron's trip to London to see the king arrive. She had wanted to go so badly that she had protested. Waldron had locked her in her room for a week, taking away her books as well as her freedom, ending the matter. And there had been no trip to France for Waldron that year; he rarely traveled. She also remembered distinctly that her husband had made no mention of a reunion with his brother. He had, in fact, never told her his little brother Morley was, indeed, alive rather than dead, as reported.

Ellen turned her attention to Gavin as he went on with his story. "That was the last time I saw Waldron alive." He smiled at his memory. "We supped together, talked like old friends. He was instrumental in helping me get my land so quickly. Then I set sail for the American Colonies with my land grant in my hand and he returned home to his young wife to take her to tour Europe."

As Ellen listened to Gavin's story, not only to his words but also to his tone of voice, she imagined the Waldron Waxton whom Gavin must have known . . . or thought he knew. The Earl of Waxton he spoke of sounded like a kindly elder brother, almost fatherly in his devotions. He sounded like a sensitive, dedicated husband who took his wife on tour.

Of course, it was all lies. Ellen knew him . . . or at least Thomasina had. The memory of her old name brought tears to her eyes and she looked away so that Gavin could not see them. It had been a long time since she had thought of Thomasina, poor little Thomasina, sold by her father at thirteen to be the bride of a man old enough to be her grandsire. Poor Thomasina, who had spent so many years in Havering House a prisoner not only of the walls but also of her husband's whims.

Ellen didn't want to hear any more. She didn't want to hear Waldron's lies and deceptions. She didn't want to remember the pain. But she was compelled to hear the whole truth. She had to understand Gavin's position. She had to know if he was involved with Hunt. "You said she murdered him . . . the wife?" Ellen heard herself say softly.

"In cold blood." His voice was bitter and raspy. "She set fire to his lab and pushed him out the window. He fell several stories and broke his neck. He lived but a few minutes."

*Long enough to tell Hunt about the letter*, Ellen thought.

"I've since found out that their fight was probably due to his discovery of her infidelity to him. Of her many infidelities."

*Liar!* Ellen wanted to scream. *Bloody whore-mongering lair! I was true to you, husband, and you knew it!*

"Where—" Ellen's voice stuck in her throat, "where is she now?"

"I don't know. In the confusion of the fire and my brother's death, she escaped and was never found."

"If she was never found, she might well be dead," Ellen offered. *Thomasina is dead. Long dead and gone. How could you pursue the woman who had to defend her own life? How can you persecute her after all she suffered at that beast's hands?*

Of course, Gavin didn't know the truth about the circumstances. No one knew but she and Richard

216

and, of course, Hunt.

Gavin flexed his hands, as if he could strangle the life from his brother's murderess with the motion. "I hid my identity, Ellen, because I wanted to find her. I wanted to see justice done. I wanted to see her hang for her crimes."

Ellen knew she was not past the point of no return. She would know all Gavin knew, or at least would admit to. If she was going to carry on this dangerous relationship, she had to at least know the odds. "And have you found her?"

"Perhaps."

Her brow knitted. "You don't know?"

"I'm very close. The thing is"—he met her gaze with his steady one—"since I've met you . . . since I've come to realize I love you, I'm not certain I care about Thomasina Waxton anymore."

A shiver coursed through Ellen's limbs at the sound of the man she loved speaking her name with such rancor. "I . . . I don't see what I have to do with this woman. Why lie to me?"

"It's difficult to explain." He came up out of his chair and slid into hers, wrapping his arm tightly around her.

Ellen could feel herself trembling. On the one hand, she was almost repelled by Gavin. He was the enemy. He had admitted by his own words that he sought her and that if he found her, he would see her hang for her alleged crime.

But from the utter desperation she felt at this moment, she needed his touch. Even knowing what she did, she still loved him. How ironic it was that the man who pursued her for Waldron's death was the only person who could wash away the memories of the anguish her husband had inflicted upon her. Not even Richard could make her safe like Gavin could.

And she felt for Gavin's pain. No matter how wrong he was about his brother, his pain over his loss was genuine. Instinctively, she reached out to caress his cheek, to draw his head to her breast.

She knew now she could never tell Gavin that she was Thomasina Waxton. She could never convince him it was only in self-defense that she had struggled with Waldron. She wasn't even certain she had been the one to push him. The night was nothing but a blur now. Hadn't he just fallen?

No, the Waldron whom Gavin knew was a different man. The Thomasina Waxton whom Gavin knew was a different woman. Too much time had passed. And why try to change Gavin's opinion of his brother now if it would serve her no purpose? If she was going to lose him no matter what, why not let him believe in the good man rather than the evil?

Gavin turned his face toward hers and she responded with a kiss. As their lips met and his hand brushed against the curve of her breast, thoughts of Waldron faded. Right now she wouldn't think about her husband, or about who Gavin was, or even about dear Richard at home alone, pacing the floors and drinking too much. Right now she would think of nothing but Gavin and the taste of his lips. She would ease the pain in his heart and worry about her own later.

# Chapter Fifteen

Richard waved a dismal farewell to his companions, who rode off laughing and shouting from a rented hell cart. He took his time walking up the icy steps of the building where he and Ellen rented their apartment. A street or two over, a watchman mournfully cried out the time of one in the morning.

Richard took the steps slowly, in no hurry to be inside. Without Ellen, the apartment was a tomb. No matter how many candles he lit or how high he had the servants burn the flames in the fireplaces, it was still a dismal, lonely place.

Richard glanced up at the quarter moon that hung low in the smoky horizon over the City. He had known he was going to lose her someday; he had known it from the night he had picked her up on that deserted stretch of roadway in Essex. So why did it hurt so much?

He tried to tell himself it was the danger she was putting herself in. Hunt was a hawk with his talons bared, waiting somewhere out there. Merrick was the link. *Waxton*, he corrected himself—the brother to the man she had killed.

Gavin. Richard didn't know if he was in Hunt's

confidences, but he seriously doubted it. The man Ellen had fallen in love with was too honorable a person. Richard had done some investigating into Hunt since the man had returned from France, and he had not liked what he had found. Ellen's descriptions and interpretations had only scratched the surface of the man's true character. Hers had been the observations of an innocent woman.

Word had it that not only was Hunt a dishonorable man, but he was also deadly. He had a great deal of influence with the king and thought nothing of using it for his own means, with or without Charles's approval. It was said he was a man no man wanted as an enemy in political circles. Apparently, in the last two years, seven close acquaintances of his had died unexpectedly or been beheaded on mysterious charges.

Richard leaned on the wooden rail, taking a deep breath of the night air. As for Hunt's personal behavior, the man's background was riddled with scandal. He had been wed twice to young wealthy women; the first had died of a mysterious illness in their first year of marriage. Rumor had it the duke had poisoned her in a fit of jealousy. The second wife had gone mad with childbirth fever and had burned her infant son and herself up in her bedchamber. There were those who whispered that the duke had driven her to it after denying the child as his own.

Then, of course, there were the tales of the Duke of Hunt's appetite for the perverted. Richard had always known there were places here in London where a man could find satisfaction of any twisted sexual desire possible, but the things he had heard about Hunt, procured through bribes, had made him physically ill.

Richard started up the steps again. No. Gavin Waxton was probably not aware of Hunt's connection with Ellen, but no doubt the duke had used him to lure her into his home that night. No doubt Hunt would use him again if he chose to do so.

So was that it? Was it the danger Ellen faced that made Richard want to hate Gavin? Was he only protecting her by wanting to keep her away from him? Or was it jealousy? Was it bitter envy?

Bloody hell, yes! It made him angry that Gavin could take Ellen into his arms and touch her the way he couldn't. It made him even angrier that he liked the jackanapes. How could he hate a man he admired? How could he hate the man Ellen loved?

If there was some way on God's earth Richard could solve Ellen's problems, erase the past or make it inconsequential, he would do it. He loved her so much that he wanted her to be happy, even if it meant in Gavin Waxton's arms.

But that was an impossibility, wasn't it? Or was it? Gavin was a reasonable man. Perhaps honesty was the best answer. Or perhaps Ellen should just go to the Colonies with him, escape from the truth, and never utter a word about her real identity.

Richard wished he knew the right thing to do. He wished he could advise Ellen, in spite of these emotions that kept getting in his way.

He had been damned furious when he had gotten home the other night to find Gavin's note and Ellen gone. The note had simply read that they had gone into the country and would be back three days hence. Though there seemed to be no immediate danger, Richard was still enraged, perhaps because she'd not told him in person, perhaps because he now realized how little control he had over the decisions Ellen would make.

But once the fury had passed, once he had broken a few pieces of china, cursed the maid, and drunk a full bottle of brandy, a strange sense of pride had welled up in him.

Ellen was not Thomasina Waxton, the woman she had been that night he had picked her up on the road, wet and frightened beyond reason. Thomasina could never have made the decision to go on a jaunt with the man she loved, despite the foolhardiness of it. Thomasina could never have put her own wants and needs above those of anyone else's. No, despite Richard's anger, his feelings of jealousy and fear for her safety, he was proud of the fact that she was finally able to take control of her own life. She was not the emotionally and physically battered woman she had once been. The truth was that she was a strong, capable woman who no longer needed him as she once had. And no matter how sad that made him, he was still proud of her and of the fact she had been able to conquer such a dark past.

Suddenly feeling a little lighter at heart, Richard swung open the heavy door and stepped into the front hallway. Oddly, the usually well-lit entrance was dissolved in inky blackness. The lamps both at the bottom and top of the stairs had gone out.

Richard thought to tell Mistress Parkinson, the plump partridge of a woman who lived on the bottom floor and owned the building, but it was late and he saw no real need. Surely no one else would be coming in so late. He would let the widow have her sleep.

Running his hand along the smooth polished railing, he climbed the steps, knowing his way even in the darkness. Ellen would be home tomorrow. Depending on how her excursion with Gavin had gone, perhaps he would suggest she again consider going with him to the Colonies and simply leaving Thomasina behind. Yes. He might just do that.

At the second-story landing, Richard reached out for the doorknob of his apartment while fumbling for his key. Oddly, as his hand touched the knob, the door swung open. His brow creased in the darkness. He was usually quite careful about closing and locking the door. The street they lived on was safe enough, but thieves certainly wandered from their homes in Whitefriars to rob the fortunate.

Cautiously, Richard pushed open the door with the tip of his shoe, and it squeaked as it swung. He peered inside and swore softly. Even in the darkness, his eyes had adjusted enough for him to see that the front room was in shambles. Thieves had swept through with a vindictive thoroughness, turning over every piece of furniture, spilling books onto the floor and ripping pictures down from the walls.

Richard hit the door with his fist, pushing it the rest of the way open, and stepped inside. The first thing he would have to do was light a candle from the smoldering embers in the fireplace.

Richard was not halfway across the room when he heard a floorboard creak beside him and felt the cold steel of a knife blade against his throat.

"Move an inch and you die painfully," came a cold, almost sinister voice.

Richard stiffened. "You've ransacked my home, no doubt taking every item of any value. What else do you want?"

"A light," the voice ordered to someone else in the room.

Richard heard the door click shut behind him as a shadow moved near the fireplace. A candle's wick flared and part of the room was blessed with feeble light. The man who held the candle was big and burly, with a head full of black hair. But it was the man who held the knife on Richard that immediately caught his attention.

An albino. The Duke of Hunt. It could be no other.

"What do you want?" Richard demanded.

"You know."

"She's not here."

"I know. Gone slutting, I understand." Hunt took a step back as the black-haired man came up behind Richard. "But she's not what I seek at this moment." His pink inhuman eyes bore into Richard's. "What I want now is the letter."

Out of the corner of his eye, Richard saw the man at the door move toward them. He was as huge and menacing as his counterpart. "I don't know what letter you speak of."

The second man picked up an overturned chair and brought it to Hunt. The duke pressed his glinting gold knife and the blade retracted. He sat down, crossing his legs in an elegant pose.

"Don't be a foolish man. I know it's here. Tell me and you'll spare yourself, for I am an insistent man."

Richard took a step forward and immediately the brawny apes were on him, dragging him back. "I told you! I don't know!"

Hunt slipped his hand into his shirtwaist and removed a small albino ferret, which he began to stroke. "Pity." He gave a nod.

One henchman pinned Richard's arms so painfully behind him that if he moved, he was certain his wrists would snap. The other man raised a fist, and Richard saw a flash of metal before the brute hit him in the jaw with unbelievable force.

Richard heard his jaw snap as the pain exploded in his face, bringing tears to his eyes.

224

"The letter," Hunt persisted. "Tell me where it is and I'll get you some medical assistance. It would be a pity to mar that handsome face of yours."

"I . . . I don't know what you're talking about, you bloody white ass!" *I wouldn't betray you, sweet Ellen,* he thought as he saw the man swing again. *Not even for my life.*

This time it was the other side of his face that shattered in a mass of blood and cracking bone. Richard felt himself sag. One of the men lifted him up by the armpits so that he still faced Hunt.

The albino went on stroking his bizarre pet, obviously taking a certain amount of pleasure in the violence. "The letter, dear Chambray. You're bleeding on the Turk carpet. It must have been quite costly."

"If you hurt her, I swear to God I'll kill you!"

Hunt let out a sigh of boredom.

Without hesitation, one of the men struck again, this time bringing down the fireplace poker across one of Richard's shins.

Richard heard himself cry out as his knees buckled. The only thing that kept him from falling was the black-haired bastard who held him up.

"Keep him quiet," Richard heard Hunt bark through a veil of pain. "Someone will hear and call the watch."

As the men hauled Richard to his feet again, one of them stuck a stinking handkerchief into his mouth.

"I'm losing my patience," Hunt muttered. "Tell me where the letter I seek is, Chambray, and I'll have the boys release you."

This time, Richard made no attempt to answer. He just squeezed his eyes shut as he felt another burst of pain, followed by another and then another, until he was no longer certain where he was being hit.

Richard didn't know how long he remained conscious, but he wished he had not been a soldier accustomed to pain, because he remained coherent far too long. Finally, he felt himself slip into an icy blackness, away from the sound of his own muffled, tortured voice and the stark reality of his agony.

It was midmorning when Ellen ran up the steps to her apartment, with Gavin following. She was anxious to see Richard, because despite the wonderful time she'd had with Gavin, she'd truly missed him. She was hoping she and the two men she loved could go out for something to eat before she had to be at the theater at noon. Her thought was that if Richard could just get to know Gavin, he would understand why she would take such risks to be with him the few short months left before he sailed for the Colonies.

At the top of the landing, Ellen leaned over the railing, waving down at Gavin. "Aren't you coming?" Her gay voice echoed off the whitewashed walls.

"I'm coming, but slowly. I believe you wore me out these last few days, sweet. You have to remember, I'm older than you are."

She laughed and went to the door. Finding it open, she pushed in. "Richard?"

She gasped at the sight of the room, her hand flying to her mouth. Thieves! Someone had turned over the furniture, ripped the upholstery, broken Richard's vases, and even torn the canvas from the wall.

"Richard?"

Someone came running down the hall. "All thank the Lord above you're home, Miss Ellen!" Rose, their

226

maid, exclaimed, slapping her hands on her ample thighs. "You got to come! Master Richard, he's bad and he won't let me call no one in."

By the time Gavin reached the doorway, catching the tail end of the conversation, Ellen had already lifted her skirts and was running down the hall.

"Richard!" She darted into his bedchamber, and what she saw made her stop dead in her tracks.

Rose leaned in the doorway. "Found 'im like that this morning, ma'am."

"Oh, Richard," Ellen whispered, tears welling in her eyes.

Richard lay on his bed, perfectly motionless, a bloody sheet twisted around him. His face was a purple mass of pulp, so distorted that Ellen would not have recognized him if she had not known it could be no one else.

"Oh, Richard . . ."

"Ellen?" His voice was naught but a trembling whisper.

She went to him.

"Christ's bones," Gavin muttered from the doorway. "What the hell happened to you, Chambray?"

Ellen reached his bedside and put out her hand to touch him, unsure how. His clothes were so bloody that she couldn't see the extent of his injuries. Slowly, he lifted his hand to her.

"Ellen?" he moaned again. "Ellen, are you all right? You all right?"

She went down on her knees on the bedstool, clasping his hand to her cheek. "I'm fine, Richard. I'm fine." She leaned closer. "Who did this to you?"

He sucked in a rattling breath. "Mustn't tell," he whispered.

She leaned closer, afraid she wouldn't be able to hear him.

227

"Mustn't tell." One of his eyelids fluttered and opened. The other was hopelessly swollen shut. "Hunt."

Ellen's lower lip trembled. "He did this to you?"

"The letter." He paused. "Wanted the letter." Somehow he managed a crooked smile. "Lucky I didn't know where it was, hmm, love?"

With her free hand, Ellen brushed away the tears that ran down her cheeks. "Oh, Richard, I'm so sorry. I—"

"What happened?" Gavin appeared behind her. "Christ, Chambray. They nearly killed you."

Ellen looked at Richard. He shook his head ever so slightly.

Ellen moistened her lips with the tip of her tongue, stalling for time.

Gavin leaned over her, touching Richard's face, his arms, trying to survey the damage. "Who did this, Chambray? Cowards, obviously. Men too cowardly to fight fairly like men."

"It doesn't matter," Ellen said.

Richard's one good eye fluttered shut.

"The hell it doesn't! This wasn't just a drunken brawl between gentlemen, Ellen. It would take more than one man to do this to another. Look at these rooms! Someone was looking for something and Chambray got in the middle of it."

"Money."

Gavin lifted an eyebrow. "Money?"

She rose, laying Richard's hand down gently and wrapping her arms around her waist. "Richard left some unpaid gambling debts." She frowned. "He owed the wrong man money. You understand."

Gavin cut his eyes toward Richard. Ellen waited, praying he bought her story or at least accepted it.

228

"Well, you've got to get a physician in here. He's got to be stitched in several places and that one leg needs to be set."

She grasped Gavin's arm, her fingers tightening around the corded muscle of his biceps. "No physician."

"So what the hell do you propose we do with him?"

"We'll take care of him ourselves."

Gavin looked back at Richard, who seemed to be drifting in and out of consciousness. "He doesn't want anyone to know?"

She smoothed Gavin's linen sleeve as her dark eyes searched his face. "Would you?"

He sighed, then after a moment said, "Well enough. I'll see what I can do, but I'm going to need some things." He pushed up his sleeves. "You'll have to send the woman out with a list. Is there an apothecary you can trust?"

She looked up at him, surprised, as well as touched, by his words. "You don't have to do this. I can take care of him."

"How much experience do you have with wounds like this?" He went to the bedside and began to rip down the torn bedcurtain, so that he would have more light to work by. "I've cleaned gunshot wounds, treated snakebites, sewn bayonet gashes, and amputated legs. A sailor and soldier learns to deal with this kind of mess."

A smile touched Ellen's lips. He was a good man, Gavin Waxton. If only it could have been he her father had betrothed her to so many years ago . . . She pushed up her sleeves. "What do you want me to do?"

"I'll need hot water—boil it first. And sharp scissors to cut these clothes off him. We've got to get these wounds clean before they start festering on him." He walked to the window and yanked open the drapes. "A good thread and needle, too."

He came back toward her. "Got anything to drink?"

She turned to go. "I'll see if the bastards left anything." When she reached the door, she turned back to Gavin. "But if he's barely conscious, you think we should give him brandy?"

Gavin looked up from where he stood by the bed, carefully rolling Richard onto his side. "The brandy's not for Richard, sweet. It's for me."


Late that night, when Richard's wounds were bandaged, his leg set in a splint, and he was sleeping under the influence of a strong drug, Ellen rose from the chair beside his bed and wandered down the dark hallway to find Gavin.

The apartment was still in a shambles, but Rose had worked diligently all day, righting furniture and cleaning up broken glass. Salvageable paintings had been rehung on the walls and the soot had been washed from the floral wallpapers. The rooms didn't look good, but they certainly looked better. When the clock struck ten, Ellen had dismissed Rose, praising her and insisting she get a full night's rest. Ellen and Gavin would take turns watching over Richard tonight.

Ellen found Gavin seated before the fireplace, his long legs sprawled out, his eyes closed, a chipped glass hanging from his fingertips.

She smiled. What man would have done what Gavin did today for a practical stranger? Few would have done it for their own loved one. Gavin had been skillful and efficient in his ministering to Richard's wounds, taking great care not to put him in any more pain than necessary.

Ellen slipped the glass from his hand and rested it on the mantel. Then she went back to him, kneeling at his feet. Carefully, so as not to wake him, she rested her head on his lap. She was tired to the bone, both her energy and emotions drained. She needed to feel Gavin close to her. She needed the reassurance of his strength. "I love you," she whispered. "I love you, Gavin Merrick."

As she lay her cheek on his thigh, he stirred. "You know that's the first time you've said that in a long time," he murmured sleepily.

She lifted her head to stare up into his eyes. "What?"

"That you love me."

"Of course, I love you."

He stroked the back of her head with his hand. "I know you do. I'm just telling you, you don't say it very often." He smoothed her hair as she laid her head in his lap again. "I like it, Ellen. Even a man likes to hear those words. You're tired," he whispered. "I've had my nap. You go to bed and let me sit up with him."

She lifted her head to smile up at his sleepy face. His hair was disheveled. His stock was missing, his shirt open at the neckline to reveal a sprinkling of dark curls. "I'd rather stay here with you."

He reached out and lifted her into his arms, drawing her onto his lap. "Minx. Temptress. Witch." He nestled his face in the hollow of her neck, breathing deeply the scent of her fresh, clean hair.

She caught his face between her palms, enjoying the roughness of the stubble. "I want to thank you for what you've done today . . . for Richard, for me," she whispered. "You're a good man."

He nipped at her earlobe with his lips. "A good man who knows a good woman when he sees one."

231

She let her eyes drift shut as he pressed kisses to the tender spot on her neck. "You didn't have to stay. You didn't have to help, but you did."

His mouth found hers and he silenced her with a kiss. "Hush," he whispered, his tongue darting out to tease her lower lip. "Just kiss me, Ellen, love. Kiss me like you've never kissed another man . . . like you'll never kiss again."

Something in his voice struck a chord in her and a sob escaped her lips. The love between them was so good, why couldn't it last forever? She cursed Waldron for the hundredth time that day as she pressed her lips to his younger brother's, kissing him hard with the force of her resentment.

Gavin slipped his warm hand into her silk dressing gown and she sighed with pleasure. His rough fingertips found the bud of her breast and gently coaxed it to a peak. Ellen squirmed in his lap, molding her body to his, running her fingers through his long sleek hair as she reveled in his touch.

When Gavin leaned to kiss her breast, she arched her back to aid him. Shivers of pleasure coursed through her veins, making her heart pound and her breath short.

"Ellen, sweet Ellen," Gavin murmured as he pushed the dressing gown from her shoulders, baring her breasts in the warm light of the fire. "Tell me you'll love me always. Tell me you'll always be mine."

"No promises," she whispered huskily in his ear. "Not tonight. Just love me for who I am at this moment, Gavin. Please, just love me."

Gavin groaned in exasperation. He wanted more. He wanted commitment. But at this moment, he wanted her any way he could have her.

Ellen sat up in his lap and pulled his shirt over his head, so she could run her palms over the muscular planes of his bare suntanned chest. When he hugged her against him, bare flesh caressed bare flesh, making her skin tingle.

His mouth covered hers, his kisses deep and filled with desperation. He kissed her neck, her shoulders, the fullness of her breasts, leaving a trail of desire that burned hotter with each passing moment.

When Gavin lifted her to stand on her feet, she gave no protest. He joined her, standing face to face as he untied the belt of her dressing gown and let it slip to a silken puddle on the hardwood floor.

When her fingers found the ties of his breeches, he smiled, his heavy-lidded eyes filled with amusement.

"You've become bold," he teased as she unlaced the ribbons.

"I've had a good teacher," she answered saucily.

Gavin closed his eyes, sighing in pleasure as she pushed down his breeches and caressed his hardened shaft with her capable hands. "I love to touch you," she whispered breathlessly in his ear. "Like this, and this . . ."

Gavin groaned. "You'll be the ruination of me," he managed thickly.

She smiled in the semidarkness, her hand still moving to that mysterious rhythm all lovers know. As she stroked him, she found his nipple with her mouth and teased it to a rigid nub.

"Enough! Enough," Gavin protested weakly. "Come sit with me, sweet."

Their lips met again, their tongues darting to entwine and taste the nectar of passion. Then Gavin sat down, pulling her onto his lap, and with a little guidance she slid down over his tumescent member, crying out in delight from the new sensation.

Gavin lifted and lowered his hips beneath her until she caught the rhythm, and then they moved as one. Her hands snaked around his neck and she held on to him tightly, breathing in the heavy scent of his masculinity, wanting the pleasure to go on forever but knowing it couldn't.

When her strangled cry of sweet climax filled the room, Gavin's followed just behind her. They laughed together as they rode in the last waves of pleasure and then she sank against him, treasuring the feel of his body deep within hers.

For a long time they sat with her straddling his lap, until finally she became so groggy with satiated love and exhaustion that he lifted her gently and carried her to her bedchamber.

"Richard," she protested sleepily as she rested her cheek against his warm, bare chest.

"I'll watch now. You sleep," he told her as he lowered her onto her bed. "I'll wake you if I need you."

Her eyes fluttered open for a moment as he covered her with a soft sheet and coverlet. "Thank you," she whispered.

He kissed her forehead. "For what?"

She laughed, snuggling down in the covers and closing her eyes. "For everything. For being you. For accepting me and my secrets."

He brushed a long lock of red hair from her cheek in a tender caress. "I could be even more accepting if you'd be my wife, Ellen."

"I can't."

"Tell me you'll consider it. It's all I ask."

"I love you," she whispered, already half asleep as she rolled onto her side. "Isn't that enough?"

"No. I need a commitment. A promise."

She snuggled deeper into her pillow. "Ask me

again tomorrow."

He kissed the back of her head and leaned down to blow out the candle beside her bed. "I will. And the day after that and the day after that, until you say yes," he murmured to himself. Ellen was already asleep.

# Chapter Sixteen

Gavin slipped a clean, pressed shirt over his head and reached for his lace cravat. Somewhere in the distance he heard the ringing of churchbells. Christmastide had come to London again.

He smiled to himself as he tied his stock. Tonight he and Ellen would celebrate in her apartments. He would have preferred to bring her here to his own place, to his own bedchamber to celebrate in intimate privacy, but Richard was still bedridden with his mending leg. Ellen refused to leave him except to go to the theater and for short shopping trips, so Gavin had little choice. If he wanted to be with Ellen, he would have to share her company with Chambray, for at least part of the evening.

But forced to, Gavin would have to admit that in the last weeks, he had come to enjoy Chambray's company. The two men had much in common besides their love for the redheaded actress, and they got along well as long as both controlled their jealousies. Often, when Ellen went to the theater, Gavin came by to wile away a few hours playing slur and knap with Richard. It was odd to think of, but despite the circumstances, the two men had found friendship in each other.

Gavin sat down on the edge of his tester bed to roll on his stockings, and his heel scraped something sharp on the floor. He lifted the bedskirt to find the culprit. The corner of a picture frame.

The portrait of Thomasina Waxton, of course.

In the activity of the last few weeks, he'd almost forgotten the haunting picture. He dropped down on his knees on the floor and eased it out from under the bed. He told himself that he had placed it there not wanting to offend Ellen by having the portrait of another woman in his bedchamber, but the truth was that he hadn't been ready to share the beauty with anyone. Not with Ellen, not with a servant, and not with one of his gentleman friends.

Gavin carried the heavy framed picture across the room and leaned it up against a paneled chest of drawers. Eyeing the piece of artwork, he went back to the bed to roll on his other silk embroidered stocking. As he dressed, he studied the mysterious woman who had brought disaster to the Waxton family.

It was strange, but the hate Gavin had once felt for this woman had dissipated. Somehow his relationship with Ellen had altered his desire for retribution. Nothing could bring his brother Waldron back, not even the capture and execution of the woman who had murdered him. Ellen had somehow made him see that, perhaps in showing him that life went on and that life was good.

Yes, Gavin was beginning to think that it was time to give up his quest for Thomasina. He could have his brother's assets legally transferred to his own accounts and let the past slip into the shadow of his memory. It was time he put aside this obsession of finding the murderess and began to truly deal with the possibility of a future with Ellen.

238

As Gavin stared at the portrait, searching his feelings, he found his need for revenge was gone. Now he felt only a stirring sense of curiosity.

Who was Thomasina Waxton? Was she truly the woman Waldron had described, the woman Gavin perceived her to be? Just what did she look like? As vain as most women were, why had she turned her face away from the artist? Why had she not allowed him to capture her spirit? Judging from the name of the artist scrawled on the lower corner of the portrait, Waldron had no doubt paid an exorbitant sum for the sitting. Why had he allowed his wife to look away?

Gavin slipped his feet into his heeled shoes and walked to the portrait on the far side of the room. Thoughtfully, he ran a finger along the dusty frame. He wondered what he should do with it. Have it destroyed? Send it back to Havering House? He was ready to give up his search for her, but was he ready to give up her picture?

His gaze wandered to the paneled wall above the fireplace. An oil painting done by some obscure French artist had been hung there by the landlord or her decorator. Gavin had always detested the picture. The damned sails on the ship were blowing the wrong way!

On impulse, he retrieved a straight-backed chair from the corner of the room and placed it on the hearth. Standing on the chair, he removed the seascape and set it on the floor. Carefully, he raised Thomasina's portrait to the paneled wall and hung it.

Coming off the chair, he stepped back to admire the portrait. Twice he went back to raise a corner until it hung perfectly straight. Standing in the center of the room, he smiled. He would let

Thomasina hang there until his curiosity was gone, and then he would send her back to Havering House to be auctioned off with his brother's other belongings. In America he would have no need for stiff portraits or the priceless Oriental antiques his elder brother had been fond of.

With that settled, Gavin slipped on a burgundy shirtwaist and grabbed his coat from the bedpost. He would stop at the cookshop down the street to pick up Chambray's favorite pudding, and then he would be on his way. Just as he blew out the candles in the bedchamber, he heard a rap at the door.

As Gavin swung open the door, he couldn't resist a frown.

Hunt.

"Waxton, good to find you in."

"Your servant, sir." Gavin bowed, eyeing the two burly men that stood in the shadows behind Hunt. "To what do I owe the pleasure of this visit?"

Hunt glanced over Gavin's shoulder. "You're alone, I take it?"

"Yes."

Hunt smirked. "No ladies or strumpets in your boudoir?"

"Quite alone, sir."

"Might I come in, then? I see you've a vehicle waiting below, so I won't keep you."

Gavin stepped back, letting the paneled oak door swing on its hinges. "Yes, I do have an engagement, but I've a moment." He kept his voice cordial but none too friendly. He didn't like Hunt and he didn't want him here. At first he had appreciated his interest in Waldron's death, but as the months passed, it had become clear to him that Hunt had ulterior motives. Gavin didn't know what they were, but he had learned enough about Hunt from reliable sources,

240

including an intriguing conversation with Chambray, to know he wanted no part of the duke and his scheming.

Gavin followed Hunt into the apartment and closed the door, leaving the duke's two men in the drafty hallway. Hunt walked to the fireplace and struck one of the typical court poses that Gavin found so absurd.

Gavin crossed his arms over his chest stoically.

"I understand the king has just signed the land grants for the Maryland Colony you've been waiting on." Hunt offered a bellicose smile.

Gavin had, in fact, not been yet notified, but it was common knowledge that Hunt knew much of what went on at Whitehall, be it at the front or back stairs. "Yes . . ."

"So I would guess you'll be departing soon."

The two men stared at each other, each gauging his own position. There was obviously opposition here, but exactly what it was had not yet been stated.

"When the weather permits. Early March, I should think."

Hunt reached into the pocket of his gaudy green and gold coat and pulled out a white ferret with eyes the same pink hue as his own. As he went on to speak, he stroked the animal with a gentle hand. "I've heard nothing from you as of late concerning your brother's wife. My patience has worn thin, so I thought I would call on you myself."

"I've been occupied with more pressing matters."

"The redheaded whore at the theater, no doubt."

Gavin didn't flinch. "I can't imagine a man of your position would be concerned with the company I keep."

"You know she's not what she appears to be, your sweet Ellen." He almost spit the last words. "She has

241

secrets . . . dark secrets some are aware of while others are not."

It was obvious that Hunt was insinuating he knew something about Ellen that Gavin did not. For some reason that made Gavin furious, not because Hunt might have information that he didn't, but because the duke would think it mattered to Gavin.

"Back to the subject of my brother's wife." Gavin paused for an instant before going on. "I've three shiploads of merchandise for my Maryland neighbors to transport when I return to the Colonies. That preparation has kept me too busy to concern myself with the missing woman. My solicitor has told me my brother's inheritance can be transferred into my name without locating the wife, so it's not imperative that I find her."

"You have a duty to your brother, to your family, Waxton!"

Gavin watched Hunt's eyes flicker with restrained anger. "I am the last of my family, sir. As I see it, it is now I who decide what is important and what is not. What I don't see is why this concerns you so greatly. Surely a man of your importance must have more pressing court matters to concern himself with."

"I told you that when you located little Thomasina, I had need to speak with her."

Gavin offered a hint of a sarcastic smile. "But you see I haven't found her."

Hunt lifted the ferret and kissed it on its pinched face. "You're certain?"

Gavin looked at the clock on the mantel behind Hunt. Ellen was expecting him. "Look here, I'm tired of your innuendos. You've suggested numerous times that you have information on the slattern but you do not offer it. I've lost interest in her. The truth is that I may well be too busy between now and when

I set sail to spend any more time or money in searching for her."

Hunt glowered, his voice raising an octave. "But I told you I need to speak with her."

"So why not seek her yourself?" Gavin lifted an eyebrow. "You knew her. I didn't. You've hinted that you know she's near. If you feel a need to avenge my brother's death, why not do so?"

Hunt went on stroking his pet. "It would be *awkward.*"

Gavin's eyes narrowed. "Awkward how?"

"That, Lord Waxton, is none of your concern. What is your concern is the jade Thomasina Waxton and bringing her to me."

"I made no such promise to you, *Your Grace.*"

The duke took in a great rush of air. "Let me make this clear. I am telling you, I wish you to find her, Waxton, and bring her to me without anyone else's knowledge."

"And I am telling you, Your Grace, that I no longer seek my brother's wife."

Hunt opened his gold-trimmed pocket flap and dropped the ferret inside. "You commit a grave error in making me your adversary."

"I have done no such thing. I'm simply telling you that my interests have changed." They were playing word games now, both fighting to remain civil. Whatever it was Hunt was up to, Gavin was certain it was more than the avenging of a friend's death, and he would damned well not be a party to it.

Hunt took a step forward, his ghostly white face taking on a red hue. "You'll regret this decision."

Gavin rested his hand on the doorknob. He knew he should keep quiet. Hunt was a powerful, dangerous man, one not to be taken lightly, but he couldn't help himself. "Do you threaten me?"

"I threaten no one. You have made your choice, you witless boy. Let us both hope you can live with it!"

Hunt came toward the door and Gavin swung it open for him, clapping his heels and bowing in mock respect. "As always, your servant, sir."

Hunt stalked out the door and started down the staircase with one of his men hurrying after him, the duke's ermine-lined cloak in his hands.

Gavin closed the door quietly behind him and then went to the window to watch the duke's crested carriage pull away. *So what the hell was that all about?* he wondered. *What could Hunt possibly want with my brother's wife? What could be so important that Hunt would come to me like this?*

The obvious answer, of course, was that the little minx had some sort of information on Hunt. Gavin smiled as he dropped the heavy drape over the frosted glass window. So perhaps Thomasina had been the conniving little bitch that everyone claimed her to be.

Gavin went to the mantel and picked up a velvet jewel case. A gift for Ellen. He tucked it inside his coat. Tonight he would once again ask her to marry him. Tonight he would convince her they belonged together. He would take her to his magic Maryland Colony, away from England and her secrets, away from Hunt, away from Thomasina Waxton forever.

Gavin blew out the candle on the wall sconce by the door and slipped out into the darkness to meet his waiting coach.

Gavin pushed back from the dining table, smiling at the sound of Ellen's bright laughter. It was good to see her happy. With Chambray on the mend, Gavin could feel his hold on Ellen growing. She truly loved

244

him. She knew it. He knew it. Even Chambray knew it.

Richard tipped his glass and drank down the last drop before rising awkwardly from his upholstered chair.

Gavin immediately jumped up. "Let me help you, Chambray."

"S'death, Gavin, you're not my wet nurse." His voice was abrasive, but it was obvious he meant no ill. They spoke as men who cared for each other more than they wished to admit. "I can bloody well make it back to my bedchamber, half soused or not."

Gavin watched as Ellen took Richard's hand, squeezing it. Her cheeks were rosy from the good wine and laughter, her lips turned up in a temptress's smile. "I'll help you, Richard."

He pulled his hand away. "I can well get my drawers down without your help as well," he teased good-naturedly. "Now see to your guest. A good night to you both." He bowed stiffly and limped down the hall.

Ellen watched him go, still smiling. She was so relieved to see Richard back to his old self again. The break in his leg was healing nicely, and though he still nagged at her about fleeing to his estates in Essex, he seemed to have accepted the fact that they would remain in London at least until Gavin set sail. Having not heard from Hunt since the night he had ransacked the apartment and had Richard beaten up, both Ellen and Richard hoped against all hope that he had given up on his quest. Ellen could only pray that was the case.

Gavin came around the table to loop his arm about her waist. "You liked the present?" he whispered.

She melted at the feel of his warm breath in her ear. "I loved it," she answered, her voice husky. She

245

found the emerald necklace with her fingertips and stroked the large, dark jewels.

"Marry me and there'll be more, I swear to you."

"Gavin . . ."

"Marry me and go to the Colonies at my side"—he kissed her neck—"and I'll spend every pound I can lay my hands on on you."

"Gavin . . ."

"Say yes. Marry me tonight."

She leaned against him, pressing her back to his hard, comforting chest. "Gavin, please don't start, not after we've had such a wonderful evening." She turned to face him, resting her hands on his shoulders, brushing her lips against his in a sensual invitation. "Not when there's still more to come."

"You said you would think about marrying me."

"And I have, but—"

"But what?" He grasped her arms impatiently. "What is it? You say you love me."

She closed her eyes, wanting to block out his voice and the feelings it stirred deep inside her. "I do. So . . ."

"So? So you marry me, sweetheart. You let me make you happy the way no one will ever be able to."

"I love Richard, too."

"So if you love the bastard so much," he said, not unkindly, "bring him with us. I can live with it if you can."

She laughed without humor as she tried to step back. He kept her trapped in his arms. "That's absurd, Gavin."

"No more absurd than the thought of two people who were meant for each other living apart the rest of their lives."

She leaned forward, resting her forehead on his shoulder. She could hear the spit of the fire as a log shifted and the sparks fanned upward. She could smell the scent of Gavin's skin. Beneath her fingers his muscles were taut with anger . . . anger at her.

"We've been through this a hundred times," she whispered. "A million times. I can't go to the Colonies. I can't marry you."

"Because of Richard? Because of the theater? Because of whatever the hell it is you once did!" He grasped her shoulders, forcing her to look up at him. He hadn't meant to get into this argument. Not tonight. But it was too late to turn back now. "Tell me the truth, Ellen. Why can't you marry me?"

A tear slipped from the corner of her eye. He was hurt. She could see it in his green eyes. She didn't want to hurt him, not like this. "I told you."

"You lied because you didn't want to tell me the truth. Well, I'll tell you the damned truth." He released her and took a step back, not wanting to torture himself by her touch. "Because you don't love me. Not enough, Ellen. Not enough to trust me. Not enough to give your life to that love."

"It's not true." She brushed back a long lock of red hair that shimmered in the candlelight.

"The hell it isn't! You don't love me! You don't even love your blessed Chambray!"

"Don't say that, damn you!" she screamed in a sudden rage. "You don't understand. You don't know what I've lived through! You don't know."

"The truth is, Ellen Scarlet, that you don't love anyone. You haven't the ability. The only thing you love is your little secrets and that pity for yourself that keeps you apart from the rest of us. You don't love me because you're afraid to!"

"Get out!" Ellen shouted. "Get out if you're going to talk to me like that. Just get the hell out!"

"You send me away and you'll never have another

chance at happiness."

She grabbed his coat off the corner of the chair and flung it at him. "I said get out! Get out of my house! Get out of my life!"

Gavin started for the door. Somehow this night had turned out all wrong. He had come here to tell her about the revelation he had had about his brother's wife. He had come here to propose marriage to her . . . to make her happy.

"You send me away and I'll not come back. I'll not beg you any longer." Gavin lifted his eyebrow. "You don't think you'll ever get such an offer again, do you?"

She grabbed a goblet off the table and hurled it at his head, missing him only because he ducked. "Get out!"

"I've gotten my land deeds. I'll be leaving soon, Ellen."

"If you don't get out, I'll have Richard put you out!"

Gavin flipped his coat over his shoulder and strode toward the door. He turned back as his hand fell on the handle. "I'll play no more games with you, sweet Ellen. I'm too old. I've too good a future. Too much to look forward to." He knew he had to get out before he said anything worse, but suddenly his heart ached so badly that he wanted to hurt her. He wanted to hurt her as badly as she had hurt him tonight. He looked up at her, his eyes narrowing. "You know you'll not get such an offer again, a woman such as yourself. An actress. Surely someone else will be willing to take you as mistress when Chambray loses interest, but even those offers will wane in the coming years." He pointed his finger. "You turn me down and you'll grow old a lonely woman."

"Go to flaming hell, Gavin Merrick!" Ellen

shouted, throwing a plate of bread at him.

The plate hit the closed door. Gavin was gone.

For a long moment Ellen stood staring at the door, then desolately she blew out the candles and went down the dark hallway. She stopped at her own bedchamber door and then passed it. She stood outside Richard's door contemplating whether or not to knock. Surely he had heard her and Gavin. How could he have not?

Before she could muster the courage to knock, she heard Richard's voice.

"Come in, sweetheart." Her dear Richard. His voice was filled with compassion.

She pushed open the door. He was sitting up in bed with a silk bedrobe draped across his shoulders, a book lying open across his lap.

"Richard." Tears ran down her cheeks.

He put out his arms to her. "What, sweetheart? Tell me."

She came running to him and flung her arms around him. "Oh, God, Richard. I've lost him. He just didn't love me enough to understand. . . ."

# Chapter Seventeen

"Up and out of bed, lazy wench," Richard commanded, throwing open the heavy draperies in Ellen's bedchamber. The sunshine of early March poured through the multi-paned windows.

She groaned and pulled the counterpane over her head. "Go away. Leave me alone."

"You can't miss another day of rehearsal this week, Ellen Scarlet, or you may damned well lose your part to Lucy Maynor again."

Ellen rolled over onto her stomach, pulling her pillow over her head. "I don't care. I hate the play. I hate the theater."

"I suppose you're going to tell me you hate Gavin Merrick." Richard threw open her wardrobe and plucked out a sensible hunter-green woolen gown sewn in the fashion of a riding habit.

"I do hate him!" She lifted the pillow off her face and pushed back a tangle of red hair. Her voice softened. "But ods fish, I love him, too."

Richard tossed her dressing gown onto the end of her bed, followed by her silk mules. "So go to him. I've been telling you that for damned near two months now."

She squeezed her eyes shut. "I can't. You know I can't."

"Then shut up about it, love. You made your decision. Quit sulking and get on with your life."

She stuck her tongue out at him. "You're certainly the compassionate fellow this morning."

He ran a finger across his neck. "I've had it up to here with compassion and with you moping about. It's time you either accepted your choice, or you tracked down the bloody pirate and let him carry you off into the wilderness."

She watched him cross the room to the silver coffee set he'd brought in with him. The break in his leg had healed so well, thanks to Gavin's expertise, that he barely limped. "Gavin's not a pirate!"

"Farmer, then."

"He's not a farmer, either. They call them plantations in the Colonies. He has thousands of acres, Richard! Why, when he goes back to Maryland, he'll be one of the richest men there, save for mayhap the governor."

Richard poured her a cup of steaming aromatic coffee. "You sound as if this Maryland Colony interests you."

"Well, it doesn't." She swung her legs over the side of the bed and slipped her bare feet into the silk mules. As she rose, she threw the dressing robe over her shoulders. "I can't imagine why anyone would ever want to go there with all those savages!"

"You'd be safe from Hunt forever if you went with Gavin," Richard offered quietly over the rim of his china coffee cup. "No more looking over your shoulder every time you step out on the street. No more being afraid to come home alone at night."

Ellen frowned. Though they had heard nothing

252

from Hunt directly since Richard's beating, on several occasions Ellen was certain she had been followed to or from the theater. Now Richard always escorted her. There had also been some puzzling changes in the positions at the theater. Ellen had once taken lead roles, but for some unknown reason the size of her parts had been diminishing despite her continuing popularity with the audience. The director would give no explanation, save that Ellen was lucky she had a job at all. Of course, he wouldn't admit Hunt had anything to do with these decisions and Ellen was afraid to ask, but she and Richard were almost certain he did.

"If you want to get rid of me, just say so."

"You know that's not it!" He ran a hand through his tousled hair as he struggled with his own emotions. "I just want to see you happy, Ellen. God knows, you deserve it."

She covered her ear with her hand as she walked to the window, carrying her coffee. "Please, Richard, don't start that again, not today. My head already aches."

He watched her standing there in the stream of sunlight, a halo of dust motes cast around her bright red hair. "You know, my guess would be that your gallant Waxton is as miserable as you are."

"Hah! You heard what he said! He called me a common actress!"

"I hate to tell you, sweetheart, but you are an actress, though common I think not."

"He said I was nothing more than a dalliance," she flung over her shoulder. "He doesn't love me! Not really, else he'd try to understand."

Richard gave an exaggerated sigh. "And he says you don't love him. I don't know who is more pitiful, you or he."

253

Ignoring him, she turned away from the window. "I suppose it is time I get to the theater, though why I still go I don't know."

"You could still take my offer to whisk you off to my home in Essex. Essex is beautiful in the springtime, you know."

She stared unseeing, lost in the memory of the past for a moment. Essex had been beautiful in the springtime. She remembered picking wildflowers as a child in the meadow, beyond Havering House. She remembered riding through the forest. But that was all before her mother died . . . a lifetime ago.

"Maybe we will go, Richard," she said suddenly.

He smiled, not easily convinced. "When?"

She grabbed her underclothing he'd laid out on the bed for her and walked behind the Chinese dressing screen in the corner of the room. Since she and Gavin had formed an intimate relationship, Ellen felt uncomfortable nude in front of Richard. Somehow, even now, it seemed a betrayal to Gavin. If Richard had noticed, he had made no comment.

"When, Ellen? I could send a message to Mother and let her know we're coming."

"Not yet," she called over the screen. "Not yet, but soon."

Richard frowned. "I'll send Rose in to lace you up. The coach will be waiting, so hurry."

"Richard?"

He stopped in the doorway and glanced over his shoulder. "Yes?"

She studied him for a moment, taking in his careless good looks, his bright blue eyes, his shiny brown hair, his regal cheekbones. By any standards he was a handsome man, but in her eyes his looks didn't hold a candle to Gavin's rugged features. She smiled. "Richard, I love you."

He waved and walked out of the bedchamber, muttering to himself.

"Not those crates, you imbecile! These!" Gavin shouted from the quarterdeck down to one of the sailors stacking crates of foodstuffs on the waist of the ship.

The pig-tailed man in striped shirting looked up, squinting in the sun. "Sir?"

"I said you've the wrong crates." Gavin pointed to a stack lined up on the starboard side. "Balance, you dogsbody. We must have balance, or the futtering ship'll go down in the first wind!"

The sailor obediently bobbed his head and moved to the specified stack of crates.

Julius came up behind Gavin, giving a low whistle. "You're going to have to go easier on these men or we'll not have a handful of crewmen to sail the three ships, friend."

Gavin swung around to face Julius, his face wrinkled in a frown. "I'll not stand for incompetence and you bloody well know it! These men are my responsibility. I'll not see them starve or go down out of stupidity." He glanced over the rail at the sailor moving obediently but slowly. "We'll not be ready to set sail for Paris tomorrow. We'll be lucky if we're ready in a fortnight, as slow as these men move!"

Julius adjusted his stocking cap. "Yea, yea, yea, you can be all gruff and tough with them, but you don't fool me."

"What the hell are you talking about?" Gavin turned back to a manifest he was scribbling on. "Did you come up here for a reason other than to annoy me?"

"I don't know why you don't just go to her. If she

won't coming willing, take her. She'll see the sensibility of your wedding her twenty days out to sea."

"I told you I don't want to talk about her!"

Julius hooked his thumbs into the waistband of his sailcloth breeches and made a clicking sound between his teeth. "Don't give a hang for her, do you?"

"I told you. That's over and I'd rather not discuss the matter." He glanced up. "No, let me express myself more clearly. I will not discuss it."

"Seems to me a man who don't shave, sleeps half the day, drinks most of the night, and chews on his best friend like a hound chews on a bone needs to discuss the matter."

"I gave her a choice, Julius. I'll not force a woman to bed nor to marriage. I'm not that desperate for either. No, her decision was not to marry me. That's the end."

"Hardheaded as eels, the pair of you. Don't you think she's just as wretched as you?"

Irritably, Gavin scratched out something on the manifest. "I hadn't thought about it at all. Haven't thought about her in weeks, except when you remind me." He flashed Julius a dark warning glance. "Now if you wouldn't mind, I've work to do."

Julius heaved another sigh. "Suit yourself, boyo, but if you don't find yourself a better disposition—be it in a bottle or in a slut's bed—damned if I might not consider jumping ship with some of those other mates."

Gavin stiffened. Ellen had abandoned him. Would Julius too? "If you want to go, you know you're free. We have no written contract."

Julius started down the ladder, muttering more to himself than to Gavin. "Contract, hell, you black-

256

hearted fool. We got friendship as a contract, and if you weren't so blessed lovesick, you'd remember that."

"Are you saying something to me?" Gavin demanded.

Julius shinnied down the ladder to the deck below. "Not a thing." He smiled to himself. "Not a rotting thing."

Not half an hour later, Julius came up the ladder onto the quarterdeck again.

Gavin was still concentrating on the manifest. He'd made such a mess of it the day before that it would take him a week to straighten it out. He barely looked up at Julius. "You back again already? Don't you have any work to do, because if you don't, I can well find some. As much as I pay you—"

"Gavin . . ."

The tone in Julius's voice made Gavin look up. "Julius?"

"I just heard out on the docks"—he raised his hands—"now, it's just a rumor, but I heard there's a fire at the King's Theater."

Gavin laid down his quill. "Anyone hurt?"

"I don't know. It's still burning, they say." He paused. "They say there's some actresses caught in the dressing rooms."

Before the last words were out of Julius's mouth, Gavin was taking the ladder rungs two at a time.

"She might not even be there!" Julius shouted, watching Gavin spring across the main deck toward the gangplank.

Gavin only waved his hand. Once on the dock, he ran up to one of the merchants he dealt with. The man was chatting with another, the reins of his horse looped through his fingers.

"I have to borrow your horse, Monty," Gavin said

as he snatched the reins from the startled man's hand.

"What?"

Gavin leaped astride and gathered the reins. "I said, I have to borrow your horse. I'll bring him right back," he called over his shoulder as he egged the steed forward through a throng of sailors carrying bags of flour.

"The hell you are, Gavin! My aunt is expecting me."

Gavin tipped his hat as he flew down the wooden dock, the horse's hooves clattering on the planks. "I appreciate it, Monty! I'll be right back, I swear it!"

Gavin could still hear Monty cursing as he rode the merchant's horse off the dock, around a warehouse, and down the street toward Drury Lane, where the playhouse was located.

*Ellen! Ellen!* his mind screamed. His sweet Ellen. If something happened to her, he didn't know what he'd do. These last weeks without her had been hell. For so long he had looked forward for the approval by the king of his land grants, and now that he had them, they seemed of little importance. Without Ellen the days dragged, the nights were unbearable. He wanted her so badly, but he wanted her to want him even more.

"Come on, come on," Gavin murmured beneath his breath as he tried to push through the busy street.

A two-wheeled wagon filled with faggots pulled out in front of him, and he cursed the yeoman driver and darted around the slow-moving vehicle.

By the time Gavin veered off Fleet Street and onto The Strand, he could see smoke rising above the haphazard wooden building. Dodging coaches and men and women on foot, he slowly made his way onto Bow Street and hurried toward Drury Lane. By the time he had sight of the playhouse looming

258

above the other buildings, the crowd of onlookers had grown so large that he was having a difficult time pushing through.

"Coming through! Coming through!" he shouted above the sound of excited voices. In the confusion of the pressing bodies and shouts, the horse became skittish and Gavin struggled to keep him in control. Some people moved back to make way for the horse and rider, while others stubbornly held their places.

Gavin could smell smoke and see it rising from the rear of the playhouse, though he still saw no actual flames. Finally, when he realized he was getting no closer to Ellen astride the horse, he dismounted. He grabbed the nearest person, a woman with red hair and a redder face. "Hold my horse, will you?" He fished a coin from his purse. "Keep him from being stolen and there'll be more when I return."

"Aye, sir, that I can do." The woman beamed. "You mind if my little'ns sit atop. They's nearly being crushed by the crowd."

Gavin eyed the two scrubbed-faced children clinging to her skirts. "Just mind the horse," he muttered, grabbing both children and swinging them astride the saddle. He heard their giggles as he pushed through the crowd, leaving the redhead and the horse to be swallowed up in the throng.

Pushing his way forward, he nearly reached the playhouse, when he recognized a woman as an actress he'd seen on the stage. "Ellen Scarlet . . . have you seen her?"

The woman's face was blackened with soot save for the clean streaks of tears running down her cheeks. "She was inside with the rest of us, sir. That's all I can tell you."

Gavin moved closer to the building. He grabbed the next person he recognized, a man who played all the second leading comedy roles. Ellen had once introduced them. "Parker!"

"My lord?"

"Have you seen Ellen?"

"God's bowels, you can't see anything in there! The smoke's too thick."

"What the hell's on fire?"

"Don't know. Something near the back." When Parker saw Gavin headed straight for the door, he called out to him. "Hey, you can't go in there. The smoke'll kill you!"

"I have to find Ellen," he shouted as he pushed by a king's guard sent to prevent looting.

"I say, my lord, you'll not be entering here. King's orders."

"Is everyone out?" Gavin rested his hand on the door.

"Don't know, sir. Just doing my duty, and that's to keep everyone out. We don't want anyone hurt, you know."

Gavin pushed the guard aside. "I'll take my chances."

"Hey there! Stop! Stop, I say, in the name of—"

The guard's voice was lost as the door closed behind Gavin. For a moment he stood there trying to get his bearings. The smoke was thick, making visibility difficult, but he could still see.

Someone had said the fire was in the rear. That had to be where Ellen was. Covering his mouth and nose with his handkerchief, Gavin raced through the internal halls of the playhouse. Nothing looked familiar, but he'd been through here enough times to trust his memory.

Certain he was near the rear of the theater where the dressing rooms were, he thought he heard voices. "Ellen! Ellen!" he screamed. His voice was hoarse from the smoke, his eyes teary.

"Ellen!" He followed the source of the voices, certain they were feminine. Someone was screaming. He turned down a hall half blocked with furniture. "Ellen!"

"Here!" Gavin thought he heard.

"Ellen!"

"We're here!" she shouted.

Gavin heaved a sigh of relief as he blindly raced down the smoke-filled corridor. She was safe! Thank God she was safe!

"Ellen, what the hell are you still doing in here!" He caught sight of her silhouette through the smoke. Then he heard the screaming.

"The twits!" She banged a closed door with her fist in frustration. "They've locked themselves inside and won't come out." She rubbed at her eyes with the heels of her hands. "I can't find a key anywhere." She reached out and touched his sleeve without thinking. "Gavin, if we don't get them out of there, they're going to suffocate."

He took her arm and pushed her. "You get out. I'll take care of this."

She shook her head. "No. It's too easy to get lost in the smoke. We go out together."

Gavin cursed her beneath his breath but knew better than to waste precious time arguing with her. "Find me something solid to break down the door. The smoke is getting thicker! We've got to hurry!"

Ellen disappeared from Gavin's line of vision as he hurled himself at the wooden door, hoping the lock would break free. "Open up! Open up in there!" he shouted.

The screaming had ceased. Now the women were only sobbing.

Gavin heaved himself against the door again and

again, but to no avail. The wood creaked and the lock scraped, but the door refused to budge.

"Here!" Ellen called from behind.

Gavin turned to see her lugging a metal post used for lighting on the stage.

The post was remarkably heavy. How Ellen had gotten it down the hall Gavin didn't know. "Stand back," he shouted, coughing.

Mustering every bit of strength he had, he slammed the pole into the door at the lock plate. Wood splintered, but the door didn't break free.

"Again! You have to try again! It's working!"

"Get out, Ellen!"

"Not without you!"

He took a running start and rammed the door again. On the third try, he heard the sweet sound of splintering wood and scraping metal, and the door swung open.

Gavin dropped the pole and rushed inside. In the corner of the tiny room he found two women huddled on the floor, gasping for breath. He grabbed both of them by the arm. "Come on!" he shouted.

Both sobbed as he dragged them through the broken doorway.

"Which way?" he called to Ellen. It was so difficult to breathe now that every word was too great an effort. Gavin suddenly realized that they would be lucky if they made it out of the building before they were overcome by the smoke. "You'll have to lead us out!"

"This way!"

"No, wait." He grabbed her shoulder. "Down on your hands and knees. There's less smoke at the floor. Can you manage?"

Obediently, she dropped on all fours as he dragged the two hysterical women down with him. "What

262

about them?" Ellen asked. "You can't carry them."

"You lead. They'll have to follow. I'll take up the rear."

"I can't," one of the women sobbed, slumping against Gavin. "I just can't."

Ellen reached out and slapped her face. "The hell you can't, Marcy! You think the viscount hasn't got better things to do than save your sorry tail? Now you get down on your hands and knees and you follow me like he tells you, you understand?"

Sobbing, Marcy did as she was told. The other girl followed suit, managing only to nod with round, terrified eyes.

The foursome went down the hall on their hands and knees, then turned right. "It's not too much farther," Ellen assured them. Still, they moved slowly. The halls were lined with hanging costumes and props, as well as with bulky pieces of furniture.

When Gavin bumped into a bucket of water, he groaned, crawling around it. Then suddenly a thought occurred to him. "Wait!" he ordered. He grasped the closest woman's skirt and pulled out the knife he wore on his belt. She gave a little shriek as he ripped a good size hunk from the taffeta and tore it into four pieces. "This will help you breathe," he told Ellen as he pushed a wet square of cloth into her sooty hand. "Just press it to your face. It will filter out some of the smoke."

She followed his instructions as he dipped the other pieces of cloth and forced the other women to take them.

"Ready?" Ellen called.

"Let's go," he echoed.

Down on her hands and knees, Ellen scurried. Her eyes stung badly and her chest ached, but she pressed on until finally she spotted sunlight. Someone had thrown open the doors to let out the smoke!

"The door!" Ellen scrambled to her feet.

Gavin grabbed the two women and hauled them up off the floor and through the doorway.

The fresh air and sunshine hit him like a solid wall. He choked and gasped as the two women slipped from his hands and disappeared into the crowd. His eyes were watering so badly that he could barely see. "Ellen! Ellen!"

"Here!"

He felt her touch and he swung around, pulling her against him. "I was afraid I'd lost you," he whispered emotionally. "I was afraid you were dead."

She laughed, coughing and choking. "I'm all right. See, I'm all right."

Someone offered them a gourd of water and they shared it. Outside in the fresh air, their lungs and eyes began to clear. They stepped back from the building as men began to rush in with buckets of water.

Gavin brushed back Ellen's tangled hair. "You're certain you're all right?"

She leaned against a wagon, offering a smile. "I'm certain. Where did you come from? What were you doing in the theater?"

He took the wet cloth he still held in his hand and wiped her sooty cheeks. "It doesn't matter."

She stroked his beard-stubbled cheek, taking in for the first time his ragged, unkempt attire. It had obviously been days since he had shaved and his hair, though pulled back in a savage's braid, was none too tidy, either. "You really were afraid for me, weren't you?"

"Ellen, this is ridiculous. I'm sailing tomorrow. I want you to come with me."

She wiped her mouth with the sleeve of her gown. "Gavin, please."

"Tomorrow. Do you understand? I leave London tomorrow and I'm never coming back."

A sob rose in her throat. It was so good to see him again. So good to feel his touch. "I can't."

He threw the soiled wet rag into the back of the wagon behind her. "You'll regret it the rest of your life if you don't."

She looked away, tears welling in her eyes. She wanted to go with him, but she couldn't. She just couldn't. She didn't want to marry. Marriage was a trap. She didn't want to leave Richard. He needed her.

She looked back at Gavin, unable to hide the misery in her voice. "I can't do it, Gavin. I can't go with you." She reached out to him, but he stepped back.

"The tide turns at ten in the morning. That's when I sail." He lifted a finger. "Be there."

She shook her head. "No."

He turned away from her and began to push his way through the crowd. "Be there, Ellen Scarlet. Be there and I'll take you to the Colonies. I'll make you my wife."

Tears ran down her cheeks. "I can't," she whispered. "I can't. I'm afraid." But Gavin didn't hear her. He was already gone.

# Chapter Eighteen

Ellen tapped her fingernails on the mantel to the rhythm of the case clock on the far wall. Nine in the morning. In one hour Gavin would set sail from England, never to return again. In one hour he would be gone from her life forever. . . .

She closed her eyes, trying to block out the pounding of her heart that echoed the clock. The minutes were ticking by too quickly. She still had a choice right now. She could go with Gavin. She could go to the Maryland Colony and see his precious fields and forest. She could be his wife. But that possibility would only last this final hour and then it would be gone forever.

At the sound of Richard's footsteps, she unconsciously stood a little straighter. Somehow allowing him to know how unhappy she was seemed like a betrayal to him and the feelings she had for him.

Richard appeared from the hallway carrying her cloak and vizard, along with a small and a large bag, the latter one obviously filled with clothing. He already wore his own cloak and hat, his sword strapped to his waist.

Her brow creased. "Where are you going?" She glanced at her woolen cloak thrown over his shoulder. "Where are *we* going?"

"The wharf."

She knew she couldn't have heard him correctly. "The wharf?"

"An hour, Ellen. In one hour the ship sails and you're going to be on it."

She blinked, a little dazed. "Richard, I told him I wouldn't go. He's going to sail without me."

"Well, you can damned well tell him you changed your mind!" He tossed her cloak. "There's no time to pack. I threw a few women's things into the bags. I'll have your other belongings shipped. You'll just have to make do."

She caught her cloak in midair. "I can't go to the Colonies."

"You can and you will." He came to her to help her with her cloak. "Don't you see this is the way to escape it all? Waldron . . . Hunt . . . your past?"

"I can't marry Gavin without him knowing I killed his brother."

"Why not? You said yourself Gavin didn't know what sort of beast his brother was. The man is dead, six feet under. Why tell Gavin the truth now? It will only hurt him. Let him hold on to his precious image of his brother and you hold on to the truth."

She shook her head in confusion. "I don't know. I just don't know if I could live the lie for the rest of my life."

"Look, he knows you have a past. But he said he didn't care. I heard the words from his own lips, and I think he means it." Richard paused, then spoke more softly. "Ellen, he loves you. Don't lose this opportunity. I'm telling you, it will never come again."

She suddenly threw herself into his arms, "Oh, Richard, couldn't you come with us?"

He laughed, smoothing her hair, kissing the top of her head. "Our time together has passed, sweetheart. You've survived your trials and it's time you were happy. You deserve more than I can ever give you."

She fought back tears as she hugged him tightly. He had been her savior, her rock for so long that she couldn't imagine living without him. Yet deep inside she felt a stir of excitement. To be with Gavin forever . . . it was a fairy tale that could suddenly come true. "But I'd miss you so much," she whispered.

"And I you." He took her by the shoulders and gently pushed her back so that he could look at her. "You have to admit to yourself that your feelings for Gavin are different."

"But I love you, too!"

"I know you do, sweetheart. But it's not the same love, is it?"

She lowered her lashes. "No," she whispered.

He pulled her against him. "Ah, sweetheart, it's all right. This last year you've given me more than I had ever expected out of life. If I never experience a happy moment again, I'll still have all the memories." He kissed her forehead. "Now come, we'll have to hurry."

She looked up at him, a tear slipping from the corner of her eye. "You really want me to go, don't you?"

"I want you to be happy."

She tied the ribbon of her cloak. "You could come to the Colonies and visit. You might like it so well that you decide to stay!"

"I might at that." He grabbed her bags. "Now we have to hurry!" He paused and then looked up at her.

"Is there anything you want to take with you I might not have packed? Of course, you're free to leave anything behind."

She frowned at his cryptic comment, then smiled, putting out her hand. "The letter. Let me see what you packed."

He handed her the small bag. "Just the things off your dressing table—face paint, hairbrushes, mirror."

"You're certain the mirror is here?"

His eyes narrowed. "I could dispose of the letter for you. I need not read it. It would be better if I didn't."

She snapped the clasp in the small bag and started for the door. "Some problems have to remain my own." She smiled up at him. "Didn't you say we had to hurry?"

As Richard stepped out the front door of the building with Ellen behind him, two burly men appeared out of nowhere. Ellen heard Richard swear in French.

"Where you hurryin' off to with your bags and your woman, hmmm?"

Richard dropped the bag and sidestepped, to shield Ellen from the two men. Ellen instinctively knew these were Hunt's men, most likely the two who had injured Richard so badly a few months ago.

"Step aside and let us be on our way."

"Not just yet. We got someone who wants to talk to you." The man nodded in the direction of the alley that ran between the apartment building and a cookshop. "Don't imagine it'll take but a minute." He grinned, baring blackened rotting teeth.

"I said step aside, else—"

"Else what?" The man flashed a pistol under his cloak.

Richard glanced up and down the street. It wasn't

busy, but still there were pedestrians and an occasional coach or horse going by. It was broad daylight and there were twenty witnesses within sight. "You're not going to shoot me on the street, now, with all these people going by."

"You're right, we're not," said the other man as he made a quick movement forward, lifting his own pistol from beneath his cloak. "We're gonna shoot her."

Ellen grabbed for Richard's arm, suddenly numb. She had almost made it, hadn't she? She'd almost escaped from Hunt forever. *Goodbye, Gavin,* her heart murmured. *I love you. Please know I always loved you.*

"Now, come on with you. The duke, he ain't got all day." The first man waved his pistol, still keeping it partially concealed beneath his raw wool cloak.

Richard casually lowered his hand to his sword. "We're not going into that alley with you."

Ellen glanced over her shoulder down the alley. She couldn't see Hunt, but as sure as she lived, she knew he was there, watching her. Waiting.

"I'm telling you, we're gonna shoot the slut. Shoot you both."

Ellen could feel every muscle in Richard's body tighten. "So shoot us. Have it done with."

Scratching his head, the second man looked toward the alley. "They say shoot 'em. They ain't comin', Your Grace. Now what do we do?"

Ellen heard a string of foul curses from the alley. Then suddenly, Hunt came bursting out astride a white horse. "I'll have your livers for this!" he shouted, reining in a few feet from them all. His pink rodent eyes narrowed as he stared down at Richard and Ellen. "I want the letter, Thomasina. Give it to me without fuss, and I might well spare your life."

She laughed as she took a step forward, pushing Richard's hand aside when he tried to hold her back. What does it matter now, she thought. *I'm going to lose Gavin. He's going to sail never knowing I had tried to come to him.* So she would lose the man she loved for this white bastard. At least she would stand up to him. She hadn't stood up to him or to Waldron all those years, but she'd do it now. With Gavin gone and her life and Richard's most likely forfeited, wasn't her pride the only thing she had left?

"I don't know what letter you speak of." She gave him a coy smile.

"Do not play the innocent with me. Your husband told me you had the list just before his unfortunate expiration."

She lifted her hands to her hips. "If I give you the paper, you'll kill me."

"I cannot kill you here, little Thomasina. Not on a street corner with citizens in view."

"Mayhap not. Mayhap you would leave me be . . . for a time. But if I give you the paper, you will kill me. If I don't give it to you . . . if you don't know where it is, then you won't know whose hands it will fall into if I die. Rather risky, I would think."

"You little strumpet!" Hunt sank his heels into his mount and the horse leaped forward.

Richard grabbed Ellen, dragging her out of the path of the horse's hooves. At the same moment, both of Hunt's men leaped to protect their employer.

Richard shoved her hard. "Run!" he commanded as he drew his sword to face his attackers.

Ellen stumbled, but she didn't fall.

"The woman!" Hunt shouted, trying to rein in his spooked horse. "I don't care about him! Get the slut! Don't let her get away!"

One of the men dodged right after Ellen, wielding

his pistol, while the other barreled toward Richard. Richard spun on his heels and lashed out at the man who pursued Ellen. He heard a boom of gunfire, followed by the sound of a musket ball whizzing through the air past his head.

The man running after Ellen turned his pistol on Richard, who lunged forward in a riposte. The tip of the sword touched the attacker's chest and then Richard sank it home. The man crumbled, his pistol falling uselessly, his eyes glazing over before he hit the street.

"Behind you!" Ellen warned with a shriek.

Richard swung around, beating back his cloak to free his movement. The other man was coming at him with a clublike stick. Richard parried with grace as the man swung the huge weapon again and again. Then with a quick twist of his wrist, he sliced his attacker's arm and, in the confusion of the man's pain, managed to sink his sword into the soft flesh of his stomach.

Ellen stood frozen in terror as she watched Richard swing around just in time to face Hunt, who had drawn his own sword but remained on horseback. "Run, Ellen!" Richard shouted, sweat running from his temples. "You know where to go! There's still time!"

"No, Richard, not without you!"

"How very touching," Hunt sneered as he and Richard parried, neither yet making a serious *botte*. "Come, come, Chambray, kill me. Kill me and the harlot is yours." The swords sliced the air, clinking again and again. "But I kill you and she's mine, isn't she?"

"Coward!" Ellen shouted. "You're a coward, Hunt, to fight a man on foot by horseback."

"Ellen, be quiet," Richard snapped.

273

"But then you were always a coward, weren't you?" Ellen dared from the top step of the apartment building.

Hunt turned his face toward her in reaction. At the same moment Richard struck his sword in a broad arc, catching Hunt's cheek with the tip of the blade.

The duke screamed out in pain, his hand flying to his cheek to touch the bloody wound. "You'll die for that, Chambray!" he cried as he wheeled his horse around in fury.

The swords struck again and again, Ellen wincing each time the metal clanged. By this time a crowd had gathered in a circle around the men. Women lifted their children up on their shoulders to see the duke fight the gentleman, and several men barked out wagers.

Tears streamed down Ellen's face as she wrung her hands in utter helplessness. She knew there was nothing she could do to help Richard save not break his concentration. But just the same, it made her feel no better.

The clanging of the swords went on and on, until Ellen thought she would go mad from the sound. First Richard seemed to gain the upper hand, making Hunt sway in his saddle, then Richard began to back up, taking the defensive.

All at once Richard made a sudden swift, calculated move, and before Hunt knew what had happened, he had been unseated. He fell from his steed and hit the ground in a roll, his sword still clutched in his hand. But by the time Hunt was on his feet, Richard was bearing down on him. For a moment it seemed as if Richard had the upper hand. The duke was now bleeding from several nicks in his arms and chest, his powder-blue fringed coat splashed with crimson.

274

The crowd that had formed around the men was becoming larger and more oppressive. As the tradesmen and hawkers pushed forward to get a better look, the circle around Richard and Hunt grew smaller.

Even from the steps, Ellen could now barely see above the heads of the men and women who gathered around. Her view obstructed, she didn't see where the child came from, but suddenly a dirty-faced boy appeared on the ground between Richard and Hunt. A woman screamed.

"My baby! Sweet Mary! My babe! Help him!"

Without thinking, Ellen bolted down the steps, shoving her way through the crowd. She had just pushed through to the inner circle, when she saw Richard reach out with his free hand and drag the child out of harm's way.

Then Hunt made his move. There was a silly smile on his face as he took a step forward, sinking his thin blade straight into Richard's chest.

Ellen stifled a scream. Richard's face paled. He stumbled, pushing the child into the crowd.

"Richard!" Ellen screamed.

Just as Hunt took another step forward to make perhaps his final repartee, Richard raised his sword and sliced open the duke's thigh in a bloody gash.

Hunt fell forward, going down on one knee.

"The horse!" Richard shouted. "Get the horse, Ellen."

Ellen grabbed the reins of the white steed, which patiently waited for its master, and led him toward Richard, all the while watching Hunt, who now lay on his side, dazed.

Richard grabbed the reins from Ellen's hands and lifted her onto the back of the nervous mount. Then he grabbed the smaller of her two bags, tossed it up to

275

her, and leapt up on the saddle behind her.

"You'll die! You'll die for this!" Hunt shouted as the horse broke through the crowd. "I'll have your neck stretched for this, Chambray!"

Ellen glanced over her shoulder as they made their escape, to see Hunt getting to his feet, shaking his fist in blind rage.

"You should have killed him," Ellen murmured, tightening her arms around Richard's waist. "You should have killed him!"

"Then it would have been my head," he threw over his shoulder.

Feeling something wet, Ellen pulled back her hand. Her palm was a deep ruddy red. "Richard, you're bleeding."

"A flesh wound," he assured her, turning hard to cut through an alley. "Don't worry about me. I'll be fine. We have to get you to the wharf before Gavin sets sail."

She laid her cheek against his coat, holding him tightly. "You'll have to go with us now, Richard. If you stay in England, Hunt will track you down. He'll have you arrested for certain. You've got no choice but to go to America."

He took a shuddering breath. "We'll see, Ellen."

Before Ellen knew it, she could smell the heady scent of the wharfs, with their wet wood, raw sewage, and open tobacco crates. She could hear the sounds of sailors shouting orders, sails whipping in the wind, and wood creaking.

"Where was he docked?" Richard demanded, running the duke's horse full speed down the wide dock, dodging horses and wagons and pedestrians.

"I don't know!" She strained to look over his shoulder. "Down this way. It's the *Maid Marion*. The figurehead is a mermaid . . . red hair."

"Of course." Richard couldn't resist the caustic remark. But when he spoke again, the sarcasm was gone from his voice. "I don't see it, Ellen. Are you certain this is the right wharf?"

"I'm positive!" She craned her neck. "What time is it, Richard? Oh, God, have we missed him?"

Reaching the end of the wharf, he pulled up on the horse and reached for his pocket watch. "Ten-ten, Ellen."

A sob escaped her throat. "No, no, he can't be gone, Richard. He didn't leave without me."

Richard slid down off the horse, resting his head against its haunches for only a moment before he reached for Ellen. She rested her hands on his broad shoulders as he lowered her feet to the dock.

"He can't be gone," she whispered.

Richard brushed back a wisp of his hair. His face had broken out into a sweat. The patch of blood on his coat was growing larger, turning to an even deeper shade of red. "Let's ask someone," he said, looping his arm through Ellen's.

"There! You boy!" he called to the first person he saw within speaking distance.

The young boy in sailcloth breeches and a striped tick shirt turned. "Me, sir?"

"Yes, you." Richard took a deep breath before speaking again. "The *Maid Marion*, do you know her?"

"Lord Waxton's ship, you mean, sir? Yes, I know her. Fine ship, she is."

Ellen took a step forward, opening her arms to implore. "Have you seen her?"

"Seen her? Yes, ma'am." He turned toward the water, pointing. "Why, there she sails now. Out of the harbor. Headed for France and then the Americas, I hear."

Ellen forced herself to follow the boy's line of vision. Sure enough, there was a two-masted sailing ship, her lower staysails rippling in the breeze as she sailed down the Thames. Across the stern in gilded gold letters the words *Maid Marion* could still be seen. . . .

# Chapter Nineteen

"I'm sorry, Ellen," Richard whispered, draping his arm over her shoulder as he watched the ship slowly disappear around a curve in the Thames. His voice was hoarse. "I'm so sorry."

"He's gone," Ellen exhaled. "He's gone without me."

Richard grasped her arm, forcing her to look him in the eye. "I'll get you on another ship, Ellen, I vow I will. The boy says he's headed for France. Surely you could catch him there." He pushed a stray lock of bright red hair away from her mouth. "If you want to go, I'll get you to the Colonies if I have to carry you on my back."

Fighting her tears, she reached up to stroke Richard's cheek. For the first time she noticed his skin was so pale it appeared translucent. His eyes had a strange light in them. "He didn't wait for me. There's no need for me to go now."

"Ods fish, sweetheart! You told him you weren't coming," he said gently. "Give the man another chance."

"Yes, give the man another chance. . . ." Gavin echoed. He watched Ellen, his sweet Ellen, lift her

279

gaze over Richard's shoulder until it met his. Tears began to trickle down her cheeks. "Gavin?"

He stood there on the wharf an arm's length from her, wanting to run toward her but feeling like a fool. What if he had misunderstood? What if she really hadn't come to join him? He held open his arms for her. It was time to take a chance. "I couldn't go without you, Ellen," he said, trying to control the emotion in his voice. "I couldn't do it."

Dazed, she took a step toward him and then stopped. Richard took a step back. "But your ship. I saw it sail," she said as if she were speaking to an apparition.

"Julius went on to France without me." He still held out his hands, afraid that if he lowered them without her tucked in them, he would perish. "He sent me back to get you. Said I was to kidnap you if I had to." He gave a wry grin. "I was hoping I wouldn't have to."

She smiled a bittersweet smile. "Gavin . . ."

He didn't know how she got there. Did he run toward her, did she run toward him, or did they meet halfway? But suddenly she was in his arms. Suddenly, he was pulling her hard against his chest, enveloping her soft curves and feminine scent in his greedy arms.

"Ellen, Ellen." He squeezed his eyes shut. Men didn't cry. "I was afraid I'd lost you. I was afraid you didn't love me as I loved you." He took a breath. "Then I realized I didn't care. If you love me just a little, it's enough."

"I love you," she murmured against the soft cotton of his shirt. "I do love you more than I can express. I think that's why this has been so hard for me." She rubbed her cheek against the rough linen of his shirt. "I didn't want to love you, but I do. Too much to let you go."

He grasped her by her forearms and pulled back so that he could stare into her dark brown eyes. "You'll go with me to the Colonies, then?"

She nodded. "To the ends of the earth." She dropped her gaze, but then lifted it again. "But there's one thing. Richard, too. He has to come."

Gavin hugged her against him again in disbelief. She had come to the wharf! She had wanted him! "Of course, of course." He glanced down at her face, wiping away the tears with the tip of his forefinger. "I could use a good man like Chambray on the land. It's a great deal of business for one man to handle alone. And even if he's not willing to work with me, he'll always be welcome in my home." He leaned to whisper in her ear. "Just not in your bed."

Ellen smiled, but then her face suddenly paled. "Oh, God, Gavin. Hunt."

He frowned. "Hunt?"

"The Duke of Hunt. He and Richard had a terrible fight. Swords. Richard says he's not hurt, but I think he is." She took a breath. "We have to get Richard out of London quickly."

Gavin slipped her hand into his and called to Richard, who stood discreetly a few feet away. "You're in trouble, Chambray?"

Richard moved sluggishly toward them. Gavin took note of his gait. As Chambray's cloak swayed in the breeze, he caught sight of the blood on his chest. "Damned fine trouble this time, I think," Richard said, grimacing with each step.

"Hunt? What the hell are you doing tangling with Hunt?" He released Ellen, going to Chambray and pulling back his cloak to see the wound. He exhaled slowly at the sight of the deep red blood that stained his pristine shirt. "Your lung," he murmured so that

281

Ellen couldn't hear.

"Yes. I fear so," was all Richard could manage.

"Not now," Ellen called from behind, not hearing the exchange between the two men. "We haven't got time for talk. We've got to get Richard out of London. Surely Hunt has his men looking for him by now."

Richard grasped Gavin's shirt. "Just take her and go. I don't want you mixed up in this. I just want her to be safe." His gaze settled on Gavin's face. "You don't want her in Hunt's hands. She'd be better off dead."

Gavin stared at Richard for a moment. He didn't like this, not one damned bit. Chambray was insinuating that Hunt had something to do with Ellen, and the thought made him furious. "All right," he finally conceded, looking over his shoulder at Ellen. "Later, you can give me the particulars on just what the hell is going on here." He glanced back at Richard's face. He was growing paler by the moment. "Ellen, take this." He tossed her a coin purse he wore tied on his breeches. "Go to that ship, the *Flying Esther*. See a man called Roberts and tell him I need a good saddled horse within the next five minutes."

She caught the purse in midair. "Five minutes. How can anyone get you a—?"

"Just do as I say."

Ellen took one look at the expression on his face, and she lifted her skirts and ran down the dock.

The moment she was out of earshot, Gavin turned back to Richard. "Christ, Chambray, he caught your lung."

Richard rested his hand on Gavin's shoulder for support. "Bloody lousy luck, hmm?"

For a moment both men just looked at each other.

Both were soldiers. Both knew what a lung puncture meant. It meant death. It mean slow internal bleeding, loss of breath, lung collapse, infection. A lung wound could mean a slow, lingering death or a swift one, but most certainly it meant death.

"I want the truth, Chambray," Gavin finally said. "Is Ellen really in danger of Hunt?"

"Grave." Richard wiped his mouth with the back of his hand. He was growing weaker by the moment. "You have to get her out of here. Hide her until you can get her on a ship and then get her out of England."

"So Hunt is somehow involved in this deep, dark secret of hers?"

"It doesn't matter, does it?" Richard studied Gavin's reaction, then, seemingly satisfied, went on. "What matters is that you know and I know it's not likely I'll survive this wound. She has no other protector but you. I'm handing her over to you, Gavin." He squeezed his arm. "I'm trusting you to love her as I've loved her . . . to keep her safe, whether she ever tells you her secrets or not. Can you do that . . . friend?"

Gavin looked away, for a moment following Ellen's movement as she walked up the gangplank of the *Flying Esther*. Roberts was coming across the lower deck to meet her. Her long shining hair had tumbled from beneath the hat she wore, flowing down her shoulders in a brilliant river of red. Her gait was one of urgency, but of confidence as well. "I love her, Chambray. I'll keep her safe from Hunt and any other man or beast who tries to harm her." He looked back at Richard. "I'll make her as happy as she's willing to let me."

Richard nodded. "Good enough. No one could ask more of a man. Now, where do you intend to take her?"

"Take her? We go together, Chambray—you, I, and Ellen."

"Let's be logical here. It would be better if we separated. She'd be safer. I can manage myself."

"You may be able to deceive her, but not me. I know a man who's barely conscious when I see one." He took his arm. "We go together."

"She'd be safer—"

"She thinks you're going to Maryland with her. If she's going to lose you to Hunt's sword, she deserves some time to get used to the idea. To say goodbye. You owe that much to her, Chambray."

Richard watched a sea gull hover overhead for a moment. "You're right. If I am to die, I'd like to have her at my side my last few days. I just didn't want my selfishness to put her life in danger."

Gavin spotted Ellen coming across the dock. Behind her, Roberts followed, leading a saddled chestnut. "I know a place where we'll be safe enough until Julius returns with the ship. He'll be back in two weeks time. By then, you may be better."

"That, or six feet under."

Gavin lifted an eyebrow. "At least tell me you caught him with your own sword."

Richard grinned. "He looked like mincemeat. Nothing life-threatening, unfortunately, but I imagine he'll take a stitch or two."

The two men were laughing together as Ellen reached them.

"You were right." She smiled. "He found one. He found us a horse!"

Gavin took the reins from the old salt. "My thanks."

The man tossed Gavin his coin purse. "Keep your coin. I owed you one, anyway, boyo." Without another word, he turned and started back for his ship.

"If anyone asks, you've not seen me, the lady, or the gentleman," Gavin called after him.

The sailor threw a cynical grin over his shoulder. "Ain't seen a thing in years." He tipped his cap. "Good day to you, my lord. See ya in hell!"

With a chuckle and a shake of his head, Gavin turned back to Richard. He cupped his hands, making a stirrup. "Up with you."

With a groan, Richard managed to heave himself onto the back of the horse.

Gavin handed him the reins. "You seated? I can tie you on if necessary."

"I'm losing my patience with you, nursemaid. I've been injured worse, remember?" He tried to smile as he wheezed to catch his breath. "Just get her up on that horse and let's get the rotting hell out of here."

Gavin crossed the dock to the huge white horse that stood patiently. Ellen followed, carrying her small bag. He frowned as he caught sight of the crest embroidered into the blanket that fell from beneath both sides of the saddle. "This isn't Hunt's horse? Tell me this isn't Hunt's horse?"

Richard reined up and came toward them. "Fine. That's not Hunt's prized French horse you're going to ride out of Londontown on. It's not the horse they say he won from King Louis in a throw of dice. Feel better?"

Gavin couldn't resist a smile. Chambray was a good man. He knew that now. Even in the face of death, somehow Chambray managed to keep his sense of humor. If he died, Gavin knew he was going to miss him.

Grasping the reins of the white horse, Gavin slung

285

into the saddle. Then he reached down to pull Ellen up. "No matter what happens, you hang on, you understand?"

She slipped her arms around his waist and wedged her bag between them. "I understand."

He urged the horse forward. He knew a few back ways out of the city. Already, he was planning a route in his head. "You'd be better to leave the bag behind. We need to travel light."

She clutched the soft satchel. "No. The bag goes."

"Ellen—"

Richard came up beside them. "Let it go, Waxton." His gaze met Gavin's. "She wants to take her bag."

Gavin was surprised by the forceful tone in Chambray's voice. He nodded. "Well enough. Let's go."

They rode off the wharfs and down a side street, hugging the Thames, a few streets off the water. Gavin led them down winding back alleys, through the slums of the city. They hugged the walls of the leaning frame houses and merchant's stores, side-stepping piles of stinking garbage and gullies of sewage. Occasionally, a woman or child stuck a head out the window to see two gentlemen and a lady riding through their back alley, but Gavin threw them a warning glance and they quickly ducked inside, slamming their shutters. He wanted no loose tongues telling Hunt's men which direction they'd gone.

Just to cover his tracks, Gavin decided to take London Bridge out of the City. They would travel through Kent and then cross the Thames into Essex tomorrow. Even with stopping for the night, if they traveled swiftly, they'd reach Havering House before nightfall. If any tongues did wag, Hunt would be sent off into the Kent countryside in the wrong direction.

As Gavin led them onto Fish Hill Road, Ellen leaned forward. "You know somewhere we can go? Somewhere Richard will be safe?"

"We'll not be there until tomorrow, but he'll be safe enough." She laid her cheek against his broad back and tightened her arms around his waist. Gavin placed one of his hands on hers in a gentle caress. "I can't wait to get you alone," he said in a voice meant only for her ears. "I can't wait to take you in my arms and make love to you. I can't wait to take your nipples between my lips and—"

She chuckled, squeezing him hard around the waist. "Enough, enough," she whispered. "The thoughts are mutual, but let's stick to the task at hand. There'll be plenty of time for that nonsense later."

"A lifetime," he told her wistfully.

"A lifetime," she echoed.

Gavin glanced over his shoulder. "You still with us, Chambray?"

"I'm with you. Keep riding."

Their horses' hooves had just hit the wooden planks of the London Bridge, when the relative peacefulness of the morning was shattered by the sudden discharge of a musket ball.

The glass window of a butcher's shop shattered and Hunt's horse reared.

"Hunt's men!" Richard shouted from behind. "Go, Gavin!"

"Richard!" Ellen screamed as Hunt's white steed leaped forward and barreled down the bridge. The wooden structure with its leaning buildings was packed with mid-morning traffic. She closed her eyes in fright as the giant horse leaped over a crate of squawking chickens, the owner jumping free of the deadly hooves.

"Damnation, that was close," Gavin muttered, urging the mount faster.

Ellen tightened her arms around Gavin's waist to keep from being jarred off the mount as its hooves pounded on the wooden bridge, hell-bent on escape. The tall, cramped buildings that lined both sides of the bridge whirled by as more musket balls exploded in the air, whizzing too close to Ellen's head for comfort.

Richard and Gavin now rode side by side. They dodged coaches and herds of goats, milk carts and peddler's wagons. Gavin sank his boot heel into the right flank of Hunt's horse and suddenly veered right, missing a funeral hearse by inches.

Ellen stifled a scream as the toe of her slipper brushed the edge of the coffin. She could still hear the pounding of horses' hooves behind her as Hunt's men raced to catch them.

"How are we going to get away?" she hollered over the pounding of the horses' hooves, the blast of musket balls, and the roar of the crowded street. "They're gaining on us!"

"I've not come this far to lose you now," Gavin called back. "Just hang on!"

They clattered over the bridge and Gavin veered again, this time straight for the water. Richard's horse pounded beside them.

"Got any ideas?" Richard called, peering over his shoulder. "There's eight of them, three of us."

Gavin reined the horse down a steep bank.

"Halt in the name of His Grace, the Duke of Hunt," a man shouted from behind. "I said halt!" Another musket blast rang in the air.

Ellen thought she should pray, but no words came

to mind. Her fingers found her mother's gold crucifix beneath her smock. No prayer came to mind, but she suddenly felt comforted. She lowered her hand, tightening her hold on Gavin's waist. He was right. They'd come too far to lose each other now. He would find a way out of this. She knew he would.

"Waxton! They're gaining on us!" Richard shouted.

"Follow my lead!" Gavin shouted. He was panting now from the hard ride, his shirt growing damp with perspiration.

Ellen could hear Hunt's men behind them. They were close enough to shoot and hit them now. She didn't want to die this way. Not with a musket ball in her back.

Suddenly, they were down at the river, riding along the edge. The Thames was busy with sailing boats, rafts, and barges.

Gavin turned abruptly onto a small dock, urging the horse forward. Ellen saw the water looming ahead of them as they flew at lightning speed. He was insane! They were going to ride right off the dock and into the water!

Ellen heard herself scream as Hunt's massive horse leaped through the air and fell the distance of what seemed a hundred feet. She closed her eyes, waiting for the sound of the splash and the shock of the cold, filthy water. Instead, the horse hit something solid with a hard jolt. A second later, she heard Richard's horse beside them.

At the sound of a man's exclamation, her eyes flew open. They had landed on a moving fishing barge and were already traveling away from the dock!

She looked up to see Hunt's men pulling back hard on their mounts to keep from riding off the end of the dock. One man didn't rein in hard enough, and the horse and rider went skittering off the dock and into the water with a great splash.

Gavin leaped down off Hunt's horse and pulled Ellen with him. "Stay low!" he ordered, shielding her from the men as they fired a last futile attempt.

At the command of someone not visible, two boys with poles swung their arms in fluid, rapid motions, hastily steering the flat barge out into the middle of the river, where it could catch the swift-moving current.

"I'll be bloody damned," Richard swore as he slid off his horse, holding on to the saddle for support. "I swear by the king's cod, I thought you were leading me straight into the stinking Thames!" He gave a laugh that strangled in his throat as he broke into a coughing fit.

Ellen watched him bring a handkerchief to his mouth and saw the bloody cloth as he pulled it away. She made a sound in her throat and started for him, but Gavin caught her arm, shaking his head ever so slightly.

Ellen forced herself to stand beside Gavin, waiting for Richard to gain his composure.

Just then a tall man with a straggly beard came around Hunt's horse. "I wish you'd let me know you were dropping in, Merrick," he said good-naturedly, offering his hand. "I'd have had the woman make a lord's supper. I got nothing but rye bread and goat cheese aboard."

Gavin chuckled. "I appreciate you being in the right place at the right time, Zach." He squeezed the man's filthy hand, not caring that it had dry scales stuck to it and reeked of fish.

Zach glanced back at the shore, where Hunt's men were trying to pull the bellowing man out of the river. The horse had already begun to swim for shore. "Did I by chance hear right? Be them Duke's men?"

Gavin caught Ellen's hand. "You don't want to know, Zach. Take my word for it."

The man thought for a moment, then gave a nod. "Right you are." He grinned. "But seems they thought they was Duke's men." He gave a shrug. "But then what do I care?" He looked back at Gavin. "So where can I take you?"

"Up the river, if you don't mind. We're headed well into Essex. Can you manage? If not, I'll not be insulted. You can well put us off a few miles up and we'll ride the rest of the way."

"Pshaw! I ain't been up that way in months. I'll just stop by the house and put one of the boys off so he can let his mother know I'll not be warmin' her tick tonight. 'Sides, I seen the look on your friend's face. He's bad hurt. He don't belong ridin'."

"I appreciate it. Name a price and it's yours."

"Don't want none of your coin, my lord," Zach said, heading back toward the boys, who were still poling with all their might. "Seems to me, you done me a favor or two in the past. Just glad I can do the same for you."

Ellen turned to Gavin and laid her hand on his chest, smoothing his damp wrinkled shirt. "You said Essex. What's in Essex?"

"A place where you and Richard will be safe until Julius gets back with the *Maid Marion*."

Ellen felt a sudden ominous shudder of fear. "What place?"

Gavin draped his hand over her shoulder, looking out over the water. "My brother's old place, of course. It's not yet been sold. Havering House, he called it."

Ellen took a deep shocking breath, afraid for a moment she might faint. *Havering House*, she thought. *Not there, please heavenly Father, anywhere but there . . .*

# Chapter Twenty

The Duke of Hunt slumped into a silver chair in the opulent anteroom off his bedchamber and waved a hand impatiently. "Come, come, before I bleed to death, you little whoreson wretch!"

A teenaged boy in tight red velvet breeches came hesitantly forward with his needle and thread and a pair of ivory-handled scissors on a tray. Jason served as one of Hunt's manservants when he was needed, but he was mainly just one of the young boys the duke kept within his household to fulfill his sexual perversions.

There was a knock at the antechamber door and then it swung open. It was Hunt's secretary, a little man with an immense periwig, a hooked nose, and a dark secret . . . and an unmarked grave to prove it, which kept him the duke's servant for life. "You called for me, Your Grace?" Ludwig Robards whined.

"I did," the duke snapped, half rising out of his chair. "What I wonder is why you tarried so long! When I call you, I expect you to come."

"Your Grace, I was—"

"I don't care if you were servicing the queen! I have

need of you and you work for me!"

Robards clutched his paper and quill to his chest, his hands shaking. "Sorry, Your Grace, so sorry. What would you have me do?" He took note of the duke's bloodied clothing but made no comment.

"I want a warrant for the arrest of a Baron Richard Chambray. And I want it tonight."

"T . . . tonight, sir?"

"Did I stutter, you moronic ass? Yes, tonight!" Hunt glanced over his shoulder at the pretty boy, Jason, who was hovering behind him. "Come, come, boy, and sew this damnable wound on my cheek. I'm bleeding all over my new shirtwaist!"

"Yes. Yes, Your Grace." Jason came to the duke's side and began to thread the needle with white silk.

Hunt settled back in the silver chair. "Get me a refreshment, Robards, and a plate of pickled eels."

"I thought you wanted me to get the arrest papers, Your Grace?"

"I do want the damned warrant," Hunt exploded, "but first I want the drink!"

Robards took a step back, his eyes flicking to the silver mirrors draped in black that lined the walls like pieces of artwork. They made a strange appearance against the silver and black stripes of the wallpapered wall. "I . . . I need to know the reason for the arrest, Your Grace. To . . . to get the papers. I take it you want this done legally."

"I . . . I'm going to start, Your Grace." Jason leaned forward to take the first stitch.

Hunt barely flinched. "The filthy bastard, Chambray, killed my man Little and wounded his brother. Look what he did to me!" He indicated the gash on his cheek. "I'll be scarred for life because of that arrogant, strutting bastard!" He gave a sly smile. "But I'll fix him, I'll warrant that. First, I'll cut off

294

his balls and have them fried and served to him with supper. I'll get what information I need out of him in the Tower, and I'll see that his neck is stretched from here to Whitefriars. Then I'll have that malapert slut, Thomasina, he's been protecting all this time, won't I, Robards?"

"Yes, yes, Your Grace."

Jason took another stitch.

Hunt licked his lips in thought. "A few days in my special little room down below, and she won't be so high and mighty with her airs, will she?"

"I think not." Robards forced a smile. He had never seen the duke's special room, which was off-limits to the servants, nor did he care to. The screams he heard echoing from the depths of the dungeonlike cellar at night were enough for him.

Jason took another stitch on the duke's cheek, then licked the corner of a white linen towel and wiped the blood that dripped down his master's face.

Hunt smiled at the gesture. "How does it look, boy?"

"G . . . good, good, Your Grace. There'll barely be a scar."

Hunt slapped Jason on the buttocks with the palm of his hand. "Liar!"

Jason lowered his head. "Yes, Your Grace, I am a liar, and I deserve to be punished," he said from rote.

Hunt smiled a wicked smile. "That's just what I like to hear." He reached out and pulled the young man onto his lap. Almost as a second thought, he looked up at Robards, who had retreated to the anteroom door. "Just see to the arrest warrant, Robards. The boy here can fetch my nourishment in just a moment."

Robards slipped out the door, closing it behind him. Hunt looked back at Jason, who now sat perched on his knee, the thread and needle still in his hand, still connected to the duke's cheek. "You're a good boy, aren't you, Jason?" He ran his finger over the bulge in the boy's breeches. "You always take care of my needs, don't you?"

"Yes, Your Grace," the young man conceded, lowering his cheek to his master's shoulder. "Always."

No matter how prepared Ellen thought she was to see Havering House again, it was all she could do to hang on to her horse's saddle as she, Gavin, and Richard rode up the long drive to the place she had called home for so many years.

Havering House, more than three hundred years old, was an immense L-shaped home renovated and rerenovated throughout the years as it passed from generation to generation of the Greenborough family. Built of brick and stone, it was three stories high across the front, with towers on each corner.

As Ellen glanced up at the right tower, she grew dizzy with memories of that night she had struggled for her life there . . . the night Waldron had died. When she closed her eyes she could still smell the smoke of the burning draperies . . . she could still see the flames shooting up to engulf the laboratory . . . she could still taste the cinders on her tongue. She could even hear Waldron's scream as he fell through the glass window and tumbled to his death below.

Ellen felt a tug at her elbow and she opened her eyes. Richard was riding beside her, they behind Gavin.

"You all right?" Richard mouthed the words.

She looked up at the tower, then looked back at

296

him, nodding, forcing a smile. She knew now that Richard had not been entirely honest with her when he had said his wound was minor. Though he had been able to travel two days on horseback to make it to Havering House, it was his sheer will that had carried him. Richard's usual ruddy complexion was now pasty, his breathing erratic, his movements slow and strained.

She reached out to take his hand. "Now that we're here, we can find you a surgeon. Someone to look at the wound."

Richard shook his head emphatically. "No surgeons. A surgeon is called into Havering House, which is thought to be vacant, and the word will be out to Hunt in two days time. He'll put two and two together and figure out that it's us."

"Surely he wouldn't think I'd dare come back here, not after what happened."

"But you have. . . ."

Ellen looked at Richard again and then urged the horse Gavin had bought her forward, so that she rode beside him. He had refused to sell Hunt's prized steed, taking the silly notion that he was bringing it to the Colonies with him. "Gavin"—she averted her eyes from the house that loomed ahead—"Richard says he'll have no surgeon. You have to talk to him."

"You cannot force a man to do what he doesn't want to do." He reached out to stroke her cheek. "No more than you can force a woman."

She covered his hand with hers, touched by Gavin's gentleness. He did love her. He did want her as his wife. He truly didn't care about her past, she was almost certain of that. She lowered her voice. "The wound still seeps blood. His breathing is worse. I'm sure it's his lung, though he says not. He could well die, Gavin!"

"He could well die whether he sees a surgeon or not," he answered honestly.

She looked away as tears stung her eyes. Life without Richard was hard to imagine. "He's not going to die," she said firmly. "He's going to get better and he's going to Maryland with us."

Gavin took her gloved hand and pressed a kiss to the pulse at her wrist. "Only time and fate will tell, sweetheart. In the meantime, we'll do all we can for him. We should be safe enough from Hunt and his men here until Julius returns from France with the *Maid Marion*."

Ellen fell silent as they rode up to the front steps of Havering House. For the first time, she noticed candlelight burning from somewhere inside. *Dear God*, she thought. *What if some of the servants are still here? What if someone recognizes me?*

"There . . . there's someone living here?" she asked as Gavin helped her out of the saddle. She clutched her small bag containing all the possessions she now owned.

"A housekeeper I hired after I arrived in London. There was another man here, but he was a drunk. He was letting the place crumble." He offered Richard a hand, but Chambray pushed it away and dismounted on his own. "I wanted no looting while I waited to put the place up for sale," Gavin went on. "It was amazing that nothing had been taken already." He laughed. "The woman I hired said the villagers were afraid of ghosts up here." He laughed again. "Ridiculous, these superstitious countryfolk."

Ellen certainly wasn't afraid of ghosts, but she had no doubt they were here. How could a house with such a tragic past not have ghosts? "This house-keeper is someone who worked for your brother?" she whispered.

He led her up the winding stone steps. "No. Actually, it was curious, but I couldn't find a soul down in the village who had ever worked here. They were either dead or mysteriously gone."

A sense of relief flooded her as she flashed Richard a grin over her shoulder.

On the landing, Gavin lifted the boar's head knocker and rapped it several times. He paused, then rapped it again. Candlelight glowed through the glass-paned front windows as someone approached from inside. The door creaked open.

"Mrs. Spate?"

A rotund woman lifted a candlestand. "My lord, that you?"

"Yes, Mrs. Spate. Are you alone in the house or are there others?"

"Just me and my four young'uns, my lord. You said I could let the help go for laziness or drunken behavior. Once the place was cleaned proper, I just sent 'em all packin'. I got my boys to help me."

Gavin stepped into the front hall. Ellen followed, her gaze falling to the black and white Greek marble tiles Waldron had shipped in specifically for that area. In a flash, she remembered him once hitting her before they were married. She remembered the thump her head had made as it struck the tiled floor. She remembered sitting here on the cold floor half the night, scrubbing a white square until the blood stain disappeared.

Ellen swallowed against the bad memories. She had never thought much about her husband's physical abuse, always assuming that all men struck their women. After all, her father had certainly hit her mother on occasion, and the Viscount Greenborough had most certainly not spared his hand raising his daughter.

299

But as Ellen stood here in the hallway, only half listening to what Gavin said to the housekeeper, she looked at Richard and Gavin. Neither man, no matter how angry she had made them, had ever raised his hand to her. Striking a woman wasn't right; all men didn't do it. She knew that now.

"Ellen?"

She blinked, realizing Gavin had been speaking to her. "Gavin?"

"I've instructed Mrs. Spate to have a bedchamber opened for us and one next to it for Richard. Can you think of anything else?"

"No." She forced a smile. "That will be fine."

Gavin looked back at Mrs. Spate. "My wife will have a bath as soon as possible. We'll dine in our chambers after she's bathed."

His wife? Ellen glanced at Gavin. He must have told the housekeeper she was his wife. She must have missed it in her musing.

"The master chambers is in the back wing, my lord, but if you don't mind, I'll put you up on the second story here. The room isn't as nice but it's clean, bedlinens and all. I make my boys clean a room everyday to keep 'em outa trouble."

"I'm sure the chambers will be fine." Gavin started for the grand staircase, carrying a lit candle he'd taken off the wall. "And Mrs. Spate?"

She stopped in the dark hallway that led into the rear kitchens. "My lord?"

"I'll ask you not to let anyone know I'm here . . . or my guest. When you go into the village to buy food tomorrow, you're to say nothing. We'll eat sparsely if necessary, but I want no one to suspect I've returned to Havering House. Do you understand?"

"Clear as springwater, my lord. What's you and your lady's business ain't none of mine. You paid me

300

too good this winter past to flap my tongue."

"Thank you, Mrs. Spate. Now, if you'll see to my lady's bath, we'll find the rooms on our own."

"Down the hallway, second door, west side for you and your lady, third for the gentleman. I can send one of my boys up with you, if you like."

"That will be quite all right. Just send up the bath and something light to eat."

Halfway up the steps, Ellen caught Gavin's free hand as he led her and Richard up the dark staircase. "You told her I was your wife?"

"Yes."

"But I'm not."

"A minor detail, sweet." He looped his arm around her waist and gave her a squeeze. "A detail soon righted if I have my way." He looked over his shoulder at Richard, who was several steps behind but still following with the aid of the polished mahogany railing. "You still with us, Chambray?"

"What I want to know is why you didn't order me a bath, my lord," he mocked.

The two men chuckled and despite her surroundings, Ellen felt a warm sense of contentment come over her. Everything was going to be all right. They were going to be safe from Hunt here. She didn't care what Richard said. As long as she gave him no cause, Hunt would never suspect she'd gone back to Havering House! The *Maid Marion* would return from France, and she, Gavin, and Richard would sail to the Colonies. Ellen was going to be Gavin's wife. She was going to make him so happy that it wouldn't matter what had happened between her and his brother. That would be another lifetime, another woman. One Ellen need never exhume.

As Gavin led her up the wide winding staircase and she walked by the stiff portraits that lined the wall,

Ellen tried to hold off any memories of the past. She was thankful Mrs. Spate had suggested they use the front bedchambers rather than those in the back apartments. These rooms held no ill memories for her. They had stood vacant all her adult life, and as a child they had been used only for guests during the holidays and for the infrequent parties her parents had hosted.

If Mrs. Spate had suggested they sleep in the apartments Ellen had shared with Waldron, she might not have been able to do it. Somehow the thought of sleeping in the same marriage bed with Gavin as she had slept in with Waldron seemed blasphemous. The fact that Waldron had never actually consummated the marriage seemed inconsequential. What mattered was the way Waldron had humiliated her in that bed . . . the way she had felt about herself when she lay in that bed.

Gavin led Ellen and Richard down the hallway, going first to the room meant for Richard. He swung open the door and went to the fireplace, where he began to light several candlestands.

While Gavin brought light to the room, Ellen went immediately to the bed and began to pull back the clean bedlinens. "I'll have food brought in for you, Richard, but I want you to get into bed." She glanced up at him standing in the doorway, slumped against the door frame. His usual neatly combed hair was tousled, falling boyishly over his forehead.

He waved a hand weakly. "I'm not terribly hungry, though a brandy would do me wonders." He began to cough and drew out his bloodstained handkerchief to cover his mouth.

Ellen looked at Gavin.

"I'm sure there are libations in the cellar," Gavin said, leaning to light a fire in the fireplace where dry

302

wood waited to be tindered. "I'll send one of Mrs. Spate's boys down to the wine cellar to bring you a bottle."

"Make it two," Richard said, his coughing spasms subsiding. He meticulously folded his handkerchief before returning it to his shirtwaist. "I've a mind to get stinking drunk tonight."

In the bedchamber next door, Ellen heard movement and young male voices. By the time she and Gavin had Richard settled comfortably in bed with a good bottle of brandy and they had entered their room, a steaming copper tub of water had been set up behind a silk dressing screen. The clean bedlinens had been pulled back invitingly on the four-poster tester bed and the draperies had been drawn. A small table had been set up with two place settings, a tureen of soup, and a plate of bread and cheese.

"Be there anything else you might be needin', my lord?" A freckled-face boy hovered in the doorway, his two brothers hiding behind him.

Gavin smiled. A fire had been lit in the hearth to chase away the March evening chill and the bedchamber was quite cozy. "No, this is fine, boys, damned fine."

"If you need anything, my lord, just give us a holler." The freckled boy stared up at Gavin with rounded eyes of glorious envy. "Day or night, sir, I can get it."

Gavin went to the door and tousled his carrot-red hair. "I'm sure we'll be quite fine. Now tell me your name, boy, and then I'll have you be on your way."

"Rob, sir. My mam calls me Red Rob."

Gavin grinned. "Well, I'm partial to redheads, as you can tell." He indicated Ellen who, suddenly famished, was lifting the soup tureen lid to see what was inside. "So, you do a fair day's work for your mam while I'm here, and I'll see you rewarded."

The boy's ruddy face turned redder. "Yes, my lord. Thank you, my lord." He backed out of the room, pushing his brothers, still bobbing his head when Gavin shut the door and slid the bolt home.

"Nice boys," Gavin mused. "I'd like to have a son so well mannered."

"A son?" Ellen returned the soup lid to its original position. She couldn't resist the barest of a smile. They'd never spoken of children before. "You'd like a son?"

"Or a daughter." He came to her and wrapped his arms around her, bringing his lips only a hairsbreadth from hers. "A child of yours."

She looped her arms around his neck, the glow of the fire and her nearness to him warming her. "You never told me before that you wanted children."

"Never had a wife to want to have children with before."

Ellen laughed, brushing her lips against his in the stroke of a butterfly's wings. Here in this bedchamber with Gavin, she felt far from Havering House and Waldron. Here in Gavin's arms with Richard just down the hallway, she felt safe and loved. "But you don't have a wife," she teased.

"Now listen, woman," he said sternly. "Did you or did you not agree to marry me yesterday, there on the dock?"

She smiled up at him, enjoying the twinkle in his teasing green eyes. "I did."

He caught her hand in his and threaded their fingers together. "Then we're handfasted. In my eyes, you are my wife."

She laughed. "Many a man has told a lady such lies to wile her into his bed. No, sir, I'll have a man of the cloth speak the words just the same."

He kissed the soft hollow of her shoulder. "A man of the cloth it shall be, but in the meantime, why not a little wiling?"

Warm shivers of tingling delight were already enveloping her. It had been so long since they'd made love. So long since she'd felt his touch, his mouth on hers. Last night there had been a few stolen kisses, a little caressing in the darkness, but they had shared a bed of hay in a barn with Richard, so there had been no privacy to see them through their passions.

But now, now that they were alone, the flames of desire were burning high. Ellen needed a bath and she was hungry, so hungry that her stomach grumbled, but she was even hungrier for Gavin.

When their lips met, he kissed her hard, his tongue darting out to taste hers. "I've missed you, sweet Ellen. I've missed you so badly."

"I'm sorry," she whispered. "I just didn't know what to do. I didn't mean to make you miserable. I didn't mean to make myself so miserable. It's just that—"

"Shhh," he soothed as he tugged at the rear buttons of her gown, his mouth already finding the soft, warm flesh of her breasts. "We move forward now. The past is unimportant. What matters is us now . . . tomorrow . . . all the tomorrows we're going to have together."

His words warmed her as much as his touch. As their lips met again, she pressed her hips against him, wanting to feel the hard bulge of his loins against her. *I'm a wanton woman,* she thought as she reached down to stroke him through the tight cloth of his breeches. *But I don't care! I wasted the first twenty-odd years of my life, so what's left of it I'll enjoy to the fullest.*

Gavin groaned as her deft fingers found his

hardening manhood and stroked it. "Ellen, Ellen," he whispered. He had pulled the shoulders of her gown down and unlaced her busk so that he could catch a pert nipple between his lips.

Ellen moaned, leaning back to enjoy the flick of his tongue. "I'm going to fall," she whispered, laughing. "Let's go to the bed."

Without a moment's urging, Gavin swung her into his arms and carried her to the waiting bed. Seated on the edge, he began to yank off his boots. She rose behind him and pulled his sailor's shirt over his head, so that she could press her breasts to his bare back, teasing him and herself at the same time.

"Witch," he accused as he peeled off his breeches and stockings.

Ellen only laughed, her tongue flicking out to tease his earlobe. She could feel her nipples hardening as she stroked his back with her bare breasts.

When Gavin was completely undressed, he whirled around and wrestled her onto her back on the bed. She struggled, laughing, and then lay back on the pillows, trying to pull him on top of her. Tonight she felt no need for foreplay. She wanted him and she wanted him now.

"No clothing tonight," he told her as he tossed her silk stockings over his head. "I want to see you when I touch you. I want to see you when I taste you."

She threaded her fingers through his dark hair and pulled him down to her, kissing him long and hard until they were both breathless. Freeing her from the remainder of her clothing, Gavin stretched his body over hers, pressing her into the bedcovers. Ellen parted her legs, lifting her hips in an erotic taunt.

"Not yet," he whispered in her ear, caressing the curve of her breast. "I want you to take your time. It's

306

been so long that I want you to be sure and enjoy yourself."

"Next time we'll go slowly," she answered, her breathing ragged. She dragged her blunt nail lightly over his buttocks. "Right now I need to feel you inside me." She closed her eyes as she lifted against his hard shaft. "Please, Gavin?"

Unable to resist her pleas, Gavin lunged deep within her, smothering her moan of pleasure with his lips. This coupling was not to be one of slow, building pleasure, but rather a violent joining of bodies and hearts after too long a separation. Two long, hard strokes, and Ellen felt herself being lifted into the throes of fierce ecstasy. Unable to control her movements, she raised herself up and down to meet his thrusts, crying out his name, clawing at the hard, smooth muscles of his back.

"Gavin! Gavin!" she cried. And for a moment, she saw a flicker of Waldron's face.

"Ellen!" he called, as he, too, reached fulfillment.

But when she opened her eyes, breathless but satisfied, it was Gavin's sharp, handsome jaw she saw. It was his loving green eyes.

"Ellen," he whispered, his voice once again a gentle caress. "Ellen, I love you."

She parted her lips to receive his kiss, unwilling yet to move and release him. *Perhaps being in this house won't be so bad,* she thought, closing her eyes to catch her breath. *Perhaps with Gavin at my side here at Havering House, I can chase away the ghosts of my past forever.*

# Chapter Twenty-One

Ellen stood at the door to her old bedchamber in a wing on the third floor. Twice in the last week she had come here and stood in the hall, but both times she'd been unable to go inside. Today was the day she had decided she would do it. Julius would be back with the *Maid Marion* soon, and then she'd be off to the Colonies to begin yet another life. It was time this old one was settled.

She laid her hand on the doorknob and turned it. Before she lost her courage, she stepped inside. She took a deep breath, then exhaled with an odd sense of relief.

What had once been so familiar was now the unfamiliar. As Ellen stood staring at the pale green upholstered furniture, the green filmy draperies, and the dreary oak paneled walls, she felt like a stranger in her own bedchamber. And she was a stranger. This lady's room had belonged to Thomasina Waxton, a battered woman without hope, without strength. She was Ellen Scarlet, a woman who had taken control of her life and fought back against the men who had threatened it.

As she moved from an elaborate inlaid writing

desk to a lacquer cabinet, stroking the wood with the tip of her finger, she thought not of the past and its pain, but of the fact that she had been able to conquer it. Like the steel of a soldier's blade, she had been tempered by fire and had survived it all the stronger.

Coming to Havering House like this had actually been a blessing rather than a nightmare. Instead of being paralyzed by memories of the past, she found that as she moved from room to room, she felt a cleansing of her spirit. The drunk who had been the caretaker the previous year had been right. Ghosts did lurk here in the shadows of the dusty furniture and damp hallways, her ghosts, but they were fast fading.

As Ellen had moved from room to room in the last few days, stirring up the memories in her mind, the demons of her past had fled. As she explored the vacant rooms, the sounds of her father's harsh voice, of Hunt and Waldron's laughter, had gradually faded into nothingness. Now there seemed to be naught left in the home but a sad, all-consuming emptiness.

Ellen opened the ornately carved chest of drawers and fingered the stiff material of a somber mustard-colored gown. Thomasina's gown. It was odd, but she couldn't even remember it now. Where had it come from? When had she worn it?

She looked down at the smock and gown she had been wearing since she left London. *The practical thing to do would be to change into one of these,* she thought. But practicality be damned, she'd not so much as carry a handkerchief that had been Thomasina's! She closed the door with a smile, proud of herself, proud of the fact that she could make a decision and be content with it. There had been a time in the house when she hadn't been able to.

Moving to the writing desk, she pulled down the lid. This was where she had sat that ill-famed night and read the incriminating list of names with which she had thought to blackmail her husband. Paper and a dry inkwell still lay there. The letter, of course, was safe.

Curious, Ellen began to pull open the tiny drawers of the desk to see what was inside. Sadly, there was almost nothing. . . . No old letters; she had never known anyone to write to, and even if she had, Waldron would never have permitted correspondence. No keepsakes. There was nothing from that time in her life worth keeping. The only things she found, other than dust, were a few copies of leather-bound books never returned to the library. She began to stack them in her arms, to return to where they belonged downstairs.

"Ellen?"

She turned around, startled by Gavin's voice in the hallway.

"I'm in here." She smiled as he came through the door. These last days together had been nearly perfect. Ellen and Gavin had time to talk, to play games, to sit on the floor side by side before the fireplace and talk of their future together. The more Ellen heard about the plantation in the Maryland Colony and the kind of life she would lead there, the more she knew she had made the right decision. The only thing that had marred the gaiety of the last couple of days, as she and Gavin talked of their plans, their hopes, their dreams, was Richard's illness.

"What are you doing up here?" Gavin was dressed in a pair of Waldron's plain broadcloth breeches and a white linen shirt and lacy cravat. The first time Ellen had seen him in Waldron's clothing it had been a little startling, but now it didn't bother her. This

311

was Gavin, the man she loved, not Waldron, the man she detested. Besides, though Gavin sported a gentleman's clothing, he still wore his colonial boots and his hair pulled back in a savage's braid. Waldron would not have been caught laid out dead in such a breach of fashion.

Ellen closed the writing desk, her father's dusty volumes still cradled in her arms. "I . . ." She shrugged. "Just looking around."

"There's some women's clothing in here." He went to the chest of drawers and pulled open a drawer. "I don't know how you'd feel about wearing something belonging to my brother's wife, but—"

She wrinkled her nose. "Not my taste." She smoothed her own creased smock. "Mrs. Spate said she'd wash out anything I wished. I'd really rather wear my own things."

He closed the drawer. "Whatever you wish, love. I took the liberty of having Julius pick up some good sturdy clothing for the Colonies for you, in the hopes you'd be coming with me, so once we board the ship, there'll be clean things for you. Still, I want you to know you're welcome to anything in this house. We'll have to travel light to the *Maid Marion*, but if you see anything you want, stack it downstairs in the library with the books I've set aside on the floor. I thought I'd have some things shipped. The rest will be sold on the auction block."

Her father's home, the home of the Greenboroughs for hundreds of years, to be sold . . . She didn't even care. "I don't need anything, just you." She brushed his sleeve with her fingertips.

Gavin looked at her, then looked away. "Ellen . . ." He had a strained tone to his voice.

Her gaze followed him. "It's Richard."

He nodded.

"But I thought he was better. He's seemed stronger." She squeezed his arm. "You've done such a good job of keeping him in bed."

"That I have, but I owe him a king's ransom in gambling debt."

She smiled. "So what is it you wanted to tell me about Richard?"

"He may actually be better—it's hard to tell—but he's still in a lot of pain. There's nothing here to ease it. He's going to have to ride back into London to board the *Maid Marion* when she comes for us. Even if I can manage to get a coach, the journey's going to be hard on him."

"We need medicine."

"Yes."

"But I thought you said that if we sent for a London surgeon, we'd run the risk of having Hunt find out someone's here." She shook her head. "I don't think we can go against Richard's wishes. He trusts you. Besides, he'd not go against yours."

"No." He walked to the window and lifted a bit of drapery to peer out at the overgrown garden below. "I know we can't send for a decent surgeon. I don't know that one would make a difference; I was never one for bleeding, anyway." He let the filmy green draperies fall and turned back to her. "What I did think we could do was send for the barber down in the village. Surely he would have some powders to ease Richard's pain on the journey. Once we reach the ship, I have medicines there. Some decent concoctions brought back from the Indians in Maryland."

Ellen hugged the books she still held to her chest. "If you paid the barber well, I imagine he'd keep quiet. Mrs. Spate obviously has."

"I'm sending her oldest boy today into London to

313

watch for the ship and Julius. I don't think we'll be here much longer, so we'd better do something."

Ellen thought for a moment, then nodded. "I think you're right. Let's send for the barber."

That subject suitably settled, Gavin went to the door, then turned back to Ellen. "This was her room, you know." He spoke softly.

"Her room?" Ellen hoped he couldn't hear the tremor in her voice.

"Yes."

Ellen looked around the room, trying to see it from Gavin's point of view. "How do you feel about it?" She knew she might well be asking for trouble, but she couldn't help herself. She had to know. "About her, I mean?"

He leaned on the door frame, taking his time in answering. "I don't feel anything. I thought I hated her once. I certainly wanted revenge, but now that I'm here again, I just don't feel anything. So much has happened in the last six months that Lady Thomasina Waxton seems unimportant."

"You don't want to keep looking for her?"

He crossed his arms over his chest thoughtfully. "Why should I? Seeing her hang won't bring Waldron back. She'll sure enough get her reward in the fires of hell, won't she? So why should I worry about it?"

"You sound as if you've nearly forgiven her," Ellen suggested.

"I think I have. Hate's a heavy burden to carry, sweet, too heavy for me. What's passed has passed for both of us." He grinned a boyish grin. "Our future is in the Colonies. I just hope you love it there as I do."

She came to the door. "I'm sure I will."

He traced her chin with the tip of his finger. "I think perhaps you're right. You strike me as a

314

woman who likes an adventure, and the Colonies are just that. Nothing is predictable there. The possibilities change with each sunrise. I think that's what I like best about it. England has just grown too stagnant for me.''

Ellen looped her arm through his and led him out the door, pulling it closed behind her. "Let's go see about that barber, and then I'll play some laterloo with you."

They walked down the dark hallway arm in arm. "Chambray's already broken me. I can't afford to lose another pound to you two cheating flints, or there'll be no money for planting next year!"

"So we won't play for coin," she said, looking up at him, a playful grin on her lips.

"Oh, we won't play for coin, will we? Then what did you have in mind, my lady?"

She released his arm and hurried down the staircase in front of him. "Sexual favors?" she called over her shoulder.

His laughter still filled the stairwell when she reached the first floor.

"What do you mean, there's no sign of them anywhere?" Hunt bellowed, turning away from the glass windows that ran along the wall of his gallery. It was raining outside, the patter of the drops making a steady sound on the rippled panes.

Robards scuffed his foot on the beaded rug in the doorway. "I mean that after they made that miraculous escape on that barge on the Thames, we weren't able to locate them."

"Nor were you able to identify the man they traveled with?"

"No, Your Grace. The men didn't recognize him.

All they know is that he had dark hair and that he was riding your horse."

"My horse . . ." Hunt echoed through clenched teeth. "My prized stallion, the whoreson!"

"But . . . but we've not giving up looking." Robards tried to sound confident. "My guess is that they escaped into Kent. I have men everywhere questioning farmers and yeomen, innkeepers and such. I . . . I'm certain we're going to find them."

Hunt clenched his fists, his jaw tightening until the stitches on his cheek stung. "Damned if you won't, Robards, or I'll have your balls! There'll be no dallying with my kitchen help then, will there?"

"N . . . no, Your Grace."

The duke turned to the portrait of the three-breasted woman he had brought back from Italy. Sure enough, Buckingham had been green with jealousy when he'd seen it. He'd offered an outrageous sum of money for it, but Hunt had refused to give it up. He figured the portrait might come of some use in the future. Sometimes articles make better bribes than all the gold in the king's coffer.

Hunt waved his hand absently, not bothering to turn around to look at Robards. "All right. You're dismissed, but I'm warning you: With every day that passes, Chambray and the slut are slipping from my grasp. I told you that it's imperative I have her and her belongings, so see to it, Robards."

The middle-aged secretary mopped his damp forehead with a lace handkerchief, obviously relieved his interview was over. "Yes, Your Grace." The door closed quietly behind him.

Left alone in his gallery, Hunt walked its length, enjoying his artworks. This whole thing with Thomasina was beginning to rub his nerves raw. For the hundredth time, he wished he had actually seen

Waldron's letter so he would know who was on it rather than having to guess.

Yesterday he'd been contacted by a representative of one of the men whose name was apparently in the letter. The representative refused to give his employer's name, but the message was clear. The man who had sent the messenger was a person of great importance. Somehow word had leaked out that Waxton's letter still existed. Of course, Hunt didn't know where the leak had come from. Nearly half of the men on that list were now dead, either of natural causes or with a little help from one of Hunt's henchmen. Still, this particular person was extremely unhappy and urged Hunt to make quick work of the letter, Thomasina, and anyone else involved, before he had to take care of the matter himself and Hunt in the process.

Whoever this mysterious man was, Hunt gathered that he was closer to the king than he himself was, and that his words were not idle threats.

Hunt ran his finger absently over the silk stitches in his cheek as he turned back toward the windows to watch the rain falling from the sky in angled sheets. Chambray would pay and pay dearly for the injury he had caused him, as would the courtesan. Hunt smiled, admiring his own reflection in the window. Waldron's little slut of a virgin wife had become quite an obsession with him, and now finally after all these years he would have her. A pity she would have to die, but at least he would get some pleasure out of her first.

"Your Grace! Your Grace!" Robards came bursting through the gallery door, breathless, dragging Hunt from his pleasant thoughts.

"What is it?" he asked his secretary irritably. "I thought I had dismissed you."

"Wonderful news, Your Grace. Simply wonderful!"

Hunt ran a hand through his shock of white hair. "Yes, Robards?"

The middle-aged man nearly leaped off the polished hardwood floor. "I think I've located them, Your Grace. Yes, I believe I have!"

The duke's attention was immediately captured. He came away from the windows and started for Robards, his stride long and confident. "Where?"

The secretary held up his finger. "If you don't mind, Your Grace, I'll have the woman tell you herself. She's quite convincing."

"The woman?"

"Mrs. Bockgard, from Essex. Her husband is the barber in a little village in the country somewhere."

"And she's seen Thomasina and Chambray?"

"Not her, but her husband. As I said, he's the barber in the village." Robards clasped his hands excitedly. "It seems you may have well mortally injured the gentleman when you parried with him."

Hunt threw up a hand impatiently. "Well, don't just stand there like a dullard, Robards! Bring her in, bring her in!"

Robards ran through the doorway and came back a moment later, leading a petite woman dressed in common homespun garb with a scarf tied tightly about her pinched face. "His Lord Grace, the Duke of Hunt," Robards announced with a formal sweep of his hand.

The woman had sense enough to dip into a low curtsy. "Your Grace, sir." When she lifted her head, she gawked at the albino duke with fascination, too ignorant to know how impolite it was to stare.

"Your Grace, Mrs. Bockgard, barber's wife of Havering Village."

Hunt's pale brow creased with curiosity. "Havering, you say?"

"Yes, yes, Your Grace. Come all the way from Havering in Essex, alone I did."

Hunt walked to one of the gilt chairs that lined a wall of the gallery. He dropped into the seat, leaning back with lazy interest. "Please do come sit down, Mrs. Bockgard." He indicated a stool. He didn't normally allow commoners to sit in his presence, but he wanted to gain this woman's confidence. He wanted her to like him, or at least to be in awe of him. "Robards, Mrs. Bockgard and I will have refreshment." He flashed her a gentleman's smile that made her giggle into her woolen handkerchief. "Some white Rhenish for the lady. You know what I like. And something sweet. Pastries will suit, won't they, Mrs. Bockgard?"

"Yes, yes, Your Grace," she echoed, apparently not certain what pastries were. *"Pasties* would be good this time of day, wouldn't they?"

Hunt waited until Robards had taken his leave and then he reached out to take Mrs. Bockgard's hand in his. It was a clean hand, at least, though rough from years of work and harsh lye soaps. "My secretary informs me that you may have some information on my wife."

"Don't know if she be your wife, Your Grace." Her hand trembled in Hunt's. "All I know is that my husband was called to Havering House to see a patient."

"Havering House," he whispered to himself in amazement. *The little bold bitch had run to Havering House! He'd never have guessed it!* He looked back at the village woman. "Yes, go on."

"See, the house's been empty 'cept for a housekeeper since the earl burned up and his wife threw

319

him out of the tower. Only all of a sudden my Bobby, he's bein' called with his potion bag to the big house all secret like." She tapped her temple. "Well, I get to thinkin'. Who's up there that needs carin' for? Then Bobby comes back with a handful of coin and *he's* all secret like. Finally, he tells me there's a redheaded lady, the new Earl of Waxton, and a gentleman that's been run through with a sword up there at the big house."

"Gavin Waxton, I'll be vexed! Why didn't I figure out it was he who helped them escape?" Hunt murmured.

Robards came in with a tray, serving first Hunt and then the woman. He set the tray of freshly baked fruit pastries on a small table between them and made a hasty exit.

"Now tell me," Hunt said, sipping his wine, "how did you know I was looking for the gentleman and the lady?"

She took a gulp of the white Rhenish, wrinkled her nose, then took another gulp. "I got a cousin across the river in Kent who was tellin' me the beginnin' of last week how some duke's men come through lookin' for two gentlemen and a red-haired lady on the run. My cousin, she said there was a hefty reward." She raised a hand, pleased with herself. "I knew there couldn't be more than one bunch like that, so I come all the way here as quick as I could." She leaned forward, fingering several pastries before she chose one. "Just how much is this reward, anyways?"

"More than sufficient." Hunt leaned closer. "If this is true, tell me why you came and not your husband?"

She took a big bite of a cherry tart and chewed loudly with her mouth open. "Oh, you don't know my Bobby. The gentleman that was well paid Bobby not to tell anyone. Bobby's such a fool he'd go to his grave not tellin'." Cramming the remainder of the tart into her mouth, she wiped her fingers on the bodice of her gown. "But me, I know a stroke of luck when I sees one."

"So where does your husband think you are if he doesn't know you've come to London to seek me?"

She reached for another pastry. "Oh, the old bog! He thinks I crossed the river to go to my cousin's lyin'-in. He won't be lookin' for me for another week." She grinned, obviously pleased with herself, oblivious to the crumbs of flaky pastry that clung to the corners of her mouth.

"I see." Hunt set down his glass, deep in thought. When he looked up at Mrs. Bockgard, she was on her third pastry. He stood. "Well, I must thank you for your help. You see, these men took my wife against her will."

The woman got up, frowning. "Funny, Bobby didn't say nothin' about that. Said the three of them was pretty friendly."

"I would guess they are," Hunt murmured.

Not catching what he said, she leaned forward. "Your Grace?"

He smiled handsomely. "Nothing, Mrs. Bockgard." He laid his hand on her shoulder and guided her toward the door. "I want to thank you for all your help. It is greatly appreciated. I can't tell you what it will mean to have my wife back in my loving arms again."

"Glad I could be of some help to you, Your Grace." She stopped. "What about my re-ward?"

"My secretary will see to it. Just follow along the hall and wait in the blue antechamber. He'll be but a moment."

"Good day to you, Your Grace." She curtsied clumsily in the doorway. "And thank you for the pasties. Best I ever et!"

The duke gave a little wave, then bellowed, "Robards!"

The secretary bounded in. "Your Grace?"

Hunt lowered his voice. "Dispose of the woman. I want no one to know she's been here."

Robards screwed up his lips but nodded his assent. "It's her, isn't it? It's Thomasina at Havering House."

The duke looked down at his secretary. "It is, indeed, and she's there with the Earl of Waxton, it seems."

"So I get rid of the old woman. Then what?"

"We prepare the men to ride. I want them armed heavily. I'll not have her get away this time."

"How many men?"

"At least a dozen." The duke smiled, walking back toward the gallery windows. "We're going to take a little ride out into the Essex countryside, Robards." He smiled at his own stark reflection in the glass. "And bring ourselves home a prize . . ."

# Chapter Twenty-Two

"It would simply be more sensible if you left me behind," Richard said, sipping one of Mrs. Spate's hot brews from a china cup.

Ellen sat on a stool beside Richard's bed. Gavin stood leaning on the fireplace mantel across the room. She glanced significantly at Gavin, then back at Richard. "That wasn't the agreement. The agreement was that you would travel to the Colonies with us." She placed her hand on his pillow and smoothed the embroidery. A lifetime ago she had sewn those pale blue pansies on the hem of the pillowcasing. "You promised me, Richard."

"I know what I promised, but it just doesn't make sense. Not now." He sighed. "Tell her, Gavin. Tell her this wound is going to kill me."

She frowned. "It isn't! Don't say that, either of you. You're better today. The bleeding's nearly stopped. You feel stronger. You said so yourself."

"Today, yes." He handed her his cup. "But by tomorrow it may be far worse. Ellen, I can barely draw enough breath to get out of bed to relieve myself. I'm not going to be able to make a journey back into London and then across the Mary

323

blessed Atlantic!"

She set down the china teacup on the mahogany table with a loud bang. Tears stung behind her eyelids, but she refused to cry. "Gavin, please talk some sense into him. Those powders you gave him have made him light in the head."

Gavin came away from the fireplace to stand beside Ellen. He rested a comforting hand on her shoulder. "You get on a horse with us at sunset, Chambray, and you head for the ship with us, or none of us go."

Ellen nodded. "We won't go without you, Richard. Just as you wouldn't go without us."

Richard glanced up, his blue eyes riveted on Gavin's green ones. He gave a laugh, but he wasn't amused. "Surely you jest?"

"I should think you know me better than that. Ellen's right. We made an agreement. You'll go with us . . . or die trying."

Richard swore a foul French oath beneath his breath. "I don't know which of the two of you is more of a lackwit! Even if Ellen refuses to believe it, surely you, Gavin, know the chances of me surviving this wound!"

"Your chances aren't good. But what are your chances if you stay here? Eventually word will leak out. Eventually Hunt will find you, and then what? Hell, Chambray, what have you got to lose? If you're going to die, why not among friends with the taste of brandy on your lips, instead of alone in some stinking dungeon?"

Richard looked away. He was tired, too damned tired to fight with the two of them like this. In the last few days he had come to truly appreciate Gavin and the friendship the man had offered, not out of pity, but because he genuinely enjoyed Richard's company. Now that neither man felt he was in competi-

324

tion with the other for Ellen, they had found how much they had in common, how much they enjoyed each other's male companionship.

"All right," Richard finally conceded, lying back on his pillows. "All right, I'll go. I'll do whatever the two of you want. Just leave me the hell alone so I can get some sleep. Dragging a dying man across the ocean, damnedest thing I ever heard of . . ." His words were harsh, but his tone was one of tenderness. Richard knew Gavin was right; he just didn't want to be a burden to him.

There was nothing here for Richard in England any longer, no place to go where he'd be safe. He had no living relatives other than his mother, and she had remarried during the winter and seemed perfectly content with her new baron, who doted on her. If Richard did make a miraculous recovery, he could think of no better way to live out his life than in the company of Ellen and Gavin.

"We leave when the sun sets," Gavin said. "We'll travel through the night, take refuge during the day so as to avoid soldiers, and then ride the next night. With a little luck, we'll make Londontown before dawn. Mrs. Spate's son said Julius would be ready to sail the moment he spotted us on the dock."

"Good enough." Richard closed his eyes.

Ellen pulled the coverlet up over him and leaned over to kiss his cheek. "I love you, Richard," she whispered. "I always will."

He patted her hand. "Get yourself ready to go, Ellen. Just come wake me in an hour."

Ellen met Gavin at the door and the two slipped out into the hallway together. He caught her hand in his and squeezed it reassuringly. "It's going to be all right, sweet."

She smiled up at Gavin. "It really is, isn't it?"

"I promise." He kissed her lips as if to seal a pact. "Now I have some last minute business to attend to with Mrs. Spate. I want to be certain everything is in order for the sale of the house and goods. Why don't you go lie down and rest in our chamber. It's going to be a long night of hard riding. We may not be able to stick to the main road."

She smiled, watching him as he released her and started down the hallway. It was difficult for her to believe her fortune. After all those years of unhappiness, who would have thought her life would have taken such a turn for the good?

Still smiling, Ellen walked down the hall to the bedchamber she and Gavin shared. She packed her few belongings, including her hairbrush and mirror, in her bag and added two books from the library. For safekeeping, she also pinned her mother's crucifix inside the bag. She treasured the icon, not so much for its religious aspect as for the fact that it was all she now had left of her mother and of her mother's child, Thomasina. Ellen had broken the chain the other day and had been unable to fix it. Once she arrived in the Colonies, she'd have Gavin find her another. Her packing complete, she set the bag and her cloak by the door.

Then, instead of lying down as Gavin had suggested, she picked up several books she'd left on a table near the fireplace and headed for the library to return them. Her father had always insisted his precious books be kept in their proper places. Once when she was ten, he had taken her library privileges away from her for six months for carelessly leaving a book on the floor. As she held her father's books in her hand, books that would be sold at auction, it seemed a fitting farewell to Havering House to take care of this last detail.

Downstairs the house was quiet, save for the tick of a tall case clock in the front hall. Ellen entered the library, her slippers clicking on the cold slate floor. As she walked to an appropriate shelf on the far wall and tucked a book into its place, she looked up at the faded fresco paintings on the dome ceiling.

She had always both loved and feared this room, even as a small child. This was the room where once she had learned to read; she'd found solace in the dusty pages of other's words, in other's lives. But here had also been the place where her father and later her husband had often dealt their blows, either physical or emotional.

She stared at the dark paneled walls, taking in the scent of fresh wood polish left behind by Mrs. Spate's dust rag, which mingled with the pungent odor of mildewed draperies. She stared at the massive desk that had been her grandfather's. Her mind flickered back to the day her father had called her into his library to tell her he'd married her off to Waxton. She had been only thirteen, not yet even a woman.

She felt a lump of sadness rise in her throat, not so much for the thirteen-year-old child as for the broken man who had been driven to such drastic measures by inadequate insight and bad politics. For all these years she had hated her father for what he'd done to her, but now, standing here in his library, she felt only pity. He had been a weak man. He had been a poor decision maker. He had done what he thought was right, no matter how wrong it had honestly been.

"There you are."

Startled, Ellen turned around, wiping her damp eyes with the sleeve of her gown.

"I thought you were resting upstairs." Gavin dropped his hand on her hip. "It's almost time to go. The horses are being saddled." His brow creased as he gazed into her dark eyes. "Are you all right?"

She smiled, lifting her arms to hug him tightly. "I'm fine."

He held her at arm's length. "You're certain? You've been acting a little odd since we got here. I'm beginning to think it's me. Tell me you haven't changed your mind, because if you have, I'll be forced to throw myself from my brother's tower window—"

She pressed her finger to his lips. "That's not amusing." Her voice trembled. She touched his smooth-shaven cheek. "It's nearly dark," she said, feeling a sudden sense of urgency. "Let's get Richard and go. I want to get aboard the ship. I want to go far from here . . . with you, Gavin Waxton. I want to leave England and never look back."

Holding her in his arms, he brushed back heavy locks of bright red hair off her shoulder. "What's suddenly brought this all on? You seemed content enough to wait yesterday."

She laid her head on his shoulder. "I don't know," she answered, thinking it was only a half-lie. "Just impatience. I'm ready to begin our new life together."

He tipped up her chin and brushed his lips against hers. "No more ready than I am. I ache to see my soil again, to smell the green of the forest, to hear the voices of my friends again. I—"

"My lord! My lord Waxton!" Mrs. Spate's eldest son, Rob, came racing around the corner, sliding on the slate floor as he came to an abrupt halt. "Men, sir! Comin' up the road! I seen 'em from the hayloft of the barn!"

Ellen froze.

"Men? Speak sense, boy. What men?"

"Don't know, sir. But it don't look good. Men in uniforms with swords coming up the hill on the main road from the village."

"Hunt," Ellen whispered.

Gavin swore but didn't hesitate a moment before moving into action. "Rob, I want you to bring the horses around to the kitchen door, but don't tie them there where they can be seen." He thought for a moment. "The woodshed lean-to. Put them there. You have got the horses saddled, haven't you?"

"Yes, sir. Done just like you tole me."

"Good boy!" He patted him on the buttocks. "Now see to the horses, then get your mam and your brothers, and you run for the village and you hide there, you understand me?"

The red-haired boy stared for a minute, stunned into silence. "They've come after you, haven't they, my lord? They're bad men, aren't they?"

"Go!" Gavin shouted.

The child, frightened by Gavin's shout, spun on his heels and raced out of the library.

Gavin grabbed Ellen's elbow and led her out of the room. "Go upstairs and tell Richard to get himself out of bed. I want the two of you to meet me in the kitchen, ready to go."

"Where are you going?"

"To get my weapons, then up to the tower to see what we're up against." He started down the hall at a run, and Ellen picked up her skirts to run with him. They sprinted up the steps side by side, then parted as Ellen ducked into Richard's room and Gavin went for his sword.

Panting, as much from fear as from loss of breath, Ellen burst through Richard's doorway. He was already up and dressed, seated on the edge of the bed with a brandy in his hand. "What the hell is going on?"

She ran to a side table to get his sword belt and

329

pistol. "Horsemen are approaching. Rob saw them."

Richard leaped up, appearing suddenly unhampered by his chest wound. He strapped on his sword belt as he questioned her. "Hunt?"

"The boy didn't know. Gavin went up to the tower to see. But who else could it be, Richard?" She handed him his sword, his cloak draped over her arm. "We're to meet Gavin in the kitchen. He has horses ready for us. Mayhap we can just slip out undetected."

"Maybe," Richard echoed, but he didn't sound convinced. He looked up at Ellen. "Are you ready? Where's your cloak? Your bag? I take it you still have the letter."

"I just have to go the room and get my things. I'll meet you in the kitchen."

"No, wait. I'll go with you!"

She threw a hand over her head as she ran out the bedchamber door, ignoring his plea. "I'll see you in the kitchen!"

Ellen raced down the hall and darted into her room. She slung her green woolen cloak over her shoulders and grabbed her small carpetbag. On the bed lay Gavin's cloak and feathered cavalier's hat, forgotten in his rush. She picked them up and raced for the door. There was nothing more they needed.

In the hallway she ran for the landing, but instead of going down the steps to the first floor, she dropped her belongings and headed for the tower steps. She had to see for herself if it was Hunt. She had to see with her own eyes.

A flood of sickening memories invaded her thoughts as she hurried up the crumbling stone steps leading into the tower that had once been Waldron's laboratory. Ellen kept her back against the wall. She didn't need to see in the darkness to know that on the

330

other side of the steps lay no railing, only blackness.

Reaching the top landing, she ran through the charred doorway into Waldron's laboratory. The room was scarred black from the fire of more than two years past, and it stank of burnt chemicals and scorched stone walls.

"Ellen?" Gavin spun around from the boarded window where Waldron had fallen to his death. "What the bloody hell are you doing up here? I told you to get Richard and meet me in the kitchen!"

"Richard's on his way." She came up beside him, her fingers brushing against a strip of burnt drapery as she craned her neck to see through a break in the boards. "I had to see for myself."

Gavin grabbed her arm as she caught sight of more than a dozen soldiers riding up the long drive toward Havering House. The Duke of Hunt took the lead. There was no mistaking him. Even from here, Ellen could see the inhuman hue of his skin. She could feel his pink eyes boring into her as he looked at the burned-out tower.

"I don't know how he found us." He pulled her away from the window. "It doesn't matter now, though. What matters is escaping." He stepped over a broken stool colored black from the fire. "If we hurry, maybe we can make it out of here without him ever seeing us!"

Ellen allowed Gavin to lead her down the winding staircase, as she held up her skirting with one hand, keeping a hold on his sturdy arm with the other. "Where's Mrs. Spate and the children?"

"Safe. I told young Rob to take his mother and brothers and run to the village. Hunt won't bother with them. He'll be too busy looking for us."

"For Richard and me, you mean."

He hurried her along. "I mean for *us*. You don't

think he can be too pleased with me, do you? I helped you get out of London."

They reached the staircase landing, and Gavin grabbed his cloak and hat and her bag. "Let's go!"

They took the steps by two, running side by side. Ellen felt a sudden streak of terror as she remembered that night she had fled Havering House, the night she had killed Waldron.

Down two hallways, they burst into the kitchen. Mrs. Spate and her children were gone. Richard was nowhere to be seen.

"Christ! Where is he?" Gavin spun around in fury. "I thought you said he was going to meet us here!"

"He was! He should be here!"

Gavin thought for a moment, then pushed her bag into her hands. "I want you to go out into the woodshed, get astride one of those horses, and head for London. We'll catch up."

"No!" Ellen shook her head, suddenly terrified. She remembered fleeing Havering House that night alone. "Not without you and Richard! I won't do it!"

Gavin had already started out of the kitchen. "Now, Ellen," he shouted angrily. "Get on the blessed horse now!"

Ellen watched him disappear around the corner. She glanced at the outside door that still led to freedom from Hunt, then back at the empty doorway Gavin had gone through. She could hear Gavin hollering now, calling for Richard. . . .

"Chambray! Chambray, where the hell are you?" Gavin ran down the hall, through the front entranceway. "Chambray!"

"Up here!"

Gavin grabbed the stair railing and spun around, racing up the steps. "Where? What the hell are you doing? Do you need help?"

Halfway down the hall, he met Richard.

"I forgot this." Richard lifted a miniature portrait of Ellen, then slipped it into his shirtwaist. "I couldn't leave it behind."

"Jesus Christ, Chambray—"

At that moment, the sound of splitting wood broke the still air.

"Where's Ellen?" Richard ran beside Gavin, headed for the front staircase. Hunt and his men had reached the house.

"I left her in the kitchen. She's supposed to be on a damn horse!"

Gavin and Richard made it halfway down the steps, before the first of Hunt's soldiers squeezed through a hole he'd made in the front door. "Halt! You're under arrest, Baron Chambray," the man shouted, getting up off his knees as he lifted a sword. "Surrender and come peaceably."

"Bloody hell!" Richard cried, drawing his own blade. "Step back and let us pass, or die, man!"

Side by side, Gavin and Richard came down the steps with their swords poised. Another soldier burst through the hole in the door.

"You take the short one," Gavin ordered. "I'll take the ugly one."

Richard leaped into action, bounding off the bottom step to meet sword against sword with the king's soldier. "Cheat!" he hollered to Gavin above the sound of clanking metal. "You know I like the ugly ones!"

Though Gavin had little use for a sword in the Colonies, his parrying abilities came back to him remarkably well. His blade felt well weighted, even comfortable in his hand. He moved his feet with the instinctive grace his boyhood instructor had taught him must be the grace of a dancer.

Gavin backed his opponent into the wall, dodged left, and sunk his blade into the man's side. The king's soldier fell back against the wall, dropping his sword to clutch his wound.

"Need a little help, Chambray?" Gavin called.

The moment the words slipped from his mouth, another soldier came through the hole in the front door. Gavin's sword had just met his, when he heard Ellen's scream from behind him. He threw a glance over his shoulder to see her struggling in the arms of a dark-haired soldier.

"Release her!" Gavin shouted, still keeping his opponent at bay with the tip of his sword. "Free the woman or you'll rue the day your mother whelped you!"

Ellen screamed and kicked as the man dragged her through the doorway into the front hall. "Let me go! Let me go!" she screamed. "You tell Hunt I want to see him! I want him to come get me himself!"

Swearing beneath his breath, Gavin sliced hard again and again, taking down his second man at the same moment Richard felled his.

"Three down," Richard called, panting heavily as he clutched his chest. "I'll watch the door, you see to Ellen!"

Gavin spun around, measuring the distance between him and Ellen's captor, trying to figure out the best way to kill him without risking injury to her.

Ellen still fought, pummeling the soldier's face with her fists and kicking wildly. She fought so fiercely that it was all the man could do to keep himself upright.

"Let her go and I'll not kill you," Gavin offered.

"I let her go and the duke kills me." The soldier shrugged his massive shoulders. "What's the difference?"

Gavin swung his sword, managing to catch the soldier's arm and draw blood.

Furiously indignant, the soldier flung Ellen into the corner by the staircase and lifted his sword. "Now it is you that must die, my lord!"

Ellen gave a grunt of pain as her head hit the wall, but Gavin forced himself to focus his attention on his opponent. As their swords met for the first time, he realized this man was good, very good, much better than the others. His only weakness seemed to be his anger. Holding tight to that thought, Gavin forced himself to remain calm, parry after parry. He pushed from his mind his thoughts of the life-threatening situation he was in. He pushed away his thoughts of protecting Ellen. All that mattered now was sword against sword, as steel met steel again and again.

"What's taking so long?" Gavin heard from outside the broken door. Hunt's voice.

Behind him, Gavin heard another soldier come through the door, then the sound of Richard's sword swish through the air.

As Gavin fought his opponent, he slowly turned, trying to make his way closer to Ellen, who was trapped in the corner by the fighting men. He took his eye off his opponent for only an instant, but it was long enough to obtain a sharp sting in the arm as the tip of the man's sword sliced through the cloth of Gavin's shirt and cut his arm.

Ellen gave a muffled cry, but had sense enough to know not to distract the man she loved if she wanted him to live.

"Bring her out or I'll have all your heads!" Hunt shouted from outside as he pounded his fist on the front door.

Out of fear of his master, Gavin's opponent flinched. Gavin took advantage of the moment and

335

went down on one knee with a long, graceful repartee. The man groaned as Gavin's sword sliced through his chest, moaning loudly as the blade was withdrawn. He stood for only a second, his sword hand shaking, his other hand clamped over his breast, before he fell to his knees and pitched forward on the black and white marble floor.

"Gavin!" Ellen ran into his arms. "Thank God you're all right."

He pulled her to him in a fierce hug. "I told you to go!" he shouted, furious at her for disobeying but relieved to have her safe in his arms.

Another soldier slipped through the front door and Gavin whirled around. "Need some help, Chambray?"

Richard threw back his head in laughter, his feet barely touching the floor now made slippery with the blood of the dead men. As Gavin watched, he realized Richard parried as well as any gentleman he had ever known.

"By the king's cod, no, I don't need your pitiful help!" Richard flung. "Get her out of here! I'll meet you on the road."

"Chambray—"

"*Do as I say, Waxton. We're running short of time.*"

Gavin glanced at Richard, taking note that his chest was stained with deep red blood again. His lung wound . . . Gavin looked back at Ellen, understanding what Richard meant. His injury was mortal and he was fading fast, despite the devil-may-care tone in his voice.

Gavin could hear Hunt bellowing outside as he instructed his men to get something to break down the remainder of the door, so the soldiers didn't have to climb through the hole one at a time. Gavin knew

336

that in a moment's time too many men would burst through the door for two men and a woman to face.

"No!" Ellen screamed. "We'll not leave Richard behind! We go together or not at all!" She reached out toward Richard, but Gavin grabbed her by the waist and lifted her off her feet. "He's right. I want you on a horse before Hunt gets in here."

"No!" Ellen screamed. "We can't leave Richard! Richard!"

"Gavin!" Richard's voice was stark and strangled, his meaning clear. Run, friend. Take her to safety while you still have the chance.

Gavin carried Ellen through the door and into the kitchen. At the kitchen, he set her on her feet and shook her. "Listen to me! You've never been a hysterical wench before. Don't start now. Are you listening?"

Tears ran down her face. She nodded.

He grabbed her by her arm, snatched up her bag still sitting in the doorway, and led her outside. "Richard will catch up with us. We have to get you out of here. It's obvious it's you Hunt wants."

"But Richard—"

"Richard's dying." This wasn't the time for tact. Only action would save them now. He led her around to the woodshed, where the three saddled horses waited. "Richard's dying, and our only chance to get out of here is to go now while he holds them off."

"No. Don't say that!" She clutched her bag.

He yanked her bag from her hand, stuffed it into a saddlebag, then lifted her onto the nearest horse. "A man who's going to die anyway would just as soon die in a sword fight defending the woman he loves, Ellen."

She gripped the reins Gavin pushed into her hands. "We can't just leave him for Hunt! We can't!"

Gavin looked back toward the house as he led her horse and his own out of the woodshed. His mind was spinning. He knew that what he was doing made sense. Chambray wasn't going to survive the wound, not after it had reopened. Perhaps he'd even been hit again in the same place. It made sense for Richard to sacrifice himself for the lives of Gavin and Ellen. Were Gavin in the same position, he'd do no less.

Still, Richard was a friend.

Gavin turned Ellen's horse toward the road. "We're going to have to ride like hell out and around the village through the woods, away from the main road so we can lose them. Do you understand?"

Tears still ran down her pale cheeks, but she nodded. She understood.

Gavin glanced once more at the house, where the sound of parrying swords still rang out. Then he slapped Ellen's horse hard on the haunch and the animal bolted.

Ellen screamed. "Gavin!"

"Just go on!" he shouted after her, already turning back for the house. "Ride! We'll catch up! I swear it, Ellen!"

# Chapter Twenty-Three

Gavin knew this didn't make any sense. He should be on Hunt's white horse riding away from Havering House. Richard was dying; there was nothing he could do for him. Gavin knew his responsibility lay with the woman he loved, the woman he had promised Richard he would protect.

But some acts went against reason.

Gavin raced through the kitchen door, drawing his sword from his belt. Sometimes logic didn't figure into decisions like it should. His head told him to let Richard go, but his heart told him no man, mortally wounded or not, should die among enemies when he could die among friends.

"Christ's bones! What are you doing back again?" Richard demanded as Gavin came around the corner from the kitchen.

The duke's men had backed Richard down the hallway. His face was ashen from loss of blood, his entire chest stained crimson. He was staggering, his sword seeming too heavy for his hand. But somehow he had managed to fight off two king's soldiers this long.

Gavin leaped in front of Richard, startling one of

the soldiers and taking him down with a single well-aimed thrust.

The other soldier swore as he tripped on his companion's body.

"I suppose I enjoyed the parrying so much that I thought I'd come back for more. There aren't a great many gentlemen's sword fights in Maryland, Chambray." Gavin glanced over his shoulder as he allowed the soldier to back him down the hall. He wanted to get into the kitchen so that he would be closer to the horses when he felled this last man. "Why not wander out the back, Chambray? The moon's pretty tonight. I'll be directly behind you, no doubt."

"Lackwit!" Richard leaned against the wall, trying not wheeze as he attempted to force air into his punctured lung. "You should have gone when I gave you the chance. I'd have done it!"

"So you're a brighter man than I!" Gavin dodged left, taking a slice from his opponent's right shoulder.

Chambray backed into the kitchen, bumping into a worktable covered with vegetables for Mrs. Spate's soup. Carrots and potatoes rolled onto the floor. "What of Ellen?"

"Yes, what of her?" Hunt's form suddenly filled the kitchen door frame.

"Chambray!" Gavin shouted. "Get yourself out of here!"

Richard took a step toward Hunt. "I fear no man, least of all a coward who sends other men to do his bidding."

The soldier Gavin had been fighting suddenly stepped aside and backed up, allowing his master full view of Gavin.

"You go, Waxton," Richard said. He lifted his sword with great effort. "I'll make short work of the freak and then be with you in a moment's time."

The Duke of Hunt threw back his head in laughter as he took an easy stance in the doorway. He was dressed as splendidly as the king, in a garish blue and red suit with gold braid and piping and a matching blue cloak.

Two soldiers slipped in the back door, trapping Richard and Gavin between them and the Duke of Hunt.

"How gallant of you both, gentlemen, fighting to see who will be given the opportunity to die first." Hunt smiled a smile that made the hair on the back of Gavin's neck bristle.

"I don't know why it is you seek Ellen, and I don't care." As Gavin spoke, he began considering his options for escape. With Richard wounded as badly as he was, the choices were few. "What I find interesting, Hunt, is that you would find a woman such a dangerous adversary that you would chase her across half the countryside. I would almost think you were frightened of her."

"Oh, you don't care what it is she's done, you say?" The duke raised a white eyebrow haughtily. "Well, you cocky colonial bastard, what if I were to tell you that your little Saint Ellen is actually—"

"No!" Richard threw himself at Hunt. "No, you won't, you pervert!"

The duke and his men were taken so off guard that all Hunt could do was stumble backward to avoid a direct hit. He knocked the soldier beside him over as Richard plunged his sword between Hunt's ribs.

Immediately, the other two soldiers leaped into action. Gavin spun around and caught the first one across the throat with his sword, spewing blood over himself and the sanded plank floor. The soldier fell with a gurgle, clenching his throat.

341

Drawing his sword against the last soldier between him and the door, Gavin backed up, grabbing Richard by the collar and dragging him off Hunt, who was apparently wounded but not enough that he couldn't shout and curse as he tried to untangle his limbs from those of the soldier and Richard.

"This is our invitation to make haste," Gavin shouted, shoving Richard toward the door.

Richard, his sword lost in the scuffle with Hunt, stumbled and fell to his knees. He was gasping for breath now, his face beginning to turn a bluish tint. "Go! Go, Gavin! Tell Ellen I loved her."

"Tell her yourself!" Gavin made a sudden turn, ducked, and came up bringing his fist in direct contact with the only soldier still standing. The man flew backward, slipping on the bloody floor, his sword sailing from his hand and out of reach.

Taking his moment of opportunity, Gavin slid his sword into the belt that hung on his hips and ran for the outside kitchen door. Halfway across the slippery floor, he lifted Chambray into his arms. Richard was so weak that he put up no struggle.

"Bastard," Richard murmured, barely conscious. "Stupid bastard. We'll never get away now."

Gavin burst through the back door and headed straight for the woodshed, where he prayed Hunt's horse still stood. If the horses were gone, he and Richard were sunk for certain. "Who's the stupid bastard, Baron Chambray? You just ran one of the most powerful men in England through with your sword!"

"Did I kill him?"

"Fear not." Gavin turned the corner of the shed and heaved an audible sigh of relief. There stood Hunt's horse waiting patiently for a rider. The horse would have to carry the burden of two riders. Richard was too weak to ride alone, and there wasn't time to tie him on a horse.

"What are you doing?" Richard protested half-heartedly as Gavin heaved him into the saddle of Hunt's horse.

"I told Ellen we'd meet her." Gavin swung up behind Richard, steadying him with one hand as he reined the horse around and out of the woodshed. "I'm a man of my word, you know that."

"You'll die for this!" Hunt screamed from the back door of the kitchen.

As Gavin rode down the drive into the darkness, he took a final glance over his shoulder to see Hunt standing at the shed, shaking his fist in fury as he applied a towel to the bloodstain on his powder-blue shirtwaist.

"I'll follow you to the ends of the earth!" Hunt bellowed. "I'll find her! And you, Waxton will die. I can't tell you how much pleasure it will give me to see you beg for mercy!"

Gavin threw up an obscene gesture and laughed as he rode off into the darkness. "God's teeth," he muttered, smiling to himself as he took a sharp bend in the road and darted into the cover of the woods. "I can't believe we made it out of there alive, Chambray!"


Ellen waited near the edge of Havering Village at Mrs. Spate's abandoned cottage. When she spotted Gavin on horseback riding full speed toward her, she ran out into the center of the dusty road "You're safe!" she cried, tears running down her cheeks. "I was so afraid you wouldn't get away!"

Gavin pulled hard on the reins, forcing Hunt's steed to a halt. He reached out to wipe away her tears with the back of his hand. "Safe, but not safe for long if we don't get out of here." The horse pawed at the ground nervously, whipping its head and pulling on the reins. "No doubt the village will be the first place Hunt looks for us."

Ellen laid a hand on Richard's knee, looking up at Gavin. Richard was slumped over the horse, unconscious.

"He's still alive, but barely," Gavin said, not making her have to ask.

"He's worse?"

He nodded. "Much."

She fought back fresh tears, knowing she couldn't let emotions get the best of her. If they were going to escape, she knew she'd have to remain levelheaded. Gavin was right: She wasn't a hysterical jade and she'd not become one now. "So . . . so where do we go? How do we get back to the ship? Hunt's sure to send more men after us. An army this time, I fear."

"He wants you that badly?" Gavin's stormy green eyes met hers.

Ellen looked away.

"I can tell you where you're going!" Mrs. Spate came across the grass, her bare feet carrying her as fast as they could manage. "You go to my cousin Gelda's farm, that's where you go. It ain't but an hour's ride from here in the direction of London, but it's far enough off the road that won't nobody think to look for you there."

Ellen looked up anxiously at Gavin, who held Richard on his horse with a steady hand. "Would that work? We could have a look at Richard's wound then!"

Gavin looked away, then back at her. He burned to know why Hunt wanted her so badly. What had she done to him? Surely Hunt was involved in the dark secret she kept from him. But Gavin knew this was neither the time nor the place for that discussion. What mattered now was escape.

"Ellen," he said gently, "I don't know that Richard will live another hour. He's bleeding profusely from his chest. He just can't take in any air. I can't, for the life of me, figure how he managed to fight as long as he did."

"I guess we can't stay here," she answered softly, understanding he meant that at this point they needed to be more concerned with escaping than tending to a dying man, even if it was Richard.

"No, we can't."

"Then we'll go to Mrs. Spate's cousin's and stay there the night."

Gavin shrugged his broad shoulders. "That's as good a plan as any. Mrs. Spate, if you'll tell us where your cousin's farm lies, we'll be on our way. I don't want the duke to see us speaking to you. I'll not have your family in danger because of us."

"I can't tell you how to get there, my lord. I ain't good with directions, but my boy, Red Rob, he can take ye. I'm certain of it."

"I don't know that that's a good idea, Mrs. Spate. It could be dangerous. It would be best if the boy stayed here in the village with you."

Mrs. Spate walked up to Gavin's horse, unintimidated by his station or the size of the steed he sat on. "Beggin' your pardon, my lord, but I'm his mam. I know what's best for him. Let him take you, my lord. He'll see you get cared for right." She looked down at her bare feet, then back up at him. "Then I have to ask ye if you'll do me a favor in return."

"What's that?"

"Take my boy with ye to the new world."

Gavin was astounded. "You want your son to go to

the Colonies?"

"He ain't got nothing here, my lord. No pap, no hope of ever ownin' land, no future. If you was to take him to the Colonies, he might have a chance to make something of himself." She wiped her eyes with the corner of her apron. "He might even make out well enough to bring his old mam and his brothers to the Colonies one day."

Gavin studied the woman's plump face. "You understand the danger involved, not just between here and London, but crossing the ocean?"

Mrs. Spate laid her hand on Gavin's broad one. "What I understand is that you're a good man . . . a good man that could give my boy a chance. One his pap never to give 'im. My Rob, he's a hard worker and he don't touch the liquor. He'd work loyal for you. I know he would. He looks up to ye. Wants to be like ye when he's grown."

"I know he'd work hard. I just don't like the idea of taking him so far from home." Gavin squeezed her hand before she pulled it away.

"He'll be fine. I swear he will. He's fourteen out. Nearly a man."

Gavin looked up at Ellen. "What do you say, wife?"

If their situation hadn't been so grave, Ellen would have smiled at his endearment. "I hate to take him from his mother, but he's a good boy. He might well be of great help to you on the plantation."

Gavin indicated the thatched cottage with a nod of his head. "You heard my lady. Fetch your son, Mrs. Spate. We've no time to lose."

While Mrs. Spate ran to get Rob, Ellen caught her horse's reins and came back to Gavin. "You're a good man, Lord Waxton," she said.

He smoothed the top of her head in a lover's caress.

346

"And you, my sweet, are blinded by your love for me. I'm not as gallant as you think. I'm like any other man. I try to do what's right. I fight the good fight."

She caught his rough hand in hers and brushed it across her lips. "Say what you want. I know the truth of the matter."

Just then Rob came running up to the horses, a feed sack of belongings thrown over his shoulder. His mother came hustling behind him. "I'm ready, my lord," Rob panted, out of breath. "I can show you the way to Aunt Gelda's, I swear it!"

Gavin looked down from his horse at the red-haired boy. "Your mother told you that you're to go to America with me?"

He bobbed his head with excitement. "Yes, my lord! It's what I've always wanted. I was gonna sell myself into indenture if I had to to get there!"

"And you understand that we're to cross a great ocean . . . that you most likely will never see your brothers and mam again?"

He glanced at his mother hesitantly, then back at Gavin. "I understand, my lord. But I want to go to the Colonies! I want to make my fortune."

Gavin laughed at the boy's innocence. "There's hard work to be done in the Colonies. I'll have no laziness. You'll do my bidding or I'll ship you back to this shire on the first boat that leaves St. Mary's."

He threw up his hand, crossing his heart. "I swear on my pap's grave I'll work hard day and night."

"My boy ain't lazy," Mrs. Spate interjected. "You seen the work he done up at Havering House. You seen he's a good boy."

"Very well. Help the lady up on to her horse and you jump up behind."

Rob cupped his hands to give Ellen a boost. "Ah, no, my lord, I don't need to ride. I can run. It ain't

347

that far.''

"We've no time to dally, boy. I said get on the lady's horse.''

Mrs. Spate reached out and rapped her son on the head. "You want the earl to feed you to the fishes halfway across the ocean? Do as you're told, son!''

Rob turned to his mother. "Well, goodbye to you, then.'' He scuffed his bare foot in the dusty road.

Mrs. Spate stood looking at her eldest son for a moment as he tried to be brave. "Goodbye, luv.'' She pulled him to her lumpy breast. When she spoke again, her voice was strained with emotion. "You make your mam proud, you hear me?''

He lifted his head. "I hear ye.'' With a grin, he turned and leaped up on the back of Ellen's saddle.

Mrs. Spate looked from Gavin to Ellen. "I got no words to thank ye both.'' She sniffed and wiped her nose on the corner of her apron. "You're good people to do this for the likes of us. I'll see to Haverin' House 'til it's sold, I swear I will.''

Gavin touched his temple with two fingers. "We have to be off, Mrs. Spate. No doubt the duke will be through the village in a matter of moments. Don't speak unless spoken to, and then deny you know anything. As for the others''—he nodded at the thatched cottages that made up the small village— "we'll just have to take our chances.''

"Oh, they won't say nuthin', my lord. Too scar't. People who's scared of ghosties is certain scared of a duke. I can promise you their jaws won't flap. Be frozen shut, they will.''

Gavin steadied Richard's unconscious body with one hand and lifted his reins with the other. "Get up!''

Hunt's steed threw up its tail and leaped forward, racing down the road out of the village. Ellen sank her heels into her horse's flanks and raced to catch up.

Just as Mrs. Spate had said, her cousin's farm was no more than an hour's ride, and Rob led Gavin and Ellen directly to it without any mishap.

Gavin rode into the swept dirt yard. Chickens, ducks, and geese scattered as he leaped down from his horse. "Can you hold on, Chambray?" he murmured, close enough for only Richard to hear. He laced Richard's fingers through the horse's mane for him.

"I can sit on a horse, Waxton!" Richard didn't have the energy to lift his head, but his voice was strong enough to be indignant.

Gavin gave him a pat on the shoulder. "I'll be right back."

Ellen led her gelding up beside Hunt's horse, and Rob leaped down. "I'll just run and get my aunt, my lord. It won't take but a minute."

The boy sprinted across the yard and beat on the door of the farmer's cottage. It immediately swung open on its leather hinges. Rob and a peasant woman in her early forties, who looked much like Mrs. Spate, exchanged words. With an affirmative nod of her head, she came hustling across the yard, shaking her apron to send her fowl fleeing.

She curtsied to both Gavin and Ellen. "Greetin's to you, my lord, my lady. The name's Gelda."

Gavin nodded politely. "I suppose the boy's told you we need a safe place to rest the night."

"That he has. You're more than welcome to the house. It ain't much, but the roof don't leak, I got no lice in my bedding, and my hare stew's the best in all Essex."

349

"We don't want your house, Gelda," Ellen said as Gavin helped her down from her horse. "The barn will be fine." She indicated a small two-story frame and plaster structure nestled in a grove of fruit trees beyond the cottage.

"An earl and a countess in the barn? Holy God, no! Don't worry none about us. My children and I'll get out of the house and leave you to your business. We can sleep in the barn. Slept in straw before, we have."

"As have we, ma'am," Gavin said. "We thank you for your hospitality, but we prefer the barn. It will be safer for us as well as for you."

Gelda looked at Gavin with uncertainty, but she nodded. "Well, Rob there can you show you to it. I'll fetch some blankets and stew." She nodded at Richard. "I take it the gentleman's ill. Is there something I can get him?"

Ellen looked to Gavin at a loss, wondering what one did for a dying man.

"Do you, by chance, have any strong drink?"

The woman's eyes widened beneath her grey bangs. "Naught but some wine I made myself, I fear. It's just me and the children here, my lord. My husband done run out on me years back."

Ellen laid her hand on Gelda's arm. "The wine will be fine. Thank you for your hospitality."

Gelda smiled back, then turned to Rob. "Well, don't just stand there with your thumb pluggin' your nose, boy! See to their comfort! Take the horses and get them settled! There'll be a lamp and tinderbox on the shelf just inside the door. Clean straw for bedding be in the loft."

"Yes, Aunt Gelda!" Rob grabbed Ellen's horse's reins and reached for Gavin's.

"I'll take care of this one, boy. You just get that one

fed and watered. He'll be needing a good rubdown as well."

"Whatever you say, my lord!" Rob ran across the barnyard, pulling the gelding behind him at a trot.

Later, when Gavin had the horses cared for and he had sent Rob to sleep inside the cottage with his aunt, he and Ellen knelt beside Richard in the thick, pungent straw.

"Another sip of wine, Chambray?"

Richard shook his head, too weak to take the effort to open his eyes. "It's not bad, Waxton, but most definitely not of French vintage." He tried to laugh at his own joke but began to cough violently.

Ellen took a clean rag and wiped the blood and spittle from the corners of his mouth.

"Ellen?"

"I'm right here, Richard. Tell me what you need."

He smiled as his coughing ceased and he could again rest his head on the pillow Ellen had made for him with her bag of possessions. "I just wanted to hear your voice, sweet." He clenched and unclenched his fingers on one hand. "I can't hang on much longer for you, sweet. Can't breathe. Hold me?"

"Don't say that. Don't say that, Richard. You're just tired." She lifted his head and scooted over so that she cradled it in her lap. Her hand found his. His touch was icy despite the number of blankets piled on top of him. He was cold to the very bone. "You'll be better in the morning. You know you will."

"Waxton?"

Gavin took his other hand.

"In my shirtwaist." Richard paused for a long moment, trying to rally enough strength to speak again. "I want you to have it."

Gavin lifted the blanket, now soaked with blood. From Richard's stained shirtwaist, he brought out the miniature portrait of Ellen. "It's beautiful," he whispered.

"She is beautiful." Richard squeezed Ellen's hand. "So keep the trinket. I'll have no use for it in hell." He smiled. "Keep it and remember that she is who she is. She is who you know and love. Don't let anyone ever convince you otherwise." He exhaled, his chest rattling. "Not even her."

Gavin looked at Ellen, confused by what Richard said. But dying men didn't always make sense. He'd seen enough to know that.

"You could give me no greater gift, Chambray," Gavin said, tucking the miniature portrait into his own coat. "Nothing but Ellen herself, and that you've already given."

"Take care of her, will you? She can get sassy on you, but don't pay that any mind."

"I will care for her," Gavin responded solemnly as he held Richard's hand. "You know I will."

Tears ran down Ellen's cheeks as she smoothed Richard's dark hair. By the light of the lamp, she could see how pale his face was. His chest now barely rose before it fell again. When Richard became silent, she squeezed his hand. "Richard?" She knew she bordered on the edge of hysteria. Richard had said he was dying. Gavin had said it, too. She knew it was going to happen, but she just wasn't ready to let go. Not yet.

She didn't know if he could hear her now, but she spoke anyway. "Thank you," she murmured, bringing his cold knuckles to her lips, "for saving me that night on the road. For saving me not just from him, but from myself. For teaching me how to live again."

Richard sucked in a deep breath. "Thank you," he whispered.

She leaned over to hear his words that were barely

audible now. "For what?" she murmured, fighting her tears. "I've done nothing for you. Nothing but try your nerves and spend your money," she finished, trying to make a joke. Richard always did love a joke.

"Thank you for riding into my life that night," Richard told her. His eyes flickered open for just a moment, then closed. "Thank you . . ."

She smoothed his handsome cheek. "Richard?"

He inhaled slowly. "Thank you for just being there. You made me feel like a man again, if only for a while . . ."

Ellen watched as his chest fell again. This time it didn't rise. Tears slipped from her eyes to fall on his face. "Richard?"

"He's gone," Gavin said gently as he laid Richard's hand down. "He's dead, sweetheart."

She shook her head. "No. Not Richard. I loved him."

Gavin came around and tenderly lifted her up, resting Richard's head back on the pillow. He drew her into his lap to comfort her. "I know you loved him, but it's time to say goodbye now."

Sobs wracked Ellen's body as she clung to Gavin. He smoothed her hair, holding her tightly in his arms. "It's all right, Ellen. It's going to be all right. I'm here. I'll protect you. You and your secret. I'll love you just as dearly as Richard did. I'll try my damnedest to love you more, if it's humanly possible."

"Ah, Gavin . . . Why does life have to hurt so much?"

"I don't know, lover." He rocked her in his arms as he imagined someday he would rock their child. "I just don't know."

Finally, when her tears subsided, Ellen lifted her head from Gavin's broad shoulder to stare into his green eyes. He wiped her tear-stained face with his sleeve. "We need to get some sleep now," he said softly. "We'll deal with his body in a few hours."

She sniffed, nodding. "Then on to London?"

"Then on to London." He brushed his lips against hers and lay back in the straw, bringing her with him. "And on to Maryland, where you'll be my wife."

Ellen laid her cheek on Gavin's shoulder and closed her eyes, suddenly exhausted. So much had happened today that she was numb. "I love you, Gavin," she whispered.

He kissed her forehead. "And I you. Now sleep, and I'll wake you in the morning. It will be a long, hard day of riding if we're to outsmart Hunt and make it to London. . . ."

# Chapter Twenty-Four

Ellen rested on her side on the bunk in Gavin's ship's cabin, her head cradled in her arm. The *Maid Marion* rocked gently as it sailed down the Thames, slipping out of reach of the Duke of Hunt and his soldiers.

She closed her eyes wearily. She and Gavin had slept fitfully for a few hours that night in Gelda's barn. Then they had risen in the darkness and made arrangements with Gelda to have Richard's body buried in a little churchyard nearby. Gavin and Ellen had considered having his body transported back to his estate, where his mother resided, but for logistical reasons they decided against it. Besides, with no body to be found, Hunt would never know he had bested Richard. Ellen smiled to herself in the semidarkness of the cabin, snuggling beneath the coverlet. She knew Richard would have preferred it this way.

With that matter settled, Ellen and Gavin had sped toward London and the refuge of the *Maid Marion*. Fearing the gates into the City were being watched by the duke's men, Gavin again gained his friend Zach's assistance and they sailed up to the wharfs on the fishing barge, under the cover of darkness.

Ellen sighed, rolling onto her back. It seemed that after all these years, she was finally safe from Hunt.

The cabin door opened and Gavin stepped in. "What are you doing still awake?" he inquired softly. He came to the rack and sat down on its edge. He brushed back a sweep of her long red hair. "I thought for certain you'd be sound asleep by now."

She smiled up at him. "I was waiting for you. I think I've grown so used to sleeping in your arms that I just don't feel right without you."

"Well, let me remedy that, then." He pulled off his boots and stood to remove his clothing. "Julius seems to have everything under control topside. He'll not be in need of me."

Ellen pushed up on one elbow, pointing to the bird cage that hung from a rafter in the far corner of the tiny cabin. "Sir Gavin. How did he get here?"

The parrot squawked at the mention of his name. "Sir Gavin! Sir Gavin! How did he get here? How did he get here?" *Squawk!*

Gavin grabbed the cage cover from his chart table and dropped it over the bird. "If I have to listen to that from here to Maryland, I surely will be ready for Bedlam." He pulled his linen shirt over his head. "Julius had the good sense to go to your apartment when he reached London. There are two chests of clothing down in the hold. He paid your servants for the remainder of the year and sent them off to seek new employment with references from me." He shook his head. "I always said Julius made a better imitation of my signature than I did."

She smiled. "That was kind of him. I'll be certain to thank him."

Now naked, Gavin slipped beneath the light coverlet, pulling Ellen against him. "Why not thank me instead?" He nuzzled her neck. "I'd be far more appreciative, I can assure you."

She laughed as she looped her arms around his neck and kissed him soundly on the lips. "I fear you're trying to take advantage of me, my lord. And me an unmarried maiden."

"A wrong soon to be righted, sweet." He rolled her onto her back. "I thought Julius could marry us on the foredeck once we make it out into open seas. Then when we arrive in the Colonies, we'll have your man of the cloth perform the ceremony again if you like."

With the tip of her finger, she smoothed the place where his mustache had been. "If we're to be married again in the Colonies, I see no reason to bother now."

He pushed up on his elbow to face her, his hand glancing over the curve of her hip. "Are you saying you've changed your mind about being my wife?" His tone was teasing, but it was obvious he wanted a serious answer.

"No." She kissed his mouth. "No, that's not it at all. It's just that I know how men feel about such ceremonies. You've bedded me. You're getting nothing out of this marriage contract. I can wait until we hit land again."

"Getting nothing!" His green-eyed gaze settled on her face. "I'm getting you. Ellen, after all we've been through, I need to know you're finally mine. I need you to be my wife."

She held his gaze. "You're an odd man, Gavin Waxton." She smiled. "If that's what you want, then so be it. I'll wed you here and now if you like."

His laughter echoed in the small cabin as he lowered his head to the valley between her breasts. "Somehow I don't think that would be appropriate, you minus a wedding gown, I minus my breeches."

Their laughter mingled, as did their breaths, as

Ellen pressed her lips to his in a lover's kiss. "Never in my wildest dreams had I imagined I would be on a ship bound for the Colonies in the arms of a man like you," she whispered. "You've made me so happy, Gavin, far happier than I deserve."

"What lunacy," he murmured as his hand slipped over her bare flesh, stirring fires of passion in her and himself with each stroke. "Everyone deserves to be happy. Especially those who make others happy."

Ellen turned him over onto his back, rolling on top of him and pulling the coverlet with her. She pressed her sensitive breasts to the hair on his chest and sighed with pleasure. "Have I made you happy, then, my lord?" Her voice was silky.

Gavin let his eyes drift shut as she rubbed flesh against flesh, sending his spirits soaring. "That you have, my sweet." He cupped her buttocks with his hands, guiding the steady movement of her hips. "More than you'll ever know."

Pulling the coverlet over their heads to make a warm tent, she brought her face close to his and shrouded him in a curtain of fiery hair. She moved her hips seductively against his, her mouth touching his lips again and again.

"Witch!" he accused, his voice husky with eroticism.

She brushed her lips across his mouth, down his cheek, to his ear. "Shall I stop? You have only to give the word. . . ."

"No, no," he breathed.

"It's only that I want to please you, husband-to-be. I want to be appreciative of your attentions."

"Enough of this torture!" With one quick movement, he flipped her over on her back on the narrow bunk and pinned her down with his own body.

"You want to see appreciation?" he growled,

moving his hips against hers, his hardened shaft prodding gently between her thighs. "I'll show you appreciation, my lady!"

An hour later, Ellen fell asleep in Gavin's arms, their naked limbs entangled. Despite her loss of Richard, she felt an overwhelming sense of joy. At last her life seemed perfect . . . at least for the moment.


A knock sounded at his bedchamber door and the Duke of Hunt gave an irritated sigh. "Yes, yes, what is it?" he shouted, sitting up in his bed, each arm wrapped around a young blond woman. The women were identical twins and quite delightful. He'd had them sent from Paris just to aid him in his recovery from his wounds sustained at the hand of Richard Chambray.

"It's Robards, Your Grace."

Hunt rolled his eyes heavenward. "Is it important, Robards? I'm quite occupied."

"Well . . . well, I could come back at a more convenient time, Your Grace. I can indeed. I just thought you might want to hear the information I've found on the Countess Waxton."

"Why didn't you say so! Quit babbling and bring yourself in!" Hunt shook his head in disbelief as he turned his attention back to the women who lay on each side of him in his massive red and gold draped bed. "You'll have to excuse me, my dears." He flipped up the sheet on both of them, revealing their naked lithe bodies. "Go to your chamber and wait for me to summon you. I assure you it won't be long." He patted them both on the bare buttocks as they leaped out of his bed like young, frightened does.

The women reached for silk dressing gowns left on

the end of the bed, but he shooed them away with his hands. "No, no, just run upstairs like that." He sat back against a silk pillow, pleased with his thoughts. "You'll stir up the household a bit, give the servants something to gossip about at the Exchange, don't you think?"

Without responding, the women ran from the bedchamber door, passing Robards on the way out. The secretary's head snapped as the young women ran by. "Very nice," he commented, licking his lips. "Quite nice."

"They are, aren't they? And the best thing about them," Hunt said, "is that they're mute. Never a word out of their little whoring mouths, which is just what I like in a woman, don't you, Robards?"

Robards took a last peek at the women before closing the bedchamber door. "I agree with you utterly, Your Grace."

"Well, come in and tell me what information it is you have for me." He closed his red silk dressing gown. "But make it quick. I promised the ladies they could come back."

"Well, Your Grace, there has been no sign of Chambray, Waxton, or the Countess Waxton . . . or any appearing likeness. No one has seen them come in or out of the City alone or together, and I can assure you all gates have been watched."

The duke sipped from a wine goblet. "So?"

"What I did discover was that Waxton's ship, the *Maid Marion,* came into the wharfs, stayed a few days, and then sailed away."

Hunt sat up in bed. "You said the ship had gone to France a month ago, Robards!"

"It . . . it did, Your Grace. All three of Waxton's vessels sailed for Paris."

"You're not making any sense, Robards!" He

360

gripped the goblet in rising anger. "Explain your-self! Quickly!"

"Well . . . well, apparently three ships sailed the day you tangled with Chambray."

"Yes?"

"But one came back to London two weeks later. The *Maid Marion*."

"And?"

"And she sailed away in the middle of the night."

"When, Robards? When?"

He cringed. "Two nights after you went to Havering House . . ."

"What?" Hunt took his goblet and heaved it at his secretary. The red wine splashed across the marble floor, the silver gilded cup striking Robards in the forehead.

Robards lifted a handkerchief to pat his bleeding forehead. "It sailed, Your Grace," he said with defeat. "With Thomasina, Chambray, and Waxton on it, no doubt."

"But that was nearly two weeks ago!"

"Yes, Your Grace. Two weeks ago!"

"And it took you that long to find out?"

"There was no record of the *Maid Marion* or any of Waxton's other ships returning to port. I checked the paperwork myself, Your Grace."

"Of course, there was no record! People can be bought, Robards!" Hunt looked away, so furious he couldn't think straight. "Two weeks," he mumbled. "Two weeks they've been gone." He sighed. "And where do you think they were bound, my idiot secretary?"

"The Colonies," Robards whispered.

"What!"

"The Colonies, no doubt," he answered a little louder. "Waxton had his land grants. He took the woman and Chambray and sailed for the American Colonies.''

Hunt was so enraged he could barely think. Robards had promised him the three had not escaped by way of the Thames! Two weeks! Two bloody weeks had passed, and all the while Hunt had been wasting time and a great deal of cash looking for the fugitives.

To make matters worse, Hunt had again been contacted by the gentleman whose name was apparently on the list Thomasina still held. The gentleman was making threats now . . . threats of a leak of information that would end Hunt's life very quickly in the Tower. A threat, Hunt feared, that could possibly turn into a reality if this gentleman was indeed who he thought he might be.

Hunt threw his silk sheet aside and leaped out of bed. "I need a ship, Robards."

"A . . . a ship, Your Grace?"

"Do I stammer? Have you suddenly gone deaf? Yes, a ship! One seaworthy enough to sail across the Atlantic Ocean!"

Robards's eyes widened. "You're going to the Colonies?"

Hunt grabbed a bell off the table and rang, bringing his manservant running. He would have to dress and begin making plans for his voyage. He'd not let little Thomasina get away like this. He'd have the letter and he'd have her even if he did indeed have to go to hell to get them! "I see no other choice at this point," Hunt said venomously in reply to Robards's question. "Do you?"


Two and half weeks into the voyage, Ellen finally began to become restless. For those first few days

362

aboard the *Maid Marion*, she had been so relieved to have escaped Hunt and to now be headed for the Colonies with Gavin that she'd been content to spend most of the time he was absent from their cabin reading or sleeping.

Four days out of England, Julius had performed a marriage ceremony for Gavin and Ellen on the foredeck of the two-masted sailing ship. There on a sunny day with the wind at their backs, the two had committed themselves to each other before God, a mermaid masthead, and a crew of cheering sailors.

Two weeks had passed since the wedding and Ellen had still found no difference in the way Gavin treated her. If nothing else, he seemed more attentive. Slowly, Ellen's fears of marriage had slipped away. Now she realized that marriage was what a man and a woman made it. Marriage was an agreement with rules laid down, just as in a card game. The night of their wedding Gavin had sat Ellen down and together they had written such rules. To Ellen the idea had seemed silly, but Gavin had insisted it was important to them both to know what was to be expected. What was acceptable and what was not.

Late into the night the two discussed a wife's submission, a husband's fairness and duty to protect and care for his spouse. They talked of both parties' rights to take equal part in decisions that affected them both. They even discussed the possibility of children and how happy that would make them both. The only topic that had been difficult for Ellen to discuss was that of honesty between them. Gavin said their honesty would start at that moment. Their lives would be a clean slate, with the past erased forever. But somewhere deep inside her heart the death of Waldron still tugged at her conscience.

Two weeks after the wedding and the serious

discussion, however, Ellen had managed to nearly erase Waldron and Hunt from her mind. This morning when she woke up, she was full of hope. She realized her woman's flow hadn't come this month and she might well be pregnant. Until she knew for certain, she had decided not to say anything to Gavin.

"What will you do today?" Ellen asked Gavin as she stretched on the narrow rack the two shared.

Gavin pulled a clean shirt over his head and reached for his breeches. "There's been some shifting in one of the holds. I thought I'd give Julius some help in having the crew do some moving." He laced up his sailcloth breeches. "What about you?"

She twirled a long lock of red hair. "Oh, I thought perhaps I'd go riding." She looked up pensively. "That, or go to the 'Change and buy some ribbons."

He chuckled. "I told you this would be a long trip. I'm sorry if you're bored, but a man can only perform so many times a day."

She tossed a small pillow at him, but he ducked. The pillow glanced off Sir Gavin's covered cage and the parrot squawked in protest. "For your information, I thought I'd go down and see what it is Julius packed in my trunks. Would that be all right?"

"There's no need for you to go down in the hold, sweet. I can well fetch anything you need."

"No. I thought I'd pick through the things. Give myself something to do. It's all right, isn't it?"

He leaned against the bulkhead, stood on one foot, and pulled on a leather boot. "By all means. If you get energetic, you could even go through some of the other crates down there. They're the things I bought for the new house I'm building. There're also some items I had transported from Havering House."

She nodded, lowering her gaze, not wanting him to know the thought of going through Waldron's and her father's belongings would make her uncomfortable. "I could do that."

"Good. Give you something to do." He pushed his hands though his blue broadcloth work coat and walked by her, leaning to brush his lips against hers. "I'll let the men know you'll be down there and that they're to stay away. I don't think I'd have any problems with any of them, but I'll not take any chances. Men can be funny about women halfway across the Atlantic."

Ellen crawled out of the rack and walked him the short distance to the door. "I'll be fine."

"If you need me, give a holler. This ship isn't so big that Jules or I couldn't hear you from anywhere."

She kissed him as if she were a peasant kissing her husband before he went off to work in the fields. "Go. Do some man work. Have a drink with Julius. You'll tire of me all too soon if you don't spend some time away from me."

"Never." He stole another kiss and then was on his way, closing the door behind him.

Ellen dressed in a woolen azure gown and swept her hair back with a thick black velvet ribbon. As she rolled on her stockings, she glanced up in the oval mirror Gavin had brought up for her from his belongings in the hold.

She brushed her hair at the roots. Richard had always lightened her hair for her, turning her dark tresses to this brilliant red with a concoction applied every month or so. Thankfully, he had done it for her only a few days before he died. Once she arrived in the Colonies, Ellen knew she would have to find the proper ingredients and do it herself. For the rest of her life, her hair would be an annoying reminder of the woman she had once been.

A small price to pay for the happiness she'd found . . .

Pulling on a pair of colonial ladies' boots Julius had brought from Paris for her, Ellen left her cabin, taking a lit lamp with her. Following Gavin's directions, she went down the narrow passageway and down a ladder, through a storage room and into the small hold where he said his personal belongings were stored.

Ellen lifted her lamp and hung it on a peg on a low beam in the ceiling, filling the chamber with soft light. Wooden crates and trunks stood neatly stacked along three walls. Behind some of the smaller crates were objects covered with oilcloth to protect them from the dampness below decks.

Among the trunks, Ellen recognized her own. She smiled at the thought that Julius had taken the time, risking his own safety, to go to her apartment and fetch at least some of her belongings. She knelt on the cool, damp floor and flipped open the lid of her chest.

For the next hour she went through the clothing, folding it and organizing it into some semblance of order. It seemed Julius had just thrown open her chests of drawers and grabbed any clothing he deemed sensible. While there was a shortage of shifts and stockings, he had managed to bring most of her durable gowns, ones that would be far more appropriate for the Colonies than the ruffles and lace she had worn in London.

Finally, content with her accomplishments, Ellen rose stiff-legged and closed the trunk again. On the floor she had stacked several items to be carried up to the cabin she shared with Gavin.

Walking to stretch out the pins and needles in her legs, Ellen began to open the lids on crates, curious as to what a man would purchase to take home with him. There were dishes, a case clock, boxes of books, and a large crate of cooking utensils. There was glassware, bedding, and a case of French champagne. Ellen chuckled to herself as she carefully replaced the lid on Gavin's precious cargo.

Standing in the middle of the room, she wondered just what it was he wanted her to do with his belongings. Then the draped items behind the crates caught her eye. What were they?

She lifted the top row of heavy crates, setting them behind her, and then pulled away the squares of oilcloth. Pictures! The first was a large oil painting of the *Maid Marion* depicted at sea. Ellen smiled, recognizing the name of the Flemish artist scrawled across the bottom. But behind the picture of the *Maid Marion* was another picture, an even larger one.

Carefully, Ellen lifted the picture of the *Maid Marion* and set it aside. When she turned back to see the other picture, her breath caught in her throat.

She could suddenly hear the pounding of her heart. She held her breath.

It was her. It was Thomasina. Gavin had taken the portrait Waldron had had painted of her and had hung in his bedchamber.

Ellen stared at the portrait of the young woman with her face turned away, as if she stared at a ghostly apparition. It was an apparition. It was her past haunting her even here in the midst of her newfound happiness.

Tears collected in the corners of Ellen's eyes as memories of the past flipped through her mind. She had had the portrait painted in this manner to hide the ugly bruise Waldron had left on her cheek. She had had it painted in this way as a small defiance against the husband she had despised.

She sighed. Why in dear heaven had Gavin taken down the portrait of Waldron's wife and brought it with him? She studied the young woman in the green velvet dress, her neck laden with emeralds, wondering what would have possessed a man to take a portrait of his dead brother's wife, a woman he had never known . . . a woman he surely despised.

"Oh . . . you found it."

At the sound of Gavin's voice, she whipped around. "Yes," she said softly.

He came to stand beside her, his hands balanced on his hips as he stared at the portrait. "She was Waldron's wife—Thomasina."

She tried to hide the emotion in her voice. "I see." She looked from the portrait of herself to Gavin. "Why did you keep it?"

He studied the life-size portrait of the Countess Thomasina Waxton for a long moment and then looked back at Ellen. "I honestly don't know. I've had it under my bed since I first went to Havering House upon my arrival in London."

*All those months it's been under the bed we were making love in*, Ellen thought. *If I'd gone into Waldron's bedchamber, I'd have known it was missing.*

When Ellen said nothing, Gavin took her hand. "Don't be jealous, sweet. I suppose it was an infatuation of sorts. At first I hated the bitch for what she did to my brother. Then, I was only intrigued by her and her mysterious disappearance. When it came time to sell the portrait along with Waldron's other belongings," he shrugged, "I just couldn't do it." He crossed his arms over his chest, again looking at the picture. "I suppose it sounds ridiculous."

Ellen grasped the oil painting of the *Maid Marion* and carefully returned it to its place, covering

Thomasina's portrait. "I suppose," she echoed, tossing the oilcloth over both pieces of artwork.

Gavin caught her around the waist and pulled her toward him. "Not angry with me, are you? Because if you are"—he toyed with a curly lock of hair that had escaped the ribbon— "I can throw her overboard. I swear, I can."

Ellen smiled at Gavin. She knew she had to come to terms with her past and was not letting it affect her every waking moment. "Keep her if you like, sweet. I'm not a jealous woman. Especially when I know I'm the one who has you."

She kissed him gently. Then he took the lamp and she her clothing, and they left the storage room and Thomasina Waxton in darkness.

# Chapter Twenty-Five

Before the wagon wheels had ceased rolling, Ellen leaped to her feet, resting her hand on Gavin's shoulder to keep from tumbling to the ground. "Heavens, but this is the most beautiful place I think I've ever seen," she breathed, turning full circle. "More beautiful than you described. More beautiful than I could ever have imagined!"

Standing in the wagon, she took in the panorama of the Maryland Colony wilderness that stretched as far as she could see. She breathed deeply, filling her mind as well as her lungs with the fresh, clean air surrounding the woods. Heaven's Fate was a plantation, like many, that had been carved out of the dense forest of the eastern shore of the great Chesapeake Bay. Land had been cleared acre by acre until tobacco fields stretched from the newly constructed house and barns down to the river's edges.

The house Gavin had had built was a two-and-a-half-story rectangular-shaped structure similar to others he had pointed out to Ellen along the shore, as they had sailed out of the Chesapeake Bay down the Ptasick River to Heaven's Fate's property lines. Red brick with white shutters on its many windows, it was plain but somehow magnificent, sprouting up in a stately grandeur in the middle of what seemed to be the ends of the earth.

Gavin had explained to Ellen that though the home may have seemed meager to her in comparison to country estates in England, Heaven's Fate and ones like her were by far the finest in the Colonies. He had explained that most of the other houses along the river had been built completely from materials shipped from mother England at exorbitant costs. Gavin had glowed with pride when he had told her that Heaven's Fate had been built from the red bricks baked in the plantation's own kiln, a new fangled idea that would most likely catch on in the Colonies.

Gavin looped the leather reins around the hand brake of the wagon and stood up to take in the view that had left Ellen breathless. "She's even prettier than I had hoped," he sighed proudly, staring at the house that was now nearly complete. He squeezed her hand. "Christ's bones, it's good to be home again. I didn't realize how much I truly missed it until we reached the shore."

He jumped out of the wagon and reached up to help Ellen down. "Rob, get your mistress's bags and take them inside."

Rob vaulted out of the back of the wagon and ran to do his master's bidding.

Ellen looped her arm through Gavin's, pulling on him anxiously. "I want you to show me everything," she exclaimed.

"I thought you'd like to go inside first. You can take a fresh water bath . . . rest perhaps. My house-keeper, Mary, can see you're made comfortable."

"I don't need a bath right now! Where are you going?"

"I thought I'd ride out to the west fields and see my

overseer.'' He pushed back his battered cocked hat he told her was his planting hat. "I've a mind to ride through the tobacco. I missed last year's crop; I don't want to miss this one, too.''

"Let me go with you." Ellen looked up into his green eyes. "I want to see the fields, too. I want you to tell me everything. I want to understand what it is you do here in the wilderness. I want to understand why you love it so much, husband.''

"All in good time, sweet. Now, I know you must be exhausted. Mary could give you a tour of the house. I won't be gone long.''

She threw up her hands. "The house can wait. I want to see this tobacco of yours.''

He grinned at her. "You're a rare woman, Ellen Scarlet Waxton. A rare woman, indeed.''

"Why? Because I want to be a part of my husband's life?''

"Because most women concern themselves with homes, fashion, and gossip.''

She lifted up on her toes to kiss him. "This woman is different. I've grown so used to working in the theater that I've been bored with nothing to occupy my time." She shrugged. "Since there are no theaters here in the Colonies, I thought, perhaps, I'd take up a new occupation.''

He grabbed her hands and spun her around, finding her excitement contagious. "And what occupation might that be, my lady?''

She gave him a smug grin. "Well . . . planter, of course. I'm going to grow the finest tobacco the London wharfs have ever seen!''

Gavin's laughter filled the sunlit afternoon as he took her hand and led her toward the barns. "What makes me think life with you is always going to be full of surprises?" He was still laughing, his green

373

eyes lit up with the pleasure of true happiness.

She released his hand to run ahead. "At least you'll never be bored!" she called over her shoulder.

His reply lost in the wind, Gavin could only shake his head and run to catch up with her.


Late that night Ellen lay stretched out on the new marriage bed that Gavin's Indian friend, Azoma, had built for them. Apparently, Azoma had predicted his white friend would bring a wife home from England, despite Gavin's insistence that he needed no wife. Ellen was anxious to meet this Shawnee man, curious as to what it was about a savage that Gavin could find so much respect in.

Ellen watched Gavin as he sat at a desk under the windows, flipping through records kept by the overseer concerning the plantation and crops. For the moment, she was content to lie on the bed and watch him, as she mulled over the day's events.

Gavin had kept his promise and taken her out to the tobacco fields to meet the overseer. While he and the tall redheaded Scotsman had talked, Ellen had ridden the perimeter of the west field, watching in fascination as bond servants carefully hoed the tiny tobacco plants that had been planted after the danger of frost had passed. Come late summer and early fall, one of the men had explained to her, they would cut down the great leafy plants of tobacco and pack it into crates to be hauled to the drying houses down by the river.

After Gavin had completed his immediate business with his overseer, he had taken her on a long ride, showing her just a small portion of his property. He had taken her down to the Ptasick River, where they had explored a huge drying barn that smelled of the pungent Roanoke tobacco, despite the fact that this time of year none hung in sheaths from the rafters. She had also seen the dock where men would load hogsheads of the dry product, to be shipped back to England and perhaps to France.

By the time Gavin and Ellen had returned to the big house, it was already growing dark. They had taken a quick tour of the freshly papered and painted rooms, most still absent of furniture, and then they had retired to their cozy bedchamber for a hearty meal served by the red-skinned housekeeper, Mary.

A case clock on the mantel above the cold fireplace chimed ten o'clock. "Coming to bed soon?" Ellen asked.

Gavin looked up from his paperwork and smiled at her. "Soon, sweet."

He returned his attention to his work and Ellen lay back on her pillow, closing her eyes as the warm May breeze blew in through the open windows off the river.

Her hand fell to her flat stomach. She was pregnant. She was certain of it. Her woman's flow had never come and her breasts had become tender. Though her mother had certainly never discussed such matters with her, Ellen had heard enough kitchen chatter to know the symptoms of pregnancy.

Of course, she was overjoyed at the prospect of giving Gavin a son or daughter. It was what he wanted, what *they* wanted. Yet something had kept her from telling him while they were still aboard the ship. And something kept her from telling him now.

It was Waldron.

Ellen knew Richard had said she was never to tell Gavin the truth of her past. Richard said it would serve no purpose. But Ellen felt dishonest, disloyal to Gavin for keeping such a secret. And now that she was to give birth to his child, her lies—or at least her failure to tell Gavin who she truly was—seemed an

375

even more heinous crime.

*You should just blurt it out. Tell him you're really Thomasina Waxton,* she thought. *He told you himself that he had forgiven the woman who had killed his brother. He said he no longer sought vengeance. He said what was past was past. Surely he'll understand when you tell him what a monster his brother was.*

Hadn't Gavin told her he didn't care about her secrets? Didn't he say he loved her too much for whatever she had done to matter?

She glanced up at him. As he turned to reach for a quill, his dark, shining hair fell to brush his bare shoulders in a strangely erotic way. She sighed, her heart giving a little trip.

Heavens, but she loved him!

So what was the right thing to do? Did she confess her sin and get it over with, absolving herself? Or did she keep silent the rest of her days and spare Gavin the pain of knowing she had killed his brother? No matter what a bastard Waldron had been, she wasn't fool enough to think that it wouldn't hurt Gavin just a little. After all, he was Gavin's brother, and Gavin had never known Waldron as she had known him.

*Tell him,* a part of her nagged. *Tell him and let the past truly be the past. Don't let your secret taint the child to be born.*

Ellen closed her eyes. She could hear Gavin moving about the room now, undressing as he blew out the candles to join her in their new bed. She'd tell him, she decided. She'd have to. It was just a matter of finding the right moment. . . .

"May God commit your rotting soul to hell, Waxton!" Hunt cursed, shaking his fist as he held tightly to the ship's rail to prevent being tossed into the violent sea. The vessel rocked and pitched in the squall as the crew members rushed about the deck, swinging the yards, trying desperately to keep her from dipping down into the waves, never to rise again.

Week after week the square-rigger Hunt had hired to carry him across the ocean to the Colonies met storm upon storm on the open seas. These unpredictable tempests forced them off course, putting them days, then weeks off schedule. At the rate they were sailing, a voyage that should have taken two or three months would take four or five.

The journey seemed doomed at every turn.

Sickness swept through the ship's crew only a week out of London. The fortunate men died, while others still lay in the ship's hold, gripping their bellies as their life's blood was slowly sapped from them.

In a storm a month off the coast, the main's starboard braces snapped, causing the foredeck to submerge for a harrowing moment. In the same storm provisions that had been securely tied to the deck went overboard, severely depleting the crew's food and fresh water supplies.

The captain swore he had never seen such ill luck in the twenty-odd years he'd been sailing. The crew was beginning to mumble about witchcraft and devil's curses. They all feared the white-skinned duke and stayed as far from him as was possible.

With barely half a sailing crew, the captain had requested returning to port to replace the lost and sick men, but the Duke of Hunt adamantly refused. He promised the captain that he would pay him handsomely to take him safely to Maryland and then home again to England in a timely manner. If the captain failed, he would die.

Hunt leaned over the rail, resting his forehead on the back of his hand. He let the icy rain and seawater pelt his face, hoping it would calm his heaving stomach.

"Thomasina Waxton," he muttered maliciously as he traced the line of the raised scar that ran across his cheek. "You'll pay you, malapert slut. You'll pay dearly for the trouble you've caused me." He looked up into the noonday sky that was naught but a swirl of dark, ominous clouds as black as midnight. "You'll wish to God Almighty you had given me your maidenhead when I had asked all those years ago. You'd have been better off with me than Waldron. We could have been friends, you and I." He pulled his wet cloak up over his head and turned to stalk across the slippery deck. "Instead, you have made us mortal enemies, little Thomasina, and you will soon see just how mortal you are. . . ."

"A good morning to you, mistress," the housekeeper, Mary, called from the window as she pushed open the draperies and let in the sparkling late June sunlight.

Ellen yawned and stretched. The place beside her was empty and cool. She'd slept late again. Already, Gavin was dressed and gone on his horse to survey one of the many tobacco fields, or to direct the clearing of more land granted to him by King Charles.

*June*, Ellen thought. *More than a month has passed and I still haven't told him. Not about Thomasina. Not about the babe.* She just hadn't found the right time.

She was beginning to wonder if there was ever going to be a right time. She was now more than three months pregnant. Another month and her belly would begin to grow round with the blossoming of her child. In another month Gavin would be able to look at her and see that she was pregnant.

But she didn't want him to find out that way. She wanted to tell him herself. She wanted to enjoy the moment with him. She wanted to celebrate the miracle of life wrapped in his loving arms.

Mary set a tray of herbal tea and biscuits on the table beside the bed. She laid Ellen's robe beside her and turned discreetly away so that her mistress could slip out of bed and cover her nakedness.

"And how be your belly pains this morning, mistress?" Mary inquired.

"Fine." Ellen stood and slipped her arms into her dressing robe and tied it around her middle. She'd been plagued with nausea for weeks but was finally feeling better. "Just fine, thank you."

"Should pass soon. A mother is not sick all the moons."

"Mother?"

Mary turned with a smile. She was a stout woman with skin the color of turned soil and hair as black as a crow's wing, save for the streaks of silver-grey. Her button eyes followed Ellen. "A woman who has lived as long as this woman knows when another carries her husband's child."

Ellen poured herself a cup of tea. There was no need to lie to Mary. The Shawnee woman was one of those people a person just couldn't deceive. Ellen knew she would see through the falseness of her words in an instant. Besides, Mary was the first friend she'd made upon her arrival at Heaven's Fate. Ellen didn't want to jeopardize that, not for anything.

"So when do you tell the master? His heart will jump for the joy only a father can know."

Ellen reached for a biscuit. "I . . . I was waiting for the right time."

Mary removed clean undergarments from a chest of drawers and laid them on the bed. She came back a moment later with a simple apple-green gown made of sturdy broadcloth. "Do not wait too long to tell the master, or he will have reason for suspicion. This is not a thing a woman should hide from her husband." She spread out the gown. "It is not good for the babe that grows in the womb."

*Today,* Ellen thought. *Should I tell him today?*

But she wasn't ready! She hadn't rehearsed her speech in days!

Ellen glanced at Mary and the way the older woman looked at her. She knew. Somehow Mary knew there was more to be told than that of the babe.

"Oh, Mary," Ellen murmured, "I have something else to tell Gavin first, but I'm afraid. Afraid he'll be angry. Afraid to hurt him. To hurt what we have."

"The truth is often like the shaman's knife," Mary said gently. "It hurts as it goes in, cutting out the poison"—she twisted her hand as if it held a dagger—"but after the evil it cuts clean away, the knife is a healer. It makes the flesh whole and good. Stronger than before."

Ellen ran her fingers through her thick hair. Perhaps Mary was right. Perhaps today was the day. Since she had decided to tell Gavin the truth about who she was, it had been hanging over her like a funeral pall.

Draining her cup of tea, Ellen rose. "Do you know where my husband's gone today?"

Mary smiled. "Happened to ask young Rob as I was coming up. The boy say he's gone to the dry house in the west fields. He fix a hole in the roof. Rain on the tobacco is not very good."

Ellen reached for her clean shift. "I think I'll take a ride out to the drying house this morning. Could you have Rob fetch me a horse?"

"The boy can ride with you."

"No. I'll go alone."

"The master, he say he does not want you alone. He is afraid of something or someone, mistress, but this woman he will not tell."

For the first time in months, Ellen thought of Hunt. Would he? Certainly not. Even if he did figure out where she had gone and with whom, he'd never cross the ocean to retrieve the letter. She could do him no harm so far from London. There would be no sense in pursuing her across the sea.

"I'll be fine, Mary. If a woman's not safe on her own land, where is she safe? No one on the Eastern Shore would harm me for fear of Lord Waxton."

Mary went to the door. "I will have the boy get the horse. Then I will come back to help you with your clothing."

Ellen nodded and turned to start dressing. Now that she had made up her mind to tell Gavin the truth about her past, she was in a hurry to see it through.

A short time later Ellen rode up to the tobacco drying house down by the river's edge. She dismounted from her mare, leaving it tied with Hunt's horse. Gavin had not only insisted on bringing it across the ocean, but he now rode it most of the time.

"Gavin," she called as she approached the barn. "Gavin, are you there?"

"Ellen?"

She looked up, following the sound of his voice. She shaded her eyes from the morning sun.

There, a good two stories in the air, Gavin sat

straddling the roof's peak, a hammer in his hand and nails clenched between his teeth.

Ellen dropped her hands to her hips impatiently. "What are you doing up there? Are there no servants who can bang a straight nail? If you fall off that roof and break your neck, I'll marry again in a month's time, I swear I will!"

"Very funny." He shinnied across the roof's peak and disappeared off the back end. A minute later, he came around the barn. He was dressed much like his bond servants, in homespun breeches and white shirt, minus a cravat. A thick braid of hair poked from beneath a wool cocked hat to trail down his back.

"So, to what do I owe this unexpected pleasure?" He leaned to brush his lips against hers in a casual greeting. "The way you've been sleeping lately, I didn't think you'd be up until the noonday meal."

She laughed with him, reaching out to touch his arm, but when she lifted her gaze to meet his, she grew serious. "I came because I need to talk to you, Gavin."

His face was suddenly solemn. "What's wrong? Are you ill? Have you—"

"Gavin, please listen to me. I have to tell you something . . . something Richard said I should never tell you."

"Then don't."

He tried to hold her hand fast, but she pulled away. "I can't keep it inside me any longer. I thought I could, but I can't, Gavin. I'm not that strong. I feel dirty inside." She looked up at him. "I love you so much that I just can't do it."

"Ellen, I've told you again and again. I don't want to know your secrets. What's passed has passed. You're mine now and that's all I care about. It's all

I'll ever care about. Now I understand how difficult Richard's death was for you, but give yourself time. You're going to be all right."

Ellen could see now that this was going to be even more difficult than she had thought. Gavin honestly didn't want to know the truth. But he had to know. It was the only way to bring a baby into the world. "Gavin, you have to listen to me. Yes, I'm yours now," she said as gently as possible, "but I once belonged to another."

He lifted a hand. "Please, sweetheart. Don't do it. Don't torture yourself like this. I don't care about your secrets." He took her by the shoulders, forcing her to meet his green-eyed gaze. "All I care about is you. How can I make you understand that? Whoever you were in the past, it doesn't matter now."

"Even if I was once Thomasina Waxton?" She blurted it out. Even before she realized what she was saying, her words were hanging still in the air like the dampness just before a rain.

He let go of her shoulders. "What did you say?" He spoke slowly, as if unable to comprehend her words.

Miserable, Ellen dragged her gaze across his face. "I said, Gavin . . . I said I was Thomasina. I was once your brother's wife."

"No." Gavin took a step backward, nearly stumbling. "That's impossible."

"It's not impossible. It's true."

"But . . . but Thomasina had brown hair. She—"

"I dyed my hair. The night Waldron died, I fled from Hunt. Richard found me on the road and took me in. He changed my name, he set me up at the theater, he—"

"No." He took yet another step backward, as if she somehow poisoned the air he breathed. "You couldn't have killed my brother, not you, Ellen. Not you who said you loved me."

She clasped her hands, wanting to comfort him but not knowing how. "I do love you, more than I thought I could ever love. That's why I had to tell you. I had to tell you because we're going to—"

Gavin shook his head in utter disbelief, not allowing her to finish. "This is no joke, is it?" he spat out.

She hung her head. "No. But let me explain. Let me tell you what Waldron—"

"I don't want to hear it!" he shouted. "No more lies, Ellen . . . Thomasina . . . whatever the devil your name is!" He turned away from her and started for his horse.

This wasn't what Ellen had expected. Yes, she had expected anger, pain. But she hadn't thought he would just walk away. "There won't be any more lies, I swear it," she called after him. "Don't you see, that's why I'm telling you this. So there will be no more lies between us!"

"You killed my brother!" he roared, jerking loose the white steed's reins. "You murdered him!"

"I didn't. Not really!" She followed him, putting out her hands to implore. "Let me explain, please. Let me tell you about Waldron, about Hunt."

"I don't want to hear whatever it is you have to say!"

Tears ran down Ellen's face as she watched him swing into the saddle. "But I don't understand. You said you forgave Thomasina. You said—"

"I said my need for vengeance had passed!" He lifted his upper lip in a sneer. "That doesn't mean I want to be married to her . . . to you, you deceiving bitch!"

Ellen's mouth fell open in utter shock . . . in despair. Gavin rode away without another word.

# Chapter Twenty-Six

*Two months,* Ellen thought dismally. *Two months you've been gone, husband.* She sat in his chair behind his desk in the library she was preparing for him in his absence and ran a hand over her swelling middle. *Two months you've been gone. Where, I don't know. When you'll be back . . . I don't know that, either.*

A late summer breeze filtered through the open windows, blowing the hair gently off her shoulders. The child in her womb stirred and tears came to her eyes.

And what would happen when Gavin did return to Heaven's Fate? Would he pack her up and send her back to England to face the Duke of Hunt alone? Or would he at least feel a responsibility to the child she would bear him and allow her to live here with him, though without the love they had once shared?

Ellen wiped at her eyes with the back of her hand, not certain which would be worse. She sighed as she dried her eyes. All this time since Gavin had been gone, she'd tried hard not to feel sorry for herself.

*Richard was right,* she thought miserably. *I just shouldn't have told him. I should have taken the secret to my grave and then Gavin would still be here.*

*But you couldn't have,* her heart echoed. *You couldn't have done it to Gavin nor to the babe you'll bear him.*

"So now what?" she said to the empty room. "What do I do now? Do I pack my belongings and return to London? Or do I stay here and fight for the man I love, even if he no longer loves me?"

She stared out the open window, her chest tightening. In the distance she could hear the sounds of singing voices as the bond servants in the fields cultivated the maturing tobacco. It was almost harvesttime.

God, but she loved this Maryland of Gavin's. Dear God, but she loved the brick house, the gardens that were being planted, the rows of tobacco that seemed to stretch on to eternity.

The tobacco was what had kept her sane these last two months without Gavin. The morning after he had gone, she dragged herself out of bed and had young Rob saddle her mare. From that day forth, each morning she rose and, with the boy at her side, inspected the fields. She spoke with the overseer who, in time, came to accept her. She talked with the bondmen. And she listened. She listened not only to the men who knew about the growing of tobacco, but she also listened to the land. She listened to the wind that blew in off the river and rustled the leaves of the Roanoke. She listened to the sounds of the soil as the tobacco grew healthy and strong, rising up toward the heavens.

Ellen didn't want to go back to London. Even if she knew Hunt was dead, she'd still not have wanted to return. She knew that even with a loveless marriage, her choice would be to remain here in the Colonies . . . here at Heaven's Fate, where life was

386

ever-changing, where there was a world of information to absorb, where there were always surprises. Even without Gavin's love, which she had surely lost, she could make herself content here as she knew she could nowhere else. Though she'd only lived here a few months, she knew the American Colonies were now her own . . . the home she had never really had.

Ellen rose and went to the bookshelves she'd had built in Gavin's absence. She ran a finger over a freshly planed board; she could still smell the pungent scent of the pine. She had ordered that shelves be built from floor to ceiling on two sides of the room, and now that they were complete, she was putting Gavin's books in order for him. She hoped he would be pleased when he came home and found his beloved books so lovingly cared for and now proudly displayed.

When he came home . . . When was he coming home? Where had he gone? The day he had left, he'd simply ridden away. He'd not returned to the house nor spoken to anyone. In the first days after his departure, Ellen hadn't been quite certain what to say to the servants. But she'd soon gotten over the embarrassment, realizing that as long as he was gone, as mistress of Heaven's Fate, she was in charge.

*He's gone, and I don't know when he'll return,* she explained simply to those who worked on the plantation, then later to neighbors. And she had apparently stated the fact in such a way that no one had dared question her further.

Ellen picked up a book from a wooden crate on the floor and slid it onto a shelf. After two months of Gavin's absence, she was beginning to fear for his safety. Two months was a long time to be gone, even if he was furious with her.

Why didn't he just come home and tell her to leave?

Why didn't he come home and allow her to explain the situation between her and Waldron? Why hadn't he at least given her a chance to tell him her side of the story? Why had he assumed she was the villain?

Lost in her thoughts, Ellen had emptied an entire crate of books and started on another, when Mary came down the hallway. "Mr. Julius to see you, mistress," the housekeeper said in a singsong voice Ellen had taken great comfort in these last two months.

Ellen spun around, smiling. It was good to see the sea captain's familiar face. Any malice she had felt toward Julius in England had long since faded. "Julius!" She offered her hands and he grinned as he took them.

"You're looking fair enough," he told her, squeezing her hands.

She brought her fingertips to her cheeks. "I'm getting fat. Gavin's going to be utterly repulsed by the time he gets—" Her voice caught in her throat and she turned away with embarrassment. She took pride in her strength these days. She didn't want Julius or anyone else to see her weakness.

Julius sighed and went to the chair behind Gavin's new desk. He made himself at home, propping his worn boots on the freshly polished desktop. "I never thought I'd say it, but my good friend Gavin, as of late the Earl of Waxton, is a fool."

"I deceived him, Julius." A week after Gavin had disappeared, Julius had come to call. Ellen had found herself baring her secret to the older man, who had taken it upon himself since then to come by often and visit, to comfort in his gruff manner as best he knew how.

"Aye, aye, I know your sad tale. But it doesn't matter. I thought Gavin to be a better man. He was a

388

fool to stalk off like that."

"You think so? I hurt him so badly. . . ."

"Every man or woman has a right to have his or her say, and Gavin didn't respect that. He had this idea in his head of who this brother of his was. Truth was—and only you knew it—that the man was a bastard from the start."

"I should have told Gavin who I was when I first realized who he was."

"Should have, could have!" Julius threw up a hand in exasperation. "Water under the hull now, sweet. Maybe you should've told him, but you didn't. Why didn't you?"

Tears shone in her eyes. "Because I already loved him. I didn't want to hurt him. I just wanted to be with him a little longer."

He slapped his hand on the desk. "So there you have it. It weren't for the sake of deceit that you kept the truth from him. It makes a difference. Now me, had I been in your position, I'd've never told the truth of the matter and never thought about it again."

Ellen wrapped her arms around her waist, turning away from Julius to pace the sanded floor. "I know, I know. That's what you keep telling me. That's what Richard said. But I just couldn't do it, Julius."

He pulled off his knit cap and tossed it on the desk. "It don't matter what you did. He shouldn't have run off like that. Like a boy angry with his mama."

She grasped a bookcase for support and stared out past Julius through the open window. "Ods fish, but where is he?" she said as much to herself as to Julius. "Where did he go? Why doesn't he come home, even if it's just to tell me to pack my belongings and go? I don't know how long I can stand this waiting."

"You're a good woman, Ellen. Gavin was a bright enough boy to recognize that. He'll surely come to his senses soon and drag his tail home."

Her gaze drifted to Julius's wrinkled, suntanned face. "Haven't you any idea where he is? If I could go to him . . ."

Julius slid his feet off the desk and pulled a toothpick from his coat to push between his teeth. "He ain't been into town. No one's seen him at the docks. He ain't holin' up at some other rich boyo's plantation. I checked them all out."

Her gaze met his. "Do you think he's hurt? Worse?" The word *dead* echoed in her head, but she didn't dare speak it.

"Gavin? Dead, you mean?" Julius gave a laugh. "Too cantankerous to die." He rose out of his chair, twirling his toothpick thoughtfully. "No. I'd think he's just more stubborn than most of us. Me, I might have run off for a day or two, gotten myself really down and out soused, but then I'd have come trailin' home. I'd not give up a warm bed and a willing maid so easily, wife with child or no."

Ellen's cheeks colored but she smiled, knowing Julius meant to pay her a compliment rather than to offend her.

She shrugged. "So what do you think I should do?" Ellen paused, dreading the thought of saying it but wanting to. "Do you think it would be best for me to find a ship to take me back to England?"

Julius's brow creased. "England! Hell and fury, no, you shouldn't go back to England! You can't go back there, not ever. Not at least as long as that bedlamite albino roams the streets. I say you stay here and wait on that foolish bastard of a husband of yours, and when he does show his tail, you give him a what for. You make him sit down and listen to you. You tie him to his own mainm'st if you have to, but you tell him what a son of bitch his brother was and you tell him what he did to you."

She shook her head. "I don't want to hurt Gavin, not any more than I have. What purpose would it serve to tell him what a creature his brother was? What reason would there be for telling now that he's dead?"

"You're a great one for the truth in all matters." Julius pulled his knit sailor's cap down over his sunbleached hair. "Don't you think it's 'bout time Gavin lost those boyhood imaginings and knew the truth of his elder brother?"

She shook her head. "I don't know. I just don't know anymore."

"Well, you keep your chin up, sweet." He started for the door. "I got one thought on where the coward might have gone. Thought, mayhap, I'd look into it."

Her face lit up. "Do you? Where? Oh, please, Julius. Tell me. If I could go to him . . . If I could only explain to him . . ."

Julius put up a scarred palm, silencing her. "You stay put, missy, and keep that child you're carrying safe. I'll try and see what I can do about bringing his papa home."

Ellen smiled as she watched Julius lope out of the library. "Thank you," she called after him.

Julius just threw up a hand in reply and disappeared down the hallway.


Julius whistled to himself as he trudged through the thick forest, a light pack thrown over his shoulder. He'd been walking since sunup, and with the day nearly over, he knew he had to be nearing the Shawnee village he sought. If Gavin wasn't here, he was at a loss as to where else to look for him.

Julius heard a soft thump and lifted his gaze, to see a Shawnee brave standing in the middle of the game path he had been following most of the day. Trying not to appear startled, Julius halted and nodded his head. "Greeting to you." He gave the hand signal of peace. "I look for my friend, Gavin, of Heaven's Fate."

The Shawnee brave crossed his arms over his bare bronze chest, studying Julius with a careful eye. He replied with something abrupt in Shawnee.

Julius cleared his throat. "Have you seen Gavin? I know he's friend to your people. I thought he might be in your village." Julius didn't know how much English the brave understood, but he hoped it was more than the Shawnee Julius understood. "Gavin?"

The brave pursed his lips and whistled shrilly. An instant later two more braves appeared out of the trees, seeming to manifest themselves before Julius's very eyes. The first spoke sharply to the other two, who then gestured for Julius to follow them.

Julius gave a shrug, moved his pack to a more comfortable position on his shoulder, and started after the two Indian men. "Well, I suppose you two boyos are either leading me to Gavin or to burn me to the stake, one or the other." He chuckled to himself.

The brave ahead of him glanced over his shoulder at Julius with uncertainty. The other brave simply took up the rear.

Julius walked in silence with the two braves for another three quarters of a mile before he began to hear the sounds of the Indian encampment they approached. Stepping through a seemingly impenetrable wall of briars, Julius found himself inside the Shawnee camp.

The village was alive with the sight and sound of black-haired, sun-bronzed men, women, and children hurrying through their evening tasks, preparing to settle down to a warm meal and the company of family and friends. A group of children ran between the hut-like wigwams, chasing a speckled hound with pups. A teenage brave busied himself feeding a small herd of hobbled shaggy-haired ponies.

As Julius entered the camp with the two braves, several Shawnee men and women glanced up with curiosity to see who the white man was, but no one seemed disturbed. A toddler came out of her family's wigwam to stare with black button eyes, until her mother dragged her back inside, admonishing her for her rude behavior, no doubt.

The two braves led Julius through the camp, directly to a wigwam that was outside the seemingly haphazardly placed structures. One brave signaled for Julius to wait and ducked inside. Julius heard the Indian speak, then Gavin's own voice as he replied in the strange language.

*I'll be damned. I've found him,* Julius thought.

A second later Gavin came out of the wigwam with a great smile on his face. He threw his arms around Julius and pounded him on the back. "Good to see you, old friend!"

Gavin turned to the two braves and gave thanks for their escort. The Indians made a polite reply and then excused themselves, disappearing among the many wigwams.

Julius tossed his bag down on the ground and dropped his hands to his hips. "You're looking a mite thinner than last I saw you, friend. These savages not feeding you properly?"

Gavin laughed. "Christ's bones, it's good to hear a decent English voice, even if it is yours, you old sea dog. Some of the men here speak the king's tongue, but it's so interspersed with hand signals and

Shawnee that it's damned hard to follow!"

The two men stood regarding each other for a moment after their laughter faded. Then Gavin spoke again, the smile fading from his face. "So what brings you here?" he intoned.

"You addlepated? What do you think brings me here?"

Gavin glanced away, scowling. "You ought not stick your nose into business that's not your own, Julius. 'T'will get you into nothing but trouble."

"And you ought not be such a flaming fool!"

Gavin whirled around to challenge his friend. "I don't know what she told you, but—"

"The truth is what she told. And how did you reward her for her honesty? You run off like a little boy who didn't get his way!"

Gavin took a step backward, shocked by Julius's harsh words. "She killed my brother, for Christ's sake!"

"You didn't hear her out!" Julius shook a finger. "You didn't give her a chance to tell you what happened."

Gavin folded his arms over his chest. "She deceived me from the start."

"Seems to me, boyo, when first you came to London, you didn't tell anyone you were Waxton's brother! You skirted about, calling yourself Merrick. You deceived her."

"That's not the same thing and you damned well know it!" Noticing that several Shawnee were looking their way, Gavin lowered his voice. "And truthfully, I was Merrick. I was simply also Waxton."

"Words! Dueling with meaningless words is all you're doing, and you're doing it to keep from admitting that you might well have been wrong." The old sailor leaned over a bucket of fresh water near the door to Gavin's wigwam and ladled himself a drink. He took a long sip and then wiped his mouth with the back of his hand. "You play these word games to avoid the issue, friend."

Gavin's green eyes narrowed angrily. "And just what is the issue?"

"The blasted issue is that you got a wife five months gone with child sitting back in that big house of yours waiting for you. You've damned well broke her heart running off like this!"

Gavin's voice softened. "She's pregnant?" He looked away, suddenly deep in thought. "She didn't tell me."

"With you acting like such a jackanape, why would she?"

Gavin lifted his chin to meet Julius's gaze. "Surely she knew before I left. Before she came to me with her *confession*. Why didn't she tell me then?"

"Ask her yourself, why don't you?"

Gavin turned his boot in the hard-packed soil. "I've nothing to say to her. I want no more of her lies."

"By the king's cod!" Julius sat down on the ground outside the wigwam and picked up a stick. He began to draw pictures in the dust. "Did you ask her why she lied? Did you?"

"No."

"When you love someone the way you claimed to love her, you owe that person certain rights. The rights to explain herself bein' one of 'em."

"How could she have done it, Julius? How could she have pushed him out the window?" Gavin's voice cracked. "How could she have murdered my brother in cold blood like that? Ellen? My sweet Ellen?"

"Were you there?"

Gavin laughed, but without humor. "No, don't be

ridiculous. Of course I wasn't there. I was here, half a world away."

"Then how do you know what happened? Whose word you got?"

"The authorities, of course!" Gavin shook his head. "The king's men made a report. I read it."

"The king's men or Hunt's?"

There was a long pause of silence as Gavin swallowed that thought. Finally, he came to sit beside Julius. He drew his knees up and stared out over the trees at the setting sun. "How could I have loved my brother's wife?"

"Loved? You mean you don't love her anymore?" Julius turned to watch Gavin carefully. "Tell me, is she any different now than she was the day you married her on the foredeck? The answer is no. Nothin' has changed. Nothin' but that she wanted only honesty between herself and the man she loves. Even if the honesty could cost her that love." Julius paused. "Has her honesty cost her your love, great Earl of Waxton?"

Gavin made a fist. It was obvious from the sound of his voice that he fought back tears. "She killed my brother!"

"Mayhap she did, but killed is right, as in she did it before you ever met her. Before you ever fell for those dark eyes and that smile that can light up every face in a room."

"She lied about Waldron . . . about who she was. How many other lies were there?"

Julius went back to scratching in the earth. "I don't know. You'd have to ask her. But my experience has been that a man might be able to lie about what happened to him, about what he did, but he can never lie about who he is." He tapped Gavin's shirt with the tip of his stick. "A man or a woman can't lie about what's in the heart. Her heart's pure and you know it, Gavin. You just need to push your pride aside to see it."

Gavin squeezed his eyes shut, pressing the heel of his hand to his forehead. "I don't know, Jules. I just don't know."

"What don't you know?"

"If I can forgive her . . ." Gavin answered softly. "I hated the woman who killed Waldron for so long that I don't know if I have that forgiveness in me."

"So what was all that talk you gave me on the ship of forgiving the Lady Waxton? I seem to recall you tellin' me you no longer sought her. You told me what was past was past. *Forgive* was most definitely the word you used."

"But to forgive a stranger, a woman I would never meet, was different. This means forgiving my wife for killing my brother. I . . . I'm not certain I can do it."

"Don't you think you ought to hear Ellen out before you go decide on such a thing?"

"A child." Gavin shook his head. "A child makes everything so much more complicated."

"So whoever told you life was going to be wrapped up all neat like a hogshead of tobacco? Life ain't neat. It's sticky, and sometimes it hurts."

Gavin turned to his friend. "She told you her side of the story?"

"That she did."

"And you believed her?"

"I believed her, and were you to give her half a chance, I think you'd believe her, too."

"Tell me."

Julius shook his head. "Ain't my place. If this is to be settled, it's got to be settled between the two of you."

Gavin stared out at the Indian village, but without focusing his eyes. "My brother, Jules," he whispered. "Waldron was my brother. He protected me as a child. He funded me as a man. I loved him."

"But now you love her. And you'll love the babe she brings into this world for you." Julius laid a hand on Gavin's arm. "I'm warning you. You give her up and you'll never be the man you could have been. As much as the thought that Ellen killed your brother hurts, it won't break you in two. You lose her and you'll never be whole again." Julius rose and picked up his pack. "Now you just think about what I said here and see if you can't find a way to bring back some sense into that head of yours."

Gavin stood. "Where are you going?"

"Home. I'll not stay here and fight with you all night, friend. I came to say what I said, and now I'll be on my way."

Gavin followed him through the village. "It's near dark. . . . At least stay the night, Julius. We could share a bottle of brandy."

Julius pulled his knit cap down over his head stubbornly. "Nope. I'll just be on my way. Any brandy of yours would taste sour on my breath right now." He gave a wave as he strode through the village in the direction of Heaven's Fate. "You come to your senses, Gavin, you know where to find me. I'll be lookin' after your wife, like you ought to be."

Gavin stood in shocked silence as he watched his friend disappear into the forest. He called out to Julius once, but the sea captain pretended not to hear.

# Chapter Twenty-Seven

Ellen stood in Gavin's library, her arms wrapped protectively around her middle as she listened to the rain that pounded on the windows. A single lamp lit the room. Lost in thought, she stared at the portrait Gavin had carted across the ocean. She stared at the woman she had been.

Ellen didn't know what had possessed her to bring the picture out, to unwrap it, and to have it carried here to Gavin's study. She laughed to herself, wondering if madness was indeed taking over.

But as she studied Thomasina's distinctive jawline and the curve of her cheek, she felt something close to contentment wash over her. She no longer feared the secret of her past, because it was no longer a secret. Thomasina could never hurt her again.

The thought that she had most likely lost Gavin's love made her heart ache. But somewhere in the midst of that ache was a spark of relief . . . of accomplishment, almost joy. She would give birth to her child not under the cover of deceit, but with the honesty every child deserves from his or her mother.

As she stared at the portrait, a slip of paper tucked under a book on Gavin's desk caught her eye. It was

Gavin's writing. She picked up the paper and smiled. On one side of the paper was a list of materials needed to build a new dock down by the river, but on the other side was an old note he had left her one morning on his way to the fields. It was a silly note, meaningless now, but she tucked it into the slit in her skirting where she wore a pocket. Somehow now the note was precious.

A sound much like the whinny of a horse caught Ellen's attention and she turned toward the dark windows behind her. She listened again but this time could hear nothing but the howl of the wind.

Suddenly cool, Ellen picked up the lamp from the desk and made her way down the hall in search of her wrapper. "Mary?"

"Mistress?" A comforting call came from the direction of the kitchen.

Ellen heard footsteps, then the Indian housekeeper appeared. "What be it, mistress?"

Ellen's brow furrowed. "A noise. Did you hear a queer noise outside?"

"Heard nothing but the crack of the fire and the snore of the boy. He's asleep on his bed in the kitchen."

Ellen glanced at the darkened front hall. Julius was bedded down in the horse barn. He refused to sleep in the main house, saying it wasn't befitting.

Julius had disappeared for three days after their conversation in the library concerning Gavin, and when he had reappeared, Ellen had a feeling he had spoken with her husband. When she questioned him, he refused to discuss the subject. All he would tell her was to have patience. After a week, her patience with both Gavin and Julius was growing thin.

"Wake up, Rob," Ellen said, looking back at Mary. "I'm going to run up and get my wrap. I want Rob to go out and take a look around with Julius."

"Something amiss, mistress?"

Ellen shook her head. "I don't know. Something doesn't feel right. I'm suddenly uneasy." She looked up at Mary, feeling a little foolish. "Do you know what I mean?"

Mary nodded her head gravely. "A night like this the ghosts of our ancestors come back to haunt us. It is a night to keep close to the fire and lift prayers to the heavens."

Ellen laughed as she started up the steps toward the bedchamber she had once shared with Gavin. "I fear no ghosts, Mary."

*Only men,* she thought. *Only one man.* She didn't know what had made her think of Hunt. Of course, there was no need to fear him. He was an ocean away, and she was safe. She knew that. Didn't she?

Upstairs, Ellen found her wool wrapper and tied it around her shoulders to chase away the chill she just couldn't shake.

The storm that had been blowing in all evening seemed to be gaining strength now. She could hear the wind howling and tree branches scraping the windows. Ellen walked to a window near Gavin's desk and peered out into the darkness. Rain pelted the glass so hard that it sounded like rocks hitting the panes. Thunderclouds clashed and lightning zigzagged through the air.

A streak of lightning suddenly lit up the sky, and for just an instant Ellen thought she saw men on horseback below. She grasped the windowsill and leaned closer, pressing her face to the glass. When lightning lit the sky again, she saw nothing.

*Shadows,* she thought.

Downstairs she heard a door open and close and knew young Rob was finally making his way out

401

to the barn.

"About time," she murmured. The boy was well behaved and obedient, but like most young men in their teen years, he was sometimes a little slow to respond to a request.

Ellen had started for the bedchamber door, when she thought she heard a bang, followed by two more. *Gunshots or thunder*, she thought. She backtracked to the window, suddenly very uneasy.

"Rob? Julius?" she murmured aloud. Of course there were plenty of other men on the plantation—bondmen and the overseer—but they slept in bunkhouses or in small single-family dwellings well away from the house.

Ellen cupped her hands over her face to block out the glare of the lamplight in her room and stared down into the yard below. She saw nothing, yet she sensed a presence. It was an odd feeling for a person who claimed to be so practical.

She rolled her eyes heavenward as she spun around, dismissing her uncomfortable feeling. All this talk of ghosts! She'd soon be as superstitious as Mary!

She picked up the lamp and started down the hallway. She had just reached the top step when she heard Mary scream.

"Mary!" Ellen screamed back. She leaned over the railing to see what was wrong and what she saw turned her blood icy.

A burly sailor was dragging a kicking and screaming Mary across the polished floor of the front hall.

Hunt stood in the doorway, his shocking white hair brushed back in a wet mane, a black cloak covering his shoulders. By the light of the lamp with the flicker of lightning behind him, he appeared even more sinister than Ellen had remembered.

"Run, mistress!" Mary shouted. "Run from the ghosts!"

"Mary!"

"Run!" she repeated as the sailor dragged her from Ellen's view. "Run from the evil!"

"Thomasina?" Hunt's voice echoed off the freshly plastered and painted walls of the stairwell. "Thomasina, my dear, come down."

Ellen whirled around and ran. She knew she couldn't help Mary at this moment, but at least she could try to help her own unborn child, for Ellen knew as sure as she lived that if Hunt captured her, she'd not live a fortnight.

"Thomasina! You whoring jade! Don't make me have to come after you! Come down here, I say!"

Ellen could hear Hunt's footsteps on the staircase as she turned the corner and raced for her bedchamber.

"Thomasina, I've come too far to play your games. We both know what I want!" he shouted. "We both know what I must have!"

Ellen reached the haven of her bedchamber and slammed the door shut. She leaned to throw the lock in the darkness, then cursed as she realized the locks had not yet been added to the doors.

"Thomasina!"

She grabbed a cherry sideboard and pulled it across the floor. Pushing it against the door, she ran for another piece. She shoved Gavin's desk against the door and frantically ran to pile heavy objects on both tables. She added two chairs, a stepping stool, and several small objects.

"Thomasina!" Hunt boomed from the hallway. He gave the door a push. "Thomasina, you're being childish!"

"Go away!" she screamed.

"Thomasina, dear, give me the letter and I won't tell your new husband the truth of who you are."

Ellen began to back up, away from the door. As Hunt spoke, he pushed on it. The furniture was beginning to slide.

"Go to hell, Hunt!" she cried. "He already knows!"

"And he doesn't care that you murdered his beloved brother in cold blood?"

"I didn't murder him and you know it! He was trying to murder me! He fell, and well he deserved it!" Ellen didn't know what made her so bold. The fear of death? Or was it that she had simply grown tired of her fear of the Duke of Hunt?

"Give me the letter, Thomasina, dear, and I'll collaborate with your story. Your charges of murder will be dropped. You'll be a free woman."

She laughed at his lies as she backed up to the window. She could see his white hands gripping the inside of the door now as he pushed his way in. Dear God, but she wished she had a gun. Of course, they were both down in Gavin's library. From here she could never get to them. "You'll have me cleared of all charges, will you?"

"A fair trade, I should think," he grunted as he shoved the door open inch by inch. "You get your freedom, I get Waldron's letter?"

Ellen threw open the window behind her. The wind whipped the draperies, and rain came through in sheets to wet the floor and soak her skirts. "You would do that, Duke?" she asked sweetly. "Give me my freedom for that silly list of names?" She could see his face now as he pressed open the door. He had almost gained entry into her bedchamber.

"I would."

"But I already have my freedom. And what harm could I do you now, here so far from London and your politicking?"

With a final shove, the desk went toppling over and Hunt stepped inside the room. Sweat beaded on his forehead from the exertion. "I completely agree, dearest, but there are friends of mine at Court who are not so . . . trusting." He held out his hand. "It's for them I must have the letter. Not myself, you understand?"

The sight of Hunt here in her bedchamber made her stomach churn. Dear God, how she hated this man! She put her hands behind her back and felt the cool rain as it poured through the window. "I would give you the letter, out of kindness," she said, her gaze meeting his. For once she didn't shrink back in fear of his inhuman pink eyes. "But unfortunately, I no longer have it."

"Liar!" He grabbed a chair off the desk and hurled it at her.

Ellen ducked and the chair struck the upper panes of the window, showering her with glass. Slowly, she rose and slipped her hand into her skirting pocket. "Of course, perhaps I do have it. . . ." She pulled out a small slip of paper.

Hunt dove for Ellen.

She slipped her hand back into her pocket and spun around. If she were to die, she'd be damned if she'd die by Hunt's hand. Without another thought, she leaped through the window into the darkness.

Ellen hit the small overhang below with a crash and a grunt of pain. The front porch roof had been farther below than she anticipated.

She rolled onto her side, still stunned. Above her she heard Hunt shout her name, but in the darkness, he apparently couldn't see her.

405

She smiled to herself as she pushed up into a sitting position, taking care not to slide any farther down the shingled roof. She had lost one of her slippers in the fall but had somehow managed to cradle herself well enough to have apparently not injured the child she carried.

*So now what?* she thought. She retrieved her calfskin shoe and slipped it on her foot.

Hunt had disappeared from the window. Surely he was on his way down the steps now. No doubt he was hoping she had met the same fate her first husband had. Wouldn't he be surprised when he didn't find her lying on the ground in a pool of blood?

Of course, Ellen knew she couldn't stay here. A bright streak of lightning could light up the sky well enough for her to be seen on the porch roof by Hunt or one of his henchmen.

Her only choice, of course, was to go down, to slip off the porch roof onto the ground without being seen, then run. But once Hunt realized she'd escaped onto the porch roof, he would expect to find her on the ground.

She glanced up at the open window of her bedchamber above her. The room was now cloaked in darkness. Hunt must have taken the lamp with him. What if she went back up?

Carefully, she stood. The cedar shake shingles were slippery and difficult to walk on, but slowly she made her way up the angled roof toward the exterior wall of the brick house.

Below her she heard the shouts of men. She thought she detected Hunt's bellow as he stepped out the front door below her.

"Find her!" he barked above the clap of thunderclouds. "Find her or it will mean your testicles, men!"

Reaching the wall, Ellen stood on her tiptoes. She

406

could just reach the windowsill above her head. "Heavens, how will I get back in the window?" she murmured, fighting the panic that lurked just below the surface of her mind. She couldn't possibly pull herself up.

She ran her hands over the cold, wet brick. As if her prayers had been answered, her fingertips met with a line of decorative headers. The row of bricks, some three feet off the porch roof, had been mortared in from side to side, rather than from end to end as with most of the rows. These decorative header bricks formed a narrow ledge rather than being flush with the wall.

Ellen took a deep breath and raised her foot. Catching the narrow ledge with her toe and using the windowsill above for leverage, she stepped up onto the brick. With her arms well within the window, she somehow manged to throw first one leg and then the other over the windowsill.

Ellen hit the floor with a heave of relief. She was safe now, at least for the moment.

But now what? Once Hunt didn't find her on the ground, as he was surely discovering right now, he would begin a search.

She needed a weapon. Gavin's musket down in the library. Then she would escape through the tobacco fields, across the woods to the nearest neighbor. Without a horse it was a long way, but she had no other choice.

Shaking with cold, Ellen raised her rain-soaked skirts and ran out the bedchamber door.

The house was dark and silent now. Ellen didn't know where Mary and Rob and Julius were. She could only pray they were safe.

Cautiously, she descended the front steps, turned down the hall, and hurried for the library. Occasionally, a streak of lightning lit up the dark rooms. She saw no one. Outside she could hear men shouting as they raced about searching for her.

Ellen reached the library and slipped inside. Even in the darkness, she could find her way around. The musket was on the far wall in the corner, near one of the new bookcases. She had only to . . .

"Striking portrait, don't you think?"

The sky lit up almost as if on cue, to flash a streak of light across Hunt's pale, gleaming face.

Ellen turned her head ever so slightly to the portrait of Thomasina that Hunt pointed to. She never felt the weight of the object that struck her in the head, only the solid floor as it rushed up to meet her limp body.


Chilly and emotionally drained, Gavin urged Hunt's white steed down the dirt road that wound between two of his tobacco fields. The sun was just beginning to come up over the horizon, casting orange-gold light over the rain-glistened tobacco.

Christ's bones, but it was good to be back on Heaven's Fate again. Gavin wondered why it was that a man had to leave behind what he loved to realize just how much he loved it. That was the way it had been with Heaven's Fate when he'd returned from England in the spring. That's the way it was now with Ellen.

He didn't know what her explanation would be. He didn't even know if he wanted to hear it. What he did know was that, God save his mortal soul, he loved her. His brother's wife or not. Murderess or not. He needed her as he needed this land; he needed her more.

Julius had made him realize that. And once he

reached Ellen and made things right between them again, he would find Julius and thank the old sea dog. Gavin smiled in the early morning sunlight, grateful for the friendship he knew now was precious.

As Gavin rode into the barnyard, he heard the sounds of the bond servants in the distance, preparing for the workday. Ordinarily, Gavin would have walked out to the field with the men, but not this morning. This morning he had to find Ellen.

He dropped his reins at the front door and took the steps two at a time. He thought he would go upstairs to the bedchamber he shared with Ellen and find her asleep in their bed. He would slip into bed beside her and pull her warm, naked body against his. He would shower her face with light kisses, waking her gently. Then he would apologize for being the fool he was. She would want to talk, of course, but first they'd make love by the light of the early morning that by now was pouring through the bedchamber windows.

Gavin hurried up the front steps, not even taking the time to call out to Mary, whom he heard stirring in the kitchen. He had to see Ellen! He had to tell her how sorry he was.

The moment Gavin reached the bedchamber door, he knew something was amiss. The door was cracked open barely enough for a man to slip through. When he tried to push it open, something heavy stopped it. Gavin squeezed through the door, to find that someone had tried to barricade himself in. Ellen . . . It had to be Ellen.

The window where his desk had been was thrown open, the draperies torn. A puddle of water lay on the floor. The pieces of a broken chair lay among the shards of glass.

Gavin spun on his heels, racing down the hall and the steps. "Mary! Mary!"

"M . . . Master?" a feeble voice cried from the kitchen. "Master Gavin, is that you?"

Gavin swung around the corner into the kitchen. Mary was down on her knees tending to a still body. It was Julius.

"What the hell happened here, Mary?" He pushed back his hair, frantic. "Where's Ellen?"

"Gone, master," she sobbed.

"Gone?"

Mary mopped Julius's brow. Blood and purple bruises stained his face until it was barely recognizable. Someone had nearly beaten the life out of him.

Gavin grabbed Mary's shoulder and shook her gently. "Gone where?"

"The ghost, he took her," she wailed. "Took her far off."

Gavin looked away, then back at Julius. He went down on one knee. He could see that the sea captain was still breathing. "Julius?" He touched him gently, not knowing what bones were broken. "Jules, can you hear me? It's Gavin."

"About time," Julius croaked, not opening his eyes. "What took you so long?"

"Jules, where is she? Mary's babbling about some ghost."

"Hunt."

It took a moment for Gavin to find his voice. He knew he hadn't heard Julius correctly. He leaned closer. "What did you say, old friend? I didn't quite hear you."

Julius licked his bloody lips. "Hunt. The Duke of Hunt took her. I'm sorry, Gavin. Tried to make it to the house." A tear ran down his shattered face. "I tried, but I never made it."

Gavin's chest grew so tight that he feared he wouldn't be able to breathe. This was all his fault. Had he been here, this never would have happened. Had he been here . . .

Julius reached up and caught Gavin's sleeve. "Have to hurry. A ship. He came up the river on a ship."

"What ship?"

"Don't . . . don't know. Just heard one of the boys who popped me around. You got to hurry, Gavin. I'd help, but . . ." He tried to laugh.

Gavin squeezed his arm, hoping to comfort his friend. "You're going to be all right, Jules. Mary here will take care of you. She'll bring in a medicine man or something."

Julius smiled as he slowly opened his eyes. "Good luck. I'll be waiting for you right here."

Gavin gave Julius's hand one last squeeze, and then he leaped up and ran down the hall. First he would need weapons, then men. He just hoped to hell some of his bond servants had experience fighting on board a ship, because Gavin sensed that was the only way he was going to be able to take the Duke of Hunt and save Ellen.

# Chapter Twenty-Eight

Ellen woke slowly, as if recovering from heavy drink. Her head pounded and her mouth was dry. As she became conscious, sounds and smells began to filter through her mind. She could smell the salt of the bay, the dampness of wood, and the scent of roasted duck. Her hands and feet were tied and she was lying in a bed. The entire bed rocked gently. Occasionally, she heard the scrape of a chair or the clink of silverware. Wherever she was, she was not alone.

Hunt.

His image and memories of what had happened at Heaven's Fate reeled in her mind. Hunt had kidnapped her!

It was all she could do to remain still, with her eyes closed. But she knew her best chance for escape would be if she was well aware of her surroundings and the situation at hand.

For a long time Ellen lay awake, pretending to still be asleep. She was on a boat. She knew that. In a small room on a ship's bunk. Hunt's cabin, no doubt. And the man—she knew it was a man because she could smell his shaving soap—who was enjoying

413

the roast duck had to be Hunt.

An eternity seemed to pass before Ellen finally lifted her eyelids. She immediately caught sight of Hunt's back and his shock of white hair, and she squeezed her eyes shut tightly again.

*Dear Heavenly Father, how will I ever escape?* she thought, trying to control the panic that rose in her throat, threatening her ability to reason. The ship was sailing, she was certain of it from the sounds of the swishing water against the hull and the voices of the sailors topside.

Sailing where? Back to England? No! Not there! She would never go to London again. She wanted her baby to be born here, in the Maryland Colony. Her baby . . . Ellen slid her bound hands down to her belly, praying the child was all right.

*I have to get out of here!* Ellen thought fiercely. I've come too far to let Hunt best me now!

"Ah ha, I see you're awake."

Ellen's eyelids fluttered at the sound of Hunt's silky voice. "Let me go!" she cried through clenched teeth.

He pushed back in his chair, a gold toothpick protruding from his lips. He crossed his muscular legs and folded his hands over his flat stomach, taking his time in responding. "Now, you know I can't do that, Thomasina." He spoke to her as if she were a young child who'd been naughty.

She shook her hands he had bound with a purple silk scarf. "Untie me. I'm not a sow to be trussed!"

"I suppose there's no need to keep you bound any longer. Now that we've set sail, where could you possibly go?" He smiled, his eyes narrowing with interest. "But I must say I do like the look of you tied like that. It does something for a man." His pink-

414

eyed gaze met hers. "Do you know what I mean, dear?"

The sexual innuendo was obvious. Her face hardened with disgust. "Just untie me so I can sit up! I've lost all feeling in my feet from being bound so tightly!"

With a sigh, he rose and crossed the short distance between them. He sat down on the edge of the rack and grasped her shoulders, pulling her up into a sitting position. "Now careful"—he shielded her head with his hand—"you don't want to bump yourself on the bed above."

Once he had her seated in an upright position, he took his time in untying first her stockinged feet and then her hands. The moment she was free, Ellen slid to the far end of the bed, rubbing her wrists.

Hunt rose and walked back to the table, which had been set for a noonday meal. "I must admit that was very clever of you, producing a lover's note rather than the letter we both know I must have. I actually thought it was the letter for a moment." He pulled a white ferret from the pocket of his canary-yellow shirtwaist and began to stroke its head. "Quite clever indeed, almost amusing."

"I told you I don't have the letter!"

"I know that *now*."

Her dark eyes met his. "What do you mean?"

"Why, I took the pleasure of searching your sweet person for it while you were unconscious, of course. I wouldn't have left that task up to just anyone."

Ellen shuddered at the thought of Hunt running his white hands over her flesh . . . flesh that belonged to no one but Gavin. "So now you know I speak the truth?"

He sighed. "I have to tell you, dear Thomasina, I was shocked to find that you're breeding. A woman

415

of your talents must certainly know ways of preventing such unfortunate complications of pleasure."

"Back to the letter, Hunt." She didn't want to discuss her baby with this vile man! "You know now that I don't have it." She kept her voice on an even keel. The only way out of this now would be by wit and wit alone. "If I don't have it, if I have no proof, then I'm of no threat to you any longer. I was really of very little threat to you ever."

"You destroyed it, didn't you, puss?"

She smiled at the thought. "The very night I read it. Before I went up to the tower to speak with Waldron. But I kept the names all this time"—she tapped her temple—"here."

"Clever, so very clever." He lifted his ferret to his shoulder, allowing the little creature to climb across the brocade trim of his epaulettes. "You figured out that it would actually make more sense not to have the letter I sought, so I couldn't find it." He shook his head. "I could use a mind like yours on my staff. That secretary of mine, Robards, hasn't the sense to find his way in off the street."

"So what do you do with me now?" she asked softly. It was almost a challenge. She wasn't afraid of him. Not any more. Whether she lived or died, she would never fear him again. "Will you kill me?"

His facial expression turned to one of exaggerated shock. "Kill you! Why, sweet, how could you even suggest such a thing!"

"You are going to kill me." It was a simple statement.

His face went flaccid. "Not quite yet. I've other immediate plans."

She shook her head. "I'll not be a part of your ugly games. I'll kill myself first."

He picked up one of the purple silk scarfs he had

416

thrown carelessly on the rack. Slowly, he pulled it through his hand, taking great pleasure in the feel of the silk at his fingertips. "But, sweet, it's such a dreadfully long, tedious journey across the ocean. I should think I'll need some sort of entertainment besides the young man."

"Young man?" Ellen felt the panic rise again. "What young man?"

Hunt touched his upper lip with the tip of his tongue suggestively. "Well . . . the boy you call Rob, of course. The handsome redhead. Such a young, slim body. I can't wait to taste of him."

Ellen leaped off the bed. "This is between you and me! The boy has nothing to do with it! You can't kidnap him like this, you son of a bitch!" She reached out to strike his smirking face and he caught her wrist, twisting it painfully behind her back.

"I can do anything I wish." He grinned. "I'm the Duke of Hunt, one of the most powerful men in England. You know that." He swept his hand through the air. "Everyone knows that."

Ellen hung her head. *Not Rob, dear Lord, not Rob,* her mind screamed. *To be defiled by a man such as Hunt will kill the boy . . . the boy she was responsible for. . . .*

She lifted her chin, her gaze meeting Hunt's with defiance. Carefully, she withdrew her hand from his. "Set the boy ashore and I'll do what you ask."

A smile crept across his pale lips as he lifted the silk scarf and dropped it over the back of her neck, pulling her so close that she could feel his breath on her face. "Anything? I can be quite creative, you know."

"Anything."

Hunt leaned forward to brush his lips against her cheek, but just before he touched her, there was a loud rap at the cabin door.

He swore. Ellen took a quick step backward out of his reach.

"What in God's Holy name is it?" Hunt bellowed, dropping the ferret onto the dining table.

"Trouble, Your Grace."

Hunt took two long strides to the door and whipped it open. "Trouble? What sort?"

It was the captain's first officer. "The captain says to tell you we got a single-masted sloop sailing dead for us."

Ellen's heart leapt in her breast. She knew who it was. Gavin! He had come for her! She didn't know how he had known she was in trouble or even why he cared. All she knew was that Gavin would save her from this hideous man.

Hunt hit the bulkhead with his fist in fury. "You're certain they're bound for us?"

"It's obvious, sir." The young officer dropped his gaze to the floorboards. "I think they've come for the woman and the boy."

Hunt scowled. "Have your men weapons?"

"Aye. No balls for muskets. They went overboard in that storm months back, but plenty of swords."

Hunt reached for his sword belt that hung on a peg on the wall. "And can they use them?"

The officer dropped a hand to the dagger on his hip. "We'll see about that, won't we, sir?"

"Have your men all on deck, ready to fight. I imagine Waxton intends to board us."

"Aye, sir. I'll tell the captain, sir."

Hunt strapped the sword belt around his waist and adjusted its weight. "Tell him I want no survivors. I know hand-to-hand was not part of the original agreement, but tell him I'll pay . . . and handsomely. If the captain loses his ship but bests the colonials,

418

I'll replace the ship as well."

The young man glanced up at Hunt, but when he saw the look on the albino's face, he knew better than to question him. He only nodded his head and beat a hasty retreat back down the narrow corridor.

Taking a pistol from a drawer, Hunt stuffed it into the waistband of his breeches beneath the cover of his coat. Ellen shrank back, but he grabbed her by the arm and pulled her across the room and out of the cabin. "I want him to see you," he growled. "I want Waxton to see what he's lost and what I've gained."

Ellen dragged her feet. "We've bested you this far. You'll not win. Not now!"

Hunt spun around in fury, slapping her face hard with a pale hand. "That's for insolence . . . and a taste of what's to come. You want to be spirited, puss? Wait until this task is completed. Wait until I can give you my full attention, and then we'll see where your spirit is!"

He grabbed her by the torn bodice of her gown. "Now come along!" He started down the corridor toward the ladder that led topside. "You aggravate me too sorely, and I'll let the crew each have a piece of you while your man watches!" He shoved her ahead of him, and Ellen found the rungs of the ladder and raced upward toward the sunlight.

Once topside, Hunt led Ellen to where the captain stood on the quarterdeck of the square-rigger. Not too far in the distance was a single-masted sailing sloop cutting through the water at breakneck speed.

"She's much smaller than we are," the captain told Hunt. "Built for these colonial waters. There's no way I can outrace her."

"How many on board?" Hunt snatched the spyglass from the captain's hands to have a look for himself.

419

"A dozen men, maybe fifteen, no more."

"And your crew?"

"Counting myself and my first officer, twice that."

Hunt slapped him in the chest with the spyglass. "Kill them all and I'll double your payment when we reach London." He held up one finger. "Kill them all but for the leader. He's mine. Your men will have no trouble recognizing him. He'll be the cocky one."

Ellen stood beside Hunt, watching Gavin's sloop rapidly gain on the square-rigger. The men on deck became visible to the naked eye, and it only took a moment for Ellen to spot Gavin. He was standing on the bow of the boat, a spyglass in his hand, the wind whipping at his hair that was pulled back in his savage's braid. Ellen couldn't resist the barest of a smile.

"By the king's cod, what are you gaping at!" Hunt roared, cuffing her. "You relish the thought of watching him die?"

Ellen made no reply, which seemed to even further infuriate the duke. "Stand back!" he shouted at her, pushing her behind him. "And don't you move, else you'll live long to regret it!"

Ellen stumbled back under the force of his fist, but she caught herself before she went down. At least he wasn't going to tie her up. That would make her escape even easier once Gavin boarded the vessel.

"We'll tie lines to two empty rain barrels and heave them aft as the sloop comes alongside," the captain told Hunt. "That should bring us up short and she'll sail right by us. If the sloop's a bit slow tacking back, we'll cut her in half and let the crabs feast on colonial meat."

Hunt nodded approvingly as the sloop rapidly gained on them, approaching by the starboard side.

A moment later, the captain shouted, "Toss the barrels, lads!"

Ellen watched as the sailors threw the huge rain barrels over the stern of the ship. As the lines attached to the barrels snapped, the entire vessel shuddered, wood creaked, and the sails went slack, only to fill with wind again, creating a horrendous booming.

Ellen craned her neck to catch sight of Gavin as he ran aft of the sloop and shoved the tiller to his starboard side, turning the sloop directly into the path of the square-rigger.

The air was filled with the sound of splintering wood, and a sheet of water shot into the air as the sloop sliced into the larger vessel.

"Christ, he's mad! He'll drown us all," the captain cried as he drew his sword. "Repel boarders!"

"Tell them there'll be a gold piece for every colonial's head they bring me," Hunt boomed.

"You heard him, lads!" the captain shouted above the sounds of confusion. "Draw your weapons!"

Ellen grabbed a hemp rope to steady herself, watching in fascination as grappling hooks flew up off the deck of the sinking sloop to catch the rigging.

Ellen spotted Gavin, but then she lost sight of him as his men swung onto the square-rigger's main deck by way of the grappling lines, their swords drawn.

It was the bondmen from Heaven's Fate whom Gavin had brought with him. Ellen recognized several of them as they lashed out at the sailors with their heavy blades. The clang of metal and the shouts of men below her on the lower deck filled the air. Then came the screams . . . screams of pain so frightening that they made Ellen's heart trip in her breast.

As she saw the first man go down, a sailor, she clamped her hands over her mouth. She could smell

421

the sweet scent of his blood on the wind as it poured onto the deck in a puddle beneath him.

But where was Gavin? Surely he had boarded. She must have missed him in the mayhem! Then, out of the corner of her eye, she saw the Duke of Hunt draw his sword and turn. Gavin appeared out of nowhere, flying through the air on a line attached to rigging far above the deck.

As his feet hit the quarterdeck and he released the line, Ellen lunged forward at the duke. Hunt swung his free hand, hitting Ellen so hard across the chest that she fell backward off the quarterdeck to the main deck six feet below. For a moment she lay on the hard wood, stunned. But as her head cleared and she realized she wasn't injured, she had no thought but to get back up to Gavin.

Just as she picked herself up off the deck, she thought she heard her name on the wind.

"Mistress Ellen!"

Ellen whipped around but saw no one who could possibly be calling her. The deck was wet with blood and men still fought everywhere.

"Mistress!"

Confused, Ellen scanned the deck. Suddenly, she realized that the voice was coming from the livestock crates only a few feet from her.

"Mistress! It's me! It's Rob."

"Rob?"

Ellen raced to the crates and dropped to her knees. The boy was locked inside a barred crate meant for hogs. "Rob, are you all right?" She gripped a filthy wooden bar, staring inside. The boy was crouched on his hands and knees, his face beaten black and blue, his clothing torn in shreds.

"I'm s . . . so sorry they got you, mistress," he cried, pressing his face to the bars. "I tried to hold 'em off at H . . . Heaven's Fate, I swear by the Holy Christ I did!"

"I know you did," she soothed as she tugged at the knots that bound the door of the crate shut. "I know you did your best. And look, I'm fine."

"Loosen me and I'll fight by Lord Waxton's side. I can lift a sword, I can!"

Frustrated, Ellen clawed at the knots. They were wet and tight. She couldn't free him!

She touched the boy's arm through the bars. "Listen to me, Rob. I'll have to get a knife to cut you free. I can't untie the door. The knots are too tight!"

"No! Don't leave me, please don't leave me," he sobbed, tears running down his face. He had tried to be a man as long as he could, but suddenly he was just a frightened boy again.

Ellen put up her hand to soothe him. "I'll get a knife and come right back for you. I swear, I will."

His lower lip trembling, he nodded. "You'll come right back?"

"I'll come right back." She smoothed his bruised cheek tenderly. "I swear it."

Raising up off her knees, Ellen glanced frantically for a knife or a sword lying on the bloody deck. She had to free the boy! Surely one of the men had dropped a knife!

Though outnumbered, the bondmen seemed to be gaining the upper hand. Sailors' bodies lay in pools of blood at her feet. Another time and perhaps she'd have been sick from the carnage, but all that mattered now was rescuing young Rob.

Suddenly, Ellen spotted a small dagger only a few feet from where she stood. She dove for it, ignoring the bloodstains on the handle. Whirling around, she ran back toward Rob, her skirts bunched in her fists.

Just as she reached the livestock crate where the

boy was imprisoned, Ellen spotted Gavin and Hunt above her on the quarterdeck. Hunt had Gavin backed up against the railing of the ship. Their swords sliced the air, the clanging of metal seeming to rise above the bloody cacophony. Ellen tightened her grip on the dagger. If she sank it into Hunt's back, he'd be dead and Gavin would be safe. . . .

"Mistress! Mistress!" Rob called, rattling the wooden bars.

Ellen turned to see Rob. He seemed so pitiful and small caged as no man or beast should be.

She looked back up at Gavin in indecision. He had several flesh wounds. Sweat beaded across his face as he struggled to best the Duke of Hunt, a superior swordsman.

A race up the ladder and onto the quarterdeck, and she would have Hunt . . .

But the boy. To cut the knots would take precious moments.

Ellen suddenly dropped to her knees in front of the livestock crate. She had promised the child. She couldn't let him down now! What if one of the other sailors came for him?

She sawed through the thick wet rope that lashed the door shut. "Hide!" she ordered him as the rope fell in her hands. "The master's sloop's gone under. There's no chance but to take possession of this boat."

The boy swung open the door and crawled out. "You hide, too, mistress. I can't without you. Lord Waxton would never forgive me."

Ellen's eyes narrowed angrily. "I said hide before one of the sailors finds you," she ordered as a mother would to her child in danger. "Now, Robert!"

The boy gulped, stepping back in fear. Then he turned and ran.

Ellen watched him disappear over a stack of barrels before she turned her attention back to Hunt and Gavin.

She flew up the ladder that led to the quarterdeck. Once her feet hit solid wood, she raced straight for Hunt's broad back, the dagger clutched tightly in her hand. All the anger, all the fear of the years past, suddenly bubbled up inside her. Revenge was what she wanted now and revenge she would have!

Gavin caught sight of her as she sprinted across the deck. "Ellen! Get back!"

Hunt took advantage of Gavin's instant of lost concentration and, with one hard slice of his heavy sword, knocked Gavin's out of his hand. Ellen shouted "No!" as the sword went flying through the air and over the railing, splashing into the water below.

As Hunt drew back his sword for one final, crushing blow, Ellen screamed again, her high-pitched voice renting the air. "No!" she cried again and again, flinging herself into Hunt. But before she could sink the dagger into his back, he knocked her off balance, sending her sprawling onto the deck. Somehow he managed to still hold Gavin against the railing with the tip of his sword at his throat.

Ellen scrabbled to her feet, trying to escape Hunt's clutches, but he grabbed a hank of red hair with his free hand and dragged her to her feet.

"You dare try to strike me, Thomasina!" he spit.

"Let him go!" she sobbed. "This is between the two of us. Free him and I'll go with you. I swear, I will!"

"Ellen, no!" Gavin shouted. "Run! He'll not come after you! Not as long as I live!"

Ellen's gaze met Hunt's; his pink eyes bored into hers. Then, out of the corner of her eye, she saw the flash of the butt of the pistol she remembered seeing him tuck into his breeches as they left the cabin.

With a slip of her hand, she reached beneath his coat and pulled out the pistol.

Hunt stared at her for a moment in surprise and then threw back his head. Laughter bubbled from his tight, pale lips.

Ellen cocked the hammer.

Hunt laughed harder. "Don't be a fool, puss. Put down the gun before you hurt yourself."

"Ellen," Gavin said, his voice strained with emotion. "Just step back, sweet. I can fend for myself."

Ellen ignored Gavin's plea. "Let him go," she whispered. "Let him go or I'll shoot your head off your shoulders, Hunt."

Hunt grinned. "You wouldn't. You fear me too greatly, Thomasina. You've always feared me. You've always been a coward."

"You're right." She nodded, testing the trigger ever so lightly with her index finger. "Thomasina did fear you. But I don't." She smiled as she pulled the trigger. "This is for Richard. . . ."

Ellen closed her eyes just as the pistol discharged. She didn't see the look of shock on Hunt's face as the musket ball blew through his head at point-blank range. She only heard him fly backward and hit the deck, his sword still clutched in his hand.

For a moment Ellen stood frozen, the pistol still aimed. There was a buzzing in her ears. She could smell the stench of blackpowder and taste it on the tip of her tongue.

*He's dead,* she thought numbly. *He's finally dead.*

Then she heard Gavin's voice. She heard him call to the men below that the duke was dead. Suddenly, there was silence; the fighting had come to an end.

Ellen felt Gavin's soothing touch as he carefully removed the pistol from her trembling hands.

"Ellen?" He shook her gently. "Ellen, it's all right, love."

"Gavin?" She was afraid to open her eyes. Afraid it was all a dream.

"He's dead, sweetheart. You're safe now. The Duke of Hunt will never harm you again."

Slowly, she opened her eyes to peer up at his strikingly handsome face. "You came back. . . ."

He pulled her hard against him. "Forgive me for not having the sense to stand and listen. Forgive me for not trusting you."

"I have so much to tell you," she whispered against his chest. God, but it was good to feel his arms around her. "I want to tell all of it."

"Later."

She swayed against him. Her mind was reeling at the thought that her nightmare was truly over. "Waldron, Hunt, the letter . . ."

Gavin swept her into his arms, crushing his mouth against hers. "Later. You can tell me your tale later, sweet. It looks like my men have control of the ship. Let's just go home now."

She looked up into his heavenly green eyes and reached out to brush back a dark lock of hair that had escaped his savage's braid. She was suddenly exhausted, so exhausted she could barely think. "You do love me, don't you?" she whispered softly.

Gavin strode across the square-rigger's quarterdeck, the wind blowing off the bay to whip his dark hair against her own red locks. "I love you, Ellen"—he laughed, smiling down at her—"Thomasina, whatever the hell your name is . . ."

# Epilogue

*December 1665*
*Heaven's Fate*

Ellen pulled the coverlet over her sleeping son cradled in the crook of her arm and smiled at the sight of his little face. From the bed, her gaze instantly went to Gavin, who was seated at his desk beneath the windows. He sat with his head bent in concentration, a quill poised in his hand. The light of the fire on the hearth flickered, casting shadows across her exquisite face.

"Ready for bed?" Ellen asked. Having fully recovered from the birth of their son six weeks ago, she was anxious to be in her husband's arms again. "Ross is asleep."

Gavin laid down his quill and rose from the chair. He came across the room, his bare feet padding on the sanded floorboards. He was still dressed in a pair of broadcloth breeches and a muslin shirt he wore untucked to fall over his hips. He reached over Ellen and lifted his firstborn into his arms. "Finally a belly full?" he cooed, nuzzling the red fuzz on his son's head, inhaling that soft baby scent that enchants all

429

parents. "Going to sleep the night and give your father some peace?"

The little boy slept on, unaware of his father's words.

With a sigh and a shake of his head, Gavin carried Ross to the cradle near the fireplace and tucked him in beneath the goose feather quilts.

When Gavin turned back to Ellen, there was a smile of true contentment on his face . . . a smile few men ever found. "And now what do you want?" he teased, his green eyes flickering with thoughts of sexual pleasure.

"The same as you, I would guess," she answered in a silky voice. She lifted her arms out to him, letting the coverlet fall to bare her breasts. "Come and we'll see."

Gavin pulled his shirt over his head and let it slide to the floor. Before he reached the bed, his breeches had joined the pile.

Ellen's skin tingled with the first stirring of anticipation. As he came to her and slipped beneath the coverlet, she wondered if he would always excite her the way he did now. She hoped so.

Gavin slipped his arm beneath his wife and drew her close. His lips brushed hers. "A damned fine son you've given me, sweet," he whispered.

"Damned fine husband," she echoed, nipping at his lower lip with her teeth. *Damned fine to have accepted all I confessed,* she thought. Damned fine to have understood what had happened between her and his brother. Damned fine to have forgiven.

"I have just one question that's been gnawing at me concerning Thomasina," he told her, rolling onto his side so that he could study her face.

In the last few months, they had spoken a great deal about her life as Thomasina. Ellen and Gavin found that through their honest, open discussions, they were both finally able to accept the past and its realities, and let it rest. "And what's that?"

"The woman whose portrait hangs in my library . . . her hair is dark." He caught a lock of Ellen's shining red hair and smoothed it between his fingertips. "But this Ellen of mine, she's a redhead. My son is, no doubt, a redhead."

Ellen giggled. "I wondered how long it would be before you asked. I should have destroyed that portrait when I had the chance!"

He pressed a kiss to the valley between her breasts, his warm breath sending shivers down her spine. "I told you, I like the picture and there it will stay in my library." He raised his head, lifting a dark eyebrow. "So explain the riddle."

Ellen felt her cheeks burn, but her laughter echoed in their bedchamber. She had wondered all these months since she'd told Gavin about her past what she was going to do about her hair. It was true. Thomasina had been a brunette, but Ellen was most definitely a redhead. She knew it was vain of her, but she didn't want to let her hair grow dark again. In her mind Thomasina was long gone, along with Waldron and Hunt. With her red locks, Ellen could truly be another woman.

She lowered her gaze, feeling a little foolish. "I was born with the dark hair you see in the portrait, but Richard suggested I bleach it to make me unrecognizable to any of Waldron's cronies in London." She shrugged. "So when I did, my hair turned red. As for the boy's, my grandmother had hair the same hue." She lifted her lashes slowly. "I'll let my dark hair grow out if you wish. . . ."

He lifted up on one elbow to brush the red locks off the crown of her forehead in a lover's caress, his own long, dark hair falling to touch her cheek. "Do what you wish, sweet." A boyish grin crept across his face. "But I have to admit, I've grown fond of the fire, both in your hair and in your spirit. I'm not certain I could be content without both. Besides, if our son is a redhead, I should think we should take this as a sign from the heavens that you were meant to be a redhead as well."

She lifted her head up off the pillow until her mouth met his. "I love you, Gavin," she murmured against his lips.

"And I you," he answered, lowering his naked body over hers. "And let you never forget it, Lady Waxton of mine. . . ."